A. D. SCOTT'S NOVELS ARE . . .

"Almost perfect in every way."
—*New York Times* BESTSELLING
AUTHOR WILLIAM KENT KRUEGER

"A pleasure for lovers of a good thriller."
—*Historical Novel Society*

"Like a visit with an old friend in front of a
fireplace on a cold wintry night."
—*Suspense Magazine*

"Searing psychological portraits and vivid
portrayals of both back alley and glen."
—*Booklist* (STARRED REVIEW)

"Beautifully written and atmospheric."
—*New York Times* BESTSELLING
AUTHOR RHYS BOWEN

"Set against the bleak beauty of the
highlands while presenting a fine mystery
with engaging characters."
—*Kirkus Reviews* (STARRED REVIEW)

D0064375

A KIND OF GRIEF

Also by A. D. Scott

The Low Road
North Sea Requiem
Beneath the Abbey Wall
A Double Death on the Black Isle
A Small Death in the Great Glen

A KIND OF GRIEF

A Novel

A. D. Scott

ATRIA PAPERBACK

New York   London   Toronto   Sydney   New Delhi

ATRIA PAPERBACK

An Imprint of Simon & Schuster, Inc.
1230 Avenue of the Americas
New York, NY 10020

This book is a work of fiction. Any references to historical events, real people, or real places are used fictitiously. Other names, characters, places, and events are products of the author's imagination, and any resemblance to actual events or places or persons, living or dead, is entirely coincidental.

Copyright © 2015 by A. D. Scott

All rights reserved, including the right to reproduce this book or portions thereof in any form whatsoever. For information address Atria Books Subsidiary Rights Department, 1230 Avenue of the Americas, New York, NY 10020.

First Atria Paperback edition October 2015

ATRIA PAPERBACK and colophon are trademarks of Simon & Schuster, Inc.

For information about special discounts for bulk purchases, please contact Simon & Schuster Special Sales at 1-866-506-1949 or business@simonandschuster.com

The Simon & Schuster Speakers Bureau can bring authors to your live event. For more information or to book an event, contact the Simon & Schuster Speakers Bureau at 1-866-248-3049 or visit our website at www.simonspeakers.com.

Manufactured in the United States of America

10 9 8 7 6 5 4 3 2 1

Library of Congress Cataloging-in-Publication Data is available.

ISBN 978-1-4767-5618-9
ISBN 978-1-4767-5619-6 (ebook)

For Anna Moi

. . . No kynd of greif sall mak my hairt agast nor
earthlie cairs torment my mind no more . . .
—Elizabeth Melville, Lady Culross (c. 1578–c.1640)

PROLOGUE

~

She'd first visited the house up the isolated glen in Sutherland when she was a child. Then, in March more than two and a half years ago, she came back to decide what to do with the place she'd inherited from her grandmother. March was still winter in these parts—with snow on the hills, and the burns and rivers veins of roiling liquid peat, it was beyond dreary, it was dreich.

She smiles to herself as she pronounces the Scottish word, "dreich," with a rolled "r" and a strong "ch" at the end. None of my southern colleagues could ever say that sound; "k" was how they pronounced it when they attempted a Scottish accent.

She remembers stumbling the last mile into an Atlantic wind funneled by the steep sides of the glen, towards the farmhouse now invisible in the thick mist, a mist that became fine rain, penetrating her coat and hat, through to her woolen jumper and slacks. I almost turned back, the track so deep in mud. And with so many potholes I didn't dare risk the car. The aftermath of the visit had been a horrid sneezing coughing sniveling cold that took weeks to shake.

At first she'd thought the house had remained unchanged since the last time she'd come up this glen, as a twelve-year-old about to be sent to boarding school.

Close up, not so. The neglect was clear. Windows, two either side of the door, and the dormer windows set in the iridescent grey-blue Ballahulish-slate roof, hadn't been painted since who-knew-when. The door also.

Instead of its former cheery blue, it was now blistered and streaked and bleached out by gales and hoar frost and hailstones. Both chimneys were jackdaw's nests of vegetation. Weeds and wildflowers sprouted from the gutters.

Then a shaft of sun breaking over the hills, over the trees, over the heather, the mist lifting, spotlighted the house.

That sunbeam changed my mind. She smiles at the recollection. And dreams, dreams of comfort and safety in the house in the glen where the buildings nestled into a fold in the faultline, those dreams sustained me in the bleakest of times, times of danger, of fear, of a relentless low-level dread of being discovered.

That day, D-day—decision day—when the sun persuaded me to reconsider, in the near distance, a skylark rose from the heather. I can hear it as if it were yesterday. Singing its heart out, that tiny bird is my talisman, my link to those long-ago long summer days when true night was a scant three hours of deep twilight.

The winter nights— they last till mid-morning, returning in the early afternoon, but they're enchanting nonetheless. Fires blazing, scones baking, curled up in the window seat reading Kidnapped, I can live that life again.

She hugs herself. Then the cloud returns and covers the sun. She smiles as she remembers her initial reaction to the move back to her ancestral land. What are you thinking of? Are you insane?

Four months later, the renovations began. Three months after that, in the beginnings of a long winter, I moved in.

It was a mad decision, she reminds herself, but happy mad.

Chapter 1

⁓

Joanne Ross remembered the morning she'd first encountered the name Alice Ramsay. As she'd unwrapped a halved cabbage she'd bought at the market, the veins and cells and hollows had thrown up an image of a brain, making her shudder, making her hand stray to the scar above her left ear. But she'd snatched it away. *Leave it alone. It's still healing.*

She'd been terrified she would never recover, never be herself again. But in increasingly frequent optimistic moments, she'd decided it was no bad thing to have lost part of her old self.

That same day—four days after she'd posted the manuscript—she'd started a vigil for the postman. In the idle waiting moments, she'd smoothed out the crumpled newspaper the cabbage had been wrapped in.

"Woman Accused of Witchcraft."

The headline was large, the article a quarter of a page of the newspaper that covered Sutherland and Caithness in the far north of Scotland. It was a newspaper she had never come across before. Then again, why would she? The northernmost counties consisted of a strip of small towns on the eastern side and inhospitable mountains and glens and peat bogs stretching westwards and northwards, with only two major roads connecting them to the south. News from there was scant and uninteresting—unless you were of the Scottish diaspora researching the ancestors.

Joanne scanned the first few lines. She didn't recognize the name of the accused woman. *Probably a poor old soul who makes home potions, has a black cat, and has crossed some local worthies, therefore is branded a witch*, Joanne was thinking. *Heaven help anyone who is different in these parts.* She knew this from bitter experience. Although newly remarried, she understood that the stain of being a divorced woman could never be eradicated. Plus, she wore trousers.

The cabbage, balanced on the rounded side of the table, fell *splat* to the floor. Joanne jumped. The chair legs screeched on stone. *Some witch has cursed the cabbage.* Then she laughed at herself. But the fright had shaken her. And reminded her that even now, superstition was all too common in the Highlands of Scotland.

Next day, the headline and the cabbage still haunting her, she went to the library and took out two books. One was a history of witches and witch trials, the other a more general book on Scottish lore, *The Silver Bough.*

"I liked thon story o' yours in the magazine," the middle-aged woman with the unlikely marmalade hair color said as she checked out the library books. "I'd love to marry a man wi' a castle—as long as it has heating."

"Thank you." Joanne smiled, but her cheeks were burning in embarrassment.

And as she walked down Castle Wynd, past the *Highland Gazette* offices where her editor husband was putting together that week's edition, Joanne Ross—now McAllister, but as yet the married name hadn't stuck—dreamed of writing a book.

One book was enough; becoming a writer was too lofty an ambition.

She gave herself little credit for the acceptance of six short stories in the Scottish romance genre by a well-known ladies' magazine. But one book—that she felt she could do. Witchcraft was intriguing, and history was her passion, and it was a topic that would rile the locals, this being a town of many churches.

But the oft-felt ghost of her father whispered, *Who do you think you are? You'll never amount to anything.*

She shivered. Shaking her thick chestnut hair, she pulled a headscarf with a print of Paris landmarks from her bag and tied it under her chin. Autumn in Scotland was capricious—one minute southern sunshine, the next Arctic winds. But she knew it wasn't the cold making her shiver. *Grow up*, she told herself. *There's no such thing as ghosts and witches.*

✦   ✦   ✦

"McAllister," she said to her husband, "there's a woman in Sutherland accused of being a witch. Would a story like that be right for the *Gazette?*"

They were at the kitchen table, and as usual, he was reading the morning newspapers. "Absolutely. Nothing sells newspapers like a bit of controversy. But I'll let you deal with the letters to the editor from the Holy Jo brigade, as I'd throw them in the bin." He smiled at her.

She smiled back but had an uncomfortable thought that her new husband would be enthusiastic about almost everything she suggested.

"Witches," said Annie, "Great. I love stories about real witches."

"Don't know about real," Joanne replied to her elder daughter. "When people call a woman a witch, it's . . ."

Here she stopped; to explain the viciousness of small-town gossip to a twelve-year-old was not appropriate. But she had an idea that her daughter already knew that. Having a father who had deserted them and a twice-married working mother, the girl had overheard more than enough from the fishwives of the town.

"I'll follow it up," Joanne said. Then, seeing the time on the gold watch McAllister had bought her as a wedding gift, she started the usual morning shepherding-children-out-the door-to-school routine.

When she had the house to herself, she started making notes. Her handwriting had suffered after years as a typist, and the scrawl in her notepad offended her. But later, sitting back, rereading the opening sentences, the jottings of notes, she felt a tug of real interest in the idea. And it had been many months since she had been interested in much.

Yes, she thought, McAllister was right. Witches were an antiquated notion in the soon-to-be-1960s. Might make an amusing short story, though.

The Sutherland newspaper had been five days out of date when she'd read it, but she knew that for the locals, the story would still be fresh. Probably even less happened up there than down here. She telephoned and asked for the chief reporter.

"*Sutherland Courier*." It was a male voice. Young. "Yes, I covered the trial. I'm Calum Mackenzie, senior reporter." He didn't say he was the one and only full-time reporter, but having worked on the local newspaper, Joanne assumed this.

She explained. He listened.

"Oh, aye, the trial made a big commotion up here. Went on for two days, and everyone was talking about it."

"My idea is to do a longer piece—the background, the trial, the verdict, belief in witchcraft in the twentieth century . . . you know."

Eager for a chance at the bigger time, Calum replied, "I think I can see where you're coming from, and I don't think there'll be a problem. Of course, I'll have to ask my editor first. Give me your number. Right, Joanne Ross, *Highland Gazette*. Thanks. Be in touch."

When, two days later, Joanne received newspaper clippings covering the trial and a summary from Calum Mackenzie, she called again, asked a few more questions, and asked if he would mind if she used his report.

"We can share a byline," she said.

Calum was delighted. "You should come up and visit," he said, as they wound down the conversation. "Maybe meet Miss Alice Ramsay. Even though she's older—she's my mother's age—she's an interesting woman. Different. And she's an artist."

Joanne heard the implication that older women were not often interesting and smiled. She also heard the emphasis on *artist*, as though being an artist indicated louche behavior and made it more likely that Alice was up to no good.

"I don't know the far northeast coast of Scotland," Joanne replied, "but in the summer, I went camping in Portmahomack and couldn't miss the monument above Golspie."

"The statue to the Duke. The Big Mannie, us locals call it, him up there lording it above us all for dozens o' miles around."

"Maybe I will come up someday. It'd be nice to explore a different part of the Highlands."

He told her if she did visit, she should give him a call and he would show her around. Then he went back to writing a piece on the price of sheep at the local livestock auctions, and she went back to thinking about witches past—and perhaps present.

◆   ◆   ◆

Next morning, Joanne was again waiting for the postman. Again at the kitchen table, she straightened out the newspaper cutting to reread the story.

She jotted down "To Do" notes:

Interview Calum Mackenzie of local paper.

Interview the woman Alice RAMSAY??? Check spelling.

Talk to someone re the trial. Local police? Procurator fiscal's office?

The clock in the hallway chimed ten. No mail. Not for the first time, she wanted to smash that clock, knew she wouldn't, knew she did not even have the courage to stop the pendulum; any explanation would seem ridiculous, especially to her elder daughter, whose constant "why?" exasperated her mother. *Thank goodness for McAllister—he always has an answer.*

She pushed her notebook across the table, opened the folder with two stories she was working on, glanced at the first page, and closed the folder. She thought of making another cup of tea. Didn't. She thought of all the ironing. But didn't move.

Maybe I should stick to light romance. But I want to impress him, show him I can do more.

She knew she was being unfair, attributing thoughts to her husband, who was always encouraging. But he was a journalist, a former war correspondent, respected in the publishing and newspaper industry. He was a reader of books with words even he occasionally had to look up in a dictionary. And although she would never acknowledge the thought, he intimidated her with his worldliness.

"You give people pleasure," he'd said when, yet again, she'd made light of her own modest success.

She couldn't accept that, longing instead to write serious, intellectual work; articles, essays, a short story—anything that he would admire and be proud of. But, she reminded herself, what filled her imagination and what came out of her fingertips did not often match.

"McAllister," she said to her husband, "the woman I was telling you about . . ."

He looked up from his newspaper. The headline was once again about the upcoming general election. A Labour man, as was most of Scotland, McAllister feared the Tory Twits, as he called them, might win.

She saw the question in the raised eyebrow. "The woman in Sutherland they're calling a witch?"

"Oh, aye?"

"I was thinking I might go up there, maybe interview her."

"Great idea." He loved stirring up controversy. "Take the car. Maybe ask someone to go with you . . ."

"I'm fine by myself." That came out harsher than intended. She smiled. "I'll set off early, and I promise I'll look after your precious car."

That was unfair. McAllister had no pride in cars. Or in much else in the way of possessions, except books and gramophone records.

"Mum, I could take a day off school and come with you," Annie offered.

"Stop fussing. All of you." Her eyes felt hot and she blinked away unshed tears. "Sorry. Maybe I'll just see if I can interview her on the phone."

"Can I have more custard?" Jean asked.

Seeing the anxiety in her younger daughter's eyes, Joanne apologized. "Sorry, I didn't mean to snap."

Later that night, before going to bed and abandoning McAllister to his book and a jazz record she found too discordant a background for her reading, she again apologized.

"Sorry. It's just I don't like fuss."

"I know. But it's a long drive, and . . ." He was about to say *I worry about you.* Didn't, appreciating it would upset her. Instead he told her the deeper truth. "I couldn't bear anything to happen to you ever again."

"Me neither."

He nodded.

She hesitated. "Night night."

"Sleep tight."

A particularly tortured passage of free-form saxophone began.

She grimaced.

Then fled.

◆　◆　◆

Whereas her husband was a reluctant driver, Joanne was a natural. It was indeed a long drive, skirting around two firths, navigating through the twists and bends of the landscape, but the solitude, the warmth—like being snuggled up in a linen cupboard with clean washing—opened up thoughts and fancies and songs. A bonnie singer, she drew inspiration from the hills and rivers and the North Sea. On the three-hour drive, through song after song, mostly Scottish apart from an attempt at an aria from *Don Giovanni*, she sang loudly, and with no passenger to chide her, she would occasionally steer with one hand, making operatic gestures with the other.

After crossing the Dornoch Firth and into Sutherland at Bonar Bridge, the town was a short distance farther. Parking in the Cathedral Square as Calum Mackenzie had advised, she walked to the newspaper office, asked for him, and was offered a cup of tea by a young woman who looked like she should still be at school.

Joanne was about to say yes, when Calum arrived.

She was taken by his outdoors-in-all-weather tanned face, his smile, but taken aback at his short stature. Everything about Calum was miniature. She fancied he would fit into the school uniform of a twelve-year-old. His sandy-colored hair, in kinks no wind would ever ruffle, could have been set with a curling iron. But it was his eyes, kind and considerate eyes, that made her immediately like him and trust him.

"Mrs. Ross." He held out his hand.

"It's Mrs. McAllister, actually." She shook his hand back.

"But I thought you were . . ." He was checking the small foyer for another woman.

"Sorry." She knew she was blushing and hated it. "Yes, I'm Joanne Ross, but I'm also a McAllister, and . . ."

"You have a pen name. Me too. But mine's a secret, and only for when I'm pretending I'm a real writer."

She almost said, *me too.* "Maybe you *are* a real writer."

"One day." They were smiling at each other now, comfortable.

"Listen," he said, "there's a wee tea shop I go to—full of old ladies, usually—but it should be quiet now. Not that you're an old lady . . ."

"Lead on, Mr. Mackenzie."

"After you, Miss Ross."

"Joanne. We're colleagues, after all."

That did it. Calum Mackenzie became devoted to Joanne Ross. He remained so for years, long after what he later thought of as "the old days," when the so-called witch's trial was consigned to distant memory. And history.

Over a pot of tea and cheese scones, then a second pot of tea, Calum told Joanne of the trial before the sheriff of Miss Alice Ramsay.

His account was confusing. He started in the middle part of the trial, reliving the most memorable moments of a witness the likes of whom Calum had never before encountered.

"Calling in thon art expert did Miss Ramsay no good at all. Many of the locals, the police, the procurator fiscal, and aye, the sheriff included, were none too pleased at being shown up for teuchters. Only Mrs. Ogilvie, the district nurse, enjoyed the professor's testimony."

He saw Joanne's bewilderment and said, "Sorry, got it back to front, haven't I?" He had, but his mother's constant indignation at the not guilty verdict and her implication that Miss Ramsay had tricked the court were most fresh in his mind.

"You know how I wrote that Miss Ramsay was accused of giving thon poor woman"—his mother's words again—"the herb tea that made her lose her baby?"

Joanne nodded, not interrupting but with encouraging nods and the occasional "aye." Letting people tell the tale in their own way, listening to what they said rather than waiting for a pause to put in her opinion, was a talent Joanne had, a talent that made her a good journalist.

Calum continued, "Most of the case was about what the police found when they came to interview her at her house up the glen: skulls and animal skeletons, birds' eggs—some still in their wee nests—loads of flowers and leaves hanging from the clothes pulley above the kitchen stove. For teas and herbal remedies, she told the court. And it was a tea—raspberry leaf, she said—that got her into trouble. It is an abort—"

Joanne saw him struggle with the word. Whether from embarrassment or because he did not know the correct pronunciation was not clear. "Abortifacient," she said. After having read the word earlier, she'd looked it up in the dictionary.

"Aye, that. But Nurse Ogilvie testified the woman had previously lost two babies."

"Poor soul."

"Then the art expert, he told the court about thon painter mannie Leonardo and some ancient called Culpepper or something like that. He brought art books to prove it. Aye, the professor really got up the noses of the folk there. I only caught a glimpse of Miss Ramsay's drawings and pictures that they showed in court. I've seen a painting of hers, a nice big one, she donated to the local Old People's Home. Right professional her work looks. Even the sheriff thought so."

The town clock struck one. Calum knew his mother would have had his dinner on the table at twelve thirty, and it would take days to placate her, his being this late.

"Sorry, I have to go, but it's all here in my report."

"One final thing—a map to Miss Ramsay's farm?"

"Not that she'll see you," he said as he tore a sheet from his reporter's notebook. "And not that it's really a farm anymore. Most of the land was sold to the Forestry Commission when her family gave up the big estate and the castle. Here. It's easy. But the track has seen better days, so watch out for your sump."

"I will, and thanks."

"If you end up needing a tow, my father has the local garage. Here's his number. Not that Miss Ramsay has a telephone, but there's a phone box at the turnoff." He stood, saying, "Tea's on me—expenses."

She knew he was trying to impress her, and accepted. "Thank you."

Saying "Good luck with Miss Ramsay" and "Nice meeting you" and "Be in touch," he almost ran out the door of the tea shop, taking a shortcut through the cathedral graveyard, knowing his mother would harp on about his lateness for the rest of the week. *I was about to call the police* was one of her catchphrases whenever her son was more than five minutes late for anything.

Joanne sat in the car studying Calum's map, then drove to the main road and the few miles to the turnoff for Alice Ramsay's home in the high glen. "I'm dying to meet this mysterious artist," she said to herself, "even if she's not a real witch."

CHAPTER 2

From the kitchen window, Alice looks out over the copse of birch trees, studying how the topmost leaves, shivering in the early-morning chill, change color as the first of the sun catches their undersides before moving down, gilding the bark of the silver limbs and trunk. She'd drawn birch leaves before, and the veins, the texture, the scent, the fragile skeletons of them delight her.

The high sides of the glen, and the lower slopes of the narrow fissure that begin a scant mile from the shoreline of the North Sea continuing deep into a landscape formed in the Ice Age, begin to lighten.

The trickster of a sun extends its arc to the heather and bracken, reaching down to the boulders and rocks and stones of the river, touching the garden wall, sending out an impression of warmth, of summer extended, tempting her out into the day.

She despairs of ever capturing that light in her work. And doubts her ability to capture variegations of shades too subtle for a camera, too violent for a painting.

Staring, seeing-not-seeing, in a state of suspended remembering, in that waking dreaming the Scots called a dwam, she feels it, that early-morning chill on the cheeks, a scent of clean, the sound of quiet.

The sky feels vast in this far northern glen. As a child coming up here for holidays, she'd played under the same sky, in the same air, in the same quiet—a quiet that is not silence, that presses in on the ears so you can feel your breath, hear your heart beating, breaking. That too she first experienced in this glen.

Alice turns to lift the boiling kettle and start the morning tea ritual.

Then, teacup in hand, she sits on the bench by the kitchen door. The sun vanishes. Clouds are racing, dancing, forming and re-forming a sky-scape of grey. Rain might fall. Soon. Or not. A faint sound fills the air.

That was it, she remembered. That was what made me stay; that lark's rising song made my heart glad. She is transported back to spring, over two years ago, to the five-mile drive up the glen, a one-and-a-half mile drive along a rutted track with high vegetation growing on the middle ridge, making her fear for the exhaust pipe; it had been every bit as bad as the estate agent told her it would be.

The big gate was in such disrepair she'd been afraid to open it. So she'd abandoned her car, worrying how she would turn it around. Walking the final half mile to the house, she'd apologized to a constellation of curlews crying out at the intrusion into their territory. "I'm only visiting," she'd called back.

She remembers the old Scots name for skylark: laverock. Then and now, as it reaches for the heavens, that tiny bird with the giant voice inspires hope. She also remembers that first day and the fatal shaft of sunlight highlighting the once-white-lime-washed walls, the once-gleaming slate roof glistening with dew, multiple greens of bracken and heather and birch and rowan to rival any of the forty shades of Ireland. She remembers how it caught her in the throat, capturing her heart. And soul.

She knew then. And she knows now. She absolutely, without doubt, and without reason, knows that this is her place. For ever and ever. Amen.

"Amen." She bobs a mock bow in the direction of the distant song. "Thank you, Mr. Skylark."

The hens start clucking. The rooster cries again. And again. She shakes herself out of her dwam.

"Good morning, girls," she calls out to the six hens and that bossy-boots cock-o'-the-glen cockerel. She liberates them. Feeds them. Collects four warm brown eggs. Then starts her day.

The weather holds.

Hours later, Alice is working the fork deep into the earth, carefully lifting the potato sets, making sure she misses none of the pale yellow tubers. There were enough to keep a family fed in a long snowbound winter. "Planted too many," she says, grunting, "and enough cabbages to feed a flock of sheep." As she digs, she again contemplates the practicality of keeping a cow. Milk was one of the few reasons for her to visit the garage shop where Mrs. Mackenzie would peck at her like a carrion crow.

A cow is a good companion but too much bother, she tells herself, and too much milk for one person. A Guernsey milking cow with long-lashed eyes is a fine animal, a beast of beauty. There had been one on the estate where she grew up. With family and servants and estate workers, one cow had been just right to provide milk and cream and butter.

"Better a dumb beast than those gossips in the town," she mutters.

She ignores the noise of a distant vehicle, knowing the gate to her track was locked, knowing the Forestry Commission people worked intermittently up the glen, inspecting and planning and planting what she named an Abomination. The plantations of rigid rows of spruce lining the hillsides were no shelter for the deer, or the foxes, or the hares, or the birds, never mind the flora of the Highlands.

A curlew cries. A peewit weeps. All familiar sounds of these glens, so the other noises don't register.

She pulls a sack of potatoes to the shed. She cleans and stores the fork. Stepping into shadow, the damp around the waistband of her trousers cold now the sun is spent, she turns towards the kitchen. Something, someone, steps into the cobbled farmyard from the side of the house.

✦ ✦ ✦

The fright was as sharp and as painful as a knife thrust.

"What are you doing here?" It came out as a shout. "Who are you?"

The question was angry or anguished; Joanne wasn't certain. "Sorry. Sorry, I didn't mean to scare . . . to startle you." She was stumbling over the words, in half a mind to run back down the mile and a half of track, jump into her car, and drive the three and a half hours home. Later, she could not decide who had been more frightened, herself or Alice Ramsay. But the dog was completely unperturbed.

Alice's innate good manners returned. "Who are you?" She straightened her back from her habitual slouch, a posture developed from years of leaning over a drawing board.

Joanne saw a tall woman, perhaps in her late forties, and thin from what she guessed were hiking and climbing and working on the land. Her hair, brown with streaks of gold and grey, was escaping from the handkerchief holding it back from her face. And her skin, browned by weather, reminded Joanne of a polished hazelnut. But it was her eyes that made Joanne feel intimidated. They were sizing up her visitor, an aloof stare, an appraisal from an artist searching for the soul of a subject she might try to capture in oils or inks or with a few strokes of charcoal or pencil.

"Miss Ramsay? I'm Joanne Ross. Actually, I'm Mrs. McAllister, I'm newly married, and . . ." She knew she was blethering, still recovering from the harsh reaction to her appearance in Miss Ramsay's territory. "Ross is my professional name." At the hardening of Alice Ramsay's face, Joanne knew that had been the wrong thing to say.

"I'm here—"

"Out of nosiness." Alice finished the sentence. "Sorry, Mrs. McAllister or Ross or whoever you are, I'm not interested."

Joanne lost her smile, though she kept her eyes on Alice, noticing they shared the same shade—that green with a hint of blue, depending on the weather, not uncommon in Highlanders.

A few splatters of rain plopped loudly on the empty wheelbarrow. The wind swirled. The cold nibbled. Alice asked, "How did you get up here?"

"I drove. Then climbed the gate."

"Climbed over the sign saying keep out."

Joanne flashed a smile. "Of course."

That did it. Alice looked again with her artist's eye at her visitor's face; she was a pushover for people with intelligent foreheads. She could see the woman was weary. And something else. Wounded, she decided. Her face betrayed her reluctance. Alice did not want a wounded soul to disrupt her life, be it a bird with broken wing, an orphan lamb, or a person with a history. But she acknowledged a hint of her younger self in Joanne and relented.

"You may as well come in and have a cup of tea before you go. But whatever it is you want, I'm not interested."

The Skye terrier, who had accompanied Joanne up from the five-bar gate, made a few circles around the rag rug on the floor in front of the Aga, then settled down to sleep.

"Sit," Alice said, and pointed to a chair at the table.

For a moment Joanne wasn't certain if Miss Ramsay was addressing her or her dog.

Then, saying nothing more, Alice filled the kettle, opened the stove lid, and began the ritual of coaxing the fire back to high. Satisfied the logs would catch, she washed her hands, attacking her nails with a brush, cleaning out the soil and the ash and a long day's labor. All the while she still said nothing, only emitting small grunts as she rolled her shoulders, stretched her back, loosening the knots from much digging, much lifting, much bending.

Joanne was not uncomfortable. The quiet between them felt right, a settling-down time, an observing time, two strangers interested yet wary of each other. She unwound her scarf and took off her beret, wishing she could also take off her shoes, which were decidedly damp. Then she looked around.

The table was covered in red gingham oilcloth with paint splatters adding to the cheery color. The room smelled of wood, yeast, and drying vegetation.

There were paintings on every wall, a mix of watercolors, oil paintings, drawings, with one large oil still life in a speckled gold frame. Another cluster of paintings, which looked modern but not too modern as to be scoffed at by the hoi polloi, were propped above the stove on a timber beam nearly a foot thick and about nine feet long.

What caught her fancy most was an ink drawing of a bird skeleton—brown ink, faded ink, light-dirty-faded brown paper. The tiny bones, in profile, took up half the composition, details of the skull the other. Calum had said something about skeleton drawings being exhibited in court, and Joanne had to look away, lest she be caught staring.

Faded rugs, some rag, some woven, and some threadbare Oriental, were scattered on the slate slab kitchen floor. The covers on a sofa, set under a window looking down the glen, Joanne recognized as a William Morris print, a design she had seen in a book and always hankered after. She loved the tapestry cushions and wondered if Miss Ramsay had stitched them herself. And the paisley shawl—perhaps it was a treasure from some relative in the British Colonial Service. She felt she was in an Oriental bazaar in a story from *One Thousand and One Nights*. Entranced by the room and everything in it, Joanne did not disguise her delight. Never before had she been in a place where she coveted so many of the objects.

Alice enjoyed her visitor's obvious pleasure at her creations. As she busied herself stoking up the fire and searching for the tin

of biscuits she had misplaced, she was remembering the numerous trips up the farm track, when every visit to the town, every
hour outside the safety of her territory, was one trip too many.

She could picture her Land Rover, the rear area, the backseat,
and the passenger seat filled with the spoils of the furniture and
bric-a-brac auctions held weekly to coincide with the livestock
marts.

Nails, screws, tools, cement, curtain rods, curtain fabric, flour,
poultry feed, barley, oatmeal rough and flakes, tea—lots and
lots of tea—sugar brown and white and castor, soap, washing
soda, scrubbing brushes, sweeping brushes (outdoor, indoor, a
broomstick made from twigs), bed linen, pillows, cushions, knitting yarn, knitting needles (secondhand from a church bazaar),
thread, needles, sewing-machine needles, scissors large and small
and pinking shears, antiseptic cream, sticking plasters, bandages,
surgical spirits, and other spirits—whisky, gin, and cooking
sherry (for she was not fond of sweet sherry, but that was all that
was available hereabouts)—everything in the house and the out-
houses and the garden she had carted up the road, through the
gate, up the track, and into her life. The fencing posts and barbed
wire and building materials, the hammer, screwdrivers, a set of
spanners, and a bow saw—all these she had carried and used.
Frequently.

Joanne cut into Alice's reverie. "Miss Ramsay, I wrote to your
post office box. Is that not the correct address?"

"I haven't had time to collect mail."

Joanne knew the mail would only have been there two days at
most and didn't take the offense that was intended.

Alice put down a tray with the teapot hidden in a pale pink
quilted satin cozy, the edges of which were stained a peat color
from spilt tea. "Milk?"

"Yes, please."

Alice sighed. She may have to venture out after all, as this was the last of her last pint of milk, with not even enough for that first early-morning cup of tea. For the remainder of the day, black tea or herbal was fine. But to start the day, milk was essential.

Joanne mistook the sigh. "I'm not your enemy. I came to talk, to ask you about the trial, yes, but never to publish without your permission. Most of all, I'm interested in your art."

No answer.

"I know how it feels to be persecuted for being different." Joanne's voice dropped, her gaze concentrating on the drawing of the bird skeleton; even the bare bones held within them the knowledge of flight.

Alice noticed how her visitor faded into herself when she spoke. How her eyes would widen, soften, as she asked a question. How her head angled imperceptibly as she waited for an answer. A good interrogator, was Alice's summation. "Ah. The trial. So you understand. I can see you have spirit. And intelligence. Not a good idea for a woman to show intelligence hereabouts." She smiled.

And when Alice Ramsay smiled, a different woman appeared—as different as the shadows of light and sun in the shire of Sutherland, the place where she had hoped to remain, anonymous, unremarked upon. Until the gossip and accusations and exposure in newspapers threatened everything she had dreamed of, worked for, and almost achieved. What was worse for Alice, fear had returned.

"Mrs. Ross . . ."

"Joanne."

"Joanne, the past months have been . . ." She was about to say *stressful* but knew it was anger that had consumed her through the police visits, the accusations, the solicitor's advice to ignore the gossip, his underestimating the venom of her accusers. "I'm not interested in revisiting that debacle. And I certainly don't want any more publicity." Alice knew it was her own fault; in trying to be sympathetic, in attempting to help a woman who had tried every way to carry a child full-term. Then her kindness had been turned against her.

"Fair enough," Joanne said. "It's just that I had this idea for a story, and as this is where the last witch in Scotland was executed, I thought—"

Alice burst out laughing. "And you thought you'd interview a real live witch!"

"No!" Joanne was burning in shame, from her face to the top of the V in her white blouse, down to her breasts, was how it felt. "No, I didn't mean—"

"How homemade herbal teas and ointments can lead to accusations of witchcraft astonished me too. But I should have known; a branch of my family is from the Highlands."

Alice was riled. In the set of her face, the stiffness in her arms, her feet planted square on the floor, it was clear she was still hurting. "That poor old feeble-minded woman executed not far from here in 1728, yes, we have something in common. We were both condemned by nothing more than gossip. But I will survive. She, poor soul, was rolled in tar, put in a barrel, set alight, and burned to death."

They both shuddered.

Joanne knew gossip could kill. Gossip, innuendo, jumping to conclusions, seeing what was not there to see, interpreting a word, a glance, an animal, an object, an artifact, even a change in the weather, in a malicious way; it all could be seen as signs of witchcraft.

Alice looked at Joanne again. Sensing the combination of confidence and anxiety, she asked, "What is it you are really looking for?"

"A story." The moment she said it, Joanne knew she needed to continue. "I want to write something of worth. Something I can be proud of. I've written wee bits for the newspaper. I've had some stories published, just romance stuff, but I want to write . . ." Here she stopped. "You know."

"Yes, I do know. Congratulations. You've had work published. Not easy, so don't be hard on yourself. The more you search for your place in the world, the more elusive it becomes." She stood. "My advice is, be content with the little things, and you will make progress."

Joanne recognized the farewell. "Thank you for talking to me."

"I'm sorry I can't help you." She knew *won't* was more appropriate than *can't*. "But as an artist, I will say this. Just work, Joanne. Just keep on writing, or in my case painting, and something will come."

"I'll try. But everyday life leaves little time."

Alice laughed. "Not an excuse. Yet I take your point. We women are always putting off our dreams."

In the farmyard, with the sun gone, the wind bit.

"That's my thinking corner." Alice gestured to a south-facing spot against the wall of the outbuilding where a bench, a table, and a dilapidated deck chair sheltered in a thicket of fading chrysanthemums and climbing rose. "Next year I'll build a conservatory where I can work. Or sit for whiles doing nothing."

"Busy doing nothing, working the whole day through," Joanne half-sang. Then stopped and blushed. "*Snow White and the Seven Dwarfs.*"

Alice looked blank.

Then Joanne remembered that only mothers had to sit

through three showings of the same film. "I'm not sure I ever have time to do nothing," Joanne confessed. "I'd like to. Though if I did, I'd end up feeling I should be getting on with something, anything." Joanne knew she was blethering again but couldn't stop.

"Ah, yes, that Scottish Presbyterian guilt complex. Know it well." Alice held out her hand. "It's been a pleasure to meet you, Joanne. Sorry I can't help you find your witch. Though I'm certain you'll find your story." Alice's hands, rough gardener's hands, were warm. As was her smile. "Just listen to the wind, is my advice."

At the top of the track, watching Joanne walk on the center ridge out of the muddy ruts, Alice called out, "Your dog, where is he? She?"

"My dog?" Joanne turned back. "I don't have a dog."

"The one on the rug in front of the Aga?"

"I thought he was yours." Joanne looked around at the empty hills, the distant mountain to the west, the glint of water to the far east, and saw no sign of habitation. "He came up the glen with me, and I assumed . . ." Now the light was fading. "Sorry, I can't help you. I have a long drive."

"Yes, yes, leave him with me." Alice waved her away.

Back in the kitchen, the dog looked up at her, cocking one ear. *Yes? You wanted me?* Receiving no reply, only a long silent stare, he harrumphed softly and went back to sleep.

"One night." Alice spoke firmly. She knew how to handle dogs. "One night, then you go back wherever it is you belong."

CHAPTER 3

At first Alice had found the gossip amusing, the overheard snatches of conversations, the furtive muttering in the butcher's, the baker's, the five-bar-gate maker's, abruptly halting as her presence became known. She'd later laughed about it and shared the stories with the hens.

Alice doesn't worry when the local policeman came plodding up the track, holding on to his hat with one hand. He is not a threat, perhaps visiting to warn her of dogs on the loose worrying the sheep. Plainclothes policemen of mysterious variety are threatening; they are the ones she fears.

"Miss Ramsay. Constable Harris."

"Come in. I'll put the kettle on."

He is too much of a Highlander to refuse.

As he sips the tea, he looks around. Frankly, openly, he stares. The kitchen, with slate floors and whitewashed walls and cooking range—an Aga, he notes—is similar to most farm kitchens yet like nothing he's ever known. The bright cushions, curtains, rugs he takes no notice of. The flowers and leaves hanging from the pulley, the fresh tree branches standing in a zinc bucket in a corner, he notices and doesn't understand. However, the paintings and, most of all, the small and larger skulls used as orna-ments, and in the case of a broken fox skull, a pen holder, fascinate him. "Unusual," he was later to testify. "No normal," he was later to say.

"Miss Ramsay," he begins.

She sees how uncomfortable he is and doesn't help. Just waits, arms crossed.

"There's this woman claims she knows you, a Mrs. North."

"Yes, I've met a Mrs. North."

"And she claims you gave her some tea, herbs . . ."

"For her morning sickness. Yes."

"Aye. Right." He has his notebook open, his pen poised, but is looking down at his boots, seeing how the mud has splattered the usual high shine and thinking they need a good clean, thinking why wasn't there a woman around who could ask the uncomfortable questions. Constable Harris's knowledge of the internal workings of women's bodies was still at fifteen-year-old-schoolboy level.

"Mrs. North," Alice prompted.

"She lost the baby." He says this without looking at her.

Alice knew already. "That's sad." She remembers the timid wee woman, how desperate she was to have a baby, a son. And she remembers the fading bruises on the woman's left arm.

"I fell over," Mrs. North had said.

Alice had pretended to believe her.

"Trouble is," the young constable says, "she—well, mostly him, her husband—they're saying it was your fault. You made her this potion, and that's why she lost the bairn."

"Why on earth would I do that?"

He remembered the husband saying that because she had no man and no children, she was jealous of those who did. "I don't know," he says.

◆ ◆ ◆

At the end of the farm track, then the single-track road with passing places, Joanne turned right for the main road south. The meeting with Alice had been oddly tiring. The drive home, with the last hour in the darkest dark, she acknowledged might be hazardous. "Blast McAllister for being right," she muttered as she changed down to second gear and drew into a passing place to allow a large lorry full of frantic sheep, heading for the abattoir, and late, to speed past. The chorus of terrified bleats upset Joanne. Pulling out onto the main road again, she realized how exhausted she was, how unsafe it would be to drive nearly four hours, half of that after sunset.

Four months ago she had been shut in a cellar by a madwoman for days, and the dark was still a challenge. It would be hours until the light faded, but the final stretch on a twisting, challenging drive around two firths, over bridges narrow and humpbacked, and under the doglegs of the railway line would be nerve-racking.

She saw the signpost for the town, followed by a sign for a hotel in town, and it seemed a good alternative. And exciting. Joanne could not remember ever having spent a night alone in a strange bed in a strange place.

The reception desk had a brass bell with a sign saying "Ring." She did.

"Hello. How can I help you?" The woman was middle-aged, with brown middle-length hair, dressed in a middle-aged matron's uniform of tweed skirt and Shetland jumper and a single strand of freshwater pearls. Then she smiled with a much younger smile.

"Do you have a room for tonight?"

"We do. Lucky there's no golf tournament right now, else we'd be booked out." The woman opened the register. "One night?"

"Yes, please. Mrs. Joanne McAllister," she said, then asked, "And can I use the phone? It's a trunk call; I'll reverse the charges."

"Down the corridor, next to the snug bar."

"Yes, operator, we'll accept the charges," Annie answered. "Mum, where are you? Why aren't you home yet?"

"I'm fine." It was like speaking to her former mother-in-law, Granny Ross. "Just don't fancy the drive here and back in one day. Can I speak to McAllister?"

"McAllister! It's your wife." Joanne could hear her daughter's delight in saying that.

"Joanne. Are you OK?"

"Absolutely. I've found a fancy man up the glens and am about to enjoy a night of passion in a den of iniquity, followed by a cup of cocoa and a good night's sleep."

"Didn't know Sutherland was that exciting." He laughed. "Glad to hear you're not taking to the road this late. How was your adventure?"

"Interesting. I'll tell you all about it when I get home."

"Call me in the morning when you leave?"

"I will. And thanks."

"What for?"

"For not telling me off for not setting off back home earlier."

"I'm your husband. Not your keeper. Sleep tight."

◆　◆　◆

Supper at the hotel was simple and delicious.

"Not much call for meals this time o' year," the landlady-cum-barmaid-cum-receptionist said, "but you're welcome to a share of the shepherd's pie I made for we're own tea."

"Thank you, that would be lovely." Joanne was hungry. Dinner was served in the lounge bar, the dining room being colder than outside in the street. With a side serve of mashed turnips, the steaming hot pie—made with lamb mince, she guessed—filled her up. For the first time since her injury, she had alcohol outside of the safety of her home, a small glass of port.

"To warm me up." Why she had to explain, almost apologize, she didn't know.

"So what brings you up here?" the landlady asked as she came in to clear the plates.

"Well, I've never been this far up the northeast coast before," was all Joanne could think to reply.

"And you're here chasing witches." Seeing Joanne's embarrassment, the woman laughed; she had a good laugh and a good smile. "Don't worry. Mrs. Mackenzie at the garage told everyone her son Calum is about to make the big time." Again she read Joanne's face. "Publication in the *Highland Gazette?*"

"Big time? I'll have to tell my husband that. He's the editor," she explained. "As for witches, if they accused every woman who makes herbal teas, or those who live alone in the wilds or keep a black cat, of being a witch, well . . ."

"You're right there." The landlady let out a deep raucous laugh that could have come from a forty-a-day smoker, which she wasn't. "Och, it was never really about witches. It was stupid gossip that got out of hand." She sighed. "Sorry, I'm still right upset. Miss Ramsay is a friend."

"It must have been quite a controversy," Joanne said.

"Thon poor wifie that lost her baby, she wasn't thinking clear. As for her man, he's a right head case. It was him who called Alice a witch at the trial. The name stuck. Mind you, some folk use 'witch' when they want to say the 'b' word but daren't." She stopped. "Sorry, I'm blethering on. And no quoting me, right?"

"Not without your permission."

"She's a right nice woman, Miss Ramsay, keeps to herself. She calls in here from time to time, her and me being more educated than most o' them round here. Went to art college so she did. I could have gone too, but I met Mr. Galloway, you know how it is." Mrs. Galloway was proud that she had been to the Academy, proud she'd passed the exams. She thought of herself as educated. Though not highborn like Alice Ramsay, she was proud the artist had chosen her as a friend.

"She visits them at the local Old People's Home, talks to them. Listens to their memories. She donated one of her paintings. Right kind of her. And another thing, since you're wanting to know about her, Miss Ramsay always pays her bills on time."

Mrs. Galloway had learned this from the man and his boy who did the renovations on the estate, likewise the man who brought firewood, plus the hardware and farm supplies store. They all said she paid in cash. Even Mrs. Mackenzie, the town and county chief gossipmonger, could not fault Miss Ramsay, as she always paid the garage bills and the petrol account on the due date.

Joanne knew that in a small community where most businesses survived from one job to the next, a reputation for prompt payment put you at the top of the queue where tradesmen were concerned; it was also the measure of a decent person.

"Another thing about her . . ." Joanne could sense that Mrs. Galloway cared for Alice Ramsay and she was glad Alice had at least one friend. "Miss Ramsay was really good to my mother before she . . ." A tear glistened. "Sorry, I've said too much. She doesn't need me discussing her with a stranger." She began backing away. Gossip had condemned Miss Ramsay to months of misery, and Mrs. Galloway was not about to be another of the tongue-wagging brigade—no matter how sympathetic this Mrs. McAllister seemed.

"I would never publish anything about Miss Ramsay without clearing it with her first," Joanne promised.

"I hope all this nonsense is soon dead and buried. She doesn't deserve . . ." She shook her head, banishing the mental midgies. "If there's nothing else I can get you . . ."

Joanne smiled. "No, thanks. The pie was lovely."

"Thanks. Not very grand but filling. Breakfast's between

seven and nine. See you in the morning." She pushed the door half open with her hip, the tray in both hands. "By the by, if you want, I can point you to the stone that shows where the last witch in Scotland was burned. Only a wee bit of a marker stone, mind, but at least you can say you seen it."

"Thanks." Joanne was not at all sure she wanted to visit the spot. The story was gruesome enough, and horribly unfair was her verdict when she read that the woman was old and probably mentally unstable. The only redeeming information was that the witch's daughter had escaped the same fate, never to be discovered. *Perhaps her descendants are living hereabouts.* She grinned at the thought.

Although her legs ached from the walk up the last mile of the glen, with the left leg aching most from the endless changing of gears on the drive to the northeastern town, Joanne had no difficulty falling asleep. The bed was perfect—the landlady had put a hot water bottle in to take the chill off the sheets. Her last thoughts were of the execution.

1728. The date was branded in her memory. Janet Horne was the name. The trial documents recorded that her daughter had a withered hand. Joanne wondered if that was why she was accused of witchcraft, knowing that over the centuries women were executed based on equally flimsy justifications.

Joanne eventually slept but kept the bedside light on, and when she awoke, she was surprised by the lack of nightmares. Not even a dream, or so she thought, had kept her from a long deep sleep. She awoke at seven, and that was only because she heard men talking in the hotel courtyard and the noise of bottles clanking as the empty crates were lifted back into the delivery lorry.

After a bowl of porridge and lots of tea, Joanne listened to the landlady's instructions and walked through town to the place of execution.

All the while she was telling herself, *I do not want to do this*, yet she kept on walking. It was a blustery, cloud-racing wind-shifting rain-threatening day, and she enjoyed the air. The spot was a stone. Just a stone. She stared at it. Contemplating how a soul died in agony made her shudder. *Father was right; too much imagination, that's my trouble.*

Joanne drove to the petrol station on the main road south of town. She watched a wee woman in blue overalls come over. Her perm was so tight her silver-streaked hair made her look like an elderly poodle, and Joanne tried not to giggle. But in the woman's eyes there was no doggie warmth, rather a shrewd scrutiny as she examined the customer, the stranger.

"Fill her up, please," Joanne asked.

"Righty-oh." The woman put in the nozzle, and as the fumes drifted towards her in the North Sea wind, Joanne put a hankie to her face.

"Bother you, does it? Och, you get used to it in my job. Calum is always teasing me, saying it's a wonder I have any sense of smell working here for near twenty-five years."

"Calum? Are you Mrs. Mackenzie, Calum's mother?"

"I am that."

"Joanne Ross, from the *Highland Gazette*."

"Oh, aye, you're here because o' poor Miss Ramsay. Right terrible that trial was. Mind you, some folk have nothing better to do than gossip. Then again, the woman's aye here there and everywhere."

"Really? I heard Miss Ramsay likes the quiet life."

"You should see the size of her petrol bills." Even though Alice Ramsay was one of the garage's best customers, Mrs.

Mackenzie was tutting at another example of what she saw as Miss Ramsay's deceptions. "No, she must cover a fair distance, as she buys at least a tank o' petrol a week. Up to thon so-caa'd artist stuff, no doubt."

Joanne had to stop herself from staring. *Telling this to a stranger? Has the woman no self-awareness?* She considered herself a person who was not interested in gossip. Until Don McLeod, deputy editor at the *Gazette*, had asked her, in her early days as a fledgling reporter, how was a journalist to do their job without listening to gossip?

The trick was to distinguish between gossip and facts, he taught her, so always check, then double check, and get at least two quotes, with names and ages and addresses.

"You must know Miss Ramsay well, if you see her every week?"

Mrs. Mackenzie sensed she had said too much. "There's knowing, and knowing." She took the pound note and went inside to fetch change. Examining Joanne through the window, she decided Mrs. Ross was another of those women who didn't know her place.

"Cheery-bye, nice meeting you," she said as she handed over the coins. Watching the car pull out into the main road, Mrs. Mackenzie thought over what her son, Calum, had told her of this woman.

"It'll be good for my career to learn from Joanne," he'd said, after he'd apologized four times for being late.

Calling her by her first name indeed, Mrs. Mackenzie was thinking. *That flighty fiancée o' his is a bad enough influence. Now he's listening to a woman who should be at home minding her family, not haring about the countryside on her own, asking after witches.*

✦ ✦ ✦

The journey back felt shorter, though the drive took the same time. Joanne felt she had proved to herself, and to McAllister, that she was capable of an outing without someone hovering, their mere presence implying, *Are you all right? Are you sure you're up to it? Maybe you should . . . ?*

I'm fine! she wanted to shout. *Completely well. All I need is inspiration, a story, a plot, anything I can lose myself in, and just write.*

Driving over the Bonar Bridge, glancing at the mudflats of the Dornoch Firth, the rotting-vegetation low-tide salt stench seeping in through a third-of-the-way-open window, a notion came to her, making her smile. *If only I could ask a witch.*

She spoke to the mirror. "'I haven't been able to find a plot,' I'll say. 'Aye, I have just the spell for plots lost and found,' the witch will tell me. 'That will be two silver shillings, thank you.'"

Chapter 4

~

Next day, in the minutes before the brain and the body were entirely awake, those minutes when the tea-making ritual was accomplished in a half-sleepwalking half-dreaming in dressing gown and pajamas state, Alice discovers there is no milk—she and Joanne finished it.

"Damn and blast and drat," she mutters. "Oh, well, it's my day at the Old People's Home. I'll buy some at the Co-op, anywhere to avoid Mrs. Mackenzie."

After black tea, the routine with the hens, a quick sweep of the floor, she reaches for her portfolio, the one containing the watercolors for her book on the flora and fauna of the Highland glen—singular, her glen—a book she hopes to have published. One day.

She spreads a selection on the kitchen table. Then puzzles yet again if she should include the drawings of skeletons and skulls. She remembers the trial, "that trial of a trial," as she calls it, and the sheriff's twisted face as he looked at the drawings, the way he drew out the word "art" when asking rhetorically, "Is this really aaart?"

"Ha, what a fine mess that got me into," she says to the wee dog still there, still on the rug, going nowhere.

She is remembering Dougald Forsythe. She was scared he might come up the glen. The thought of his patent-leather shoes stepping over puddles attempting to find safe ground and failing makes her laugh.

The wee dog cocks his head.

"Don't want him examining our pictures," she tells the dog. "Though *why I thought it a good idea to call Dougie as a witness I'll never fathom. Still, he does recognize a piece of real art when he sees it. And he says good things about my work—so he can't be a complete knave."*

◆   ◆   ◆

"Hello, the McAllister household."

"Joanne. Or should I say Mrs. McAllister?"

"Sandy. Or should I say My Lord Editor-in-Chief?" When at last, after many a story, Joanne had met McAllister's best friend and fellow conspirator, she had been apprehensive, nervous even. She compared herself—unfavorably—with female journalists on the *Herald*, women she was certain were worldly and sophisticated, in clothes bought in expensive stores, not run up on an old treadle sewing machine.

Her first and only meeting with Sandy Marshall, editor of one of the nation's most prestigious newspapers, was at her wedding. She liked him, liked his wife, liked his children too.

At the wedding, Sandy was best man. He'd asked Joanne for a dance, and taking off his jacket, turning his sporran to the side, he'd led her onto the floor to join the eightsome reel. Kilt swinging, wheeching and skirling with celebratory cries worthy of warriors, he linked arms with her, throwing her around the dance floor, and she'd laughed till her jaws ached.

His wife, Morag, had said, "Whew! Thanks, Joanne. It's usually me who's the victim of his dancing."

"So how's that husband o' yours?" Sandy asked now. "Still playing that screeching he calls music?"

"He is." Try as she might to like them, some of the more esoteric tracks from McAllister's beloved jazz recordings bewildered her.

"There should be Saint in front of your name," he said.

"Listen, I'm calling about the so-called witch trial. I spoke to McAllister. He said you've met this woman . . ."

"Alice Ramsay."

"I understand she doesn't want publicity, but Dougald Forsythe, who spoke for her at her trial, writes for us."

"Isn't he a lecturer at the Art College?"

"He is, and he's also our art critic. To cut a long story short, I owe him a favor." Sandy would never reveal the story of the previous art critic cum junior reporter caught plagiarizing copy from a London art journal. Dougald Forsythe had shown Sandy the original article, saving the editor and the newspaper much embarrassment and perhaps a court case.

Then Forsythe had brazenly claimed the art column for himself. Aware of public opinion, with which he usually disagreed— he produced articles that were never less than entertaining, were often controversial, and usually resulted in irate letters from conservative art patrons and readers.

"So how can I help?" Joanne asked Sandy.

"Write me a think piece, based around what ordinary people see as art. Cite the trial. Mention the narrow-minded responses to anything modern the art galleries buy."

"Like the Salvador Dalí brouhaha."

"Exactly. Given what it's costing the taxpayers for these works, it stirs up the readers no end. Forsythe suggested Glasgow's next buy might be one of the weirder Picasso works; that stirred up plenty of controversy."

"Why me? No, don't answer—I'm the ordinary person." She was interested. An article in a major newspaper was a major coup. "Sandy, it's a huge topic. I've no idea where to begin."

It had been Dougald Forsythe's idea to publish contrasting opinions, just as it had been his idea that Joanne Ross write them.

But Sandy couldn't figure out how the man knew of Joanne. *Always has a hidden agenda, does our Dougald*, was the opinion of one of his art colleagues. Sandy Marshall would perhaps have been more cautious if he'd heard that before hiring him.

"Write in your natural style, perhaps write how modern art can offend but how tastes are changing, today's failure is tomorrow's masterpiece."

"Like Vincent van Gogh."

"Exactly. And just so you know, the fair Dougald in his next column is writing about women artists, how they are undervalued, their passion is never taken seriously . . ."

"And they are judged if they have an eccentric lifestyle. Whereas men . . ."

"Exactly. I'll pop a brief in the post, plus Forsythe's phone number if you want to chat. Best call him early. Later in the evening he's . . . he's hard to communicate with."

"Drunk?"

"Aye, and maudlin, and full o' himself. So, can you knock out fifteen hundred words? There'll be a picture to go with it."

"Promise me no Highland cows in misty glens."

Laughing, Sandy said, "You've got the gist of it already. Forsythe suggested *Starry Night* as an example of work no one wanted when it was painted."

"Good choice." Joanne liked how this would tie in with an article about art and the "eye of the beholder." They settled on a publication two weeks away, delivery in five days' time.

Fluctuating between excitement and anxiety, fearing she wasn't up to the standard of national publication, Joanne began mentally composing the piece the minute she put down the phone. She wanted to ask McAllister's advice but suspected he would be less than helpful, saying *Write it your own way.*

Curious about Forsythe, she phoned Calum Mackenzie to ask about the art critic.

"Forsythe spoke in big words, he mentioned all sorts of artists no one up here has ever heard of, and he was wearing a strange outfit."

That was of no help. "Calum, do you know how, or if, he and Alice Ramsay are acquainted? And why she would have asked for him as the expert witness?"

"No idea," he replied.

And you, a reporter, didn't inquire? she wanted to say.

"Quite a character, though," Calum continued. "He turned up to court wearing an Inverness cape over a blue velvet jacket, a mustard-colored waistcoat, and tartan trews." The wonder in his voice told Joanne that if it had been Oscar Wilde himself in the witness box, it would have caused less of a stir. "And he spoke pure Glasgow. When I asked around about Forsythe for my article, I found out he'd annoyed most everyone."

Calum mentioned him in the golf club bar. If the speaker was a man in male company, allusions to his sexual preferences were immediately joked about. In mixed company, the speaker chose to comment on his clothes. Or his shoes. Even Calum, a reporter supposedly trained not to use adjectives, couldn't help returning again and again to Forsythe's appearance and gestures, using the word "colorful." When he'd asked Mrs. Galloway for an opinion, she'd said Forsythe was "full o' himself," an expression Joanne loved, it was so apt.

Calum was unable to recall the essence of the man's testimony. The disruption Forsythe caused to the flow of the case and the time wasting, with the sheriff constantly telling the witness to stick to the point, irritated the sheriff. It also, Calum thought, made him hurry his verdict.

"I do remember one part clearly," Calum told her.

He recounted how the sheriff had asked, "Mr. Forsythe, are you are saying that anatomical drawings, including this exhibit . . ." He had held up and then quickly turned down the drawing of a fetus in the womb, as though the subject of pregnancy was distasteful. "That these are usual subjects for art students to study?"

"Life drawing is an essential part of an artist's education," Forsythe had replied.

The sheriff, who had never seen anyone naked, not even his wife of thirty-two years, had shuddered. "What you are saying is that this is a normal course of study at an institute of art?"

"Just so. The great classical traditions of art, from the Greeks onwards—"

"Thank you. That will be all."

It had taken some moments to dislodge Dougald Forsythe from the witness box. When he was gone from the courthouse, disgruntled because he was not allowed to give his speech on Scottish Philistinism, and when the atmosphere had returned to the solemnity expected in a court of law, the sheriff had summed up.

"Taking the testimony of Nurse Ogilvie, an experienced midwife, plus the plaintiff's medical history, and disregarding the prejudices of some in the medical community against more traditional remedies"—he was referring to the procurator fiscal, who had pressed the charges against Alice Ramsay—"I find no connection between a cup of herbal tea and the subsequent miscarriage." He had not mentioned that the ointment his wife had persuaded Alice to concoct for his arthritis was, in his estimation, a miracle. "As for the art, I find no connection between Miss Ramsay's work and the charges brought against her." He could not bring himself to mention Dougald Forsythe's name. "I therefore find the defendant not guilty."

"So," Joanne now asked Calum Mackenzie, "what did *you* make of the trial? How did it go down with the locals?"

"The trial was right interesting," he replied, "Most locals thought the charges ridiculous. But some . . ." *Mostly my mother and her friends.* "They were not happy she 'got away with it.'" Again a direct quote from his mum.

"It must have been a big story," Joanne commented.

"Oh, aye. For months."

When she put down the phone, she was wishing she'd been there or that *Highland Gazette* reporter Rob McLean had covered the trial. Extracting information was a slow process with Calum.

Plus, she was frustrated. There seemed to be no way into a longer story, one she could use as a plot.

✦   ✦   ✦

A few days later, when Dougald Forsythe telephoned, Joanne was surprised. And wary. But after the long phone call, she felt enchanted.

"Hello, the McAllister household."

"May I speak to Joanne Ross?"

"Speaking."

"Dougald Forsythe, Glasgow College of Art and the *Glasgow Herald* here."

"Oh. Hello. I've heard about you."

"Aye, people who are educated know of my work." He laughed, and she thought he might be tipsy. "I'm calling to introduce myself and to ask if I can check your article before it's published. Not that I think it will need changing. Sandy told me you're an experienced journalist, but . . ."

He blethered on, boasting of his role as arbiter of art for the Scottish nation.

He must have heard her sigh, as he stopped and turned on the charm. "So, Joanne, I hear you're a real writer, not just a small-town journalist."

"Don't know about that," she said, "but yes, I'm hoping to publish a novel." She had no idea why she'd said this and was immediately cross with herself for sharing her ambitions. So she told him of her meeting with Alice, her delight at Alice's home, her work, and her kindness.

He listened, commented on her observations, and commended her appreciation of the paintings. "Not many recognize real artistic merit, especially when the artist is a woman."

When she put down the phone, she couldn't decide whether to be flattered or furious. "Condescending" was one word that came to mind. And "charming." So why she was suspicious of him she had no idea. Then telling herself not to be so distrustful, she went back to baking a Victoria sponge cake.

◆　◆　◆

That Saturday, a week earlier than Joanne had expected, an article on Alice Ramsay was published in the *Herald*.

McAllister spotted it first. Breakfast finished, on his second cup of espresso made in the stovetop machine—a much-appreciated wedding present from their friends the Corelli family—he was reading the Glasgow newspaper.

"See the Forsythe character is stirring it up again: 'neglected women artists.' He's right, but he leaves you wondering if he's only out to impress his female students."

"Meow." Joanne laughed, making a clawing gesture with her hands.

"He has a lot to say about the Sutherland trial, specially his part in defending a poor misunderstood woman artist: 'defending her from the uneducated gossips of a small Highland community.' That won't go down well."

"Let me see." She grabbed the newspaper from across the table, skim-read the piece, then, staring at her husband, exhaled loudly. "How dare he! The man is appalling."

"His writing is a bit florid, I'll grant you, but—"

She scanned the article again. "He's named her. He's identified her, made clear where she lives. He's stirred up the witch accusation, sensationalized the trial. All this is yet more gossip, a repetition of the ridiculous charges in the guise of defending an artist. It is everything Alice wants to avoid." She read the piece again. "Some of these lines . . ." The newspaper was trembling. "He used me. He asked about her house, the glen, and her connection with the community. He told me he wanted a better picture of an artist's life but only as background. I fell for it. I betrayed her."

McAllister put a hand on her arm. "Joanne, it's not your fault. You weren't to know he—"

She ignored him. "No. I promised Alice Ramsay I'd never identify her, never publish anything without her say-so. Reading this, Miss Ramsay will know the information came from me, know I'm just as much a gossip as those who accused her of witchcraft."

"Maybe Forsythe visited Alice after the trial and noted those details himself."

"No, he said he'd never been to the glen. That's why he needed me to describe it."

She remembered Forsythe's charm offensive: *I've read your work; Sandy speaks highly of you; neglected women artists; time they were recognized; my article needs a female input.* And she'd fallen for it.

"He even describes the William Morris cushion covers. I only mentioned them because I wanted to buy the same fabric." And she had been showing off her recognition of Morris's work.

The second half of the article concerned the court case, how, by appearing as the star witness at her trial, one Dougald Forsythe, hero, connoisseur, and art expert, had single-handedly rescued Alice Ramsay both in the sheriff's court and in the court of public opinion.

"The cheek of the man!" Joanne exclaimed. "Look how he mocks the locals."

"It is obvious the local judiciary knows nothing of art," he wrote in one nasty paragraph that parodied the sheriff and his questions. He described the local community as insular, stuck in the Middle Ages.

"How dare he repeat that nonsense about Alice being a witch!" Joanne's cheeks were burning with fury. "I told him clearly that the sheriff dismissed the husband's accusations as malicious."

"There was a headline using that word in the local paper," McAllister pointed out.

"Aye, and again it was *me* who told Forsythe about that." Joanne was so ashamed she'd been hoodwinked, she could say little more.

McAllister took the newspaper from her. "To any intelligent reader, it's clear Forsythe's aim is to show how he, the great art critic, rescued a woman artist from the ignorant populace of the Highlands."

"I can see that. But the details of Alice Ramsay's life up the glen came from me. How could I be so stupid?"

"I'll talk to Sandy."

"No! I was the one commissioned to write a piece. I'll phone Sandy."

McAllister nodded. Seeing how upset Joanne was, knowing

how much she wanted to have her work published, he felt sorry for his best friend. "He won't be at work until Monday morning." *Just as well*, he was thinking. *Joanne can put the fear of the Wee Man into the best of us when she's riled.*

Annie came into the kitchen. "Mum, we're off to the Saturday matinee." Then she stared. "Have you two been fighting?"

"No." Joanne realized she was too abrupt. "No. It's just some idiot man who used my information in his work without my permission."

Annie shrugged. "When I grow up, women will do the same jobs as men, only better."

Joanne snorted. "Aye, that'll be the day."

Over the weekend she stewed on Forsythe's article. Many times she came to the same conclusion: she had been gossiping on the telephone, and in doing so she had betrayed Alice Ramsay. Do as you would be done by. That was how Joanne tried to live her life. *And I failed.*

◆   ◆   ◆

On Monday morning, McAllister telephoned Sandy Marshall. A hatchet job, McAllister called the article, "an exercise in self-promotion at the expense of a woman who has already been crucified by some in the local community."

Sandy agreed. "I don't know how it was passed, but it was not the article I read." McAllister knew some poor subeditor would pay for the oversight.

"Disaster" was Joanne's word when she spoke to Sandy.

"Smug, self-satisfied, full-o'-himself wee shite" were some of the words Sandy used. "He's finished," was the editor's pronouncement on the fate of Dougald Forsythe.

Not that that was any comfort, Joanne decided. She'd already lost any chance of friendship with a fascinating woman. And lost her self-respect. "I'm sorry for being upset with you, Sandy. McAllister did say there would be an explanation."

"I'd never have published if I'd seen it before it went to print. No excuse, I know, and I can't apologize enough." He'd promised not to tell Joanne that he'd already had a blast from McAllister over the article. *Not what I need first thing Monday morning.*

"Sorry, I should have trusted you." Another "sorry." She knew she should stop apologizing.

"I know what I'd like to do to that man . . ."

She listened. Then began to giggle. "No, Sandy! You can't send his you-know-whats in a parcel. My postie might guess. Or the cat. She'd definitely sniff them out."

◆   ◆   ◆

On Tuesday morning, the letter with a Sutherland postmark arrived. Joanne instantly knew whom it was from. She took it into the sitting room. She sat in the big armchair with the high back and deep arms, a chair that gave a sense of support, of safety. She took the folded page out. Took a deep breath. Opened it. It was all she had dreaded. And more.

Joanne, it began—no date, no address, no "Dear."

The newspaper article has caused me great distress. It has also revived the gossip about myself. Again I have to put up with strangers and neighbors and acquaintances discussing me, my life, my past, my reasons for living here, alone, in a remote glen.

On closer reading of the offensive piece, I have detected details that few could have known about, such as the paintings on the walls of my home.

Only you could have provided the author of this piece with such details, which he has used to illustrate his self-aggrandizing article.

I thought better of you.

Please do not reply. Please do not contact me again.
Alice Ramsay.

That phone call, Joanne was thinking. The way he'd charmed her. The way she'd fallen for it. And he'd promised—"cross my heart and hope to die," he'd said when she'd told him, twice, that he could never use Alice's name or identify her whereabouts.

What was I thinking?

The phone rang out. "Yes?" She didn't mean to be abrupt, but she was feeling . . . abrupt.

"Calum Mackenzie here. Sorry, is this a bad time?"

"Sorry. I thought it might be someone else." Not that the great Dougald Forsythe would ever apologize. "What can I do for you, Calum?"

"Thon article in the Glasgow newspaper, it's stirred up a lot of interest."

"I can imagine."

"And I'm hearing there might be some as want to stop Miss Ramsay from visiting the old folks, maybe even shopping at the local shops. Feelings are running high." He didn't say it was his mother who wanted to ban Miss Ramsay from their premises, but for once, his father had stood up to his wife.

"Miss Ramsay wrote to me. She's furious. Quite rightly." She took a deep breath. "I can't be responsible for small-minded small-town gossip. It's not my fault that traitor Forsythe broke a confidence." As she said this, she knew it was untrue. In discussing Alice Ramsay, she was as guilty of gossiping as Calum's mother.

Calum said, "Mum doesn't mean any harm. She's lonely and likes to talk about people and . . . you know."

She heard his voice, quiet, apologetic, with a hint of sadness, and was immediately contrite. "I'm sorry, I'd never betray Miss Ramsay. Or anyone—not deliberately."

"I know."

She sighed. " I hope it all blows over soon."

"Hope so too." It was his turn to sigh. "Bye-bye for now."

"Bye. And Calum, thanks for listening." She meant it. She did not really know him. She would probably never work with him. But another journalist's opinion mattered.

Joanne found herself standing in her hallway, the receiver in her hand still purring, telling herself, *I'm no better than those gossips I condemn.*

CHAPTER 5

~

Alice is distraught. And afraid.

She remembers being at the garage shop to pay for petrol and pick up the newspapers. How Mrs. Mackenzie had handed her the Herald, *open at the article, saying, "You're famous and, from what this says, too good for the likes o' us."*

She remembers the woman's malicious smile. Not wanting to satisfy her, Alice had said, "I can't help what others say, or write."

"But," Mrs. Mackenzie had said, "it mentions you by name, so maybe you should be interested." And she'd shoved it into Alice's basket, along with the milk, charging her for a newspaper she didn't want.

"How could she? How could she? How could she?" Alice shouts this to the wind, hoping it will carry all the way across two counties into what she imagines is the smug-snug home of Joanne Ross.

Publishing my business in a local newspaper is one thing; publication in a national newspaper that is read even in London is another.

Later, deliberately letting go of her fury, knowing how much it damages the tranquillity she needs to paint, she remembers those who spoke up for her. Nurse Ogilvie and Dr. Jamieson, both were called for the prosecution, both turning out to be her best witnesses, best allies. She remembers the kindness and friendship from Mrs. Galloway. The support, with a squeeze of her hand, from the young nurse who works with the old people. Alice had heard she was engaged to the reporter, that short fellow. Heaven help her, with Mrs. Mackenzie as a mother-in-law.

"Good people. Nurse Elaine, she's young, but she's kind and clear-headed." She scratches the dog's ears. "Listen to me, will you? Talking to a dog. First sign of the mind going, they say."

The wee dog cocked his head, wanting her to continue scratching. If he could, he would tell her he understands. He cares. So he whines.

"Sorry," she says, "I should be used to betrayal by now."

Next day, Alice picks up her letters from the post office, thankful the boxes were in the entranceway and she would not have to endure the stares, the sideways glances, from other customers. She uses her key, removes the letter she had half-expected, half-dreaded. She goes to her Land Rover and writes a reply on a sheet from her drawing pad. She knows he is not interested in explanations, and certainly nothing is ever to be said in writing. Or in telephone calls. Not even from public call boxes. Never know who is listening, he'd taught them.

She doesn't want to see him. Yet she misses him. Misses the life she used to have.

Drat! She realizes she needs a stamp and will have to go into the post office after all.

She assumed he will come by train. So she suggests a time, one week hence, and a place, far enough away but convenient for both of them.

◆   ◆   ◆

The encounter with Alice Ramsay in the Station Square was much worse than Joanne had imagined. She knew that after Forsythe's article, she was unlikely to meet Alice Ramsay again, as any contact would be fraught with misapprehensions. Yet she longed to explain. In her mind she had written a letter, she had rehearsed the conversation, she had fantasized the outcome: Alice was understanding, forgiving, and they became friends. In her mind.

The day was dreich—damp, cold, with intermittent rain. The figure crossing the square towards Joanne had her umbrella tilted forwards partially covering her face, so the women did not recognize each other until they almost collided.

Joanne instinctively said, "Lovely to see you, Miss Ramsay."

They were standing at the base of a statue honoring a Highland soldier killed in some forgotten war.

Alice stared at Joanne. Not cold, not warm, just a clear, calm stare. "I have nothing to say to you."

She walked away to the steps of the Station Hotel, where a gentleman in a suit, also carrying an umbrella, joined her on the top step. The doorman took both umbrellas. The gentleman took Alice's hand, smiled at her, then they disappeared through the large brass-handled doors.

Joanne was trembling and needed to sit down. Across the street, at an entrance to the covered Victorian market, was a tea shop. She ordered and took a seat as far away from the window as possible. It took two cups of tea and a sticky raisin bun for the hurt to subside to a slow-heartburn ache.

On the bus home, she stared out the window into a day half lost in mist—mist from the river, mist from tears. Going over and over the encounter, it was the tone of Alice's voice that hurt. *I've nothing to say to you.* There had been a hint of pity, of disdain. Or was it indifference?

Walking the last stretch from the bus stop to home, Joanne again considered her part in the betrayal of Alice Ramsay.

She owned up to being foolish, naive even, admitted she'd been flattered by Dougald Forsythe, seduced by him calling her a fellow artist. When she'd protested, he'd said, "You are a writer, therefore an artist." Fatal word, that, *artist.*

Her loneliness she considered. Then dismissed. *I have a husband who is not only the man I love but a friend. I have Chiara Kowalski.* Her friendship with the Italian refugee and incomer to this insular town was warm and true. But since Chiara's marriage and the birth of her son, they met less frequently. Joanne had a sister she saw less than she should. She had a mother she barely communicated with. The violence in her first marriage had isolated her. The common knowledge of her divorce made her reluctant to seek new friends.

Meeting Alice Ramsay was like having a character in a story come to life. Her independence, her home, her books, her work, her way of talking, and her dedication to her art were familiar to Joanne only from novels or articles in one of McAllister's literary magazines. An artist was not someone she expected to meet in the wilds of Scotland. Paris or London, yes. Edinburgh even. But to know one herself had always seemed like too great a dream for Joanne to harbor.

I was wrong. I made a mistake. And it has cost me a possible friendship.

She couldn't yet recognize it, but in accepting the loss and acknowledging her part in the debacle, Joanne had changed. Healed. She was leaving behind, slowly but surely, her former self, a woman with no identity except that of daughter to a tyrant father, wife to an equally cruel husband, and mother to two young girls. To see herself as a writer, an artist even, was her dream. Meeting Alice Ramsay, seeing how she lived and worked, had made that fantasy seem possible.

Write, Joanne told herself. *Escape into the romancing of a bonnie lassie by her Highland hero. Write anything and everything to block out the glums.*

So she did.

Joanne knew that her husband would have good suggestions, good insights into her struggles to find a plot for a novel. But she knew she wouldn't ask. To show him a finished manuscript, for him to be overwhelmed with admiration, that was her fantasy.

After three days of thinking and two more days of anxiety, she decided she had to talk to someone who knew about writing.

"*Highland Gazette*. How may I help you?" It was a new girl on reception, and Joanne couldn't remember her name. That made her sad. The *Gazette* had saved her, made her who she now was.

Having started as a part-time typist and evolved into a part-time then full-time journalist, her work had given her an income and an escape from her former husband. Initially, she had been intimidated by the new editor, John McAllister. Marrying him had been beyond her imagination. *A man like him marry a woman like me?* she would have asked. For a man to take on a divorcée and two children was rare, especially in a society decimated by war, where women outnumbered men. For a man as respected and accomplished and prosperous as McAllister to do so was practically unheard of.

She missed working, missed the day-to-day chats, the laughter, the controlled chaos of deadline day. Don McLeod, the deputy editor, and Rob McLean, friend and fellow reporter, even Hector Bain, the all-round nuisance but brilliant photographer—she missed them.

What she didn't regret was not working with McAllister now that their relationship had changed. He made her nervous; nothing intentional on his part, it was she who had lost her spontaneity and her confidence. And she hated how solicitous he became when she couldn't find a pencil or a phone number or the right word for a sentence. He too was terrified the operation on her brain would leave her diminished, but she knew it was simply who she was, who she had always been, but forever searching for more.

About to ask for Rob, she found herself saying, "Mr. McLeod, please."

Someone picked up the phone and answered with an irritated "Aye?"

"It's Joanne."

"Lass. How are you? Where are you? No lost in the wilds o' Mackenzie country, are you? Right funny people up there." As a McLeod of Skye, he had the right to joke about fellow clansmen.

"I'm at home. And I need your advice." She was smiling as she spoke, knowing she'd called the right person, knowing Don cared for her. Much shorter than her, his head reaching her shoulders, partial to a drink and a bet, and a chain smoker, he was not a man she would have imagined as a father figure. If someone had described him as such, she would have protested, saying he was a friend. But father figure he had become, a person who gave her painfully honest advice, a friend who cared for her as a daughter.

"I was just about to go and have ma dinner break, so why don't we—"

"I am not going to the Market Bar."

"Pity. The Station Hotel? You can have tea, I can have a dram."

"Not there either." She was scared Alice Ramsay might still be there. Joanne could only think of tea shops. "No, you're right. The Station Hotel, just not the bar."

Half an hour later, she and Don met up. Lunch was being served to the worthies of the county and what looked like commercial travelers, which they turned out to be, as there was a sales conference of insurance agents going on. That and a Liberal Party meeting made the place much busier than usual. Joanne was uncertain if she was relieved or disappointed when she discovered no sign of Alice Ramsay.

"You're looking well," Don said as he looked around for an empty table. He spotted one, and as they reached it, a man in a navy-blue suit with a shiny tie swept in and pulled out a chair. But when he saw Don's face, he stood aside.

That glower from Don McLeod would have made Joe Louis stand aside, Joanne decided.

"I'm glad to see you're looking the same as ever," Joanne said as she looked at him over her menu.

"Pity. I need to look ten years younger." Seeing the question in her eyes, he continued, "The high heid yins in the board of management want to give me my gold watch." He took a long glug of his beer. "I ask you, what eejit came up wi' the idea o' giving a person a gold watch on retirement? To count down the hours to the grave? Nah, I'm hanging on as long as I'm standing."

"McAllister will be pleased to hear it."

"Aye, and so he should be. No one knows this place like I do." He looked around at all the strangers. "Or like I used to. Nearly the end o' another decade, but too many changes too fast for my liking."

She was quiet. Joanne did not want a discussion on the pros and cons of progress, Don's pet peeve, as she, for one, hoped the new decade would bring changes. And she felt in her bones, in the air, on the television, in the demolition of the old buildings on Bridge Street and along the river, that changes were indeed coming.

"I wanted your advice."

"The case in Sutherland? The woman some say is a witch? Are you still following it? It's a good story, that."

"After the disaster in the *Herald,* no."

Don nodded. McAllister had told him already.

"I'm interested in using the burning of the last witch in Scotland for a short story, maybe even using it for . . ." Her voice trailed off. She was unable to say the word, fearing it was an ambition too far.

"A book," he said. "Aye, why not? Witches is always interesting, specially if you make it spooky. Mind you, I'll never be persuaded thon poor woman was the last witch hereabouts. If you read some o' the letters to the *Gazette* you'd be convinced the town and county is hooching wi' them."

"Don!" She laughed, but recalling the trial of Alice Ramsay, "witch hunt" was still an appropriate term.

"So, how are you going to tackle the idea? Historical? Romantic? Base it on the mean-spirited gossip o' those who condemned Miss Ramsay just as they condemned thon poor auld wifie that was burned alive centuries ago?"

"You are completely incorrigible!" The laugh burst out of her, making those around look up, making Don grin, making her cover her mouth with one hand and smile with her eyes.

"Incorrigible but right."

"Aye. Maybe. And thank you. I needed to be reminded there's lots worse troubles than mine."

"With writing, it's a good idea to begin at the beginning," Don continued.

"Starting with the last witch in Scotland?"

"Maybe no that far back. Ask why was the Ramsay woman accused? How come it went as far as a trial? Seems a bit far-fetched that the police would be involved if it's only tea she was making. Naw, there's got to be more. Research, then do what I always told you. When? Who? What? Why?"

"I'll never be able to use it. But yes, the why is what interests me."

"Write it for no other reason than to put it to rest. Ask questions in a big sense. Why do small communities turn on those who are different? Is it malice? Idleness? And if a person is seen as suspicious, are they? If someone is acting weird, do they have something to hide? Or are they just plain weird? Sometimes something—animal instinct, call it what you will—is behind the gossip and speculation, an' it turns out to be true, or partly true."

"Alice Ramsay was guilty of being a woman alone—no man, no children, even her dog is a stray. She is, was, content. That's all." Joanne knew her voice had risen and sat back to calm herself. "Thank you, o Great Wise One, it's good to talk it over."

"For that you can fetch the next round." He looked towards the bar and the barman, who had known Don for at least thirty-five years, nodded. "Ach, no need. But I have to warn you, this is the last time I buy you lemonade. Any self-respecting writer knows it's the hard stuff you need to be a novelist, ladies included."

As she walked up the hill to home, she felt lighter. Don was right. She was assuming Alice Ramsay had nothing to hide. So what evidence did the police have that made the procurator fiscal decide to go ahead with a trial? What didn't come out? It was then that she realized she knew nothing about the prosecution's case.

She was panting by the time she reached the top of Steven's Brae. Still not completely fit, she could walk for miles on the flat, but the steep brae and the cobblestones were a challenge. By the time she reached home, she was desperate to write. Afraid that the words and ideas might escape, like dandelion seeds in the wind. She fairly flew into the sitting room to her typewriter.

◆　◆　◆

The Sutherland Case.

The woman lived alone. She was content with her life, and said so. Fulfilled in her work, never seeming to need a husband or children or the company of others, at first she attracted the curiosity of her neighbors. Then suspicion.

CHAPTER 6

～

It had been five days since the meeting in the hotel. She enjoyed meeting him again but wondered if she was not being paranoid. Life was now returning to normal, and she was keen to add the final touches to the manuscript.

Then I'll make a decision whether to spend another winter here. I do so miss the sun.

Alice looks around at the bright, late-autumn, gold-red day and resolves to walk, to tramp to the high moors, and take pictures before resuming work. She laces up her stout brown boots, slings her smallest camera around her neck, and calls the dog.

She is about to set off when she hears a vehicle in the distance. So does the dog. His ears prick up, but he is silent.

Shading her eyes with two hands, she scans the moorland. Nothing. She looks down to the dip where the burn runs to meet the river and continue to the firth and the sea. Again, nothing. Along the tree line all seems as deserted as ever. She considers fetching the binoculars.

Don't be so silly, she chides herself.

"Must be a Forestry vehicle," she tells the wee dog. He wags his tail, then bounds off. She takes his lack of alarm as a sign that all is well.

No one is out there, she tells herself. You are being ridiculous.

◆   ◆   ◆

"Gazette."

"It's me."

"I'll be home for lunch."

"That's not why I'm calling," she said. "Sorry. It's just such a shock and—"

"Joanne, what's wrong?"

"I'm fine. Well, not really. But I will be."

McAllister sighed. "I can't help if I don't know."

"Mrs. Mackenzie from Sutherland called. She says Alice is dead."

"Alice Ramsay?"

"And the way she put it . . ." She hesitated. "She says Alice died the day before yesterday and the police think Alice killed herself. The story is in today's Sutherland newspaper."

"Are you sure?"

"Yes. No. I can't believe it. Not Alice. She is so . . . was so . . . she'd never kill herself."

"You never know who, you never know why someone takes their own life."

Joanne flinched. She could say nothing to that. His younger brother had let the river swallow him. McAllister was intimate with suicide—a word never uttered, a word always in the air, a kite of doom floating above her husband. And his mother.

"Why would Mrs. Mackenzie call you?"

"A tip. Thought you and the *Gazette* might be interested, she said, and she implied her local newspaper couldn't function without her input."

They both knew that with a huge geographical area covered by their local newspapers, informants could be time-wasting but crucial.

"How, exactly, did Miss Ramsay die?" he asked. "Did the newspaper say?" He quickly answered his own question. "No, of course not." This was Scotland. This was 1959 and a local newspaper. Nothing direct could be printed. But the code words, the conventions of reporting suicide, would make it clear. "Joanne, I am so sorry. I know Alice Ramsay meant a lot to you." Bloody clichés, he thought, and you, a journalist, you should know better. He too was shaken—partly by the mention of suicide, partly because he feared for his wife's well-being.

"I only talked to her properly the once." Joanne's voice trailed off. She couldn't say what she was really thinking, that Alice was a woman with a life she would have liked for herself—if she hadn't been trapped by an early marriage and children. "I wonder what will happen to her pictures."

"I'll come home."

"And her hens. She'd never abandon her hens."

"See you in about twenty minutes."

"No. Come back at the usual time. I need to think."

To mourn, he thought. "Are you sure?"

"I'm fine. See you later."

Joanne remembered word for word what McAllister had said, and it didn't help. *You never know who, you never know why someone takes their own life.*

Joanne was pacing. Shivering and pacing. She knew it was not her fault. But she also knew she had been complicit.

If I hadn't talked to that beast Forsythe.

The phone rang. *It's McAllister checking up on me.*

"What?" she shouted down the line.

"Joanne? Calum Mackenzie here. Sorry to call you at home, but . . ."

"Sorry, Calum. I just found out about Alice. Your mother told me."

"Aye, she would. She likes to pass on information to the paper." There was a hint of impatience in his voice, and Joanne sensed that it was something Calum would be teased about. "Joanne, I'm sorry I didn't tell you sooner." He couldn't tell her he'd been too shocked to talk.

"Well, I know now."

"Erm, I'm not sure how to tell you this . . ." He sniffed as though he had a cold, and Joanne wanted to tell him to use a hankie, just as she would to her daughters.

She waited. She heard him taking a deep breath.

"Alice Ramsay left a note—more a message, really."

"How do you know that?"

Calum went silent.

"Sorry. I know how it works in small towns." She guessed someone he had been at school with or a neighbor or a relative working with the police had told him. "What did it say?"

"The police found the page from the *Herald* with Forsythe's article on the kitchen table. Her notebook was on top, open at your name and your home and *Gazette* telephone numbers."

"I see." She couldn't process the news. Not yet. Not in a conversation with a twenty-two-year-old who was almost a stranger. After a moment, she gathered herself to ask, "How did Alice die?"

"I heard that she hanged herself."

"No!" Joanne moaned. "That's horrible." She always assumed that when women killed themselves, they took tablets of some kind and drifted away in their sleep. A coward's way out, it would be said if the victim was a man. But hanging? That was so brutal, so judicial. And final.

"Joanne, sorry, I have to go now. I just wanted to let you know."

"Your mother beat you to it." Joanne didn't mean to sound so bitter but was shocked that a stranger should take it on herself to spread the news.

"I'm sorry." Whether for his mother or for Alice wasn't clear. "I have to finish ma report. I'll send you a copy if you like."

"Yes, please." Her voice was a whisper.

"I'm sorry, Joanne," he said again before he hung up.

Not knowing what else to do, she put on her coat and hat and half-walked, half-stumbled to the *Gazette* office. She stopped at the bottom of Castle Wynd to take some deep breaths, not wanting her husband to see the depths of her distress. And guilt. But she needed company.

"Shocked" was not a word that could describe her feelings; "complete disbelief" was closest. She couldn't believe Alice Ramsay would kill herself. She was so alive; she'd created such a beautiful home. Leave the glen, yes, that she could understand, especially with winter coming on. But kill herself over some ridiculous gossip? No, not the woman Joanne had met.

McAllister was in the reporters' room with Don McLeod and Rob McLean. Hector Bain, the photographer, was there too.

"Hiya, Joanne. Nice to see you." Hector's grin was reminiscent of a Halloween turnip lantern. His hair color also.

"Good to see you, Hector."

"Are you all right?" McAllister asked.

"We've heard," Don said. "Calum Mackenzie called." He didn't mention that Calum had also asked if the *Gazette* would be interested in publishing the story. Joanne was glad she did not have to explain why she was there.

"Sad business, suicide," Rob said.

"It wasn't." Joanne, her back straight, her lips pressed tight as though keeping in the anger, the sadness, and the indignation, continued, "No matter what anyone tells me, no matter what the note implies, I will never believe she killed herself."

"Note?" Rob was interested. At the age of twenty-four, he

had finally grown up but still couldn't disguise his eagerness for a story.

"It wasn't a note. It was only the newspaper with that stupid article left on the kitchen table with my name and telephone number beside it." Her voice was flat. Deliberately so. She wanted to shout, *It is not my fault!*

Don said, "I never met the woman, but with suicide, you can never pick who will—"

"Don, she just wouldn't. Believe me."

McAllister took her arm. "Let's walk."

"The girls will be home from school soon."

"I'll call Annie," Rob volunteered, "tell her you're finally off on your honeymoon." Even that did not raise a smile.

As they walked down the stairs, Joanne ahead of him, Mc-Allister heard Hector asking, "What was that all about?" *Indeed,* McAllister was thinking, *what is this all about?* He hated not being able to protect Joanne from bad news; his greatest fear was that an upset, a scandal, would affect her, depress her, in ways he couldn't anticipate.

They walked across the castle forecourt, not seeing the view or the statue or the river. They walked down the steep brae to the riverbank and followed the path towards the islands.

No matter how many times they walked this walk, it always soothed them, putting fear and worry in perspective, gladdening the heart. Joanne had a dream of living on a river. *Much too pricy for us*, she'd said often as she admired the mansions of the wealthy townsfolk.

He had the good sense not to speak. And she didn't want to talk. So, in silence except for the quiet roar of rushing water, they crossed the bridge, walked over one island, and crossed a smaller bridge onto the next. At the final bridge, Joanne turned around and began walking back the way they had come.

Keeping to the middle of the path, avoiding the deep banks of autumn leaves lining the sandy walkways, she was looking up through the tunnel of bare branches. She watched one solitary leaf that had survived wind and weather come twirling down to fall at her feet. She couldn't resist. She jumped into them, began kicking up leaves, stirring up small clouds of red and orange and gold and dust and sand and a smell, a damp dank earthy scent. She relished it, until the memory of her father's funeral hit, the smell of freshly turned earth in a freshly dug grave.

"I wonder who will bury her," Joanne said. "She told me she had no one."

"I don't know," McAllister replied. He was not one for funerals. He believed in the memory of the person, not the worship of a body when it was all too late.

"I will be there."

He said, "I'll come with you."

"Thank you."

They didn't take the river path back, instead walking up the steep hill that wound through woodland to their home. Not until they reached Drummond Road and had their breath back did she speak.

"You'd have liked her. Like you, she lived in Europe for years. Before and after the war, I think. She spoke Italian, she said. And I think she spoke French—she had French books, anyhow. I can see her there. Living in the sun. Painting. Visiting art galleries and churches and . . . Sorry, McAllister. It all seems so wrong."

"I know."

The funeral would not be immediate; this they both knew.

The procurator fiscal would institute a fatal accident inquiry, starting with a postmortem. Only after the finding—suicide, natural causes—would there be a funeral.

"We'll wait till the legalities are over," McAllister said. "Then we will go to Sutherland to say farewell."

✦ ✦ ✦

Next morning, Joanne was once more on the phone to Calum Mackenzie. "It's about the trial," she started—no need to say which trial. "I wanted to ask . . ." She had no idea what she wanted to ask; she just couldn't let go of Alice Ramsay.

"I don't mind. Maybe we could meet up?"

Joanne dreaded the thought of another drive. The last one had been fun, but it had taken her three days to recover.

"Me and my fiancée, Elaine, we're coming down your way," Calum said. "She has a training day at the hospital, and I'm driving her down in ma dad's car, so I've all day to kill."

"When?"

"Friday coming."

"Perfect." Joanne was pleased. "Phone me when you arrive, then come for a cup of tea. No, better still, let's meet at the *Gazette* office. I can show you around, introduce you to everyone."

Now it was Calum's turn to be delighted. "Elaine has to be at the hospital at nine o'clock, so let's say . . ."

"Ten o'clock at the *Gazette*."

✦ ✦ ✦

Joanne sat in a visitor's chair in her husband's office, Calum in the other. Purloining McAllister's chair was one step too many. She had her reporter's notebook and a pen. She put on reading glasses. They reminded her that the surgeon had feared for her eyesight.

In her thinking, however, she'd reached a turning point in her recovery. For a long while, she'd believed that the attack was her fault. She wrestled with different scenarios in which she should have done this, could have done that, changing the outcome. She wrestled with what she should have said, or done, and after the fact decided that she was not clever enough. Or brave enough. Until McAllister showed her different.

Joanne guessed he would be unlikely to support her investigation into Alice Ramsay's death, but she was determined to find out more, if only to lessen her own guilt.

That stare, that sentence uttered in a cold voice on a cold day in the Station Square, would not go away. *I thought better of you.* Joanne had been, and still was, the victim of small-town gossip. And she in turn had gossiped with Dougald Forsythe. That she could not forgive herself for.

"The trial of Alice Ramsay," she began. "Why was she prosecuted?"

This was a question that flummoxed Calum still. The charge was an obscure one; even the procurator fiscal had wrestled with it. Calum hated to think about the miscarriage, deliberate or otherwise. Anything to do with what he called "women's plumbing" he avoided.

"When you asked to meet, I gathered it might be about the trial, so I looked at my original notes." He pulled out a small spiral-bound reporter's notebook. "There was the husband called for the prosecution. And the wife. There was Dr. Jamieson and Nurse Ogilvie." He turned a page. "After the woman lost the baby, she didn't go to the hospital. The husband went with her to the doctor. The doctor said nothing could be done. The husband accused Miss Ramsay. The doctor apparently dismissed the notion. So the husband, he went to the police, saying Miss Ramsay gave his wife some medicine to make her vomit and cause an abor—"

"A miscarriage."

"Aye, that's the word." Calum was grateful. That was not the word he had been thinking of, and "miscarriage" was much preferable to the other term for losing a baby. "The husband insisted it was deliberate. But Elaine says—she's my fiancée—she says why would Miss Ramsay do that? For months, she'd been helping some of the old folk, giving them home-brewed tea and medicines. No one objected. Nurse Ogilvie said it was all harmless stuff like her granny used to make. And many women, so I'm told, suffer terribly from sickness when they have a baby."

He remembered his mother gossiping about how Miss Ramsay was always interfering, especially at the old people's home, formerly the workhouse, and how she was only helping because she was after some old person's inheritance. Calum knew, as did most in the district, that this was a Council Home, and people there had nothing. Some didn't even have visitors, Elaine told him, and they were happy to see Miss Ramsay because she listened to their stories about the old days.

"The doctor gave evidence for the prosecution. He was their first witness." Calum was remembering the morning session and how, in spite of his education and his reputation as a good doctor, he did not go over well in the witness box. "Too sure of himself" was his mother's phrase, and in this case she was right. The defense had torn him to shreds.

"You have the toxicology report on the mother's blood?" the fiscal had asked.

"The patient came to me too late to do tests," Dr. Jamieson had replied.

"In other words, no."

"Herbal concoctions can clear the blood quickly, and—"

"This herbal concoction Miss Ramsay gave the unfortunate woman, was that identified?'"

"Yes."

"And?"

"It was *Rubus idaeus*."

"Otherwise known as raspberry leaves."

"Yes. It is suspected that in sufficient quantities, and taken early enough in a pregnancy, they can affect the tissue of the womb, causing—"

"Suspected? I see. And in what quantities are we talking about, a cup full, a pint, a gallon?"

"It's not an exact science, but a large dosage," Dr. Jamieson, young, red-haired, impulsive, sure of himself, had now been defeated. Then again, he had not agreed with the charges against Miss Ramsay to begin with.

"Next they called Nurse Ogilvie," Calum told Joanne.

"For the defense?"

"No, the prosecution. But it may as well have been for the defense, for all the good it did the fiscal's case."

"Miss Ramsay was in the habit of visiting strangers in the old people's home, was she not?" had been the first question.

"I'm not sure if you could say they were strangers. Miss Ramsay comes from a well-known family who, up until the war, were major employers hereabouts, so as a child she knew many of the old people she visited, or their families."

"But why would she visit them?"

"Simple charity." Nurse Ogilvie had supplied the answer from her personal standpoint, from her understanding of the Gospels. It had been said with such conviction, such directness, it had taken the procurator fiscal some moments to recover.

"Now, these teas she supplied. Did you know about them?"

"I did."

"Did you approve?"

"I approved of the chamomile tea to calm the nerves. And the cocoa she made in the nurses' kitchen. And the soups she brought in a flask—chicken soups, vegetable soups. She always made sure they was not too hot, not too cold, and she spoon-fed those who couldn't manage themselves."

"Yes, yes. But how can you be sure they were not tainted in any way?"

"Why would they be? Besides, Miss Ramsay always brought some for the nurses. Delicious they were too."

"So Miss Ramsay, a self-styled recluse, would often visit the hospital to sit with old people?"

"Not often. Mostly on Sundays when we were short-staffed as—"

"Was she supervised?"

"The residents' areas are open."

"And these teas, these herbal medications?"

The sheriff had intervened. "We've already covered this."

"The procurator fiscal is an experienced prosecutor," Calum told Joanne, "but he was beaten by Nurse Ogilvie's honesty. It was hard to see why the charges went to trial."

"Agreed." Joanne could not see why either.

"It was said Miss Ramsay was doing . . ." Calum hesitated. "It was rumored that girls who wanted rid of their babies could go to her for help."

"Was there evidence of that?"

"No," Calum said, "but that didn't make the stories go away."

"The defense witnesses, tell me about them." Joanne needed to hear the positives of Alice's trial.

"Mr. Dougald Forsythe." Calum grinned. "He took up so much time no further witnesses were called. A right bit of entertainment he turned out to be. But first up was Mrs. Galloway telling everyone what a good person Miss Ramsay was. How Miss Ramsay looked out for her old mother, made her smile, how she'd made tea that was good for the nerves—calmed her mother right down, Mrs. Galloway said. Next and last was Mr. Forsythe." Calum paused. "I told you about his testimony, how he annoyed the sheriff an' all."

"I know," Joanne said. "It's just that I'm trying to find how—"

"How it connects with her death?"

"How it could lead to her death."

"No idea." Calum then recounted how Forsythe had first made sure his name was spelled right. Then he'd had the ushers set up an easel with the drawing of a bird skeleton and a bird's wing. Then he'd made certain the sheriff had the portfolio of numbered references to hand.

"I hope this won't take long," the sheriff told him. Forsythe paid no heed.

"He went on and on," Calum said. "Boring everyone wi' lectures about art and the like, mostly talking about himself and how much he knows. Didn't go down too well with the locals, being called ignoramuses."

"And she was found not guilty."

"Aye. Only took Sheriff Anderson a few minutes to decide."

"Thanks, Calum." In spite of the verdict, Joanne knew, as Alice probably did, in the eyes of some she would always be guilty.

"How does knowing about the trial help?" he asked.

It was Joanne's turn to say, "No idea."

CHAPTER 7

~~~

Alice decides to re-hang the skeleton drawing, this time above the sideboard where she keeps the crockery. After the derision the small delicate bird skeleton sketch had caused in the courtroom it felt tainted by the memory.

Every time I need a cup or a plate, every time I look across, it will remind me I was once the best, she tells herself. Here in the glens, no one knows how valuable my talent made me, how they sought me out, asking for my help, because I was the best of the best.

Of course, when he asked, I said yes, without thinking of all the ramifications. I have to admit I was flattered. I never thought this one small favor could be so disastrous.

She hammers the picture hook in without measuring, her eye sure.

Alice notices the light darken, and seeing the purple bruise across the skyline, she knows that one of the frequent fierce cloudbursts typical of the glens is imminent. A bird is huddling on the windowsill. She opens the kitchen door to throw out a crust. But the sparrow has flown.

She steps out, gathers an armful of logs. A flash—she counts the seconds to the thunder-roll, watching as the storm moves towards the mountains. Something moving on the edge of the Forestry plantation registers in the corner of her eye. Another crash of thunder startles her. And the dog; he hates thunder.

She looks again but sees nothing. "Probably some deer," she tells the Skye terrier. Deer hate thunder too.

• • •

The weather had been abysmal for days—sky collapsed, drained of color, no wind, no breaks in the suffocating canopy of persistent rain.

Joanne was trying to write at the kitchen table; keeping two fires burning in two rooms was too hard. In these dreich days, fetching coal and logs from the shed chilled her, making her fear in her weakened state she'd catch a cold. The kitchen was warm, but with the wood-burning stove stoked up, wash hanging from the pulley, over the backs of chairs, on an old wooden towel rack, and the girls' school socks pegged to a length of string hung over the mantelpiece, the smell and feel of damp were thick and cloying. Everything smelled damp, she noticed, even the newspaper was warped, and there was at least four months of winter to come.

One letter and one bill and McAllister's political magazine arrived in the mail. She'd given up waiting on the publisher, consoling herself with the thought that she'd submitted to a major British publication, not a Scottish one, and to have them accept one of her stories was an ambition too far.

The letter was from Calum Mackenzie. She unfolded a cutting from a newspaper. Classified ads. There was a note with it.

Thought you might be interested.

Yours sincerely,

Calum.

The ad read: "Auction 21st October, Inchdarroch House, auction of goods and chattels of the late Miss Alice Ramsay. Items include one Land Rover, furniture, paintings, household equipment, garden equipment, and sundry bric-a-brac."

Joanne realized the twenty-first was this Saturday, three days

away, and she knew she had to attend. Not just out of curiosity—
she coveted that drawing, the one of the bird skeleton.

It had been weeks, yet still she held to the belief that she was
partly to blame for Alice's death.

When she'd said this to McAllister, he'd said, "How can you
think that? You can't blame yourself for this . . . this . . ."

"Tragedy." She knew he was right, but she couldn't shake the
conviction that her role in Alice's last days was not an innocent
one.

Still staring at the paragraph on the typewriter, wondering
where next to take her latest story—about a local postie who
served the remote communities up the glens and was the community lifeline for news, both written and oral—she heard the front
door open and close.

"Is my beautiful wife at home?"

She laughed. Then shivered. His voice made her want to grab
him and tell him how happy she was, how very glad she was to be
his wife. Instead, she said, "I'll warm up some soup."

"No," he said. "You stay there. I'll get it."

And he did, but not before reaching down, kissing her on the
top of her skull, enveloping her in a current of cold and rain and
his own particular scent of wet wool, cigarettes, and a very un-
Scottish cologne he bought whenever he was in Glasgow.

When they finished the soup, served with buttered brown
bread and lashings of parsley, he asked, "How's the writing?"

"Slow." She never liked to talk about her writing, so she
quickly passed over the newspaper cutting. "Calum Mackenzie
sent me this. I'd like to go, so I thought I'd leave the girls with
their granny and granddad Ross and drive up."

"I'll come with you. I've never been to that part of the world."

"I'd like that." She looked out at the steel sky, felt the damp wash pressing down on them, and said, "Let's hope it's not raining in Sutherland."

◆　◆　◆

Back at the *Gazette*, McAllister mentioned the trip to Don McLeod.

"We're driving up to Sutherland on Saturday morning. Joanne wants to go to an auction, Alice Ramsay's estate."

"Take the Nuisance with you. There's a junior golf tournament up there this Saturday, our lot versus theirs. I need better pictures than thon disasters the club secretary sends us."

Do I have to? McAllister was about to say, then remembered this was Hector's catchphrase.

Coverage of local sporting events mattered to the newspaper. Intercounty games were often played in wee communities, in remote parts of the Highlands, so the editor knew the logic in taking the photographer with them. The thought of being in an enclosed space with Hector for hours, with Hector endlessly discussing lenses and camera angles and light, or lack of in this weather, bothered him. He cheered himself up with the thought that while Hector covered the tournament, he could wait in the nearest bar.

◆　◆　◆

Saturday morning was still wet, but occasional breaks in the cloud cover made Joanne optimistic. "You never know, it might be nice in Sutherland."

"Considering it's farther north, I doubt it," McAllister said as he parked outside Hector Bain's house—or, rather, his granny's house, where Hec and his wee sister still lived.

"Eeyore," Joanne said, and stuck her tongue out at him.

"For that, you can drive." He honked the horn for Hector,

then opened the door to change seats. Joanne slid over, saying nothing, but she was relieved. McAllister could drive well enough, but she was better. He saw it as a way to get from place to place. She actually enjoyed it.

Hector came running through the rain, a duffel bag over his shoulder. He knocked on the driver's window. "Want me to drive?"

"No!" Hec's driving petrified Joanne. "Hector, get in. It's pouring."

They hadn't covered half a mile before Hec began to blether. "I see there's some camera stuff for sale at the auction. Maybe I'll get a bargain."

"Maybe," McAllister said. He knew that all the photographer needed was the occasional "aye," or "maybe," or a grunt, as nothing would stop the flow. He adjusted the seat to his six feet two inches, settled back, and let the road and Hec's words flow over and around him, much the same way as the rain was enveloping the car. And with the heater up full blast, the radio playing country dance music, and Joanne's steady but fast driving, they were at Bonar Bridge sooner than he expected.

"So then she'll be finished her studies, and she'll move in with me and ma granny."

"Will the wedding be before Christmas or next year?" Joanne asked.

"April," Hec explained. "The light's perfect an' the trees just right and—"

"Hec, a wedding is more than photos." Joanne laughed.

"Aye, there's the church ceremony an' all that, but . . ."

McAllister switched off again.

The farm sale would be signposted, Calum had explained when Joanne said she might not remember the turnoff.

Sure enough, there was a SALE sign. The notice was fixed to

a board, which was fixed to a fence post, which was close to disintegrating back into pulp. Joanne thought to herself that if you didn't know where to look, it would be missed. Then again, everyone in the county—and beyond—was curious about the farm, now a place with a lurid history, always to be mentioned with *Isn't that the place where . . .*

Visibility was poor; little could be seen except short stretches of the road ahead as it twisted and climbed through low-lying cloud. There were no farmsteads, fences, sheep, or militant ranks of Forestry plantations in sight, just bog cotton and ferns and heather rolling across the hills like a mantle of rotting carpet.

To an outsider it was a remarkably unremarkable landscape at the best of times, Joanne was thinking, and this was definitely not the best of times.

Three miles up the tarmac road, they came to the five-bar gate leading to the property. It was open. Tracks from other vehicles making their way to the auction made the drive muddy, and Joanne knew that the ruts and puddles hid holes too deep for a saloon car. She drove slowly, carefully, wishing she had a vehicle like Alice Ramsay's Land Rover.

Reaching the farmyard, they were surprised at the number of cars and vans and at least two tractors, one with a trailer with chickens in coops and the cockerel in a coop of his own; Alice's chickens had already been sold.

Joanne backed into a narrow space in the line of cars along the garden wall and switched off the engine. She took a deep breath and said, "Right, let's join the body of the Kirk."

McAllister smiled at her use of one of Don's favorite phrases. Glancing at her, he could see she was nervous.

She sensed his scrutiny and nodded. "I'm fine. It just all seems . . ."

"Such a waste." He knew.

And she knew he knew and put her hand out to touch his.

Hector clambered out the back of the car, leaving his duffel bag inside but with a camera concealed under his mackintosh to keep it dry. He was delighted with the scene: locals in their Sunday-best overcoats and hats, farmers in their wellie boots and tweed jackets with nonmatching deerstalker hats, some with fishing flies embedded in the band. He loved the backdrop: tumbledown outbuildings, the new slate roof on the barn glistening black and grey and petrol green, and the old cobblestones, treacherous in rain but a photographer's delight. "This is really atmospheric."

Joanne opened the boot to change her shoes for wellies. McAllister adjusted his hat to an angle that Joanne considered French. They set off towards a roofed but semiderelict former barn where much of the goods had been set out.

The auctioneer had finished with the garden implements and was moving on to the furniture. His assistant called out a lot number. The bidding began for a well-loved kitchen table and a set of mismatching chairs, now looking like the relics of a bombing. Joanne half-listened as the price rose swiftly and still ended in what she considered a bargain; the wood was oak, and with a polish, the table would be handsome.

She and McAllister looked around at the crowd, some of whom were bidders and some of whom were just plain curious. The very ordinariness of the crowd struck her. *Yet some of these people condemned Alice as a witch.* Joanne shivered at the thought. Then, looking at the individuals in the crowd, seeing the ruddy-cheeked Highland farmers, the women out for an enjoyable morning's entertainment, she was more charitable. *Don't be so judgmental,* she lectured herself. *Gossip can't kill.*

The roof on the barn was obviously new, the concrete floor clean. She found herself gazing at the wooden beams, fancying she could smell the wood. The thought came like a poisoned dart. *She hanged herself from one of these beams.* Panic flashed from her stomach to her throat. She dug her fingernails into her palm. Remembering her doctor's advice, she took a conscious breath and swallowed.

The realization that panic tasted of bile distracted her. She needed tea. Or water. There was no one she recognized to ask, and she certainly wasn't about to ask McAllister. Then, from across the room, standing between two wardrobes and a sideboard, she caught Calum Mackenzie waving at them. She waved back.

He gestured to an open space near the kitchen equipment, then pointed with his forefinger to the pictures stacked on the dresser. She nodded and began to edge towards him. "Excuse me. Sorry."

McAllister followed. The crowd parted to let them through, though not without some curious looks and some muttering. Strangers this far up the glen were unusual.

A wee round woman was sticking to Calum like a limpet mine. Joanne recognized his mother from their brief encounter at the garage. When Calum was in conversation with friends, acquaintances, and professional contacts, his mother had the good sense to say little, but she would watch the speaker, follow Calum's replies with an "aye" or "that's right" or, most frequently, a smile and a chuckle that said, *That's ma boy, isn't he grand?* It wasn't that Calum didn't notice, just that he accepted that she was his mother and this was how she was.

A pretty young woman—too healthy and capable-looking to be called beautiful—a few inches taller than Calum, also caught the wave. Joanne smiled back. With a flutter of a raised hand, Elaine introduced herself as Calum's fiancée.

"How are you, Joanne?" Calum asked when at last she made it over to them.

"Where's your manners, Calum?" his mother hissed. "It's Mrs. Ross to you."

"Actually, it's Mrs. McAllister." Joanne smiled. "But as Calum is a friend, I told him to call me Joanne."

To Mrs. Mackenzie the idea of friendship between a man and a woman of differing ages and differing social status was outside of her understanding. Therefore somehow wrong. She said nothing, but Elaine, who'd overheard the exchange, knew that later much would be made of Joanne Ross McAllister.

"Elaine." Calum's fiancée formally introduced herself. "Calum's told me a lot about you."

"And you. He's really proud of you," Joanne said. "This is McAllister."

"Your husband?" Mrs. Mackenzie asked. She looked up at him. Seeing no indication of status, she was about to dismiss him. Then she remembered he was the editor of a newspaper. "I'm Calum's mother," she said. "My Calum's done right well for himself. When he was at school, he passed all his exams wi' top marks. An' one o' his essays was printed in the paper an' him only fifteen. Then he was champion o' the junior golf team. That's before he was made chief reporter and—"

"Next lot, number ninety-seven, cameras and equipment," the auctioneer announced.

Hector pulled at the editor's sleeve as if he were a wee boy trying to get the attention of his granddad. "Will you bid for me? I'm scared I'll mess it up."

Thanks, Hec, for saving me from that woman, McAllister was thinking.

Calum spoke up. "I'll bid. None o' the locals will go against me. What's your limit?"

"Who'll offer me five pounds?" the auctioneer asked.

"Five pounds is fine," Hec said.

"Wait," Calum told him.

"Come on, ladies and gentlemen. An excellent wee camera, German-made. And lots of equipment, extra lenses. Three pounds? No? Who'll start me at one pound?"

"Ten shillings!" Calum shouted.

"Come on, the bag's worth more than that." Still no reply. And the sound of rain on car roofs drumming a tattoo made the auctioneer want to finish before the pubs closed. "Ten shillings. Sold to Calum. Now, this nice mirror, antique, looks like . . . five shillings?"

"Ten shillings?" Hector's eyes were popping.

"Wheesht," Joanne told him. But she could see him trembling and the raindrops coming off his mackintosh like a dog shaking off the rain. "Maybe you should bid for me too, Calum."

"What do you want?"

"The drawing of the bird skeleton, the one in the plain wood frame."

"The one used in evidence in court?"

"Was it?"

"Nasty old thing, thon," Mrs. Mackenzie muttered. Calum nudged her with his elbow. "But there's no accounting for taste," she added.

"I'll bid for it," McAllister said.

They waited as a few more items were presented—an

Edwardian water jug and bowl, brass fire tongs and dustpan set, a half tea set. "Royal Doulton," the auctioneer said, but still couldn't raise more than five shillings. "Sold to Nurse Ogilvie," he announced.

A prosecution witness at Alice's trial, Joanne was thinking. She watched as the nurse made her way to the bookkeeper to pay for the china. With her was a young man, tall and very thin, his skin white in a redhead way. She sensed a nervousness about him, reminding her of a highly strung greyhound, one that had been overraced and was now on its last legs. Then, as though sensing someone was watching, he turned around, scanned the crowds, and seeing Joanne, one of the few strangers at the gathering, he paused.

She could feel him trying to place her. And almost smiled as if to say *friend*. Then he was gone.

Next came a set of tools—hammers, a hand saw, a bow saw, various screwdrivers and pliers, all in a nice folding wooden box with compartments of various size. The auctioneer expected brisk bidding, as they were all of superior quality. Three competing bidders dropped out when they saw who was determined to have them.

"Twa pund an' five shillings? Do I hear ten? No? Sold to Mr. Novak." *Bang* went the hammer.

Calum leaned closer to Joanne. "Mr. Novak, it was him who had helped Miss Ramsay renovate the house."

Mrs. Mackenzie heard her son even though he had spoken quietly to Joanne. "Another one o' they foreigners," she commented loudly. "And, so I heard, she and him spoke German thegether."

"Mum." Calum was smiling when he chastised her. She took no offense. Or notice.

"Next, this wee drawing—some o' you will recognize it." The

auctioneer's assistant was holding it high. A murmur ran around the steading. "Nice frame, though no so sure about the picture." That raised a laugh. "Five pounds? No? Three? One pound?"

A local antique dealer nodded.

"One pound thirty shillings?"

Now McAllister joined in.

"Two pounds?"

Another figure, male, standing in the gloom of the far corner, raised a hand.

The auctioneer continued. "Three pounds?"

McAllister.

"Four pounds?"

The stranger.

"Five?"

McAllister.

Joanne was staring at the other bidder. There was something about him. "Calum, do you know that man? The other bidder?"

Calum stared, then whispered, "Aye, it's Dougald Forsythe, the man from the Art College. But why would he be here?"

McAllister didn't hear. Thank goodness, Joanne thought. She was uncertain how her husband would react but knew it would be on the high end of the wrath scale.

The bidding had reached twenty pounds in about fifty seconds. Then forty pounds. There had been a buzz of conversation amongst the onlookers and not a few comments on the reappearance of the art critic, but when the bidding reached fifty pounds and kept climbing, the intakes of breath over every ten-pound rise in the bidding was as clear as the hissing from a flock of geese.

At eighty pounds, Joanne said, "Stop, McAllister, I don't want it that badly." But her husband was dogged when he wanted something. He had his hands in his pockets, she knew his fists would be clenched, and his voice had dropped to almost a growl. She knew when that happened to let him be.

At one hundred pounds, he dropped out.

"At one hundred and ten pounds, to the gentleman in the far corner . . ." The auctioneer looked at McAllister, who shook his head. "Going once, twice, sold."

A huge upswell of voices greeted the price. Even the auctioneer had to pause to recover his breath. He took out a large spotted hankie, wiped his forehead, and nodded at the equally astonished spectators. This was a tale he and they would be telling for a long time to come. *One hundred and ten pounds for a scribble o' a deed bird that they ca' art*—that would be the least of the comments. Already one wag had called out, "Aa' daft them southerners."

"Psst, Hec." Joanne bent over to whisper to him, right in his ear, as she sensed Mrs. Mackenzie's interest. "Get a photo of the man who won the bid. But don't let him, or McAllister, know what you're doing."

"I won't."

When it came to his profession, she trusted him absolutely and knew from past experience that once Hector was decided, he was as obstinate as her husband.

"What is it about that drawing?" Elaine asked, stunned by the price.

"Absolute nonsense, if you ask me," Mrs. Mackenzie replied.

Elaine had put herself deliberately between Calum's mother and Joanne and had addressed the question to McAllister.

He shrugged. "No idea." Then he went out to stand under the barn eaves, light a cigarette, and ponder on the same question.

"Lot one hundred and seven, some oil paintings and three watercolors o' the glens, nicely framed." They were being sold as a job lot, as the auctioneer had earlier decided they were too hideous to fetch a decent price. The antique dealer joined in at five pounds, and Joanne put up her hand.

"Seven pounds I'm bid on my right. Sir?" the auctioneer asked the dealer. He shook his head. "Seven pounds to the lady." The hammer fell.

"Eight pounds." A voice came from the back.

"Too late," said the auctioneer.

Joanne was pleased. She at least wanted a reminder of that afternoon.

"They're nice, those pictures." Elaine smiled at her.

"I couldn't bear them being thrown out, seen as only worth the price of the frames."

"Next lot. Writing box, pens, and inkwell."

McAllister bid and won.

Joanne said, "No more; we haven't room in the car boot." She then turned to Calum. "Maybe you could introduce us to Mr. Forsythe. And I'd like to meet Nurse Ogilvie."

"What would you be wanting to meet her for?" Mrs. Mackenzie asked.

Calum frowned. "This is work, Mum."

"I'll introduce myself to Mr. Forsythe." McAllister had come back and immediately wanted to escape again. "And I'll pay for the pictures. Coming, Calum?"

Elaine jumped down from the bench where she had been sitting with Joanne. "Come on, Joanne, let's get out of here. This place gives me the creeps."

Naturally, Mrs. Mackenzie had to say what Elaine and Calum and most of the crowd knew but would not say, not to a stranger. "I heard it was on thon beam over there, right above Mr. Duncan the auctioneer's head, that she hanged herself."

Joanne had had to look up the word "schadenfreude" when

she first came across it in a book. Confronting an example here, in real life, made her shiver.

"Come on." Elaine tucked her arm through Joanne's. "You and me can check the farmhouse kitchen for the nurse. There's tea and biscuits set up over there."

With everyone deserting her, Mrs. Mackenzie looked lost. Poor soul, Joanne thought. *She's no idea how she comes across.* But as she followed Mrs. Mackenzie's stare and saw the woman's look of malice fixed on the back of Elaine, her future daughter-in-law, making her way through the crowd, Joanne's sympathy vanished. *Oh dear, there's trouble brewing there.*

Joanne and Elaine dashed across the yard to the back door leading into the kitchen. The stove had been lit, and a tea urn and pink fishy-smelling paste sandwiches were there for people to help themselves. It reminded Joanne of an after-funeral spread. And depressed her just as much.

Elaine said, "Thanks. You handled the old witch well."

Joanne had no doubt to whom she was referring. "Divide and conquer." She smiled at Elaine, seeing a pleasant young woman. *She has gumption; she'll make Calum a good wife, as long as she can cope with a mother-in-law who will never let her son have his own life.* As she was thinking this, she was scanning the empty hooks where the paintings had hung. And the room itself, empty except for a trestle table where the kitchen table and chairs had been, was just that, a small farmhouse kitchen, practical but with no charm. And no life.

An immense sense of loss overcame her. "Sorry, Elaine, I have to sit. It was a long drive up, especially in this weather." Joanne took a chair at the table.

"You just need a cup of tea," Elaine told her.

Again Joanne was reminded of the universal—at least in

Scotland—remedy for trouble, a nice cup of tea. She sighed. The only time she had been here in this glen, in this room, it had enchanted her; it had given her an immediate sense of home, of refuge. It had been warm, not just in temperature but in the love put into a collection of bric-a-brac and furniture and rugs and pictures. All the objects, old, new, and found, made the house a home. It was a place where you could dream, find inspiration, she thought.

Now, with no rag rugs, their color breaking up the grey of the stone floor, the boot marks and mud offended Joanne. Alice would never allow that, she was thinking, when she noticed the dog. Standing alone but not lonely, not wet, clean and brushed and obviously well cared for, the Skye terrier was observing the many visitors, not at all what he was accustomed to in the home of Miss Alice Ramsay.

"Hello," she called to him. "Come here, boy."

He did. He stood looking up at her. She saw the collar, blue for a boy. She tickled him behind the ears.

"So you've met Rover," a voice behind her said.

Joanne turned and looked into lovely warm brown eyes and a lovely smile in a pale face.

"I call him Rover because he is always wandering."

"I thought he was Miss Ramsay's dog."

"Oh, no, he lives with me. But she did take him in one time. Not that I had ever been up here before now, so goodness only knows how he found his way." The woman took the seat beside her. "I'm Janet Ogilvie, but everyone calls me Nurse."

"Joanne Ross. Sorry, McAllister. Och." She was shaking her head at still not being certain of her own name. "Just call me Joanne."

Nurse Ogilvie smiled back. "Yes, Mrs. Mackenzie filled me in on the confusion over your name."

"I bet she did." Elaine was there with tea and a plate of scones for herself and Joanne. "Can I get you tea, Nurse Ogilvie?"

"Thank you, dear, that would be lovely. Nice girl, that," she said as Elaine left. "Now, you wanted to talk to me?"

"I did, but . . ."

"But not now," Nurse Ogilvie finished for her, looking towards the doorway.

Mrs. Mackenzie had just bustled in like a hen in search of a lost chick. "Have you seen Calum?" she asked.

"He's in the storage place out the back," Elaine told her.

"He's—" Nurse Ogilvie looked up at Elaine. "Thank you for the tea, dear."

"I know, I know, he's in the other room," Elaine whispered. "I couldn't help myself."

"Listen, we're supposed to be off to a golf match this afternoon, so how about we all get a sandwich at the hotel?" Joanne asked Elaine. "Then we can talk."

"Better still, Calum can sign us in at the golf clubhouse. His mother won't follow us there. She thinks she's so important that she shouldn't have to pay the annual fees."

"I'll round up my husband, then. And Hector the photographer. If we squash up, we can go in our car."

Arrangement agreed, Joanne turned back to Nurse Ogilvie. "Do you mind if I ask you a bit about Miss Ramsay?"

"Not at all."

"She visited the residents in the hospital?"

"Aye, but we're not strictly a hospital, we're an old people's home. Alice would visit the residents, mainly the ones who have nobody or are a bit doolally. She would sit with them in the common room, listen to their stories, sometimes sketching them—though I don't know why, because there are none o' them any oil painting."

"And Miss Ramsay made them herbal tea?"

"Miss Ramsay would make them ordinary tea, herbal tea, cocoa, sometimes Horlicks. She baked Victoria sponge cakes for the residents—seeds and fruitcakes are no good with their false teeth."

"So is that how the rumors started? Of her poisoning people?"

"Oh, no! Whoever gave you that idea? No, the poor lassie, or at least her man, they made the accusations. To be fair, she'd lost a baby, her third miscarriage—although no one knew that at the time—and she was right depressed. But the husband, he's . . . well, a bit o' a bully, so I heard." She'd heard more than that but, unlike some, wouldn't repeat it.

Joanne could see Nurse Ogilvie was flustered and was trembling when she put down her teacup. Whether it was from passion or anger or perhaps grief, Joanne couldn't yet distinguish, and she was loath to ask the next question but went ahead. "And Mrs. Mackenzie, didn't she say Miss Ramsay had poisoned the woman?"

"Mrs. Mackenzie—you mustn't pay any heed to her havering. A woman in her situation, I'm surprised she . . . people in glass houses and all that." The way the nurse spoke almost made Joanne laugh. Nurse Ogilvie would have been more charitable to the cannibal Lizzie Borden. "Who told you about Mrs. Mackenzie saying that?"

"I can't remember where I heard it." Joanne was fibbing; she had heard it from Mrs. Galloway, the landlady at the hotel, who'd been furious at the gossipmongering from Mrs. Mackenzie and her clique.

Elaine came back. "Sorry I took so long. More tea, Joanne? Nurse Ogilvie?"

"Is that the time?" Nurse Ogilvie was consulting the upside-down brooch-watch she habitually wore even when not in uniform. "Thank you, Mrs. Ross, you've reminded me I need to be back for the residents' afternoon tea. We're short-staffed with Elaine on her day off and Miss Ramsay now gone." At the door she paused, looking around the kitchen, perhaps sensing, as Joanne had, that the house was only walls and a roof without the presence of Alice Ramsay.

More people cared than you will ever realize, Alice, Joanne thought.

"Ready?" McAllister appeared.

"I'm coming with you to show you the way," Elaine said.

"Good," McAllister replied. He was also thinking she could protect him from Hector.

Joanne asked her husband when they reached the car, "Do you have the paintings?"

"In the boot. Mind you, one of the antique dealers was keen to buy them off me. Offered me double what we'd paid."

"You didn't?"

"Too scared of my wife to sell, I told him."

Joanne poked him in the ribs. "Quite right."

◆　◆　◆

They drove to the golf clubhouse, where Calum Mackenzie—miraculously without his mother—was waiting in the foyer to sign them in.

McAllister went with Calum to the bar to order. At the opposite end of the long curved counter, he spotted Dougald Forsythe. The editor knew it was not advisable for him to go anywhere near the man and had to turn away before he did something he knew he should regret but wouldn't—like punch the man's lights out.

Apart from being trounced by the art critic at the auction, the pain the newspaper article had caused Alice and Joanne were still sore subjects in the McAllister household. That revealing the life and locality of Miss Ramsay might have contributed to her death McAllister was uncertain, though his wife was not. But he had no doubts about Forsythe's unprofessional, self-serving attitude.

"Keep me away from that man," he muttered to himself.

Calum overheard. "Aye, I will." *Who signed him in?* Calum was thinking.

Ten minutes or so later, Calum watched an obviously inebriated Forsythe weave his way through the tables.

"Sorry, really sorry," he said when he bumped a table, rattling the drinks.

McAllister had his back to the room and was contemplating the vista of a sea more white than grey, gorse bushes bent landwards by ceaseless weather, and huddled competitors waiting their turn to tee off only to have the balls return in their direction in the fierce wind.

Calum contemplated waylaying the art critic, but as the man was six feet tall and drunk, he hesitated.

Too late. Forsythe was standing there, swaying slightly from his heels to the balls of his feet. Calum longed to check if the southerner was wearing the infamous patent-leather shoes, but he daren't duck beneath the table.

"Mrs. Ross, isn't it? Joanne—you don't mind if I call you Joanne?" He didn't wait for an answer. "Mad at me for outbidding your husband for the drawing?" He had turned the straight-backed chair around and sat. Joanne thought the pose ridiculous. In other circumstances, she would have laughed, but she was aware of her husband's anger and afraid of a scene in a crowded room in a distant county in an incident that might attract the police. And be reported in the local newspaper.

"Who invited you?" McAllister snapped.

"Wheesht." Joanne put a hand on McAllister's sleeve. "Mr. Forsythe, I wanted that drawing as a reminder of a lovely lady and a true artist," she said. "You betrayed her. You don't deserve to have her work." She straightened her neck and glared at him, waiting for him to deny the accusation.

"I never meant to harm her."

"But you did. As my husband indicated, you are not welcome."

"All I wanted was a reminder of a talented but sadly unacknowledged Scottish female artist," he countered.

Joanne waved her hand, swatting him away as though he were a fly on a sandwich. "We bought some of her other works, so no problem." She was angry, yes. And upset. But seeing him now, she thought him ridiculous. His sitting on a reversed chair, his ruby-red cravat, his overlong hair, brought to mind one of McAllister's words, said in a strong Glasgow accent: "poser."

Caricature of an artist was Joanne's kinder assessment.

Different, Elaine was thinking.

He's a right character. Dougald Forsythe dumbfounded Calum.

Now is not the time or place to give him a good hiding, McAllister was telling himself. But his hands were shaking in the effort to keep them under the table.

Hector had no opinion of the man but had taken plenty of pictures, as requested. All Hec could think about were the canvas and leather bag—a poacher's bag, he thought—and the camera and equipment, still marveling that such a precious camera and lenses were now his.

"Well, nice meeting you," Forsythe said. His long face and his downward-turning eyes showed a weariness that almost made Joanne relent. His red-veined nose indicated years of drinking. In Joanne's opinion and experience, drink was never an excuse for bad behavior.

"I can't say the same, Mr. Forsythe," she told him. "You betrayed me. Most of all, you betrayed Alice. I hope you can live with that."

He took a step backwards, her words landing as squarely and as painfully as any punch.

No one at their table or the neighboring tables saw him leave—they were too busy admiring Joanne.

"Jings!" Hector's eyes were round and bright, his grin almost reaching his ears. "You terrified me as much as him."

McAllister's shoulders were shaking in his attempt not to laugh long and loud. "That's him told."

Elaine and Calum were looking at each other, smiling. "Good for you," Elaine said.

"Ever since the trial, I've wanted to pay back that man," Calum added. "He made us out to be an ignorant bunch of teuchters."

Joanne said, "If I wasn't driving, I'd have a port to celebrate. Instead, I'll have a shandy."

Hector went to talk to the tournament organizers and take pictures of the returning golfers; no way would he risk his cameras in the salt-laden air. The talk returned to a discussion of the auction and the ridiculous amount Forsythe had paid for the picture. McAllister joked it might be an unknown masterpiece.

"I was sure it was Alice's work," Joanne said. "At least, that was the impression I got when I saw it in her kitchen."

As they waited for Hec to return, the conversation slowed into more personal exchanges between the couples. In the far corner, next to the picture windows overlooking the first tee, McAllister noticed the man with whom he'd had an encounter in Alice Ramsay's farmyard. He was sitting with two gentlemen. Locals, McAllister decided, though he wouldn't have been able to say why.

McAllister had been carrying a box of books he'd purchased as a job lot after hearing they were to be thrown out. Reaching the car, keys in hand, he had been fumbling to open the boot quickly to avoid the rain.

The driver of the car next to him started the engine and began to move out, almost running over his boxes—and his feet.

"Hey, watch it!" he'd called out to the driver. But there was no slowing down, no acknowledgment, and the car continued on into the yard and down the track to town. McAllister had seen that the driver was in a chauffeur's uniform, with a cap placed on the passenger seat. The passenger, sitting in the backseat, was as unmoved and uninterested as a shop-window dummy. This was the man now seated at the far corner of the bar. Even though he was in the company of two men who, from the way other customers addressed them, were frequent visitors of the club, the man from the car remained still and silent. Watchful.

"My round." McAllister stood. "Calum, will you help me carry them over?" As they waited on the order, he asked, "Do you know those gentlemen over there?" He nodded towards a corner.

"Oh, aye, the big man is the chief constable, the old man is the sheriff, and the other man, I've never seen him before." Calum looked carefully in the mirror to avoid turning around. "But he looks English."

McAllister had to smile at that; any person with pale skin, a perfect suit, and a perfect haircut, perhaps even a manicure, had to be English to a young man who'd never been anywhere.

To McAllister, the man looked official. What sort of official he could only speculate, but from a branch of some government office was his supposition. Or perhaps a relative of Miss Ramsay's? He remembered Joanne saying she thought Alice was wellborn.

Three rounds of drinks and sandwiches later, Hector returned. "Calum, I need your help wi' names o' the competitors. Everyone's a Mackay or a Mackenzie up here." He wanted to rope Calum into writing down the players' names, the scores, and a brief commentary that Hector would pass off as his own work, as he had no time for golf.

"Oh. Right. Aye." Calum wanted to stay; to be in the company of Mr. John McAllister, famous journalist, was an honor. And an opportunity—or so Elaine had told him.

"Hec, take a couple of interior shots," McAllister instructed. "And"—he dropped his voice so Hector had to stand closer to hear—"get me a shot of the trophy board at the end of the room and those men sitting under it. But discreetly."

"Hector" and "discreet" only belonged in the same sentence when applied to his photography. His art, as Hec preferred to call it.

It was midafternoon before they were ready to leave, and McAllister was not looking forward to the long drive ahead. As they walked towards the car, the clouds parted. A rainbow appeared. And in the near distance, the beach and the dunes lightened up to golden and green moving strips of color, stretching southwards to the mudflats of the mile-wide firth.

Standing atop the dune bordering the car park, surveying the empty seascape, Joanne took a deep breath, filling her lungs with the chill, ozone-laden air. Letting it out in a long, slow, deliberate stream, she exhaled the melancholy of the auction. She tried to banish thoughts of a desolate Alice Ramsay. And to dismiss the encounter with the preening peacock that was Dougald Forsythe.

In the cocoon of the car, lulled by the sound of tires on tarmac and wind rushing by, Joanne dozed, and Hector slept deeply, stretched out on the backseat with his head resting on a camera bag. She knew only the apocalypse would wake him.

She jerked to full consciousness as McAllister braked. Then cursed.

"Watch out, you bloody idiot!"

A black saloon car, driving fast, surged around them on a blind bend, before disappearing towards Dingwall. McAllister was certain it was the car he'd had the encounter with in the farmyard. But he said nothing. I took your plate number, he thought, and I will find you and report you for dangerous driving.

Joanne said, "The train south runs about now. Let's hope he's held up at the level crossing."

McAllister smiled. "That's another thing I love about you—you know all these wee bits of information."

"Aye," she agreed. "I don't know a lot about anything, but I know an awful lot about nothing."

"You're too unkind to yourself." He said it lightly, but it hurt him nonetheless to hear her talk like this.

"What gets me is what on earth made Alice do it?"

The swift shift in subject he was used to from his wife, but he wished it wasn't this particular subject. And he knew she was not asking him for an answer, just thinking aloud.

"She had everything she wanted," she continued, picturing the house, the kitchen, the garden, as it was before the auction. "A home. A beautiful garden. From what Nurse Ogilvie told me, she had friends. So why?"

"I think everyone wonders that when a person takes their own life." McAllister spoke quietly. "And we know nothing of Miss Ramsay's past."

"You're right. Why would you come back here when you could be living somewhere in southern Europe in sunshine?"

"With wine and song and art galleries," he added.

"There is something about these mountains, these glens," Joanne began, "this empty landscape. It gets into your heart, your veins. It mesmerizes you. Perhaps Alice was seduced by the landscape."

"She either forgot or had never spent a nine-month winter up here," he joked. Then, more somberly he added, "When it comes to the dead, there are always questions and seldom answers."

Knowing that this was an eternal struggle for her husband, with his younger brother having taken his own life, she said no more. She was about to say, I'm so sorry, but knew he was trying to heal her of her constant need to apologize. Sorry is such an inadequate and overused word, he'd told her. Instead, she reached over and squeezed his hand. She was right. The touch of her skin expressed more than could ever be said.

CHAPTER 8

Alice has on walking boots and a waterproof jacket—the disreputable one with the many pockets for camera and film, sketchpad, pencils, pen, magnifying glass, penknife, big red-spotted hankie, and chocolate. Her smaller camera, on a strap fashioned from a torn strip of silk scarf, is around her neck.

She watches her visitor glance at the pictures on the wall,. Then pause before a slight painting of wildflowers in a blue-and-white-striped milk jug. Done as an exercise in mixing color, Alice knows it is appealing—if you like pretty.

She knows her visitor has little interest in art. Just as well, Alice is thinking, because the treasure is hidden in plain sight.

"The frames are nice," the visitor says.

"Made most of them myself," Alice replies.

She sees the visitor glance at the Herald article pinned to the edge of the easel.

"Absolute rubbish," Alice says.

"I haven't read it," her guest says.

She knows this isn't true. How else did they find me? she is thinking. Then wonders if this person right here is the one who is spying on her; that she has a watcher she no longer doubts.

No, he's a friend, she tells herself. Though how anyone can have true friends in our business is always the question.

◆ ◆ ◆

Over the next few days, singly and together, Joanne and McAllister would ponder their trip to the glen. It was only Hector's photographs that brought all the loose thoughts, ideas, and speculation together.

Tuesday morning, the day before deadline, McAllister, Rob, and Don were working together at the High Table, Don's name for the long narrow high bench in the long narrow high-ceilinged reporters' room where they worked side by side.

"These are the best I could do in thon rain," Hec said, laying out the photographs of the golf tournament. "Ma notebook got soaked through, so I'm no sure who anybody is."

"Looks like you took the pictures through a cloud," Don said, examining them. "There's nothing usable here."

"I didnay want to get ma cameras wet," Hec complained. "It was bucketing down."

"How about the pictures of the auction?" McAllister asked.

"Now, there the light an' shadows wiz great. Got some brilliant shots." Hec's grin would win a gurning competition. "Here's a great photo of thon Forsythe mannie."

McAllister agreed it was a brilliant photograph, but he could not think how to use it. Hec had captured the art critic in full flow, hands sweeping out in a Shakespearean gesture. Richard in want of a horse, the editor thought, although he was certain Richard III would not wear a paisley cravat.

Other pictures were of locals: the auctioneer, local farmers in a huddle over some garden implements, women poking around in the detritus of another woman's life—her hair combs, her jewelry, a silver hairbrush, a bundle of lace-edged hankies. He put the photographs facedown on the pile. Knowing that the woman who had once handled these objects was dead by her own hand made it all feel so poignant, so wretched.

There was one photograph of the person McAllister had encountered in the farmyard. "Have you a better one of this man?" he asked, pointing to the shot of the surly driver of the black car, a car he now thought might be the same one that had overtaken them, at speed, on the Dingwall road.

"Naw," Hec replied. "He caught me lifting the camera and turned away."

The editor turned over more shots from the sale, most taken outdoors, and most featuring stone walls and cobbled surfaces and other creative compositions. He liked the pictures of the caged cockerel but knew they were of no interest to readers of a local newspaper.

"These three pictures, I like them."

"Aye, that's those gadgies in the golf clubhouse. Not much good, really—unbalanced, too much light coming in from the window and not enough on the right-hand side."

It was the men that interested McAllister. Calum had identified the sheriff and the senior policeman but didn't recognize the other man. Their guest, perhaps? They were certainly comfortable in each other's presence. Then again, he thought, men of their class always had something to connect them, mostly their former schools or a passion for grouse shooting.

One August, he had seen a party of men such as these alight from the London train. As resplendent as the birds in their tweed plus-four suits, with matching grouse-shooting hats and waistcoats, they had voices, used to commanding soldiers or the lower orders, that made him want to join the revolution—any revolution that would rid Scotland of the braying asses of privilege. *And you can relocate those bloody grouse to Hyde Park or Wimbledon Common.*

The visitor was interesting in his ordinariness. A cultivated ordinariness, McAllister decided. Compared with the lined or unlined, the animated, or quiescent faces of the locals, his expression was blank, more mask than face. His suit, plain, unremarkable, had an air of money. McAllister was more intrigued than ever, but he would not share his fascination with his wife.

"Hiya." Joanne came in with a blast of cold fresh air. "I'm here to meet my husband." She gave him a peck on the cheek.

She nudged Rob with her shoulder. "Fit like?"

"Brawly guid," he answered, echoing her east coast dialect.

She grinned at Don. "Don."

"Lass."

Seeing the prints spread out on the high table, she asked, "More genius pictures, Hec?"

"The auction sale," Hec said, nodding in agreement to the point where his neck was in danger of dislocating. He too thought his work genius.

"Aye," Don told her, "but nothing usable of the golf match."

"These pictures from inside the clubhouse are good. Since it's so historical, maybe do a feature on the club?"

"So you'll write it up?"

"No, Don, you're not roping me in. Ask McAllister. He was there."

McAllister was about to protest when he saw the photograph of the nineteenth hole. "Maybe I will. And we'll use this." He pointed to the shot of the bar, where a collection of silver cups and shields was prominently displayed. On one side of the trophy cabinet were framed boards with the names of past champions listed in gold lettering. On the other side were the three gentlemen huddled together in conversation.

He was about to ask Hec to crop the men out of the shot, but there was something about them—the closed pose and what appeared to be a grave discussion whilst people all around were chatting, drinking, celebrating the home team's success. It was a clear picture of the club but not of the men; they were barely recognizable.

Unless you knew them.

Shake the tree, sees what falls, he decided.

Joanne was leafing through the rest of Hec's prints and looking carefully at the contact sheets. "More or less the whole community was there." She was talking to herself. "Probably everyone who was at her trial or involved in the case."

"No doubt the sheriff and the fiscal and every worthy of the county are members of the golf club," McAllister added.

"With our ridiculous licensing laws, there's nowhere else to get a drink outside of closing time, so who can blame them?" Don said. Like most men who worked unsociable hours, he was of the opinion that closing bars for the afternoon and shutting altogether at ten in the evening were a major infringement on his liberty.

McAllister suspected that the man had been the passenger in the car that had scared him on the blind bend, but with the speed of the moment, he wasn't entirely sure there *had* been someone in the backseat. And although he was curious, his overriding concern was Joanne. No more potential dramas, he'd vowed after seeing her lying in a hospital bed, head bandaged, unconscious, and with no certainty she would recover.

He left the photograph with Don, who was sizing up the dummy page with an em ruler, mentally composing a story on the golf club and the tournament for the sports section.

"Right, Mrs. McAllister, are you ready?" McAllister asked.

"Where are we going?"

"To choose curtains," he said, turning once more to a contact sheet. "Hec, can I borrow these prints for a day or so?"

"Aye, no problem."

Joanne was staring at her husband. "Since when are you interested in curtains?"

"You'll see." He smiled at her. Patted his pockets for the car keys, put on his hat, and they went out, leaving Don and Hec staring at each other.

"Curtains?" Hec asked. "Is that a code word for . . . ?"

"I'll explain once you're safely married," Don told him.

* * *

Joanne returned home with two large envelopes; one contained Hector's pictures, the other details of the house. McAllister went back to work after the property inspection, saying they'd talk about it when he came home. He could see how, after the initial surprise at the style of the building, she had begun to look at the rooms, particularly the summerhouse, with increasing enthusiasm.

"What are we doing here?" she had asked when they stopped on a street a short distance from where they lived.

"I promised when we married to find you a home that is ours, not mine. Now we are looking."

She hadn't forgotten; but she'd not given the idea much thought, especially as their garden was now finally responding after years of indifference on McAllister's part. Not that she faulted him. He'd confessed that the garden had almost stopped him from buying the house. City men saw grass as useful only on a football pitch.

"It looks expensive," she said as they turned into the driveway to an angular white building that looked more like a marooned ocean liner than a home. Joanne could not tell him that she was slightly intimidated by the house.

It was large, on huge grounds, and in a style of architecture she had only seen in magazines; deep inside, she felt it was too grand for someone like her. The words, the put-downs—*who does she think she is?*—were always there to ground any woman who seemed to be living "above their station," a phrase that she equally delighted in and detested.

Standing in the empty sitting room, seeing the sun streaming through the windows, even this late in autumn, giving the room a warm light glow, she began to feel the possibilities of the house. Almost Mediterranean, she thought, not that I know what Mediterranean light feels like. But she had read of it in magazines and decided it was a style she could make her own.

McAllister had read the contract and the details of the house, had checked it from the outside, but this was the first time he'd seen the interior. And he liked it. Walking around, checking out the rooms, ignoring the kitchen, he examined the sitting room in approval, and ditto the four bedrooms. Standing in the study, he liked the warm honey of the parquet floor, the built-in bookcases, the French doors leading out into the garden.

He was not a practical man; poking about in plumbing and electric wiring, checking for dry rot or woodworm or whatever else could be wrong with a building, was not his forte. But the light, the spaciousness, the clean white lines, inside and out, with nothing to remind him of Scottish baronial architecture, of damp, of mean wee rooms, there was a sense of future to the place.

Joanne went into the garden to inspect the summerhouse. It felt perfect. She could see herself there, at a desk, pen in hand, notebook spread open, a comfortable armchair in the corner, pictures on the one solid wall, a rag rug. She shivered, imagining what Alice would have done with the empty space. *Alice. What made her so desperate she'd abandon her retreat?*

"I like it." McAllister returned from a stroll around the property's perimeter walls. "The garden is a bit big. The bedrooms are nice . . ." He tried to think of what else to say about places he had barely glimpsed, like the kitchen. "The study is grand. And since you're working at home, it's just right for you."

She laughed. "McAllister. Don't. You know, and I know, that is your room. I'll even knit a PRIVATE sign for the door. No." She looked out of another set of French doors leading to a stone terrace and summerhouse beyond. "Out there, that wee place in the garden, that's my—"

He wrapped an arm around her shoulders. "Room of one's own," he finished, knowing how much Joanne enjoyed the Virginia Woolf book.

"I hadn't thought of it that way, but yes."

"Do you want to think about it and come back again?"

"I want to think how we could live in a place this big. None of your, our furniture or curtains would fit the style of this place. Then we'd need a new cooker, rugs . . ."

"That's your department." He was remembering Angus MacLean the solicitor's opinion that as the house was so unusual, there might not be a great deal of interest. Most people prefer traditional stone-built houses, he'd said, and the size of the grounds might attract a builder who'd tear the house down and subdivide for two, possibly three new homes.

McAllister hated the idea of moving and saw nothing wrong with their present home. Yet he would suffer the catastrophe of packing and unpacking and decorating and spending months trying to remember where everything was stored, if it made Joanne happy. The possibility that his wife might become distracted and drop the Alice Ramsay obsession was also a motive for moving.

"I need to get back to work," he told Joanne. "Can you pop in and see Angus and arrange another viewing?"

As he drove down the hill to the Castle car park, she said, "I kept thinking about Alice Ramsay—how she set up her own house, was in the midst of renovating the byre, planting fruit trees and bushes. The book she was working on was almost finished, so she said." Joanne saw the question from his eyebrows. "Nurse Ogilvie, the landlady at the hotel, Elaine, they all said people liked her. The old people in the home too."

"Then the court case came along."

"Alice hated that. But at the same time found it amusing. It was a local scandal, nothing more, she said. Then I . . ." She flushed at the memory of her complicity. "That traitor Forsythe used me. He published her name, her location, exposing her . . . Sorry, I just can't see . . ." But she could. At the auction in the barn, seeing the solid beams cut to last a hundred or more years, she had imagined Alice up there, swinging.

"Alice killed herself. There is no evidence of anything or anyone . . ."

"It's just so hard to believe."

"I know." He parked the car, wanting the subject over, finished, done with. "So, do you like the house?"

"It's a lovely house." *But . . .* she was thinking and didn't say.

"Good. I like it too. Don't get your hopes up, though—you never know how many other possible buyers are out there—but fingers crossed, yes?"

"Thank you." She smiled. "I'll try not to be too excited, but that house would be fun, a new beginning."

And a new obsession, he was wise enough not to say.

✦ ✦ ✦

"How did it go at the solicitor's office?" He kissed the top of her head, breathing in the smell of shampoo and Joanne. Being a Thursday, the usual quiet-after-publication day, McAllister was home early.

"Interesting. I've an appointment to look at the house again tomorrow, so let's hope it's raining; then I can really see what it would be like to live there. And I've asked Chiara to come with me."

"Good idea." McAllister felt that Joanne's best friend, Chiara, being Italian, would love the light in the house.

"So what did Angus MacLean say?" He was watching her, her glasses perched on the end of her nose, her hair falling forwards as she reached for her notebook.

"There are two other bidders and no allowance for a building inspection. So he's going to try to find out if it is in good repair and let us know."

"Good enough." He knew how Scottish property sales worked, knew the hazards of the sealed-bidding system.

"Angus showed me this. He knows from Rob the story of Alice and . . ." She didn't want to say *her death*. "It was sent to him by a solicitor in Dornoch who's acting on behalf of the estate." She handed over a document relating to the sale of Alice Ramsay's house and land. There was also an asking price, and the price was low. "How come it's so cheap?" she asked.

"Too remote for most people. Probably gets snowed in in winter. And that track up there will put most potential buyers off."

"It's all so sad. By the way, don't mention the new house in front of the girls."

They heard the front door open. When the girls came in, McAllister asked, "How was school today?" It was a question their mother had long given up asking, as the answer was always "fine," or "the same" or "OK."

She now knew to be specific. "Did you have PT today?" she would ask, knowing the answer was "today was art" or "singing" or any subject more interesting than English or arithmetic.

Annie said, "I'm top in French class."

"Well done!" McAllister was delighted; fluent in French, he enjoyed helping his stepdaughter and had promised her a holiday in France next year if she came in the top three in her exams.

Annie secretly thought her new father would take them to France no matter her exam results. But, she thought, maybe not if they bought that house.

What Joanne didn't know was that Annie, with her usual inquisitiveness, had seen the papers describing the house, had jumped to the correct conclusion, and had already gone to Culduthel Road and inspected their potential new home from the outside.

"Milk and a scone?" Joanne asked the girls.

"Yes please," they chorused.

"Start your homework, and I'll bring a tray into your room."

Girls fed and watered, she asked her husband, "Did you unload Alice's pictures from the car?"

"I'll do it later." He had had enough of Miss Alice Ramsay for the time being. "Let's talk about the White House." That was his name for his dream home.

The House—in capital letters was how Joanne thought of it. She liked the house, just couldn't quite see herself in such a grand setting. The cost of moving would be astronomical. "Fine," she replied. Then, even though she knew her heart's instinct would overrule the reality, she said, "Let's discuss the practicalities."

♦ ♦ ♦

That week, as was true even in wartime, the *Highland Gazette* came out on time, no problems, few letters to the editor, and then only complaints about the chaos and destruction of Bridge Street and the delays from the temporary bridge across the Ness while a new one was being built.

The sports section carried a summary of golf tournament results for the Highlands. Don had used the picture of the cabinet of trophies to illustrate another year of successful results for Dornoch.

In the classified section, a notice had been placed stating that a solicitor in Dornoch was handling the affairs of the late Miss Alice Ramsay and any who might have a claim on the estate should contact the office. As the solicitor was legally bound to place this notice, it was not unusual, but with the connection to the "witch trial" and the subsequent suicide, it would attract interest.

Joanne read it. She felt a sense of desolation at the abandonment of a place of such geographical beauty, a place that Alice had been renovating, turning an ordinary Scottish farmhouse of no heritage value into an enchanting refuge. Joanne remembered Alice's plans for a conservatory, another reason to doubt the suicide verdict. No matter how mistaken it was to see such tragedies as anything other than despair, Joanne couldn't shake her conviction that killing yourself was much worse than any other death.

But in the spirit of Alice Ramsay, Joanne resolved she would create, in the open space of the shiplike house, a refuge as beautiful as the farmhouse far up the Sutherland glen.

✦ ✦ ✦

Next morning, Joanne helped McAllister lift the boxes of books and papers from the car into the sitting room. Thoughts of Alice once more intruded. But this time, Joanne told herself, *Stop it. You hardly knew the woman. Stop being so maudlin. And forget witches—find something cheerful to write about.*

McAllister was leafing through history books, art books, and four books of botanical illustrations, one very old.

Joanne was wiping the dust from the writing box the auctioneer had included in the job lot of books and papers, hoping to finish the auction sale before the pubs shut for the afternoon.

"The box is beautiful. Cherrywood, I think." She loved the swirl of the grain, the deep red of the wood, the little inkwell, and the groove for the pens, and she appreciated the slope of the writing surface. "The box is old. Sir Walter Scott might have used a traveling desk like this."

McAllister smiled; his wife's flights of fancy were yet another part of her that he enjoyed.

"What's this?" She unlocked the desk with the brass key still in the lock and took out a thick cardboard folder tied with brown twine. It was heavy. She put it on the floor and sat down on the rug. Opening the folder, and finding a bundle of loose papers, she immediately knew what it was. "It's Alice's manuscript, the one she said was almost finished."

"Looks more like a portfolio of paintings."

"Sort of. But see, the paintings are numbered on the back, and on each painting is a description of the plant's location. It seems she intended it to be an illustrated book on the flora of the Highlands." She turned over more pages. "Look at this." She held out a painting of a tiny wild orchid. "It's beautiful and, from what she writes here, pretty rare."

"It is lovely," he agreed. "Let's finish unpacking the boxes. Then we can lay the manuscript out and have a proper look. If at all possible, we will do something with it."

"Have it published?"

"Maybe."

The idea gave Joanne more pleasure than the thought of having her own work published. "That would be wonderful. It might make up for—" She shook the guilt out of her head. "McAllister, the note, or rather that article and my phone number, will it be part of the evidence at the fatal accident inquiry?"

"Possibly."

She saw his face close. "What if that was a message to me? What if she was saying she wanted me to question her death?"

McAllister doubted this greatly. But he welcomed anything that made the love of his life feel less responsible for the whole nightmare. "From what we know, the findings of the inquiry are almost certain to be suicide. It would take a professional to fake a . . . that type of method." Even he balked at the word "hanging."

◆　◆　◆

The house was silent apart from the rustle and groan and creak of windows and doors and floorboards. Not that it was old, only a hundred years or so since it was built, and the noises were nothing Joanne didn't recognize; the familiar whispers and grumblings made her feel safe. She rolled paper, interleaved with sheets of blue carbon, into the portable Olivetti, then picked up a pencil opening her reporter's notebook to summarize what needed doing to Alice's manuscript.

"People" was the heading. She stopped. *Get on with the manu-script. Stop procrastinating. Stop obsessing with the court case.* But she needed to revisit the trial, if only to clear her thoughts.

She found the envelope of Hec's pictures still in the bureau. She spread the contents over the table and began to list all those she recognized, making note of others she needed Calum to identify.

Humming, she continued with the list. "The auctioneer. Connection to Alice? None that I know. The doctor . . ." On the column opposite his name, she wrote, "hostile witness." Nurse Ogilvie. Mrs. Galloway. Forsythe. The sheriff." She crossed out the sheriff. "Now you're being ridiculous," she muttered. *Right. Now what? OK, cross-reference all those involved in the trial with all those who were at the auction.*

That evening, McAllister asked Joanne how her work was progressing with Alice's manuscript.

She smiled. "Early days."

The tranquillity of working with the color and beauty of the illustrations made her feel a connection to the woman. It also helped her in her own work; enthusiasm, energy, thoughts, and ideas seemingly coming from outside of herself.

Earlier, in that precious first hour of writing time, ideas poured out. The central character was a postman working in a re-mote community up the glens. The words had flown off the ends of her fingertips onto the keys, onto the paper. This she also kept to herself; more from superstition than logic, she felt that talking about it might make the muse desert her. How to fit in the topic of witchcraft she had yet to figure out.

A letter rejecting a story she had submitted three weeks ear-lier had arrived that morning. With a ring at the bell and a cheery "How are you today?" the postman she was basing her character on handed it over. For one moment, she was worried he might guess she was studying him.

She smiled. "Thanks, Archie."

"You look like you're doing well." His grin and his wind-sun-rain-red cheeks cheered her.

"Thanks for noticing. I am."

She and all the neighbors knew that he kept a check on anyone elderly or infirm or, Joanne suspected, anyone who might give him a quick cup of tea on winter days.

She read the letter quickly, and the disappointment didn't overwhelm her. *I can do better*, she told herself.

The letter was on the hallstand when McAllister came home for lunch. He would never read his wife's mail but was curious.

"A rejection letter," she said.

"May I read it?"

"If you like."

He did. "This is not a rejection letter. It's . . ."

"They don't like my story."

"No. And yes." He held out the letter at arm's length. He would never admit he needed reading glasses. "It says he? She? Anyhow, Drummond says this particular story doesn't fit in with the editorial thrust of his magazine, too much in the romantic vein for them, but he likes your style, particularly your characters. He goes on to say if you want to submit stories with more reference to place—I think he means more Scottish—featuring your obvious talent for character development, he'll be happy to consider them. Joanne, this is extremely positive, particularly from this magazine. It publishes some of the best writers around."

"I know. I thought when I posted it I was being overambitious."

"You can write. I know you don't believe me, think I'm biased, but you can write. From this letter, the editor thinks so too."

"So I should write what I know?"

"Start there. See where it takes you. Now, wife, where's ma dinner?" He thumped the table with his fist. She laughed and stuck out her tongue.

An hour later, and with her husband back at work, she took up the rejection letter and read it again, thinking, *I'll start again. Maybe that postman idea will work after all, if I can find a twist. Maybe the postman can be a postwoman—and a witch.*

Neglecting the lunch dishes and leaving the ironing for another time, she settled down to work. Again, she couldn't concentrate.

I'll clean Alice's pictures first. Maybe they will inspire me.

She dusted them. Next she polished the glass with a vinegar and water mix, finishing off with a final rub using an old copy of the *Gazette.* The middle-sized paintings, two of them in simple wood frames, she propped up on the sideboard behind the decanter and glasses and an empty flower vase.

One in particular she loved. It was a still life of a kitchen table with checked cloth, a wicker basket with grapes, a string of red onions hanging off the table's edge, and three flowers in a vase filling the top corner. The other, a simple depiction of wildflowers, reminded her of what little she knew of the work of Charles Rennie Macintosh.

Tackling the larger oil painting was hard, as it was too heavy for her to lift. Kneeling on the floor, she pulled it towards her. The ornate gilded frame was a boxlike construction, perhaps two inches and a half deep, perfectly in keeping with the subject, a gloomy portrait of the Virgin and Child. It was not to her taste or that of the Scottish Presbyterian Church.

No wonder that antique dealer only wanted the frame; baby Jesus looks more like twenty years old than twenty months.

She did not know this was a convention of the time and might date the oil painting to the sixteenth century. It couldn't be valuable, she decided; not even the fair Dougald had bid for it. Then again, a real work of art would not be for sale at a local farm auction.

She wanted the other large oil painting—of a clergyman skating—above the mantelpiece, but it was also too heavy to lift. She left both propped against the wall.

She was curious about their provenance and resolved to borrow a book from the library. *Can't ask Dougald Forsythe. He and people like him, all those arty types, they'd turn a simple question into a lecture, making you feel a right Philistine.*

Joanne was interested in art but acknowledged she was woefully uneducated. At boarding school, there had been occasional visits to the art gallery in Edinburgh—until the headmistress discovered the many nudes on display, some of them naked men with not even a fig leaf. The trips were soon changed to visits to the Royal Observatory.

What Joanne liked most was the manuscript with Alice's botanical watercolor illustrations. She admired how the flowers were drawn, or a tree, or a leaf, with a color wash light and free over the top of the pen-and-ink outlines.

One illustration had an ink drawing of a section of the plant, showing the leaves and roots, and the plant in full bloom. There was a date and a map reference of where the plant had been collected. "Bladderwort," it said, with "Butterwort" in brackets, and the pale gold wash over the flowers reminded Joanne of sun and summer.

Maybe I should identify the work with a map reference. Ordinance survey maps fascinated Joanne; the shading of the color to accentuate the contours of a landscape spoke to her, helping her visualize the glen or the mountain or the seashore.

Maybe the postman, or postwoman, in my story covers a big district.
The flower illustration was sparking off more ideas. *Maybe he*
checks how everyone is and carries the news and the gossip as well as let-
ters and parcels.

Grabbing a notebook before the idea vanished, she began to
scribble, her pencil flying across the lined paper. Only when her
wrist ached did she stop. Then, stretching her back, she grinned.
She had once told her daughter Annie that catching ideas was
as hard as chasing and catching a wild rabbit. Today, at least, she
could say, "Got it."

In this fugue, twenty-three minutes passed, and she captured
the postie's route as though she had been in the passenger seat
with him as he drove up into the hills, crossing burns and rivers,
driving through fords, through mist and rain and deep shafts of
sunlight. She breathed the air, smelled the heather, the rotting
bracken, the fresh-tilled earth. And as she imagined his cheery
wave, his voice as he called out, "Fine day the day," she experienced
his life and his part in the life of the scattered community.

People informed her writing, people she had met or merely
observed. The secrets of total strangers, seen from the top deck
of a bus or on walks through the islands or spotted through
the window of a tearoom or café, set her mind racing as she
invented lives for them. But what inspired her most of all, what
infused her work over her twelve years in her adopted home
in the Highlands, was the splendor of the lochs and glens and
mountains.

Getting up from her chair, she glanced again at the pictures
on the floor. *They look lovely there; maybe no need to hang them.* Then
it hit her. If someone came forward to claim the estate, could they
claim the manuscript too? It hadn't been part of the sale; it had
been inside the box, and not acknowledged as part of the estate.

After the initial flash of panic, she knew she wanted these papers more than anything.

She telephoned Calum Mackenzie.

"The paintings and books and papers we bought, has anyone a right to claim them back?"

"You bought them fair and square," he said. "Whoever inherits would receive the proceeds of the auction, or at least I think so. I'll check with the newspaper's solicitor. I did hear that someone got in touch with the solicitor about the estate." That he could find out nothing frustrated him, and for once his mother knew nothing.

"Really? That's interesting." *That is very, very interesting, Calum, so why didn't you tell me immediately?*

"I'll see if I can find out more," he offered. "Anything else?"

"Not that I can think of. Thanks, Calum."

She was struck by how uncurious Calum Mackenzie seemed. Yes, he did his job, but information came to him, and he followed leads only after being asked to. Probably hadn't ever had to investigate, she guessed. He had his mother to do it for him.

CHAPTER 9

I should tell him.

"Anything, anyone unusual," he'd said, "write. In an emergency, call. You have the number. You know the protocol."

She puts the binoculars back on the hallstand. Then, changing her mind, she hangs them around her neck, tucking the leather strap under the collar of the soft checked Viyella shirt, a man's shirt that she uses as an artist's smock.

"I'm probably imagining it," she says to the wee dog. There's no actual sign of anything, she reminds herself, or anyone unusual. But I can feel it in my bones—I'm being watched.

He whines his agreement. He too is restless, ears pricking at shifts in the wind, at distant unheard sounds.

Jumping onto the window box seat, he watches, gives up, goes back to his bed, then repeats the ritual five minutes, or half an hour, or two hours later. She, like him, had her ritual: pace, stare out the windows, grab the binoculars, walk down to the heather line, sweep the edges of the woodland, the ridges above, the burn down below, the track scar across the landscape. Once she watched a small herd of deer—six of them, five does plus one magnificent stag—pick their way down to the water. Apart from them, nothing. Yet still she searches.

Framed by the window, in a not far distant fold made by an intermittent burn flowing to the larger burn, almost a river, that dissects the glen, a last gasp of heather is in bloom. The bright of the blue far above, the ink *stain of the conifered horizon, the dirty stain-splotch-splash pink-purple, grips her heart.*

That's my cover illustration.

She loads a new roll of film. Takes her binoculars.

"Come on, boy," she says. "I need to take photographs. Let's go for a walk."

He only heard "walk."

◆ ◆ ◆

On Monday, in his office at the *Gazette*, and an hour or so after the sacred Monday Morning Meeting, McAllister was visited by Detective Inspector Dunne. His past experience of many police officers was not positive; his experience being that journalists and policemen were on opposing sides. But although they were wary of each other in a professional setting, the inspector and the editor had worked together before and respected each other.

"First, I need to say this is an unofficial visit." Dunne had his overcoat buttoned up over his plainclothes detective's uniform of navy-blue suit, gleaming black shoes, white shirt, and regimental tie.

McAllister waited, saying nothing.

"There's been some concern shown over a picture you published," Dunne started, "but . . ." He hesitated. Not because he was unwilling to share the information—he was here, after all, in the editor's office—but because he did not know what to make of the summons he'd received from the chief constable.

"I've been asked to explain why, how, you came to publish a photograph of the chief constable, and the sheriff of Sutherland-shire, in a bar."

"We didn't . . . Oh, you mean the golf clubhouse shot?" McAllister was thinking fast. *What is this about?* "That was taken in Sutherland, so what's it got to do with here?"

The detective didn't—couldn't—answer.

"Let's get the photograph, and you can point out what has offended such high panjandrums."

They examined the picture in the sports section of the *Gazette*. Neither subject was holding a drink. Neither had a finger near his nose. Or his flies open. The third man in their group had his head turned away; it would be nigh impossible to identify him.

"These men are background only. You could only make out their identity if you were looking closely and knew them. So where's the problem? Is it because they are in a bar? Offending the Temperance League? The Kirk?"

"I don't know." Dunne was shaking his head slowly.

"The third man." McAllister was poking at the image with a pencil. "I think it was him in the car that almost ran us off the road."

Dunne was surprised. "I never heard about that."

"I didn't see the point in complaining. It was on the Dingwall road, after that photo was taken. The car was traveling well above the speed limit."

The detective was looking closely at the photograph. "It would be hard to identify anyone from this."

"Aye. So why the complaint?"

"I don't know. I was order—*told* to talk to you and tell you to never print pictures of senior police officers without permission."

"Tell your chief constable the *Gazette* will never publish pictures of him again. Or his wife."

"I'll let him know." Dunne smiled; he and McAllister knew the policeman loved having his picture in the newspaper, handing out cups and medals and handshakes. His wife even more so.

But from the way the detective was looking anywhere but at McAllister, he knew there was more.

Dunne was visibly struggling with the task given to him by his superiors, so he came straight out with the statement. "You signed the Official Secrets Act in 1942 when you were a war correspondent. I've been told to remind you that the agreement still stands."

McAllister stared in astonishment. The Official Secrets Act was only invoked in the protection of matters of national security. "Are you implying we are on a war footing here? That publishing that picture in a local newspaper is of national importance?"

Dunne didn't answer. He had been as astonished as the editor. In all his years in the army, then as a police officer, he had never come across a matter of state security. And he did not believe that he, a provincial policeman, should be involved in state secrets. Heavy-handed and a major breach in protocol, he thought. He also resented being treated as an errand boy with no reason or explanation given. "That's all I know."

McAllister knew that the "ours not to reason why" ethos pervaded the police force as much as it pervaded the army. "Why warn me?" he began. "If you want to keep something a secret, why raise the issue with a journalist? Red rag to a bull, that."

"I considered that, and . . ." Dunne was fiddling with his hat. His hat had no answers either, so he stood. "I'm just the messenger, McAllister." He held out his hand. "Thank you for your time."

Seeing this as official police-speak for *Consider this a warning, but we will talk more when I'm off duty,* McAllister joked, "Message received, DI Dunne." And in no way understood, he implied with a shake of his head.

He saw his visitor to the door.

"Miss Alice Ramsay, her trial, her death—it's all very interesting, don't you think?"

The inspector gave no hint that he'd heard. "Thank you for your time, Mr. McAllister."

Once alone, with the photograph from the golf clubhouse propped up against the cigarette box, McAllister wondered why the fuss. He leaned back in his chair in his favorite thinking position. *Perhaps Joanne is right; perhaps the death was . . .*

He was unwilling to consider that possibility—that someone had caused harm to Alice. And he was decidedly unhappy at Joanne involving herself in a story that might be even remotely dangerous. He decided not to tell her of the inspector's visit. If she was ignorant of the visit, she would have no reason to suspect that the fate of the late Alice Ramsay now also intrigued McAllister and DI Dunne. The man he'd seen in the car, and at the golf clubhouse, only added to the mystery. Who was he? Was he at the auction? McAllister couldn't remember seeing him, but as it was crowded, it was possible he had been there.

As for Dunne's invocation of the Official Secrets Act, that practically guaranteed that McAllister would look for answers.

Perhaps that was the intention.

◆　◆　◆

On Tuesday morning, McAllister took a phone call.

"Mr. McAllister, it's Calum Mackenzie."

"What can I do for you, Calum?" He leaned back in his chair, trying to avoid a fierce draft coming in the half-open door he'd been too lazy to get up and shut. It felt as though the North Sea gale was coming through every crack in the walls, every window, every skylight in the old stone building. "Calum? Are you there?" He was hearing weird snuffling noises down the crackly telephone line, voices fading in and out as though they were at sea. *Is he crying? Can't be.*

"I've lost ma job."

"What?"

"I've been fired." There was a sound of someone blowing his nose. "Mr. McAllister, I can't work out what's happening. The editor . . . I told Elaine, and she said I should talk to you, you being a newspaper man. But I canny use the phone at home cos my mother—"

"How can I help?"

"I think it might be to do with me asking questions about Miss Ramsay." Calum didn't say *at your wife's request.* "Can I talk to you? If I leave now, I can be down in three hours."

"Come straight to the *Gazette* office." McAllister was about to put down the receiver. Something stopped him. He listened. No dial tone. Not yet. A silence, thick and dense, seemed to be radiating out of the black Bakelite receiver. And in that void, he felt another person . . . persons? Spirits? Spooks? Witches? He shook his head. *Get a grip*, he told himself. And hung up.

"Don!" he bellowed.

"Give us a wee minute!" Don shouted back.

When his deputy came in, the first thing they did was light up. Then, cigarette smoke spiraling upwards, they talked.

After McAllister related the gist of DI Dunne's warning, the sacking of Calum Mackenzie, and his suspicion about the man seen in the company of the worthies of the county at the golf clubhouse—and after he told Don he'd been warned not to discuss it with anyone—he sat back, knowing Don was now as intrigued as he was. And as Joanne had been all along.

"Reminding a journalist of the Official Secrets Act, eh? I like it." The news cheered Don up greatly. Over the last few weeks of rain and gloom and the depressing sight of demolition crews tearing down the historic buildings on Bridge Street, and along the river below the castle, he was in the mood for some mischief.

"One other thing," McAllister said. "If he's interested, do we want to offer young Calum a job? Joanne says he's a hard worker. The advert for a junior reporter has run for weeks and no likely candidates."

"I've read a wee bit o' young Mackenzie's work—pedestrian but nothing that can't be fixed. Will he want to leave home though, move to another county?"

"Does he have a choice? Newspaper jobs are rare. For us, the chance of having inside knowledge of a story that might involve a shady section of the establishment . . ."

"That's settled, then." Don grinned. "The lad starts next week."

McAllister was about to say, *What about his mother?* But he was sensible enough to stop himself. *He's a big boy now.*

◆   ◆   ◆

On the long drive down through Sutherland and Ross & Cromarty, over the pass, and all along the coast, Calum saw nothing of the towns and villages and scenery so spectacular it would lift any gloom. Indeed, his sense of grievance was so heavy it hurt his bones. One time, he had to stop the car, as he felt physically sick. His nose was blocked from crying, and even with the windows wound down letting in blasts of icy North Sea air, he felt claustrophobic.

Never once did he dream that that morning he would lose his job. And that same afternoon, he'd be offered another that would be, to him, a huge promotion.

◆   ◆   ◆

Don asked Calum the questions. McAllister observed.

"So, what's this I hear about the *Sutherland Courier* kicking you out?" Don began.

"I don't understand. I had a meeting with my boss just last week. He was telling me how well I was doing."

"How long are you into your cadetship?"

"That's why we were chatting. I've been there since I left school, five years, and I finished my training a few months back. The editor promised me a wee pay rise. Now he says he has to let me go."

The red around Calum's eyes was threatening. McAllister could barely cope with a crying woman, much less a crying man. "Probably why he fired you. Doesn't want to pay more, so he gets rid of you and hires a junior."

"Aye, I've heard all you Northerners are tightfisted." Don was grinning, trying to make a joke of it.

"Really?" Calum doubted that, but to save face and have an explanation for his mother, he would grab any excuse.

"Let's go over it once more. And try to remember word for word what your editor said," Don told him.

"And try to think about what was *not* said," McAllister added.

"Like what?" Calum was lost.

We'll need Rob or Joanne to train him in observing between the lines, McAllister was thinking. "Like was the editor nervous? Did you believe his story?"

"Come to think o' it, he wasn't himself. I thought it was because . . . because he doesn't like my . . . ." He was about to say *mother*, remembering how Mrs. Mackenzie had once implied the editor was "fond o' the lassies," even though he was a married man. "It could be because he doesn't like firing anyone. I've been there since I left school, and nobody's lost their job."

"Tell us what happened." Don was trying not to show his impatience. As he barely knew Calum, he didn't snap as he would if it were Rob, or more likely Hector, meandering around the heart of a story.

"It was first thing this morning. I came in, on time," he added to impress the editors. "The receptionist told me to go to the editor's office. He's a nice man, ma boss, and I knew right away something was wrong, cos he never even asked me to sit down. He just said, 'Calum, I'm sorry, I have to let you go.'"

Calum didn't say that his instinctive reaction was to ask, *Go where?* He continued, "Next, he said, 'Your work is fine, but it's just, we have no room for you at the moment. Maybe in another year or so, you can come back. So I've asked the pay office to make up a month's wages in lieu of notice. I'm sorry.'"

Again, Calum didn't relate how he'd almost fallen into the visitor's chair, his knees were so shaky. He didn't say how he was almost crying, asking, "You're firing me? But why?"

"Cutbacks," he'd answered. The man Calum had worked with, respected, and admired couldn't—wouldn't—look at him directly. But Calum could see that he too was feeling wretched. "It's best you go now, lad. I've written excellent references for you. I'll put them in the mail. Good luck." And he'd left his office, leaving Calum too shocked to move.

"That's all?" Don asked.

"Aye, that was all." Calum folded into himself, making himself smaller than his already fourteen-year-old size.

McAllister was stumped as to what to ask next. Then he remembered the game he played with Annie when helping her with her essay writing. "Your editor . . ."

"Mr. Watt."

"You think he was upset when he spoke to you?"

"He seemed to be."

"Unhappy?"

Calum nodded.

"Uncomfortable?"

Calum seemed to catch on and thought for a moment. "Shifty," he said finally. "He couldn't look me in the eye, and his explanation was . . ." He searched for a word. "Stupid."

Oh, dearie me, Don was thinking. There's a lot we need to teach him.

Almost as though he had read the deputy editor's mind, Calum began thinking aloud. "We had all the excitement of Alice Ramsay's trial. The editor was happy with my work. Then it went quiet. Then we had her—her death. Then the auction. Then there was the Fatal Accident Inquiry."

"Wait. Already? We never heard about that."

"It was held at five o'clock in the afternoon with no notice given to the newspaper. We were sent a statement. Suicide while the balance of the mind was disturbed. The hearing only took fifteen, maybe twenty minutes."

"I wrote up the FAI verdict," Calum continued, "but it didn't run. Not a good subject for a family newspaper, I was told."

"What about the police?" Don asked. "Surely they were there as witnesses? And whoever found the body? They would have to appear."

"I was told the police found the body," Calum said. Though which policeman he didn't know, as it wasn't one of his friends or contacts. He couldn't admit this to his potential new bosses; who found the body and in what circumstances were the first questions any half-decent reporter should ask.

McAllister nodded, thinking that was something that definitely needed investigation. Why would the police have just shown up at Alice's farm without any notification? He knew from his own experience how far it was off the main road, and no neighbors nearby. "And the funeral?"

"I've heard nothing."

McAllister hadn't moved. His eyes were fixed on the junior reporter. Calum felt it and began to perspire. *Not sweat, Calum—horses sweat, gentlemen perspire.* He could hear his mother's voice, and his hands were now clammy, his tie too tight. How she would react when she heard his news terrified him. Plus he couldn't fathom out what the older men wanted to know. He looked at Don, hoping for a cue.

Don saw and nodded.

"Thon stranger in the golf clubhouse, the man in the picture Hector took," Calum began.

McAllister still didn't move. But his eyes were boring into the slight figure of a journalist, drowning in the visitor's chair.

"I was wanting to find out about that man—no for a story, just interested—an' I'd noted the car numberplate like I always do . . ."

Don was shifting in his chair. *Get on with it, laddie.*

Calum took the hint. "So I asked a pal at the police station to check it out, and the registration number is English. From London."

McAllister realized he'd forgotten to check the numberplate himself.

"That's all my friend could find out before his sergeant—his boss—stopped him." He saw the look between the two journalists. "There's another thing. On my way out, I asked the deputy editor why I was being fired. He was really surprised, said he knew nothing about it."

Don knew that if an editor, without his knowledge, fired one of his journalists, he would be more than unhappy. He tucked away this information, and would call his colleague in Sutherland to check.

The Church Street clock chimed four.

"Anything else?" Don asked.

Calum was fooled by Don's soft Skye accent, and the deputy editor's eyes reminded him of his granddad, and he found himself saying, "When I spoke to my friend in the solicitor's office about—" He stopped. "Sorry, I promised I'd no tell." Promised who what, he didn't elaborate.

"Quite right. A good reporter always protects his sources." Don looked at McAllister. They knew each other so well; McAllister recognized it was his turn.

It took Calum less than two seconds to say yes to the job offer. He did not consider his fiancée, his mother, where he would live—there was nothing else he wanted to do with his life except work in a newspaper and play golf. "One thing, is it easy to get into the golf club here?"

McAllister was startled. "I don't know."

"Don't you worry, Calum, I can fix that," Don told him. "So now you're one of us, you need to put us in the picture. The information from the solicitor?"

"I'm sorry, Mr. McLeod, I don't know names, so it's not really helpful."

Don had run out of patience. "I'll be the judge of that."

"Oh. Right." Calum heard the reprimand. "Someone put in a claim on Miss Ramsay's estate. It's being checked—at least, I'm assuming it is."

Don was thinking, *When he hands in his copy, I'm sure to need ma wee red pencil through at least half of his words.* "McAllister? Any more questions?"

"Welcome to the *Gazette*, Calum. And get me that car numberplate, will you?" McAllister asked.

Don stood. "So, laddie, let's you an' me meet the others and tell them the good news."

As they walked the few steps to the reporters' room, McAllister could hear his deputy saying, "When can you start? Next Monday?" He knew this was Don's way of keeping their source close and agreed it was a good tactic.

They needed Calum Mackenzie as a contact in that community. News of the goings-on in a county in the far northeast was usually of no interest to neighboring counties, yet this story had potential. Threats to him, and to Calum, were suspicious; visions of front-page headlines and a coup worthy of a national newspaper filled his mind.

◆　◆　◆

McAllister was in the hall hanging up his overcoat and hat when Joanne appeared. "Calum called. He's been fired from his newspaper."

That Calum had called her before phoning her husband she didn't share.

"We've offered him a job." McAllister wished he'd made it clear to Calum that Joanne was not to be involved. Too late now, he thought. He told her all he knew from Calum. Told her about a claim on the estate.

"I know about that," Joanne said. "Sorry I didn't tell you, but Calum told me about the claim a few days ago. I asked him to try to find out the name. I was worried I'd lose the manuscript." When she said it, it sounded like an excuse. Even to her.

"Did you ask anyone else to help?"

"I phoned Mrs. Galloway at the hotel. I phoned the nursing home and asked Elaine, Calum's fiancée. No one knew anything, and they promised to keep it quiet."

Was that why Calum was fired? Asking about the estate? No, that would be normal for a local reporter. It had to be something else. "I had a visit from DI Dunne yesterday." Again, it was information he'd had no intention of sharing with her. But if somehow she found out on her own, he knew what her reaction would be. There should be no secrets in a marriage, she'd say. And he couldn't tell her not to keep information to herself if he was guilty of the same.

When he'd finished, she said, "The Official Secrets Act?" It came out as a whisper, as though she might be overheard. "That's . . . that's very important." And terrifying. There was no word she could think of to convey her alarm.

"One very big mystery, I agree," he said. "But until we find out more, it's best you do absolutely nothing. No more questions. No more phone calls about Miss Alice Ramsay."

"And you? What are you going to do?"

"Nothing."

From the way she looked up through a stray strand of hair, her eyes holding his, questioning his decision, he could see she was disappointed.

"I'm not ordering you to do or not do anything, Joanne. But this is way beyond a small-town newspaper affair."

"I know. The Official Secrets Act is the realm of spy stories and national newspaper headlines."

"So for once in my life, I must listen to the advice of the police." He was shaking his head, grinning as he said this.

She smiled back. "Not at all like you."

"Next week, we should be back to normal, and young Calum joining the staff should make life easier. I have a feeling he'll need some training. He's selective in the information he shares and doesn't always realize the importance of what he knows."

"Back to the beginning for Calum, then." Joanne knew that feeling. There was no need to add that without his mother as his main source of information, the newly hired reporter would have to cultivate his own contacts in unfamiliar territory. "Look out for him, will you?"

"I will." Her thinking of others before herself was yet another reason he loved her. And respected her. "As well as a job, Don has promised Calum a membership at the golf club."

"In that case, Calum Mackenzie will be at the *Gazette* for life."

CHAPTER 10

The color of autumn is magnificent up here, especially in the woodland at the beginning of the glen, she is thinking. Winter is creeping in, seemingly overnight; that wind this morning, even the hens felt it.

"Let's hope we don't become snowed in," she says to the wee dog.

She sighs at the idea of encountering Mrs. Mackenzie but knows she has no alternative. "I'll take the Land Rover to Mr. Mackenzie and have him put on heavy-duty tires. And I'll dig out the snow chains just in case."

Then the thought of North Africa intruded, remembrance of warm star-studded nights, of cocktail parties and New Year embassy balls. And winters in Italy. And Turkey. It can snow there, she remembers, but it's definitely warmer than up here in the glens.

She looks at the dog. "Don't worry, boy, I won't abandon you."

◆　◆　◆

Don watched McAllister staring out the high window. Looking like he'd found a sixpence and lost a pound, Don decided. He glanced up and could see nothing of interest. A lack of pigeons, maybe, he thought, as not even they were out in rain that had started days ago and seemed set to continue for the biblical forty.

The view was even more dreich when seen through the ever-present cloud of cigarette smoke, as thick and as threatening as the weather outside. The half light in homes and offices and schools, too dim to be comfortable, too bright to turn on the lights, was depressing. "Dreich," that good Scottish weather word, rolled off the tongue and was descriptive of the feel, the sound, the shiver of weather not quite dramatic enough to call a storm. Dreich—miserable enough to require liberal amounts of whisky. Or start arguments. Or cause road accidents. All three combined could end up a large-font front-page splash.

When the editor slid off his stool and went out without a word, Don didn't question him. *I'll find out soon enough.*

He turned to the others. "Rob, when you get back from covering that court case, will you give Calum here an hour or so of your time? Frankie, two o'clock for that update on the dummy. Calum, phone your mother—but only this once. Keep your private life out of the office." At the sight of two bright spots of red blooming on Calum's cheeks, Don stopped himself from saying, *You're twenty-two, not twelve.*

"Use the phone in my office downstairs," Frankie offered. "It might be important."

And Calum stopped himself from saying, *It's not important; it's my mother.* He'd been forced to take a job away from home, and he saw it as a chance to start again, only better, a chance to lose his reputation as a mammy's boy. "Thanks, Frankie."

In his private office, McAllister shut the door in a do-not-disturb-on-pain-of-the-sack notice to all. Knowing the number as well as his birthday, he dialed an outside line and rang the Glasgow number.

"*Herald.*"

"Sandy. I got your message."

"You, now *we*, have a problem."

"Tell me."

"That numberplate you asked about, it rang all kinds of bells. My contact in the police is furious, says he might lose his job over it."

McAllister said nothing.

"Do you want to share?" Sandy Marshall could smell a story. But if it was going to bring some shady arm of government down on himself, he wasn't certain he needed the bother.

"Considering I have no idea what's going on, no. Besides, I've been warned off."

"Since when did that stop you?" When his friend said nothing to the teasing, Sandy changed the subject. "I'm hearing our Mr. Forsythe is up to something."

"Him of the velvet jackets."

"Aye, and purple at that. No one knows what bother he's up to now, but . . ."

"I don't want to think about him." Talk of the man irked McAllister. "In resurrecting the witch accusations in his article, some might say he harried a woman to her death."

"That was my fault," Sandy said. That the final responsibility for every word printed in a newspaper legally rested with the editor they were both aware.

"Done now," McAllister told him. "Thanks, Sandy."

"Not so fast. I want to know more about this numberplate."

"If I find out more, I'll call."

"Maybe we need some secret system—you call me, give me ten minutes, and I'll call you back from a phone box. Maybe you do the same."

Silence.

"Just kidding." The concern in the editor's voice was soft and clear.

"Aye. I know. Thanks again." McAllister hung up, reached for another cigarette, and was practicing blowing smoke rings when there was a knock. Without waiting for an answer, Don came in. He sat, lit up, and waited.

McAllister couldn't remember what, and how much, he had shared with his deputy, so he began at the beginning.

"It was at the auction in Sutherland."

Don knew immediately but said, "Refresh ma memory, starting wi' the court case."

McAllister summarized rapidly and succinctly.

Don digested it all—or at least all he could take in. "So all those involved in the trial were at the auction?"

"So Calum says."

"Then we publish thon photo, then DI Dunne warns you, then Calum starts asking questions . . ."

"About the car and the numberplate."

"The bit that intrigues me," Don said, "is the rushing through of the fatal accident inquiry. That there is no information from whoever found her or why they were up at her place, no results of the postmortem made public, you have to have some major influence to keep that quiet." He sighed. "Doesn't feel right."

"No, it doesn't." And Joanne, in asking all those questions, put herself in the thick of it.

McAllister didn't need to explain this to Don; the deputy editor was sharp, and he was protective of Joanne. Rolling his shoulders, which were hurting from too much bending over proof sheets, Don continued, "Another thing: Calum tells me Alice Ramsay was cremated here in town."

"Really? Why down here and not nearer her home? And why wasn't anyone informed? There's a good few would have liked to say farewell." Joanne included.

"Why here? Don't know. With no relatives coming forward, I'm told the sheriff decided it was the best option." Like most of his generation, and many of the younger generation, Don was not in favor of cremation.

"Maybe the sheriff was ordered to dispose of the body discretely."

"By whom? And why?"

"No idea. But it's done."

◆　◆　◆

That evening, when the girls were in bed, in that time when the streets were empty, the house quiet, the sitting room smelling of wood smoke and whisky, when Joanne had her knitting, he his novel, and music, a piano concerto Joanne had requested, was swelling and fading, matching the dancing blue-red flames from the pine logs, McAllister told Joanne.

He spoke softly, stating the facts, telling her that Don knew and neither of them had an explanation as to why it was done so secretively.

"Cremated?" she asked. "With no one at the service?"

"That we don't know."

"Poor Alice." She turned away to face the painting of the clergyman skating. It was not her favorite—perhaps because she was not too keen on clergymen. She wouldn't tell McAllister—not yet—but she would find and claim Alice's ashes. Somehow. And she would scatter them in the glen. In the wind. And the sun. And a lark would rise; of that she was certain.

◆　◆　◆

Next afternoon it was still raining heavily and McAllister arrived home to a deserted house and a kitchen smelling of damp wool. Leaning over a drying rack laden with wet washing, he checked the wall calendar. Piano lessons. Joanne and the girls would be home in an hour. He put the kettle on. He took the mug of tea into the sitting room, drew the curtains, and then, catching sight of the picture on the floor behind his armchair, he paused. It was the painting of the clergyman skating.

When it hit him, he went up close, examining the paintings one by one.

He knew that painting. He looked again. It had to be a copy. He looked at the others. Maybe they were all copies.

Joanne's favorite, the still life with red onions, he thought might be from the Bloomsbury school. Why hadn't he noticed? *The Skating Clergyman*, a picture beloved by many a Scotsman, admired by many an art lover, reproduced in magazines, in newspapers, in schoolbooks. Why hadn't he seen it?

His thoughts at fast gallop, he felt his hand shake. Cigarette smoke swirled above him in a cloud worthy of an Atlantic cold front. He was annoyed with himself. And disappointed.

He opened the folder Joanne had left on the bureau and leafed through the manuscript. No, these looked original; the writing, the drawings, they were fresh. Then again, he knew nothing about art. He examined pages of script, paragraphs written in different styles. He admired how Alice was trying out different styles, matching handwriting to subject. The penmanship was exquisite; even the spaces between lines seemed planned, exact, with a sense of an assured artist at work. An artist who loved her subject, who took joy and pride in her talent.

Seeing the pile of books he had yet to sort—art history books, books in English, a few in French, more in Italian—he began to speculate. Was she a teacher? A lecturer? An art historian? Didn't someone say she spoke German? Whatever Alice Ramsay's past, she knew her subject. It all added another layer to the mystery.

He knew he would have to tell Joanne that some, possibly all, of the pictures were fakes. How she would react he couldn't guess.

"Well," she said when he told her, "it all seemed too good to be true in the first place." She looked around at the paintings. "I still enjoy them. And they brighten up this gloomy old house."

"That they do." He enjoyed yet another discovery about his new wife; she constantly surprised him. "Then it's definitely time to move to a new place."

She said nothing. The idea of a new house she loved. The idea of packing up and moving she hated.

◆   ◆   ◆

Even though the rain had lessened, clouds were still hovering over the town, scowling, threatening, and Joanne refused to miss the ritual Sunday walk.

They headed for the Islands. To their surprise, Annie accompanied them with no objections or moans of *Do I have to?* The girl had on her Timex wristwatch, a present from her grandparents for passing her eleven-plus and becoming a Royal Academy pupil. She noted the time they left. Noted the time they reached what she thought of as their new house. Only seven minutes extra to get to school. She was delighted.

Joanne asked as they passed the high walls and gate, "When will we get news if your bid has been accepted?" She was trying not to look interested in the property, not wanting to alert the girls.

"Soon."

"Did you do as I suggested?"

He laughed. "I did. And why not? When I went to write it in full, I couldn't decide how much over a round figure to add to the offer. So I used the house number—eighty-nine—and hopefully your intuition will make the difference."

"The solicitor is duty bound to accept the highest bid, and as people always put round numbers, why not?"

He put his arm around her shoulders. "Why not?"

"I wonder what will happen to Alice's house? Maybe . . ."

"Not today. Sunday is a day of rest, and that includes a rest from talking about work."

I wish it included a rest from thinking, she didn't say.

"Maybe Angus MacLean knows who put in a claim on Alice's estate."

He didn't reply.

"Sorry. We should have the equivalent of a swear box—any talk of work on a Sunday, and we fine ourselves a sixpence," Joanne said.

"Are you certain you want to continue working on Alice Ramsay's manuscript?"

After the first flash of doubt, and fear that he might tell her to stop, followed by an understanding that he was not a man who would forbid his wife to follow her dreams, she answered, "Yes, I am."

They were now at the War Memorial. The girls had run on ahead to the Infirmary Bridge, where they would enjoy jumping along the length of the suspension bridge's span, trying to make it buckle but seldom succeeding, as they were too light.

"I know the other pictures are copies . . ." Joanne began.

"I'm told 'studies' is the correct word—exercises in painting and drawing technique."

"I glimpsed a half-completed landscape painting on her easel. It was a wee watercolor of a wren. She did small sketchbook-sized paintings of birds or flowers or buildings and gave them away as presents. Even Mrs. Mackenzie has one in her shop. No, the manuscript is original, so I'll finish it as best I can. The other paintings? I like them; that's enough."

She didn't say, as it hurt too much, that she knew the

manuscript was original because the signature and writing were the same as those on the envelope and the angry letter Alice had written her. The hand, the ink, and the signature were identical to those in the manuscript.

The experiments in writing styles she assumed were just that, experiments to determine what worked best with each illustration. It was clear also that Alice intended to publish her work in book form. That drove Joanne on. Guilt and regret had been the initial motivations. Now it was a sense of duty. And, increasingly, pleasure.

They reached the center of the long, narrow suspension bridge. The rain had paused. The wind was barely perceptible, the temperature mild for November. Yet Joanne shivered. "To do what she did—it makes no sense. Her work is so full of life. Love, even. The flowers, the light in the birch trees, on the hillsides, on the rocks, it makes me feel—I don't know—connected?" She was shaking her head; "beautiful" was too vague a word to describe the paintings. So simple, so clean, there seemed less than a dozen brushstrokes in the more dramatic paintings, especially the ones with heavy hurrying clouds.

McAllister supplied the word. "There is a reverence in those works of the hills above her home." Having seen many religious paintings in churches in Spain, in art galleries in France, and the Salvador Dalí in Glasgow, he understood what Joanne responded to in Alice Ramsay's original work.

"Maybe that's why I want to complete her project. It's a need to understand."

"There is sometimes no reason we can understand," McAllister said. "In my brother's case, it was his shame at being abused that made him drown himself."

Sixteen, Joanne was thinking. *What must it be like to be so desperate at only sixteen years of age?*

"And in Alice Ramsay's case, we may never know her reasons. After years of reporting or, rather, hushing up suicides, it is always the same question: why? It can obsess people, consume them. I know that was my reaction."

Another suspension bridge crossing the river to the first of the islands was satisfyingly shaky. The whoops and yells from the girls made Joanne laugh. "As you said, it's Sunday. No more thinking." She hurried off to join the girls, calling out, "Race you to the next bridge!"

He watched her coat fly open, her hair escape the headscarf; he saw her skip off to join her children. Under the tunnel of barren trees, with the hushed roar of the river falling over the shallow weir filling his ears like a constant comforting tinnitus, he caught a distant glimpse of Annie's red jacket. As he watched Joanne and Jean shuffle through the dank carpet of leaves, he was engulfed by a happiness he had never previously known. *This is my family.*

◆   ◆   ◆

The week passed quickly for Joanne—an hour or so each day on Alice's manuscript, around two hours on her linked short stories in the not-totally-imagined world of a remote glen still stuck in a prewar time warp. How to use the subject of witches she could not fathom, so she wrote about what she called the Celtic Twilight, adjusting to the loss of the old ways, bracing itself for the coming decade of electricity and, maybe one day, television. It was a world she wanted to document before it disappeared entirely. Much as Alice had done in her paintings.

Do not *lapse into Brigadoon,* she repeated to herself as she typed. Often. Much as she loved Gene Kelly, the Hollywood depiction of Scotland, with the fake accents and the terrible tartans, had her squirming in her cinema seat in embarrassment—unfortunately in the company of Rob MacLean, who'd laughed out loud at the more mawkish sequences, causing the woman in front to turn and shoosh him so often Joanne thought they'd be thrown out. Not a good look for representatives of the *Highland Gazette*.

In between organizing the chapter layout, which was clearly scripted in Alice's notes, Joanne saw to the shepherd's pie or perhaps mince and tatties, or a pot roast, or bramble and apple crumble, or jam roly-poly. Cooking, washing, cleaning, ironing, mending and darning, checking the girls' homework—writing had to be fitted around the more important role of mother and housewife.

She joked with McAllister, "Unlike Mr. Wordsworth, I do not have a household of a devoted sister, wife, and helpers to allow me all the time in the world for art."

He offered to pay for a housekeeper. She refused. "A weekly cleaner is all I need."

She went over to her desk bureau, a lovely piece she had bought in the auction rooms in Church Street and restored with many sheets of medium, or fine sandpaper, and liberal applications of elbow grease. She took out her reporter's notebook. But her pencil remained in the pot. The notepad unopened.

"Alice," she said aloud, "I know I wronged you. But I know you didn't kill yourself, and I can't let your death go. Please help me find who did it."

The clock ticked. A car passed. A flicker out the corner of her eye startled her. Someone behind that cypress tree? The wind rattled windowpanes, shook the trees. *If we don't move house, that kirkyard tree comes down.* The girls came home. Then McAllister. And nighttime. And still no answer from Alice.

CHAPTER 11

Alice remembers Mrs. Mackenzie as an annoying child always on the edge of everything. In games in the woods and castle grounds, in the sand dunes, running and leaping, arms outstretched pretending to fly, she was the one who would complain about the sand down the back of her dress. On excursions up the glen to the waterfall, she was the one to complain the paths were too muddy, or too steep.

Father encouraged me to be friendly with the locals—as long as I didn't learn to talk like them. Or forget my manners. The summers were long, and boring, for an only child like me, so even though it was a long time ago and I hardly knew her, I remember her—Mackenzie was her maiden name as well as her married name—as someone to be pitied. Though why I couldn't exactly say.

At the end of the summer holidays, when we packed up to go back to London, Nanny McNeil would parcel up my old dresses and coats and give them to the Mackenzie family. "Always help those less fortunate than you," she'd say.

Mrs. Mackenzie's grandmother was one of our housemaids, and her father worked on the estate. There was some scandal about him, but I never knew what, just some overheard remarks that meant little to me as a child, phrases hinting that he was "soft in the heid." Father had explained, "He was never the same since he came back from the Somme."

Now, knowing her present family circumstances, I pity her. But I've discovered, much to my detriment, just how dangerous she can be.

* * *

Frankie Urquhart, the *Gazette* advertising manager, found accommodation for Calum. It was off Island Bank Road, the route to the south side of Loch Ness. The short street ended at the rock face of the ridge above the river. With the castle to the left and the prison not far above, the small enclave of terraced and semidetached houses was within walking distance to the *Gazette* office and the town center.

A war widow ran the three-room boarding house, and Frankie knew she'd recently renewed her classified advertisement in the Rooms to Let section. "Respectable gentlemen only."

Calum was delighted. Then terrified. He had only ever spent four nights away from home, at a Boy Scouts camp near Aviemore. Even then, his mother was one of the volunteers, helping with the cooking and general minding of seventy twelve- to fifteen-year-olds from all over the county.

Elaine had tried every which way to prevent her future mother-in-law from coming on the trip.

Calum agreed. "I'll tell her no," he'd said.

"That'll be right," she'd replied. To herself.

She'd also appealed to Mr. Mackenzie. Such a nice man, she always thought, but the way she treats him, no one blames him for straying. "I won't see Calum for weeks," she'd told him. "It'd be really nice to have the day to ourselves."

"Leave it with me," he'd replied.

When Calum came to collect Elaine, Mrs. Mackenzie was in the front seat.

"Hello, Mrs. Mackenzie," Elaine said through the front passenger door. "Are we dropping you off somewhere?"

"I'm coming to see ma boy settled in."

"Really? And how will you get back?"

"The train."

"Elaine is driving Dad's car back home. I told you, you can go with her," Calum pointed out.

"It's no I don't trust you, dear, it's just I'm no keen on women drivers."

Elaine saw how her less-than-full-sized fiancée was trying to disappear into the leather of the driver's seat. She saw how he couldn't look at her and how white his knuckles were as he held on to the steering wheel. *Poor Calum.* She refrained from making a sarcastic remark and resisted the urge to reach across and shake the woman. *His new job is step one in the escape plan,* she told herself, *so be nice.*

Approaching the outskirts of the town after a mostly silent journey, Elaine said to Calum, "May as well open the present I got you."

He glanced in the driving mirror.

She held up an envelope, with red ribbon around it and kisses and "S.W.A.L.K." across the back. "It's a book of maps of the town and county."

"I could have got you that," Mrs. Mackenzie said.

"That's brilliant. Thanks, Elaine." He was smiling that silly smile she loved. "Open it."

Elaine blew him a kiss, opened the book, and found the map of the town. Using her forefinger, she traced the route to the boardinghouse. "Keep on the main road down Kenneth Street. Left at the T junction." She continued, "Go straight ahead, and after crossing the river take a hard right."

Mrs. Mackenzie was silent. From the set of her shoulders, Elaine could see she was in a huff and ignored her. Even Calum wasn't his usual "Are you all right, Mum? What's the matter,

Mum?" Maybe he does see her tricks, her constant need for attention, Elaine thought.

"Now, follow the river, then turn left at the War Memorial, and left again. Then it's the third street on the right." Before they stopped, she added, "Good location. Only a short walk to your new job."

"If he lasts," his mother muttered.

They heard. But didn't comment.

"I don't usually take young men," the landlady told Calum. Examining Elaine—as though she was something the cat brought in, Elaine later joked—the landlady added, "And no female visitors allowed."

"Don't worry, I live in Sutherland. I'm only helping my fiancé move in."

"My Calum is a well-brought-up boy. He'd never dream of . . ." For once, Mrs. Mackenzie couldn't find a suitable word.

When the landlady showed him the cupboard containing the vacuum cleaner and the ironing board, Calum knew not to ask, in front of Elaine, how you worked an iron. The gas cooker, as ferocious a nightmare as a fire-breathing dragon, he instantly decided was not for him. As for the twin-tub washing machine, Mrs. Addison's instructions on its use were more complicated than a service manual for a Spitfire.

"Post your washing home," his mother told him.

When he replied, "Thanks, Mum," he caught the glance between landlady and fiancée and didn't care.

Lodging arrangements finalized and three suitcases lugged up three flights of stairs to the attic room, they went back to the car. Calum driving, Elaine navigating, Mrs. Mackenzie criticizing, the trio arrived at the McAllister residence, where they were expected for afternoon tea.

Joanne had invited Calum Mackenzie for a welcome tea, as she would any newcomer to the *Gazette*. When Calum asked, she said she would be delighted if Elaine joined them.

Annie answered the door. "Hello. Hiya, Calum. Come into the sitting room."

"It's Mr. Mackenzie," Mrs. Mackenzie said.

Annie pretended not to hear. She looked at Elaine saying, "Calum told us you're a nurse. My wee sister wants to be a nurse."

Joanne had come into the hallway and watched as her daughter seized Elaine's hand and dragged her towards the dining room cum television room cum girl's den.

"Annie . . ." Joanne began.

"It's fine," Elaine replied.

"I'll serve tea in a minute, so don't be long."

A few minutes later, Joanne called out, "Elaine, can you give me a hand with the tea?"

"Your girls are lovely," Elaine said as she helped butter the scones. "And so bright. All those questions took my mind off . . . family stuff."

Joanne put her hand on Elaine's arm. "Poor you, is it really that bad?"

"Och, not really. I'm used to it. With Calum down here, well, I'm hoping we can escape her clutches." Elaine looked around to see if any more help was needed. Spying the Dundee cake, she said, "Shall I cut it?"

"Please."

"Aye, and what Mrs. Mackenzie doesn't know is that I've put in for a transfer to the hospital here."

"It's your life." Joanne did not want to become involved. Her own experience of families was mixed. Luckily, she adored

McAllister's mother. "Elaine, I heard Miss Ramsay was cremated here in town. Did you know?"

"Never! I heard nothing about that." She looked close to tears. "Cremated, you say? That's terrible. We were waiting for news of the arrangements. Me and Nurse Ogilvie were going to go. And a few of the residents wanted to pay their respects. What will I tell them?"

"I was shocked too."

Elaine thought about it. "I can't believe that happened without Mrs. Mackenzie knowing—and if she did know, it would've been all over the town by midday and the county by evening."

"See what you can find out."

Elaine spotted two of Alice Ramsay's watercolors that Joanne had propped up on top of the kitchen dresser.

"That's the nursing-home garden. Miss Ramsay was right fond of the trees there, and she loved that old monkey puzzle, always drawing it. On sunny days, she'd sit with the old folk, them blethering away, her sketching and listening . . ." She looked away. "We miss her. The nurses always say good night, but we've no got the same charm. No, that's no right, it was more than charm. Miss Ramsay cared."

"It's such a loss," was all Joanne could say.

"This wee one." Elaine was staring at a watercolor where bright new-wound blood-red geraniums made a splash against whitewashed walls, and a small fountain stood in the center, no water falling and dried leaves in the bowl. "That's never Scotland," she said. "England, maybe?"

Joanne glanced at it. "Somewhere warm, certainly." She lifted the tea tray. "My husband thinks somewhere in the Middle East, Mediterranean. Talking of McAllister, we'd better rescue him."

"And my fiancé."

When they came in with the tea tray, Joanne could see McAllister had that glazed-over gaze that descended whenever he attended Town Council meetings.

Mrs. Mackenzie had the officious look of a welfare officer who knew an unsatisfactory household when she saw one. It was taking her every ounce of self-control not to swipe a finger along a chair back checking for dust—of which there would be plenty, she'd already decided.

Calum looked lost; between his boss and his mother, he could find no topic of common interest, so he'd given up. At one point, McAllister caught Calum looking at the door, much like a dog longing to be let out for a walk.

When Calum caught the editor's frown, his unsaid *Don't you dare*, he made some attempts to interrupt his mother. "But Mum" or "Mum, Mr. McAllister was telling me," or "Isn't it interesting that."

Nothing stopped her.

Mrs. Mackenzie had been boasting about their garage, their house, her father, her grandfather, her uncles, her charitable works, her prizes from the Women's Guild for her cakes. "I use four eggs in ma Victoria sponge."

She detailed the traffic on the A9 trunk road, the road works, the accidents, the speeding lorries, how sheep were still herded on the main road, often blocking the traffic. "No many vehicles passes by that I don't know about," she told them. "As for thon convoys of carts and caravans when the tinkers take to the road, an absolute disgrace. There should be a law against them!"

She has enough breath to climb Everest without oxygen, he was thinking when Joanne came in.

"McAllister," Joanne said, "I didn't make tea for you, as I thought you'd have it when you come back." She was enjoying his discomfort. And he knew it.

"Come back?"

"Aren't you taking the girls to the Islands for an ice cream?" She turned to Calum. "Why don't you and Elaine go too? The Islands is a favorite spot for courting couples."

Thank you thank you my dear dear wife. McAllister grinned at Joanne. And stopped himself whistling. "Annie. Jean. We're off out for a walk."

"Maybe we can wait until after we've had our tea?" Mrs. Mackenzie suggested.

"Och, no, you and I can have tea now," Joanne said. "The young ones need time to themselves, don't you think?" McAllister was already in the hallway putting on his coat and hat. "I remember when McAllister and I were courting, you couldn't keep us away from the Islands." Thank goodness Annie didn't hear that, Joanne was thinking.

"Calum and Elaine will enjoy a walk there. It's really bonnie," she said, seeing McAllister and her daughters and the courting couple walk down the path to freedom—and envying them.

Her husband, as though sensing her gaze, turned around at the gate and tipped his hat at her. The rush of joy at the sight of her man made Joanne decide that an hour or so with Mrs. Mackenzie was worth that grin of complicity that had radiated across the garden, through the sitting-room window, straight to her heart.

But soon they had run out of conversation. Or, rather, Joanne had. After a second slice of cake and a third cup of tea, leaning back, tiny in the armchair, her thin wrists and skinny ankles reminding Joanne of the bird skeleton drawings, Calum's mother simply began repeating herself.

Whether this was because she had forgotten what she'd said earlier or whether she could not stop the flow of sentences describing the minutiae of a life where little happened, a life only lived through discussing others, Joanne couldn't say. But what she did recognize was the loneliness leaching out from the woman, as palpable as a haar on the firth, and as clammy. Joanne found herself pitying Mrs. Mackenzie. And counting her own blessings—until one phrase struck her. Then all sympathy vanished.

When the clock chimed five and still no sign of the wanderers, Mrs. Mackenzie began to be anxious. "I knew I couldn't trust that Elaine." Her scorn, as she said her future daughter-in-law's name, would wither roses off the bush. "She'll make me miss my train."

Joanne said, "I'll drive you to the station."

"And miss my boy?" She continued, "Of course, *she* thought herself too good for the likes o' us. After the trial, when thon eejit o' a sheriff let her off, that was when she realized few o' us had the time o' day for her. So what else could she do but kill herself?"

It had taken a moment for Joanne to grasp the change of subject, to understand who was the subject of the woman's venom. "Are you saying that animosity from the community drove Alice Ramsay to kill herself?" Joanne kept her voice flat. Low. She was holding on to the arms of her chair to stop herself trembling.

"Anim—what? You're like our Calum, full o' big words." A hint of censure was there, but her snobbishness won out. She relished the chance to show off to neighbors and customers, whether they wanted to hear or not, that her boy was coming up in the world, promoted to a bigger newspaper, and keeping company with people who owned a big house and drove a smart car.

"Anyhow, no matter what the Sheriff Court decided, thon Ramsay woman did what they said. That poor woman lost her baby because of her wickedness. Aye, there's no many mourns her passing. And I did hear someone is claiming her estate. I have an idea who it is. Hopefully someone decent. Not like *her*."

Joanne wanted to know the identity of the claimant. But wouldn't ask. As Mrs. Mackenzie offered no more information, she guessed the woman didn't know. Or was making it all up.

It was a long hour and ten minutes before the front door opened and Jean came running in.

"We had a brilliant time, Mum. McAllister let us have a double cone with a chocolate flake. And a chocolate frog."

"Where's Mr. Mackenzie?" Mrs. Mackenzie asked.

"You mean Calum?" It was Annie who answered. She had flung herself onto the sofa, kicking off her shoes without undoing the laces, and was busy licking the last of the melted chocolate off her fingers.

"*Mr. Mackenzie* to you. It's bad manners to call a grown-up by their first name." Mrs. Mackenzie's eyes narrowed, her lips disappeared, and her hand was straying outwards as though it had a mind of its own, a mind wanting to slap the girl.

Annie saw. Or guessed. And said, "Calum told us to call him Calum." Then added, "He said to tell you they'd meet you at the station."

Normally, Joanne would reprimand her daughter for her lack of respect and manners. But the words, the tone, the sheer lack of compassion from Mrs. Mackenzie over the death of Alice Ramsay, had horrified her. She wanted the woman out of her house. Immediately.

She met her husband in the hall. "I'm taking Mrs. Mackenzie to the train," she explained.

"Make sure she catches it," he murmured.

On the short drive to the station, and to stop Mrs. Mackenzie's relentless muttering about children and manners, Joanne said, "I thought Miss Ramsay had no living relatives."

"There's a lot about Miss Ramsay you don't know. When the

truth comes out, I promise you'll be shocked." Mrs. Mackenzie was clutching her handbag close, as though guarding the family secrets.

From her voice, Joanne didn't need to see her face to know it would show a smug expression saying, I know everything. And you know nothing."

Joanne could not bear another minute with the woman. "I'll drop you off here," she said, pulling into Station Square.

"Shameless!" The word exploded, ringing around the car.

Joanne followed the pointed finger. Elaine and Calum were in a corner, arms around each other, kissing—not long deep passionate kisses, more sweet-friendly kisses. The height difference caused Elaine to bend down towards her fiancé, giving the impression that she was the instigator of their passion.

Joanne knew kissing in public was disapproved of, but she smiled, glad the young couple had had time to say good-bye in private. "Young love," she said.

"But it's Sunday!" Mrs. Mackenzie spat out the words as though she were a sheriff handing out a sentence for immorality. Or witchcraft, for that surely was what she believed: Elaine had bewitched her innocent boy.

Mrs. Mackenzie got out of the car, slamming the door without saying good-bye. Or thank you.

"Manners," Joanne muttered.

She watched the woman try to reclaim her son.

But Elaine deliberately let go of Calum's hand slowly, smiling, and blowing kisses in a gesture that said she had won. After a final wave good-bye to her fiancé, who was now buying a platform ticket so he could see his mother safely onto the train, she walked to the Mackenzie family car parked nearby.

Joanne wanted to wind down the window and shout out to the nurse, *Well done, Elaine!*

She didn't. She didn't wait to offer Calum a lift to the boardinghouse either. On the drive home, up the hill, past the castle, along Crown Drive, Joanne kept bursting into giggles. She couldn't stop grinning when she told the story and the comment to McAllister: "But it's Sunday!"

"Sunday, Monday, any day, if that woman is in town again, warn me, and I shall take a long, long walk."

Annie looked at her stepfather and said, "Or we could drive to Nairn."

Joanne agreed. "We'll all go."

CHAPTER 12

~

Alice is at the window, her hands wrapped around a mug of tea.

I can't believe I thought asking Dougie to be a witness was a good idea. We had some good laughs when we were students together, but he's turned into such a pompous ass. Dougald indeed! And an added "e" at the end of Forsythe. He comes from some mining community in Ayrshire, and was proud of being born in Burns country. Now he's less Rabbie Burns and more Oscar Wilde, but without the wit of either.

As for the drawing, it didn't occur to me until too late that the procurator fiscal would use it as evidence. "Evidence of what?" I asked the sergeant. He didn't reply, but my solicitor said, "Evidence of bad character."

The policeman had the grace to smile when I burst out laughing. "So collecting skull and skeleton drawings is the mark of a bad person?" I asked. Only later, at the trial, did I understand it was more than that; it implied witchcraft.

Now I have Dougie back in my life. The man won't give up until he gets hold of that drawing.

◆ ◆ ◆

"McAllister household."

"Morning. How's my pal treating his bride? Lavishing you with sweet words? Showering you with exotic presents?"

Joanne laughed. "I'm fine, Sandy. And McAllister is the same as ever."

"You should have run away with an Onion Johnnie—the French are good at romance." Sandy Marshall knew his friend well. "Anyhow, what I'm phoning about might give your man a heart attack. So . . ."

She was thinking no editor of a national newspaper rang to waste time, so why was he blethering away like this?

"Mr. Dougald Forsythe . . ."

"No, Sandy. I will never work with the man ever again."

Sandy continued, "Don't blame you for being upset—he's an infuriating wee nyaff. No, it's this latest piece Forsythe has written for the *Herald*. He's claiming he discovered a Leonardo da Vinci drawing."

"What?" Joanne knew immediately which drawing but could hardly speak, she was so flabbergasted.

"It was the drawing used as evidence in the trial against Miss Alice Ramsay. Forsythe had it authenticated in London. Seems to be the real McCoy, so he intends to sell it at auction down there."

"At the sale of Miss Ramsay's possessions, he outbid Mc-Allister for that drawing."

"Aye, I know—though in my hearing, Forsythe had the good sense not to crow about that. He also writes that he would have donated the sketch to the city of Glasgow, but because of the 'reactionary attitude towards art from the worthies of Glasgow,' he's keeping it. As it's been declared genuine, he'll make a very tidy profit and stir up the art world. Though I suspect what he really wants is to stick it to all those who don't listen to him or value his judgment."

"Where would a Leonardo drawing have come from?" Joanne still couldn't take in the idea that Alice Ramsay had such a valuable work of art and kept it secret.

"After the war, 'lost' artworks were, still are, being bought and sold with no questions asked about how they were acquired."

Joanne could hear the quotation marks around "lost." "In that case, how can Mr. Forsythe sell it?"

"Finders keepers, he says." Sandy sounded annoyed. After the last debacle and the letter from a furious Alice Ramsay that arrived only a few days before the news of her suicide, he had little time for the art critic. But the man stirred up debate, and that sold newspapers. "Talk it over with McAllister. Let me know if there's anything to add from your end, a valedictory article perhaps. 'The Mystery of Miss Alice Ramsay.' She's gone, so it won't hurt."

Joanne knew how newspapers worked, but she knew Alice would have hated any more publicity. Then again, maybe she could avenge Alice's treatment by Forsythe; he had exposed her and used her, making himself out to be an arbiter of all things artistic. Now he would profit from her death. "Thanks, Sandy, for letting me know rather than . . ."

"Rather than having McAllister read over the breakfast table that he's been bested by Forsythe?" He laughed. "I was tempted."

Joanne put down the telephone and stared at the small oil painting they'd hung in the hallway. She loved it. A copy of a Pierre Bonnard painting of a vase of flowers, she'd decided, after finding his work in an art book.

She wandered into the sitting room. Leonardo da Vinci? Sandy Marshall's revelation made her fear that the two small drawings she'd found amongst the papers in the writing box might also be genuine. Although taken with them, she hadn't given them much thought. But what if they were genuine Leonardo works? She was too nervous to take them out and examine them. Even the thought of holding such ancient pieces of paper, of reading the notes, the thoughts of the great man, made her tremble.

The artworks hanging on the walls now seemed larger, brighter. *I know they are copies, but what if even one of them is genuine? And how would I find out?* She dismissed the idea. Mr. Fancy Wes'coat Forsythe would have bought them if they were.

She opened the portfolio of watercolors. *These are real.* She remembered glancing at a notebook on the kitchen table in Alice's farmhouse, admiring a half-finished sketch of a vase of flowers.

She opened the writing box and brought out another folder. The drawings were small; their simple lines, the handwriting, and most of all their possible provenance imbued them with a spiritual value no anonymous artist could command. The paper had seemed dirty when she first looked at it. Now she knew the discoloration was age. The ink seemed to float on the surface as lightly as a thought. She held her breath; a puff of wind, a drop of moisture, and, she imagined, the writing and images would dissolve.

Who could tell me if they are genuine?

She closed the folder, closed the box. She turned the brass key in the brass lock. Her hands felt clammy.

She walked across to the painting of an unknown but definitely Continental countryside. The painting was set back in a gilt frame with elaborate gilt carved-wood curlicues, a fitting piece for a baroque theater. She brought over the footstool, kicked off her shoes. One foot on the tapestry cover, her knee began to tremble. She paused. Stepped up again. She dropped the key onto the top of the frame.

As she stepped down, she thought of her former mother-in-law's expression, "a right palaver." She shook her head. *Stop being so suspicious.* Forsythe was a man obsessed, certainly. A killer? Surely not.

✦   ✦   ✦

She waited until that precious time, the time between the girls going to bed and McAllister putting on a record they would both enjoy. He would pour a whisky, although more and more lately it was wine, and they would talk. These shoes and ships and sealing-wax conversations she so loved.

Having hoarded the tale tight to her all afternoon and into the evening, the sentences burst out rapidly, breathlessly, and absolutely clearly.

"Sandy called. That drawing you bid against Forsythe for, the one I wanted, it's a genuine Leonardo Da Vinci."

"It's a what?" He'd heard her, just needed to process the information.

She looked at him, shaking her head to one side, seeing in his face a reflection of her earlier shock. "I know. It's incredible."

"So does that mean . . . ?" He was gesturing around at the walls with a whisky glass in hand, but practiced Scotsman that he was, not a drop was spilt.

"I don't think so." Even after only a short few months together, they communicated in that verbal shorthand of most married couples. "But maybe."

"Crivens."

"Aye, crivens."

Neither could have said who started laughing first. "Crivens," McAllister repeated, shaking his head, bemused by the idea of a genuine old master, albeit a sketch, being discovered in an auction sale up a Highland glen. "Tell me exactly what Sandy said."

She did.

"So Forsythe must have known," he commented when she'd finished, "but how?"

Of all the thoughts Joanne had had, this was not one of them. "How? I don't know." She jerked up in her chair, spilling the art book she'd been examining. "Did he know her before she came to Sutherland? Or was he just an acknowledged art expert appearing for the defense at her trial?"

"Miss Ramsay's solicitor might know. I'll get Calum to find out."

"Perhaps we should ask Mrs. Mackenzie. She's bound to know how he came to be at the trial." Seeing his expression whenever Mrs. Mackenzie was mentioned, she grinned. "Only kidding." Her misgiving at voicing the question was overcome by a need for her husband's opinion. "I was wondering . . ."

He could see it was more than wondering.

"Would someone . . . I mean, do you think a person would do something bad for that drawing?"

"Forsythe?" He didn't use the word either. But the possibilities were between them: steal, kill, murder. "I don't know. Some would. It's not only the money, it's the prestige of recognizing a wee drawing for what it really is."

She knew to not say this proved Alice didn't kill herself, for she knew that was illogical.

But McAllister guessed. "Concentrate on the manuscript. Then we'll try to find a publisher. It's the best we can do for Alice Ramsay."

♦ ♦ ♦

Alice's work was taking most of Joanne's time and concentration. Her own short stories—some no more than extended captions or chapter ideas—she allowed to float. When they were ripe, she would catch them, as though plucking some literary fruit from an ideas tree. Some days it was only a heading. "When Mrs.

MacGillivary Dropped Her Wedding Ring Down the Well." Some stories were a line or two, and two of them were a few paragraphs. The postman's story was almost ready to be edited and retyped. The witch idea had yet to find a plot.

She started every story idea on a fresh sheet of paper and wrote by hand with a fountain pen in black ink. Blue ink was for correspondence with friends and family; black ink was serious.

Notes on Alice's manuscript she typed. The artist's system was logical, starting with the species' names in alphabetical order, making it easy for an editor and a reader to follow. Usually, the flowers and brackens and trees were identified initially by their Latin names, then the common names, then the Scottish names if different from English. There was a note from Alice with a line crossed through it: "arrange by color?" That had made Joanne smile, as she liked the idea, but could see it would be hard to persuade a publisher to agree.

Today, though, was different: no work on the manuscript, no work on the stories. All Joanne could think of were the two small, faded drawings. Why hadn't she shared her discovery with McAllister? And should she have the other artworks evaluated in light of the revelation? She had no answer to the first question and, for an answer to the second, didn't know where to turn. *Alice Ramsay, what secrets were you hiding?*

The telephone rang.

"Hello."

"Hiya."

"Rob. What's up?"

"I hear the joker in the velvet waistcoat found a Leonardo."

"The distinguished art expert, you mean."

"Aye, him. McAllister said your paintings might be fakes, but—"

"Studies!" a voice she recognized as Hector's shouted in the background.

"Shut up," Rob said. "Sorry, not you, Joanne. The pest is really excited. It seems we have a distinguished art expert in the office—or so he tells me. And after hearing the news of a genuine Leonardo, he's desperate to check out your pictures."

"I know my stuff." That was Hec again.

"Really? Truly?" Joanne was delighted.

"We're coming over," Rob told her, "so put the kettle on."

"I can go on ma own," she heard Hec complain.

"I wouldn't wish that on my worst—" Someone cut off the conversation. She guessed it was Hector.

She was still in her pajamas and McAllister's dressing gown. The kitchen was a mess. The sitting room needed Hoovering. She was debating whether to tidy or to dress first. Dress, she told herself. It's only Rob and Hector, and they won't notice if it's untidy.

There was something in the way Hector would examine her that always made her straighten her shoulders, push back her hair. With people, Hec saw a subject, an object even, and when he took a shot, often sneakily, he could bring out that indefinable something that revealed the essence of the person.

She was leaning forwards, her head upside down, to brush her hair, when she heard the distant throb of Rob's pride and joy, a red Triumph Bonneville motorbike.

Opening the door for them, she watched Hector hop off the bike. With a camera bag around his shoulder and a woolen balaclava hiding his marmalade-colored hair, he trotted up the path. Rob sauntered behind, his bike jacket and boots and airman's goggles giving the impression he'd stepped off the page of a Biggles book.

"Paintings first or tea and gingerbread?" she asked.

Hector hopped from foot to foot. "Gingerbread, I can smell it."

"But you can't eat it, not with that thing on your head." Rob yanked off the woolen helmet.

Hec yelled, "Ouch! You pulled ma hair out!"

Joanne smiled, envious of the easy, teasing camaraderie. She missed working, joking, thinking, sharing ideas, worries, front-page scoops, and coups in the cramped reporters' room that smelled of men and cigarettes, the place where she met McAllister, the place where she grew up—finally, at the age of twenty-nine.

She made Hector sit at the kitchen table to eat his gingerbread; she had no energy to Hoover the carpets after his visit. Finished, he washed his hands thoroughly at the kitchen sink. He might be clumsy, but when it came to his professional persona, he was neat and knowledgeable.

Joanne and Rob followed Hector into the sitting room. He stood in the center of the washed-out Persian rug and slowly turned in a complete circle, eyeing the paintings and sketches at a distance, murmuring all the while, "Right. I see. Uh-huh. Och-och." Then he stepped towards the paintings propped up on the mantelpiece. "Can I?" he asked.

She nodded. "Of course."

He lifted what she considered one of her favorites, the still life with onions. He turned it around. "Aaah." He made the sound softly, slowly, and then he put the picture back. The perhaps Picasso he was quicker with. "Mmmm." He examined all the pictures plus the Bonnard look-alike in the hallway. Back in the sitting room, he said, "I'm pretty sure most of them are studies— really good ones, though."

"Aye, they'd have to be copies, otherwise that fox Forsythe would have snapped them up at the auction," Joanne agreed.

"They are not copies; they are studies." Hec went into lecturing mode. "See, when you study art, you—"

"What about these?" Rob had been half-listening, more interested in nosing around Joanne's manuscript and the books in the boxes McAllister had yet to finish unpacking.

"Don't have enough bookshelves," he'd replied when Joanne asked for the fourth time when he was going to unpack them.

"Rob!" she called out as he tried to open the writing box.

"It's OK, I won't read your private stuff—well, only a few paragraphs." He leaned over a page still in the typewriter. "This is good. I like the opening."

"These watercolors are really skillful," Hec said. "The page composition an' all." He was holding the pages by their edges, laying them carefully on the tablecloth. "You need to put acid-free paper between the sheets. It costs a fortune, but I get it on *Gazette* expenses, so . . ." He winked at her. "Then you need to photograph them." He reached for another illustration, this one of a clump of bog cotton. "I can do it for you if you like."

"Would you?" She lifted a folder with a selection of Alice's watercolors of the glens and the beach and the cathedral for Hector. The drawings locked in the writing box were what she really wanted to know about but daren't ask. "I'd love to see Miss Ramsay's manuscript published as a memento." *Of a life ended so horribly*, she didn't say.

"I'm your man." He grinned at her, that half-boy half-man mad-troll grin, and seeing his enthusiasm, she was all the more determined to see the work published.

"I have to get going." Rob had had enough of the pictures; fakes, studies, whatever they were they were not genuine, so he lost interest.

"See ya," Hec said.

Rob shrugged. "Any chance of another slice of gingerbread?" he asked.

Joanne watched him lope down the garden path, bike key in one hand, and a fat slice of gingerbread in the other.

"Hector . . ."

He squinted up at her. He knew that tone; it was the same when his wee sister wanted something but was too shy to ask.

"Hector, there are two wee drawings I think might be important. No one knows about them. I locked them up and hid the key, and . . ."

They fetched the stepladder from the laundry. Key retrieved, she took out the folder and laid it on the table.

He opened the folder carefully. Touching only the top and bottom edges, he separated the drawings, and Joanne felt guilty she hadn't thought to put tissue between the pages. He stared. For almost two minutes, he did nothing but stare, turning his gaze from left to right, from top to bottom. He peered down. He stood back. "Do you have a magnifying glass?"

"Somewhere," she answered, knowing the only one they had was with Annie's abandoned stamp-collecting project. "I think there is writing on the back." She went to turn a drawing over.

"Don't touch." Hector was a man transformed, green eyes shining like a cornered wildcat's, every freckle in his pale face sharp as stars in a clear midwinter midnight sky. "These are special."

She stepped back. "Sorry." She blew out a long, deep breath. "Sorry, Hector, it's just I'm scared they might be . . . you know."

"Real. I know."

He bent over the drawings once more, examining them through the glass.

Much as a surgeon might examine the insides of a brain, Joanne thought.

Holding a page between thumb and forefinger, he held it up to the light. He put it down. Then sat down, staring not at the drawings but into another time. All he could eventually say was, "Crikey!"

All she could say was, "Fancy another cup of tea?"

"That'd be grand."

She went to the kitchen. Filling the kettle, she could feel the excitement as a knot, a twist, in her stomach.

They didn't speak until halfway through the first cup.

"I'm no certain. But if I am right . . . seeing yon . . . and . . ."

His eyes seemed wet, but she couldn't be sure. She shared his feelings. "For me, it's cathedrals. I stand in them and am completely overawed."

"Does anyone else know?"

"McAllister knows about the paintings. But not the drawings. I kept them hidden because . . ." She glanced up at the clock. Her husband would be home soon. "I don't know why I hid them." Not completely true; she wanted to keep them to herself for as long as possible—to enjoy, to marvel, to feel a pleasure as high and as clear and as uplifting as any visit to a cathedral—knowing that when she told someone, even her husband, she would have to give them up. To whom, she didn't know.

Hector was also feeling covetous of the drawings. "Keep it that way for now. We'll work out what to do later."

She was flicking a pencil between her fingers, the frustration and the distress over Alice's fate gnawing at her. *All very well for my husband to tell me to let it go, but there had to be a reason for her to kill herself. If in fact she did.* "Hector, why do you think Miss Ramsay killed herself?"

"I've never given it much thought."

"She was really distressed by the gossip about her before and after the trial."

"Aye, Rob told me. But what other people say and think is no reason to kill yourself."

Joanne was startled by Hector's conviction. Her own experience of malicious tongues was partly the reason she was so obsessed with the fate of Alice.

"I'm sure people say things about me, and I know for definite some call ma granny an old witch."

Joanne smiled. Hec's granny would be a star in a production of *Macbeth*.

"So why bother giving them harpies the satisfaction of gaining a hold over you?" he asked.

"Thank you for saying that, Hector."

He stared at her. To him it was so obvious.

"I know, sticks and stones and all that. I've experienced how much malicious gossip hurts. Maybe that is why I am . . . why I am so sympathetic to Alice Ramsay." *Obsessed*, she was about to say but didn't. "Do you think the drawings and these paintings might be connected to her death?"

She watched as Hec, his head cocked to one side like a blackbird listening for a worm, considered the question. Remembering the solid beams and the height of the barn roof, he could visualize the *how* all too clearly. The why was beyond him.

"Sorry, I'm not one for thinking. Images is how I figure out the world. But whatever caused her to do it must have been serious—hanging is pretty final."

Thanks for the reminder, Hec, she wanted to say. But didn't. His cutting to the quick of an argument or an idea was what she valued most in the photographer. She knew how scatty he could be. And that he suffered from foot-in-mouth disease. But in this, the manuscript, the drawings, the secret, she knew she could rely on him. Absolutely.

The doorbell rang, startling her out of her dwam.

"Mrs. McAllister?" a man with a suitcase asked when she opened the door.

"Sorry, I'm not interested."

"I have some great household gadgets you might want to take a look at." Ignoring her, he opened a suitcase in which brushes and mop heads and all manner of cleaning products in bright plastic bottles were neatly arranged. An Aladdin's case of chemical delights. "Let me demonstrate how good this is, best furniture polish ever, and a lovely fragrance." He began to insinuate his way into the porch, intent on gaining entrance to the hallway. "That mirror, I have just the solution to make it sparkle."

Joanne said, "Sorry, I have to go. I have guests."

He stepped back. "Another time. Let's fix an appointment."

"No, sorry. I've everything I need."

When he'd gone, she looked at the mirror. It was dusty. In the reflection, Alice's painting seemed to fade to the color of another country. Another century.

"Who was that?" Hec asked.

"A brush salesman."

"My granny buys from them. Says they're good."

McAllister came home. They talked about Hector helping Joanne with the manuscript. McAllister said he was delighted. And he was.

Nothing was said about the drawings.

Hector said he had to get going.

McAllister offered him a lift.

He said he'd rather walk.

They trouped out to the hall to say good-bye. The stained-glass door panels were aglow in the last of the sun, a sun that disappeared in late afternoon in the Highland autumn, and the world seemed brighter, washed clean by all the rain.

Hector Bain walked down Stephens Brae, along Eastgate, down the High Street and Bridge Street, across the river. He walked almost the length of Tomnahurich Street—in a complete dwam.

Joanne was much the same. Mostly studies, she was thinking. Mostly. So does that mean one might be genuine? She told McAllister. Yet she kept back the real secret.

He didn't notice; hands clasped behind his back, he stared at the paintings, as though in Kelvingrove Art Gallery, attempting to guess which might be authentic.

"I give up," he declared—to an empty room. He hadn't noticed that Joanne had gone to bed ten minutes earlier.

Chapter 13

Alice steps into the farmyard and sniffs the wind. "Maybe it's time to move on," she tells the dog, "but not yet." She inspects the new roof on the barn. Nods at the excellent result of hard work, much money, and Ballahulish slate.

I've always known I might have to leave. But not yet—I won't give Mrs. Mackenzie the satisfaction of driving me out.

Somewhere warm next time. She smiles to herself, somewhere with a better climate to grow tomatoes and herbs. Basil, I've never been able to grow basil this far north—let alone find the seeds. Up here, basil is a man's name. As for olive oil—you can only buy that in tiny bottles in the chemist's shop.

Maybe I should move to a place where I barely speak the language, then, when the gossiping starts I won't understand what's being said. Or care. I can be an eccentric old woman, lost in her memories. Heaven only knows how many of us there are—widows, mothers, sisters, daughters, bereaved and bereft by two world wars, and the century only a decade past the halfway mark.

She tries to shake the thought. Soon, she tells herself, a new decade will arrive, bringing a new civilization. It should be time to put an end to wars. But she doubts that will ever happen. Like the wind, this new war is cold, invisible, and insidious, penetrating the cracks in our civilized exterior, revealing us for the warmongering creatures we still are.

A blast of freezing air, blowing straight across the ocean from the wastes of Labrador, rattles a loose tile above the porch. She makes a mental note to fetch the ladder and fix it.

"It is indeed a cold, Cold War." She says this aloud. The dog looks up, head cocked to the side. No "walk" in the sentence, so he drops down on his haunches. And sighs. She mistakes his sigh for a sign of understanding.

"Don't worry, boy," she tells him. "If I ever leave, I'll find a good home for you."

She shivers, whether from cold or a premonition, she can't tell. She crosses her arms, hugging herself, before turning back to the warmth of the kitchen and a cup of tea.

✦ ✦ ✦

The following Tuesday morning, Calum's second day in his new job, in a new town, and after another terrifying night in his new lodgings, McAllister asked, "Settled in, have you, Calum?"

How could he explain that the strange bed, strange sounds, strange smells all terrified him? "Thanks, Mr. McAllister, it's great." Calum looked around at his colleagues, saw everyone busy with notebooks, photographs, copy, the layout spread on the table awaiting decisions, and felt better. This was what he knew.

The morning discussion of the front page had barely finished when the new receptionist, Lorna, marched into the reporters' room. She distributed one telephone message to McAllister, two to Frankie Urquhart, and a pile to Calum Mackenzie.

As she handed them over, she said to Calum, "Please tell your mother I do not lie. When I say you are in a meeting, you are in a meeting."

Calum blushed. Rob looked at his boots, Frankie at the ceiling. Hector didn't notice. Don, who initially thought Lorna might not last long at the *Gazette*, especially as her eye makeup made her look like a terrified panda bear, changed his mind. *With an attitude like that, she stays.*

"Rob, give the new lad here an hour or so of your time," Don said. "Frankie, two o'clock for that update on the layout. McAllister, the editorial."

"Calum, let's get a coffee. Bring your notebook, and we'll go over stuff you need to know." Rob put on his motorbike jacket and grabbed his tattered leather fighter pilot helmet, saying, "We'll take my bike."

Halfway down the stone staircase, Calum whispered, "Is it OK to leave the office without permission?"

Rob could think of no answer except *we're not at school anymore*, and was too kind to say so.

*   *   *

On Thursday, publication day, Lorna put a call through to the editor. He was busy on the *Herald* crossword and hated being interrupted. "What?"

"It's important. A policeman from Sutherland."

There was a pause, a change to a vacant whisper down the line. As he waited, he thought about Lorna—eighteen years old; an A pass in English, history, and French in her Highers exams; sharp, efficient, and unafraid to speak her mind to anyone, even him. He valued that in an employee. Plus, she didn't gossip. Listened to it, yes; repeated it, no.

"Hello. Hello?"

"John McAllister, *Highland Gazette*."

"Sergeant Black, Sutherland Constabulary." The policeman cleared his throat. "I gather Calum, eh-hem, Mr. Calum Mackenzie, is working with you."

McAllister instantly knew this was not good news. "He is."

"I'd appreciate if you ask him to call us. No, what I mean is . . . och, maybe you should tell him first, better than hearing on the telephone. It's his mother, she's in hospital, in a bad way."

McAllister knew this meant possibly fatal. "What happened?"

"She was knocked down by a car. Hit-and-run. But maybe no say anything about that just yet." There was a hint of a command in this request; the sergeant realized he should not have given out the information to a journalist. On good terms with the local newspaper, he'd forgotten the outside world was not always as biddable.

"I'll let Calum know immediately."

That Thursday was a special day for Calum; his first story for the *Gazette* was running, a minor report on the Forestry Commission plans to plant a particularly beautiful glen with a vast plantation of conifers, much to the disgust of wildlife lovers.

Calum had looked at the article numerous times, and although there was no byline, he knew his mother would cut it out and add it to the scrapbooks of his articles in the Sutherland newspaper, his essays from high school, even his homework from primary school she had saved and put into the book of her boy's achievements.

Hector was also in the reporters' room, looking at the photographs in rival newspapers. "Rubbish," he'd mutter. "A joke," he'd say, chortling. "Would you look at yon?" he'd ask of no one in particular. As Calum was not yet accustomed to Hector's constant havering, he dutifully looked at each offending photograph—and saw nothing remarkable.

The phone had been ringing a full minute. Again, Calum wasn't to know Hector never answered the phone.

Lorna yelled up the stairs, "Calum, it's not your mother, so pick up the phone."

"Hello."

The caller sounded as though she were laughing. "Sorry, Calum, I have a wee bit of a cough. It's Joanne Ross."

"Uh-huh?" He had no idea what to say. Yesterday morning, he'd been feeling lost. The phone call to his mother had been three minutes of her sobbing and wailing, when all he'd wanted was to know if he could send his washing on a Thursday and have it back by the following Monday. It took three minutes of him saying "I have to go now" before he could hang up. Shopping, cooking, washing, sleeping in a strange room, all the unconsidered disadvantages of living away from home, had hit him after the call. Now, with an edition printed, with a sense that he was part of the team, he felt better. But no closer to finding a solution to his domestic problems.

"Would you like to join us for supper, a small celebration as it's your first edition of the *Gazette*?" Joanne asked.

"Supper?" In Calum's parlance, lunch was called dinner and supper was tea. But breakfast was always breakfast.

"Tea."

"That would be great." A home-cooked tea, he was thinking. Can't wait.

"Come back with McAllister," Joanne said.

Thirty seconds later, McAllister walked in from his office. "Calum, I need to talk to you."

"It's OK," Calum said. "Joanne—sorry, Mrs. McAllister—she's just asked me."

"How does she know?"

"Mrs. McAllister invited me for tea, and I said—"

"Come into my office."

When McAllister broke the news, Calum's first thought was that he'd miss being fed properly for the first time in almost a week. Then it hit him. Paralyzed him. So used to his mother organizing his life, he had no one to ask, *What do I do now?*

McAllister told Calum to phone Sergeant Black in Sutherland. Seeing that Calum could barely dial the number, he also offered him a lift to the station.

On the way there, Calum repeated what he'd been told, talking as though reading aloud from a book that made little sense.

"The sergeant said that last night, after my mother closed up the shop and petrol pumps, she was walking home." He was visualizing every step she would take. "It's not far, only five minutes to our house, so all she had to do was cross the main road." He shivered. "It was dark, it was raining, must be the driver didn't see her." He closed his eyes. "But I don't see how, cos there's a big streetlight right out front o' the petrol pumps." He stared at the rain and the streets ahead, seeing nothing.

McAllister was driving cautiously over the cobbles in the lane beside the Station Hotel, looking for a free parking spot.

Calum was seeing, in slow motion, his mother, her wee scurrying walk, her handbag with the day's takings clutched tightly to her, seeing her sprawling, her crying. And although the sergeant hadn't mentioned it, he was seeing blood. "Maybe they skidded when they braked." He was trying to find a reason, avoiding the thought of a hit-and-run. Or worse. "Probably they stopped to check she was all right and panicked and . . ." To not stop was beyond him. "She's got broken bones and . . ." He was not distraught; he was bewildered. "It's the hypothermia the doctor's most worried about. All that time and no one found her. She'll be fine eventually, he said, even though it was a right bad accident."

If it was an accident, McAllister thought, recalling his brief conversation with the policeman. "Wait, last night?" He somehow had assumed it was this morning.

"Aye, she wasn't found until the back o' seven this morning. The petrol station wasn't open, so someone phoned Dad."

McAllister wanted to ask, Didn't your father notice she didn't come home? But he didn't. "I hear it's a good hospital," he said. Why come up with such an inane statement, he asked himself; he had no idea if it was a good or an indifferent hospital.

After buying a ticket for Calum, he waited until the train left. He could find little to say beyond remarks on the weather and good wishes for Mrs. Mackenzie's recovery. He felt he should have said more, should have given the young man some advice, some comfort. Knowing he was inadequate in emotional situations, knowing Joanne would have been better, yet not wanting to involve her in anything to do with accidents, hospitals, grief, he told himself, Elaine will be there; she'll comfort Calum.

Back in the office, his newspaperman's antennae on alert, he wondered—*hit-and-run*—and decided to telephone his counterpart in Sutherland. Then changed his mind. This was a task for Don McLeod; Highlander to Highlander, his deputy would find out more than a southern interloper.

He guessed that when the news about Mrs. Mackenzie came out, few would feel sorry. Titillated, yes. Satisfied?—perhaps. Shocked that such an event could happen in their small community more likely.

In a small community, two unfortunate events could be seen as just that, unfortunate. Unconnected. In McAllister's brief acquaintance with a town he formerly knew only as a place with an ancient history and a golf course, there were too many riddles: the life, the trial, and death of Alice Ramsay; mysterious strangers; bizarre events; now this.

* * *

Next day, Joanne was shopping in the town's only department store for new slippers. All the styles reminded her of Mrs. McAllister senior. Her own mother thought it vulgar to wear slippers in the house. Even at thirty-two, the learned-by-osmosis rules of her upbringing still cast a shadow.

She tried the chain-store shoe shop in the High Street. Better but still not right; pink faux-fur trim was not for her. Leaving the shop, she squeezed past a woman in a navy-blue trench coat buttoned high against the weather, who was struggling with an umbrella.

"Sorry," they said in unison.

"Joanne!"

"Elaine!"

"You're in town for long?" Joanne asked.

"Just for the day. I had an interview at the hospital. Now I'm going to treat myself to those shoes in the window."

"If you've time, we could go for a coffee afterwards."

"Love to."

Joanne enjoyed shopping with Elaine, enjoyed the pleasure the young nurse conveyed as she stood in front of the mirror three inches taller. She noted how Elaine counted out the money, mostly in small notes and change, telling Joanne how she had been saving for months, how the shoes were entirely unsuitable for work, but gorgeous for dancing, but that Calum didn't dance, so maybe spending so much money was silly.

Joanne reassured her. "Gorgeous shoes are always a good idea, although—" She bit back the thought that wearing them, Elaine would be a foot taller than her fiancé.

"I agree."

Elaine laughed, and Joanne smiled, and the seriousness of the days and weeks past vanished. Temporarily.

Shoes purchased, umbrellas open, they walked quickly through the back lanes, through the covered market, running the last yards across Queensgate, holding on to their hats, nervous the umbrellas might turn inside out in a gusting wind blowing from the Atlantic straight up the Great Glen, ripping through the town before joining its little brother, the North Sea squall.

"Whew!" Elaine laughed. "And I thought it rained up our way."

The conversation started on Elaine's plan to move south to the town. Inevitably the subject turned to Mrs. Mackenzie.

Elaine said, "Mrs. Mackenzie being injured, Miss Ramsay being . . ." She was mopping a small smear of spilt coffee with a paper napkin. To say the word "murdered" would make true her fears. Like Joanne, Elaine could not believe Alice Ramsay had killed herself. She had no explanation for the death, only a firm belief in the impossibility of a bright, alert, caring woman, with a passion for her art, ending her own life.

"The old people miss her. Nurse Ogilvie does her best. Me too. Mrs. Galloway has a word with most of them when she comes to see her mum. But Miss Ramsay had that special touch."

Joanne told her about working on the manuscript and asked her not to share this with anyone.

"I won't tell Calum, then." Elaine smiled. "I swear his mother can read minds."

"How is she?"

"Bones take time to heal. The bruising and swelling have gone down. But her mind is as full of the same old nonstop nosiness as ever." Elaine looked up at Joanne. "Sorry, I shouldn't be so uncharitable. Mrs. Mackenzie has a hard life, so I can't condemn her. But Calum needs to get back here soon as possible, or else she'll never let go." She smiled. "The interview for a transfer—I think I did well. Fingers crossed. Eyes too."

Her face and crossed eyes were funny and guileless, as was her laughter. Joanne was glad she'd bumped into Elaine. "Don McLeod, the deputy editor, will love you for life if you persuade Calum to come back to work."

"I'll do my best."

After they parted, Joanne regretted not asking what was hard about Mrs. Mackenzie's life. The woman had an attentive son and a husband, a business, a home. Joanne knew the same mores that made her embarrassed to wear slippers stopped her from asking direct questions.

Walking back through the market, it came to her. *Ballet shoes. Thin black ballet slippers. And if I can't find them, I'll buy Highland dancing shoes.* One hour later, black Highland dancing shoes wrapped in brown paper in her shopping basket, she went into the newsagent's, bought five magazines that published short stories. Along with a fresh ream of typing paper, she was ready, and went home to write.

Before beginning, she put on Scottish country dance music, laid out crossed walking sticks, and practiced a sword dance.

"Hopeless," she said, laughing, when she kicked a stick for the second time. Still panting, she sat down to write. The scene came easily, vividly. *A village hall, a ceilidh, the wee girls onstage dancing a Highland fling. A stranger comes in, back from some foreign campaign, sees the crossed swords, and remembers his regiment dancing the dance, the regimental warrior Highland sword dance. But the woman he sees across the room—he remembers her, remembers she is the granddaughter of a famous singer, and healer, and perhaps witch.*

She wrote and wrote, the *ping* of the return carriage ringing out a fast rhythm. She kept typing until she was making too many spelling errors to continue. She took the typed sheets, put them into a folder, kissed the folder, and locked it in the writing box along with the manuscript. And the drawings.

"That felt good." She did a wee skip. "When I write, I'm always going to wear dancing shoes," she announced to the room.

The accident. Once more, the fixation with all matters Sutherland intruded. *I wonder if it's connected. But if so, how?*

She reached for an art book that McAllister had dusted, then placed it on a lower shelf. It was a large, heavy format, the full-color illustrations printed on thick paper. She checked the index. No references to Leonardo. Not wanting to go back to the library in the rain, she began to leaf through the color plates, hoping to find examples of paintings similar to the ones she'd bought at auction. Nothing matched. She looked at the frontispiece, then the dedication page. It was written in Greek. Above was an inscription in elegant handwriting: "To my dearest A, from your cousin D." Then a date: "Cambridge 1936." Cambridge? How was Alice connected to Cambridge? Was her cousin up at Cambridge? Was Cambridge her family home? The inscription was yet another mystery in the life of Alice Ramsay.

Joanne needed to find out more. Her promise to McAllister loomed in her mind, but, she reasoned, she wouldn't be looking into Alice's death—she'd be trying to discover more about her life.

CHAPTER 14

I was always good at drama. Starred in the school play every year. I suppose that's why subterfuge comes easily to me.

Alice is looking at the painting in progress—a small illustration of a tiny wren sitting on a nest as small as a child's hand—remembering her school days, remembering writing, in her best hand, to various aunts, pleading poverty, or family quarrels before asking for cash to be sent inside a card or a box—anything to fool that prying dried up stick of a devout Calvinist form-mistress.

It's easy to deceive when you have practiced for years on family members. And men. Alice chuckles to herself.

The dog looks up. Five minutes, she promises, then we will walk.

Finishing off the delicate cross-hatching lines of the nest, Alice thinks of her archenemy.

Poor Mrs. Mackenzie. My nemesis. Little does she, or anyone, know that she is right. Not in what she has accused me of, but she knows there is something not quite genuine about me. She smells it, senses it. Perhaps she is the witch.

⋄　⋄　⋄

Don was shouting, "How do you expect me to fill these pages when I've no staff?"

Frankie Urquhart shrugged. "It's my job to bring in the advertising. How else can the *Gazette* pay the wages?"

Fortunately, this was all he said. Pointing out that being understaffed was editorial's problem and not advertising's, would not have gone down well with the increasingly frazzled deputy editor. With Calum back in Sutherland and Joanne retired, filling the pages in the season leading up to Christmas was not easy.

"I've a picture of a two-headed sheep," Hec said, chortling. "It's a trick o' the light, but it's funny."

"Get it," Don ordered. "Nothing like a shaggy sheep story."

Hec squinted at his boss, trying to figure out if he was serious.

"Get on with it, laddie!"

Don had reached growling point, so Hec knew it was time to run. He did, straight into McAllister. "Sorry, I have to fetch ma two-headed sheep shot."

The editor was so inured to Hec's bizarre behavior he didn't comment. "Don, I need a word."

"Unless it's you offering to give me two five-hundred-word pieces, I haven't time."

"Done," McAllister said. "You'll have them when I get back."

Don peered up through the bifocals perched on the end of his nose. And waited.

McAllister jerked his head to the left. "My office."

Frankie said, "I was just leaving."

Don knew it was impossible to shut the door to the reporters' room. Age and damp and a good few kickings had left it hanging squint on the frame. Then the thought of the whisky decanter in the editor's private lair made him climb down from the high stool and follow him.

"I've a summons from DI Dunne," McAllister began. "A gentleman from London wants a wee chat. Says it can't wait till tomorrow. Then I've an appointment in town." He didn't share that he was off to discuss the sale of his house and the purchase of another, not until he knew if his offer had been accepted.

"Aye, well, we've a newspaper to turn out, and it can't wait either." Don raised the decanter. McAllister shook his head. Not because it was too early, more that he needed a clear head for Dunne and company. The inspector had sounded most official when he'd asked for the meeting. He'd been ordered to do this, McAllister guessed.

"I told Dunne that."

"Better to go to him than him come to the office." Don was now intrigued. "A story in it, you think?"

"I doubt it."

Don knew McAllister was telling him the details on the remote chance the editor would need bailing out. "Och well, if you're not back in two hours, I'll send for some o' ma clansmen. Didn't work out too well in '45. But maybe this time."

McAllister knew his colleague meant 1745, not the last war. "I'll have those articles ready by two," was all he said. He took his hat off the stand. He pocketed a notebook and pencil. He thought again about a quick dram. But as it was ten past ten on a Wednesday morning, he resisted.

♦ ♦ ♦

"Sorry, but an interview room is the only private place in the station." DI Dunne ushered them into a small cramped space off the winding stone staircase. The police station was in a building similar to the *Gazette* office, and it smelled the same: cigarettes and damp.

"Plenty room for two," the gentleman said.

"Inspector Dunne stays." McAllister nodded towards the policeman. "Otherwise no interview."

"This isn't an interview, more a friendly chat."

The man was smooth. Oily as a cormorant's back, McAllister was thinking. "Nonnegotiable."

Dunne took a chair on the editor's side of the table. He clasped his hands, not to lead them in prayer but in an *I'm waiting and this better be good* gesture.

"We haven't all been properly introduced," Dunne began. The room was chilly and damp. The atmosphere and the detective's voice were equally cold. "You both know who I am. No doubt you've checked up on Mr. McAllister." A slight bow of the head from the stranger acknowledged he had.

The visitor was silent for a moment. "Call me Stuart," he replied.

"Of the Skye Stuarts? Or is it London?" McAllister asked.

"My name doesn't matter."

"You could have introduced yourself before now. Not at the auction, I grant you, and perhaps not at the golf club, but sending the inspector to issue your threats, that was clumsy."

"It was. I apologize."

McAllister did not actually remember seeing him at the auction, and his remark was a guess, so the confirmation only added to his suspicions.

Stuart leaned forward from the chest, his hands beneath the table, his face in a practiced, *we are all friends* expression. Seeing that it wasn't washing with the Scotsmen, he sat back. "The person you know as Miss Alice Ramsay was a former colleague. I am greatly saddened by her death."

There it was, out in the open, released into the stale air of the small room in the small town that felt as claustrophobic as the weather—cloud cover lowering the sky by miles, rain imprisoning all but the foolhardy.

" 'You know as Miss Alice Ramsay,' you said? So she went by another name?" McAllister asked.

"Naturally."

"So if she went by a pseudonym, how did someone know the article was referring to the same person?" And why were they interested? he didn't ask.

"That is all highly confidential." Stuart glared at McAllister, unhappy that the roles were being reversed and he was the one being interrogated.

From the sharp staccato reply, McAllister deduced Stuart didn't know the answer either. *So that's why you are here.*

"What department do—did—you and your former colleague work for?" Dunne had on his formal policeman's voice, betraying nothing of his frustration. He had been seconded by his chief constable to facilitate this investigation but given no information.

"We are a branch of the Civil Service, in a department in Whitehall. Very boring, really."

"Boring, maybe," McAllister remarked. "Secretive, certainly. And, it seems, dangerous."

"No, no. We are of no great importance." The round head that seemed too small for his shoulders, the pale face with dark darting eyes, the mouth that barely moved as he spoke, were all the more memorable for being unmemorable.

McAllister fancied he could feel sorrow from the stranger, who would not, could not, say from where he came. "I'm sorry you lost a colleague," he began. "She was a talented woman, and interesting. My wife certainly thought so."

"Yes, she was a hugely talented artist." Mr. Stuart—if that was his name—looked directly at McAllister, ignoring the inspector. "You are a signatory to the Official Secrets Act. DI Dunne is a professional police officer here as a witness." Something in the set of his mouth and eyes indicated a change of attitude.

McAllister said nothing. Waiting.

"What I'm about to tell you concerns matters of national importance." Stuart let that hang for some seconds.

McAllister smothered a smile; the theatricality of the man he found ridiculous.

"The woman you knew as Miss Ramsay worked for us during and after the war. Her role was to forge documents, passports, identity papers, letters from family, household bills, bus and train tickets—all the minutiae that make up a person's history, their backstory."

"Is that why she collected old paper?" McAllister asked, his mind racing.

"Yes, we—she—collected paper of the correct ages and types for the documents. We employed a former forger for watermarks. After fifteen years in the department, she resigned, saying she'd had enough of the city and wanted to pursue her dream of living simply and painting. I—we—told her we would miss her and asked her to reconsider. But she was determined. Had enough, she said, wanted to discover if she was talented enough to earn a living as an artist, she told us."

That "us" again, McAllister was thinking. And no doubt Miss Ramsay was also warned that the Official Secrets Act was a lifelong pledge. "Is it departmental policy to keep a watch on your colleagues even in retirement?" McAllister was thinking how their watchfulness hadn't protected the former forger.

"A distant watch, yes. There are emergency procedures, if required. Alice invoked one a week before her death."

"Why?" He wasn't sure the man would answer truthfully.

"She felt she was being observed."

"Did she report this to the local police? Or anyone else?" Dunne was asking from a police perspective. "Did she have proof of her suspicions?"

"No. And none." With a flick of his left hand at the questions, it was clear Stuart did not welcome Dunne's intrusion into his performance.

"But still it had you worried enough to come north to meet with her." Dunne was not deterred by the visitor's dismissal of him; this was his police station, his territory.

"In the past, documents of an extremely sensitive nature passed through her hands, so yes, we took her concerns seriously." He would not share, not even with his colleagues—especially not with them—that after Alice's retirement, a departmental inventory had revealed the loss, or removal, of particularly sensitive material. And if she had not taken the material, the ramifications were even more worrying.

"The identity papers she worked on—were they used recently? Perhaps illegally, if you can call using forged documents illegal?" McAllister asked.

The man jerked in alarm. "Why do you ask?"

"No reason. Been reading one too many Ian Fleming spy thrillers, I suppose." McAllister was enjoying the stranger's reaction.

"That traitor. Done more to harm the service than . . ."

McAllister wanted to tease him with the names: Burgess and Maclean. As a newspaperman and someone who avidly followed the news of the Cold War, he was fascinated by the revelations of spying. The defection to Moscow of the Cambridge spies had occurred in early 1951. Yet the story was not confirmed until 1954. He had been on the news desk of the *Herald*. The headlines were sensational. The statement from the prime minister confessing that the spies had escaped on the cross-channel ferry to France was splashed across front pages, occupying the nightly television and wireless news bulletins. It had almost brought the government down and jeopardized their relationship with the United States secret services.

He remembered how many "D" notices, which banned publication of stories of "national importance," were issued at that time. Even more than in wartime, it had seemed. And according to journalists' and commentators' gossip, there was still much information that the government was suppressing or that hadn't yet been discovered. Rumors of a third traitor had circulated. Eventually, when none was discovered, they were no longer discussed in public. McAllister had heard from Sandy Marshall that it was still a topic of speculation and gossip and rumor in newsrooms and journalists' clubs from Washington to Hong Kong and all territories in between.

Perhaps Miss Ramsay knew more? he wanted to ask, but didn't, deciding the risk of a note in his secret file, or worse, wasn't worth the fun of provoking a man who had been born lacking a sense of humor. That there was a file on him McAllister didn't doubt; his time in the Spanish Civil War, if nothing else, would warrant at least a security check.

"So why are you here?" The deadline for two articles by two o'clock was pressing down on the editor.

"The paintings you bought at auction. I was distracted by the drama of the bidding for that one drawing and the antics of that art expert, so I missed the bidding for the job lot of pictures."

McAllister bit back a quip, didn't say, *Careless. You also missed the boxes of books and papers the auctioneer threw in when we won the bid.* He was desperate to ask if Stuart knew of the manuscript Alice had been working on, but he didn't dare alert him if he wasn't already aware.

Stuart's face resumed the oily-feathers-bird's-back look. "I'm afraid I have to insist you turn those paintings over to the Ministry."

"Do you now?"

Stuart possibly understood and chose to ignore the threat in McAllister's low, slow, drawn-out drawl, but Dunne heard it. "And by what authority can you do this?" the inspector asked. "I would need a good explanation should you seize those pictures." He added, "Mr. McAllister's solicitor would also, I'm certain, want to see the appropriate paperwork."

Stuart looked ready to reprimand the policeman, but his training overrode his arrogance. "I'm sure Mr. McAllister and his good wife will cooperate."

McAllister shrugged. "If, and when, you present the appropriate legal documents, I will give them to my solicitor. If he says we have a chance of fighting said documents in a court of law, I will. And remember, here we are under Scottish law, not some opaque, made up on a whim regulation."

"It's not the paintings as such," the stranger began. Then stopped. "Official Secrets Act, remember?"

Silence.

"Miss Ramsay had information that could severely compromise other . . . officers. You needn't know the details." McAllister was certain he had been about to say *operatives*. "She may have concealed some material for safekeeping."

"For God's sakes, man, why didn't you just ask?" McAllister was fed up with the game of amateur spies. The window was too high to see out of. And the grille in the door made him feel he was a prisoner. He wanted out of this place and away from this man. "All this palaver—warnings, threats—why not come straight out and say, *May I examine the paintings you bought fair and square at that auction where I was so busy lurking, trying so hard not to be noticed that I made myself all the more noticeable?* As for forcing Dunne here to deliver a threat over that photograph at the golf club, that was a total embarrassment." He was shaking his head at the ham-fisted fiasco, asking himself how a secret service could be so inept.

Stuart, if he was a Stuart, smiled with his lips only. "You are right. We should have sent an experienced operator. I'm only an office wallah myself." The smile meant to reassure did not work, and he could see that. "I apologize, Mr. McAllister, Inspector Dunne. And I accept the offer to examine the pictures."

McAllister suspected Stuart seldom apologized. He also knew he had little choice but to let the man, or his minions, inspect the pictures. So he relented. "You can do that, but in my home."

"I will need to request expert help."

"Fine. Let me know when you'll be coming round. In the meantime, I have a newspaper to put to bed."

They all shook hands. McAllister left first.

Dunne remarked to the visitor, "You and your colleagues would do well to remember that we Scots don't take kindly to threats."

"I promise to remember."

The inspector did not believe him. They left the room, both glad of fresh air. The London man invited the inspector to lunch. Dunne refused. Holding the man's umbrella, watching him as he put on an overcoat the inspector knew would cost a month's salary, he asked, "So does the attack on Mrs. Mackenzie have any connection with your inquiries?"

"I beg your pardon?"

"You don't know?" Dunne saw confusion, the first and only sign of emotion, in the blank canvas of a face. *Doesn't want to admit he's missed something else.* The policeman sighed. "You'd better sit down again."

* * *

McAllister was usually late home on Wednesday evenings. There was no need for him to stay in the office, but when the presses started to roll, he and Don had a little ritual. The first proof pages would be printed off and checked. Barring last-minute adjustments to be corrected on the stone, Don would give the Father of the Chapel the nod. Then the presses would roll.

Against all union regulations, McAllister was allowed onto the print-room floor. He was wise enough to keep out of the men's way as they went about the controlled panic of the countdown to the printing run. The hammering and clattering of the printing press, the race of the machine that layered and folded, shooting out the warm, ink-damp newspapers onto the conveyer, always entranced him.

Watching the men and apprentices parceling, labeling, and loading the awaiting delivery vans gave him a satisfaction that could never be bettered. His words, his newspapers, were now on the journey to the people of the towns, the islands, the villages, to be sold in large news agents' or wee general stores where everything necessary for the rural communities was available, except on Sundays, when even the petrol pumps were locked.

Then the two men, a Highland Stan and Ollie, would trudge up the stairs into the editor's office and share a dram of a good whisky, a single-malt from whatever small distillery in the area they were of a mind to sample.

This time, McAllister brought out a favorite, a twenty-five-year-old Talisker. He felt he deserved it after the morning's interview with the "Man from the Ministry," as the deputy editor had baptized him.

Don lifted his glass. "Slàinte." He took a sip. "A fine drop from the shores of my homeland," he pronounced, then settled back to listen to what he expected to be a fascinating account of the morning's interview. He was not disappointed. "The Cambridge spies?" He whistled. "Not what I expected to hear of in the Highlands of Scotland."

"Me neither," McAllister agreed.

"Aye. Fits, though. Some o' them lords and lairds that come up here for the fishing and shooting, they were, and are, the regimental chiefs who used our young men as cannon fodder."

McAllister knew the truth of Don's statement. "Aye, but the spy scandals center around London, Berlin, Moscow, Washington, even Istanbul. It's quite a leap from there to a glen in Sutherland."

"Not for the aristocracy or royalty, it's not. They own more than eighty percent of our country." McAllister knew he meant Scotland, not Great Britain. "As for the traitors in their ranks turning up here, stranger things have happened an' a' that."

"So?"

"So let's wait an' see."

Don's pronouncement made sense to McAllister. Since arriving in the north from the city of his birth, Glasgow, he'd learned the Highland ways. He didn't always follow them, but he appreciated the lesson of sit back, do nothing, and wait for what unfolds.

♦   ♦   ♦

Next morning, McAllister waited for the girls to leave for school and a second pot of coffee to brew before he told Joanne. He skimmed over the details of the interview, although "interrogation" would be a truer description of the meeting. There had been no overt threats. He understood the directive: *This is none of your business; if you try to publish anything, we will issue a D notice—a legally binding edict that stated "publish and you will be prosecuted"—perhaps in secret.*

When he'd finished, he saw that *we have to do something* gleam in her eyes. He said, "Joanne, we cannot continue to be involved in this. Making ourselves of interest to whoever—"

"Whoever killed Alice."

"If I thought for one second—"

"It's fine. I don't believe government people would leave us exposed to danger."

He didn't contradict her. He didn't express his opinion that that was exactly what they might do. In his darker thoughts, he had considered that perhaps he—they—were being used to draw out traitors. Why else allow a journalist the freedom to keep asking questions? Why else share highly confidential information?

But protecting Joanne was all he cared about. "I don't want strangers in our home, so I've asked for the paintings to be taken to the town art gallery and examined there. They've agreed."

That the discussion had become heated and that he'd asked DI Dunne to back him up, he didn't share. He also omitted to mention that at Don's suggestion, he'd typed up a statement of the events, leaving it with Angus MacLean, their solicitor, and made sure Stuart was aware of those actions.

Joanne looked once more at the paintings she had grown to regard as theirs forever. "We don't have a choice, do we?"

"Not really. They'll be collected later this morning, so I'll stay home until then."

He was firm, decision made. She didn't object. He was her

husband. He had the right to decide what happened in their household. "Alice's manuscript, can I keep that?"

"Nothing was mentioned about the manuscript or her books." He grinned at her. His eyes, deep dark blue, crinkled with mischief, and she saw the little boy, the one his mother said was impossible to say no to, and she grinned back.

"What the eye doesn't see the heart doesn't grieve over?"

"Something like that." He was certain the manuscript was nothing more than what it appeared to be. And he enjoyed how much pleasure it gave his wife.

"Right, we'd better get started." But she didn't move. She was gazing around the room, taking in each painting, every splash of color. She tried to imprint the images in her imagination, in case—in case of what, she didn't want to think about. Every thought of Alice Ramsay was tinged with regret, shadowed by the what ifs. "I uncovered a newspaper article wrapped around a cabbage. I followed it up because I was appalled that a woman could be openly called a witch in this day and age."

McAllister was listening without comment, watching Joanne as she stared at nothing in particular, recounting what had led them to an encounter with an unknown government organization.

"I met Alice Ramsay. I liked her. I think she liked me. Then I betrayed her trust—or at least, I allowed myself to be duped into betraying her—and her name was splattered across a national newspaper. She died. We bought her pictures. And now you say the secret service thinks that classified information could be hidden within these pictures?" She was shaking her head slowly, slightly. "It's hard to believe."

"I was thinking the same."

Joanne didn't want this happening. That she was hiding two potentially valuable drawings, so mesmerized by them, so covetous of them, that she was possibly committing a crime—that was something she was not ready to admit, even to her husband. "Right. Let's get started. You lift the paintings off the wall. I'll stack the others in the hall. I'm not having strangers tramping through my house."

"Your house?"

"Our house."

"Does that mean you don't want the other house?"

"Yes. No. I don't know."

"When the pictures are returned, this affair will be over. We can return to normal."

"Never thought I'd hear my husband say that." She grinned. She knew what he meant yet gave no indication she agreed.

"I'm serious. No investigating, no poking around, no asking questions."

The flash of defiance in her eyes did not escape him.

"Joanne, I'm not ordering you to drop it. I would never do that. But after all you went through the last time you investigated a crime . . ." He stubbed out his cigarette, not wanting to look at her. "I can't bear the thought of anything happening to you again."

"Me neither."

The doorbell rang.

"If it's that brush salesman, tell him no thanks."

The bell rang again. It was two men with a van to fetch the pictures.

Joanne called out, "Tell them to take their boots off." Perhaps she needed that carpet sweeper after all.

✦ ✦ ✦

That night, in bed alone, McAllister downstairs with a book and his music, Joanne tried to sleep. Couldn't. The images of the drawings came to her. A desire to creep down and open the box, open the folder, stare at them, perhaps touch them, was overwhelming her. That and a guilty conscience.

The key was in the small snuffbox on the mantelpiece. She'd told Hector she didn't have the head for heights anymore, and climbing up every time to fetch a key from on top of the picture frame was silly. Hector offered to take the drawing to his studio-cum-washhouse at his granny's place.

"They stay with me," she'd snapped.

She remembered him staring at her, then shrugging, saying, "I know. Gets to you, a really fine work of art does."

Possessiveness was new to her; acquisitiveness had never been her nature.

Wrapped in McAllister's dressing gown—she loved the smell of him that clung to the wool—she went downstairs. The sitting-room door was shut; he didn't want the music to disturb her. She went in, saw the top of his head above the armchair, and she melted. I love this man, she thought, and now I have to disappoint him.

"Can't sleep?" he asked when she took the chair opposite his. "I'll make some cocoa."

"No. Sorry. I know I should have told you before."

She explained about the drawings.

"I'm sorry I didn't tell you sooner," she finished.

"Maybe just as well. I would have had to inform *that man*." He looked at her sitting, waiting, like a small girl in front of the headmistress or her father, awaiting punishment. "I'd love to see them," he said, and smiled.

She smiled back. What flashed between them were the small steps, the vital, crucial, accumulative steps in a new marriage, a friendship, a relationship that held people, families, together. She watched him as he examined the pages, the small sketches that might, just might, she told herself, have been created centuries ago.

"Interesting." He sat back, the closed folder on his lap. "I'd like to check the legal position first. We bought them fair and square—not that that is a defense in a court of law. How Miss Ramsay acquired them is another matter. If she obtained them illegally, we might be guilty of receiving stolen goods."

"So shouldn't we tell the official from London about them?"

"The way it was put to me was that they wanted to examine the paintings we bought as a job lot." He smiled. "It could be said I'm being obtuse, but I'll risk it."

She sighed. "It might be better if we handed them over." She meant safer.

"We will. But not yet."

From his smile, from the way he was nodding his head slightly, she guessed he was plotting something. And she knew not to ask. Her husband's phrase "not yet" delivered when her eldest, Annie, would ask, "When are we going . . . ? When are we getting . . . ? When . . . ?" drove the girl crazy. Joanne now knew how she felt.

She stood and laid a hand on his shoulder. "Night night."

He covered it with his. "I'll close up the house."

"I'll wait."

CHAPTER 15

∿

Alice looks up from her handwriting exercises. The cloud cover is lifting, the light softening to pearlescent greys. She puts down her pen, chooses another nib.

What would my teacher, Mr. Smith—formerly Mr. Schmitt—say now?

The training had lasted only two weeks, but in that time she'd learned the basic principles of the psychology of handwriting.

She remembers how he had surprised her when, after asking her for a brief handwritten curriculum vitae, he'd guessed that although she was a native English speaker, she was not entirely English. Irish perhaps? Or Scottish? With a French education?

Swiss boarding school, she'd told him.

He even guessed I was estranged from a parent, or parents.

Mummy was too busy to look after me I told him. Daddy was a career soldier and died in the war. "My father also," Mr. Smith had said. From the number tattooed on his wrist, she suspected more than one parent had perished.

Mr. Schmitt was the one who started me on a new passion, the study of graphology. His ability to discern, through handwriting, the sex, age, physical type, native or nonnative speaker, even a person's weight, was astonishing.

After a further two weeks of training, I began to grasp the tricks of replicating a person's handwriting.

We practiced with private correspondence obtained from who-knew-where. "Intimate letters are best," he said. "See here, in the first paragraph, the letters are upright, evenly spaced, the handwriting clearly stating the writer's intention. Then in the middle section, the writing is looser."

See this—*he was using a letter with sections blacked out by the censors.* "See how in the first paragraph the man is in control. The second, he is in a hurry to describe his situation. In the third, he slows down, the writing is sprawling, lingering, intense with longing for the person, the place, from which he is parted."

"Perhaps written by a man who isn't certain he will return," I commented.

"Just so," my teacher said.

At the end of the training, I was deemed competent enough to work unsupervised. Star operative, Mr. Smith called me. I never heard from or of him again.

• • •

The paintings were returned.

"The still life painting of the onions, it's not here," Joanne told the delivery man.

"Nothing to do wi' us," he said.

She read the document that accompanied the inventory. "Says here they have shipped it down to London for 'further examination.'"

"At least it's not off to Glasgow and the esteemed Dougald Forsythe to pontificate over it," McAllister commented.

"Meow." Joanne laughed.

"Why that one?"

"It had such a beautiful frame," she answered. "Maybe it's genuine."

"Hope so. It would go well over the mantelpiece of our new house."

"Have we got it?" It wasn't that she'd forgotten. More that she didn't want to think about moving. She dreaded packing up, clearing out. She had married a man who could afford professional help, not hire a man with a van and a boy and a dog. But the thought of strangers poking through her possessions, except for the lifting and carrying, she hated.

"I haven't heard," he said. "I was expecting to know by now. I'll call Angus MacLean tomorrow."

She could see he was distracted. The rehanging of the pictures had motivated him to unpack the last two boxes of books. That most of the volumes had gone to the attic—another place that needed a clearing out were they to move—McAllister thought logical.

Joanne didn't. After her father had died, after her mother had had to move out of the manse, her sister was left with the job of dealing with the detritus of thirty-two years in the same house. Joanne hadn't been allowed to help, but her sister's stories of the woodworm in the furniture, broken crockery, moldy books, and moth-infested rugs and blankets and curtains being carted off to the town dump were a warning to both sisters.

"If you don't use it, look at it, care for it for more than a year, then give it away, or put it in the church jumble sale," her sister had said.

"That will be my motto," Joanne agreed.

But how to enforce that with a husband who'd had so little in his childhood he was now the proverbial jackdaw? As for her younger daughter, Jean kept everything—broken crayons, almost-finished coloring books, and a toy tea set with only one cup remaining. When she and the girls had moved from their wee Council prefab to McAllister's house, she'd found under Jean's bed an ancient knitted bear that a mouse had attempted to make a nest from and was well beyond repair. After a prolonged crying fit, her daughter had agreed to keep all her old treasures in a tin trunk, not scattered on the alternative cupboard, the bedroom floor.

"This is interesting," McAllister said. He was leafing through a leather-bound book. It was translated from German. "It's a system, graphology, and seems to be a method of deducing personality traits from handwriting."

"Alice was experimenting with different handwriting for her illustrations."

"Hmmm. Stuart said she was an expert in falsifying documents."

"The book is a remnant from her colorful past, then."

"I wonder if . . ."

"McAllister! Now you are doing what you told me not to."

He looked up at her.

"You are speculating. Come on, admit it. You're as fascinated by Alice Ramsay as I am."

"I am." He stood. Taking the book to the table, he laid it on a sheet of paper. "Everything about Miss Ramsay is intriguing. But the more we know, the more dangerous it seems."

"I listened to you. I had no intention of becoming involved." She gestured around to the books, the paintings, the manuscript snug in the writing box. "But now that we know a little of her past, these papers are very interesting to a nosy journalist and a budding author."

"And to Mrs. Mackenzie," he added.

"I can't see how she is connected to Alice, apart from being chief gossipmonger."

"Neither do the police."

"Elaine thinks or at least wonders if Mrs. Mackenzie saw something."

"Or someone."

"And doesn't recognize the connection, the significance."

"Or she does."

"But what could Mrs. Mackenzie have seen that would make her a target? Wouldn't she have told everyone? Or at least told Calum?" Joanne dropped into the chair. "If her accident does connect with Alice, this is . . ."

"Serious."

"Mrs. Mackenzie could still be in danger."

"Not if it was a warning."

"Do you think that would stop that woman?"

He had no wish to think further about Mrs. Mackenzie. "I have to go into the office. I'll finish unpacking the books tonight."

She knew he wouldn't. He would start to read, and somehow, whilst still reading, get up, settle in the armchair, the books from the box scattered on the floor awaiting a decision—keep or donate.

After a sandwich lunch, she spread a newspaper on the sitting-room floor and, with a duster and a damp cloth handy, began unpacking the remaining volumes. She rifled through the pages, small puffs of dust falling onto the newspaper, then stacked them according to size. Arranging alphabetically or otherwise, she'd leave to McAllister.

In one box she found a book written in Latin with many pages missing. But as the book was hand-stitched, with any glue long since disintegrated, she thought little of it. As she fanned the pages of some smaller books, she could feel where pages were also missing. After a fifth book in the same condition, a thought struck her.

Too intrigued to wait until McAllister came home, she called the *Gazette*.

"He's out," Lorna informed her.

"Is Hector in?"

"He is. But I'll have to run upstairs and make him pick up the receiver."

"Tell him to call me back."

Joanne smiled. When working at the *Gazette*, she'd tried to make the editorial staff function efficiently. And she'd succeeded. Mostly. Hector, however, was not a person who could be organized.

"You wanted me?" Hec sounded astonished that anyone should ask for him.

"Do you know anything about paper?" Joanne found herself reflecting Hec's abrupt speaking patterns.

"Maybe. Try me."

"Old books. Could you date them?"

"I thought you said paper."

"I've a collection of old books." Telling him how she'd acquired them was a longer conversation she had no time for. "Sheets of paper are missing. It seems to be a pattern."

"At the beginning and end of them. At chapter breaks."

His confidence startled her. "How did you know that?"

"It's what people do when they need old paper."

"Why?"

"Well . . . Look, I'm free for the next hour. I'll come over."

◆ ◆ ◆

After Hector left, Joanne was confronted with yet another puzzle.

"Elaine, I am so sorry to bother you at work. Maybe I can call back when you're free?"

"Don't worry," Elaine said. "Dinner is finished, so most of the residents are having a nap."

Joanne was about to say, *But it's only half past twelve*, then remembered how at old people's homes, the residents were fed early: breakfast at seven, tea at five o'clock, and in bed and lights out by eight.

"How is Mrs. Mackenzie?" Joanne asked out of good manners, not because she was interested but more because she'd heard her husband complain that once again they were without a junior reporter. When she'd offered to help out, he'd said, "Your work comes first," and when she'd understood he was referring to her writing, her editing the manuscript, she'd been thrilled. *Yes, I am working, I am writing.*

"Not much wrong with her tongue." Elaine laughed. "And poor Calum is scared he'll lose his new job."

"Tell him to come back. Monday, if possible."

"I'll fib a wee bit. I'll say you said he needs to be back by then. It might be the only way to persuade him to leave."

"Tell him *Mr.* McAllister said it, not Mrs." Joanne knew Elaine would know why. "What I wanted to ask may seem strange. Did you ever hear of old books being sold from up your way? Maybe a private collection?"

"I'll ask around, maybe start with the auctioneer. Lots of old stuff comes up at estate sales."

"Thanks, Elaine."

After a minute or so of pleasantries, Joanne put down the phone. She caught her reflection in the mirror. Dust coated her hair. A smudge was on the tip of her nose. *I'm a mess—and Hector said nothing.*

But he had been absorbed in the books, examining the paper,

the writing, the printing style, so she shouldn't be surprised that he'd barely noticed her. Hector was on a mission to date the books, the paper and the ink and everything about them.

"Why are you so interested in these ones? They're mostly in Latin," she'd asked as he put back another desecrated volume of religious tracts.

"Because there might be a Leonardo notebook in amongst this lot."

"Really?" The thought thrilled and appalled her equally.

"Highly unlikely, but . . ." He went back to examining one particular volume that was older than the others, before sighing and returning it to the stack. "Forsythe had that bird drawing authenticated. Then there are your two wee sketches. If we found the book they came out of . . ."

Hector had left her with more questions than answers.

Joanne had to rush to bathe and wash and dry her hair, to be ready for the two o'clock appointment at the hospital. It was a routine checkup of the almost-healed injury she'd received five months previously.

Maybe I should mention I'm seeing shadows. She was certain she saw movement when no one was about. The feeling of being watched was never strong enough to mention, yet frequent enough to make her uneasy. "It's only birds," she'd mutter. "Wind whistling. Rain drumming. Cloud shadows."

Maybe we need a dog after all, she thought. She wondered what had happened to the wee Skye terrier she saw at Alice's. There would be plenty room for him in the new house.

◆　◆　◆

On Monday, Calum came back to work at the *Gazette.* He lasted all of three days. It was Lorna who precipitated the crisis.

"Good story on the golf, Calum," Don told him.

Calum went pink.

"Made a deadly boring game sound interesting," Rob said.

Even though miffed at his description of golf, Calum was more thrilled by praise from Rob McLean than from the editors.

"Even though the paper's only been out a few hours, I've had phone calls objecting to Mr. McAllister's editorial," Frankie Urquhart told them. "They're mostly for, not against, the new shops and offices."

McAllister grinned. He liked to stir up controversy.

Frankie continued, "It's progress. High time this town caught up with the rest of the country." He was in the destroy-and-rebuild camp. "Got to move with the times," he told his father. Frankie was a modern young man. "Soon be 1960," he'd say, "a new world." The destruction of historic buildings didn't matter to him. His obsession with Elvis, with clothes and haircuts and suede winkle-picker shoes, annoyed his father and his sister, who said his feet and his hearing would be damaged forever.

"I'm more interested in how many believe in the two-headed sheep," Don said to Frankie. Any reply was lost as Lorna came in, and, stating the obvious, she placed the envelope in front of the editor. "A telegram," she said. She didn't linger to find out what was in it. Another point in her favor, Don decided.

The telegram was addressed to McAllister. He was concerned but not overly, as he'd spoken to his mother two days ago and all was well. After two wars where the news, always bad, came by telegram, receiving one was always unsettling.

He read it silently. The others in the reporters' room tried to pretend they were not curious. "Calum." McAllister looked up, and trying not to laugh said, "Your mother wants to know why you don't return her phone calls."

Rob and Frankie caught each other's eye and had to look away.

"I do, I always do." Calum switched from a happy man, delighted with his new job and new colleagues, to a short-trousered wee boy.

Don lifted the telegram, read it, and sighed. He needed a junior reporter, not a junior schoolboy. "I think I know about this." Taking the telegram with him, he went downstairs.

"Lorna."

"Aye?"

He handed the telegram over.

"Oh," she said. "Right." From under the desk, she produced a stack of messages and handed them to the deputy editor. Each one had a date and a time and a similar message. "Mrs. Mackenzie called." "Calum's mother called." "Calum's mother." "C's mother."

Don sighed again; he was doing a lot of sighing over Calum Mackenzie.

"I give him at least three a day; that's enough." Lorna was looking at Don through black-rimmed eyes, through a thick fringe of hair that reminded him of a Highland cow—only no Highland cow had eyes as blue as Lorna's. "I haven't the time to keep answering the woman and keep this office running properly. We're a newspaper, no the loony bin."

"Lorna."

"Sorry." Her pale-pink-lipstick mouth set straight, she was trying not to grin.

He expected rebelliousness from her, as that seemed to be Lorna's default setting—weird makeup, weird clothes, and a taste for American poetry and novels that only McAllister had heard of but even he hadn't read. As for Lorna's "Ban the Bomb" badges pinned to her overlarge jumpers, her home-knitted hats, her duffel coat, Don ignored them, on McAllister's instructions.

He said, "Lass, no matter how tempting, it's not for us to interfere in someone's private life."

"It is when it interferes in the running of the office, specially on deadline day." She rifled through the stack of messages, putting the Wednesday pile separate. It was thick. "This is from yesterday. Today's pile is beginning to mount." The phone rang. "*Gazette*. Good morning, Mrs. Mackenzie. Yes, I'll give him the message." She disconnected the line. She said nothing but stared pointedly at Don.

He sighed. "I'll deal with it."

Her sniff said she doubted it. "You'd better give him these." Then she took the pile back. "On second thought, maybe not. I'll give them to him when he comes by," implying there was no need to further humiliate poor Calum.

Don nodded. Another act in her favor.

"One other thing," Lorna added. "I've had a few phone calls asking for Mr. McAllister, and when I ask for a name, he says, 'A friend,' and I say, 'Putting you through,' and then he hangs up. One, even two calls like that I don't notice, but there've been a few. Maybe it's a burglar checking if the boss is at work or something."

"Thanks, Lorna."

Don walked up the stairs, thinking, *or something*. And not at all pleased with thoughts of what that something might be.

"I have to go home," Calum said as the deputy editor walked into the room.

"Aye, I guessed that," Don told him. "Take a half day tomorrow. Go home for the weekend. But I expect you back first thing Monday morning." The *or else* went unsaid but was understood. "McAllister, can I have a wee word?"

McAllister assumed the wee word would be about Calum. When he heard about his own phone calls, he asked, "What do you think?"

Don replied, "Nothing good."

McAllister felt sick. "I've had enough of this." Without an explanation, the editor left.

For home, Don assumed. He guessed he might have to put out a newspaper without Calum; one good reporter, half an editor, and an enthusiastic sales manager meant a major headache. Hector didn't count, as he couldn't write. "I'm too old for this," Don muttered.

The solution came from Lorna.

When he asked her to put in an advertisement for a cadet reporter, she said, "I'll do it. I'm good." He was thrilled. She'd scare the life out of the members of the town council—and maybe bairns and the churchgoing—but he liked the solution.

Don replied, "You're not good yet, but you will be," and began composing an advert for a receptionist.

◆ ◆ ◆

Late that afternoon, McAllister was summoned to the police station for a "chat." He was not happy.

"I'm not yours to command," McAllister said as he greeted Mr. Stuart.

"This is important," Stuart said.

The lack of an apology annoyed McAllister. "Before you start, I have a question. Did you, or your cohorts, kill Alice Ramsay?" He'd had no intention of asking the question. He didn't even believe it probable. But the man and his arrogance, his upper-class Englishness, riled McAllister. A lot.

"No, we did not kill Alice Ramsay." His clear distaste for the question from a mere editor of an insignificant local newspaper pleased McAllister.

Looks like he's sooking on lemon sherbet. The formal tone, the word choice and phrasing, alerted McAllister. And the "we" meant it was unlikely that the man was a lone operator with a private grudge—unlikely, although not impossible. Did not kill her, he accepted. But did something to cause her death, directly or indirectly? He wouldn't rule it out.

"Again, I will remind you that you're bound by the Official Secrets Act."

"Get on with it, man."

"As you now know, Alice Ramsay is not the name she was using when she worked for us." Her family surname carried the ancient Scottish title "of that Ilk." It had always amused him. "However, some of the persons she came into contact with"—*concocted false identities for,* he didn't share—"knew her from the past."

"Knew her by her real name, Alice Ramsay?"

"Quite. When she left us, she took some of the tools of the trade with her. Whether she used them for private commissions we don't know." He hadn't shared his concern—later, anger—over the missing passports with his superiors. Nor had he mentioned the paper, the specialist ink, and watermark tools she had also purloined.

Neither McAllister nor DI Dunne commented. They could guess at the larger implications of false passports and faked identities, but the inner workings of the world of Mr. Stuart, the Man from the Ministry, were too remote, too murky for them.

"Our operatives and support staff such as Alice have as little contact as possible. Her job was simply to provide the necessary identification; she was not to intermingle with the individuals themselves. But as they were from the same social circles, it was perhaps inevitable. Then the scandal involving those persons . . ."

McAllister and Dunne had been speculating which governmental scandals Alice Ramsey had been connected to. Moscow, they both concluded, knowing this would never be confirmed or denied.

But now this.

"Did Alice Ramsay know the Cambridge spies?" McAllister knew he was unlikely to hear the truth, but he had to ask.

"That is classified information," Stuart snapped. His body stiff, his eyes blank, the anger was clear, the affront at being questioned by a mere provincial journalist with a working-class accent.

McAllister and Dunne exchanged glances. Both well versed on the spy scandals, they were aware that one of the traitors who had defected to Moscow had the Scottish name, Donald Maclean.

McAllister tried again. "So Alice Ramsay *was* involved in the Cambridge spy ring. Interesting."

Stuart jerked back in a motion that reminded McAllister of a man hit by a sniper's bullet. "I never said that." He glared at both men. "That matter is over and done with. The traitors have escaped, and if I ever hear that either of you share such wild speculation or attempt to publish . . . If information should come your way, anything unusual, especially any documents, perhaps someone asking intrusive questions, I need to know. Immediately."

"I know, I know," McAllister said. "We'll be clapped in irons and thrown in the Tower of London if we don't."

"Why did you want to talk to Mr. McAllister?" Dunne intervened. He could feel the animosity between the men building, and wanted Stuart gone; a quiet life in a quiet town was the sum of his ambitions.

Stuart cleared his throat, the nearest to an apology the inspector would receive. "Miss Ramsay's manuscript. We'd like to examine it."

"How do you know about the manuscript?"

The involuntary tilt forward, the blood draining from the

editor's face, the heel of his hand pushing hard against the table scared Dunne. "Manuscript?" the inspector interjected.

"It wasn't mentioned at the auction, so how do you know we have a manuscript?" McAllister's question came out as a hiss, as vicious and as fierce as a swan defending its young.

"One of our operatives was on the removal team that collected the pictures."

McAllister thought back to that day. Had the manuscript been out on display? He didn't think so. Could he prove it had been locked in the writing box? Not without asking Joanne. Scaring her.

"I assumed you acquired it along with her books."

McAllister did not believe him, and the sight of his eyebrows rising towards his hairline made Stuart realize his mistake. "It was Alice's plan to paint the flora of her glens and perhaps make a book of her work. Part of the reason she retired, she said." He looked away. She had spoken of her progress the last time they saw each other. But that brief meeting in the Station Hotel he hoped to keep secret. "I told her I could perhaps help find a national publisher, in a private capacity, of course—our department does not deal in original works."

This was as close to a joke as the man was ever likely to make, and Dunne, for one, was grateful.

McAllister nodded. His suspicion that the man somehow knew about Joanne's project had been confirmed. He wanted out of this room. Away from this man. He wanted to be home, music playing, girls laughing, Joanne looking up from a book or her knitting or the dinner table, looking at him with those green eyes, smiling. And him smiling back.

"I have a newspaper to attend to," he said. "I hope we don't meet again, Mr. Stuart, or whoever you are."

As he walked down the stairs, he heard nothing from the open door of the interview room where they had been for the last hour, only the constant ringing of telephones from below and the murmur of voices. From the remand cells in the dungeons, shouts from a prisoner echoed up the staircase. McAllister sympathized. *Poor sod, but it's probably better than freedom in the open prison of Moscow.*

CHAPTER 16

~

Getting low on stock. The new commission needs nineteenth-century paper. Not that that woman would know the difference between eighteenth-, nineteenth-, indeed twentieth-century stock. But I have my standards, and it's fun going to auction sales looking for old books, old manuscripts, even old letters. It still startles me what treasures people throw out. I might ask Muriel Galloway to come with me if she can take time away from the hotel.

We could reminisce about that summer such a long time ago. Our last year at school ended, long light nights when you could read your book outdoors at midnight, when we would sneak out and roam around the sand dunes.

We were friends—of sorts—but I was the outsider. They had known each other since babies. It was a time of first boyfriends and girl-friends, of holding hands and chaste kissing. There was some scandal involving Mrs. Mackenzie's father; I don't remember the details, if I ever knew. Shot himself was the story I heard.

That was the last summer I spent at the big house—before war and debts and death duties lost us the family estate that had been ours for generations. With Daddy off somewhere on that horrendous campaign in Italy, and Mummy dying so soon after, the estate had to be sold. The new owner is an insurance company and runs it as an investment, and for the grouse shooting.

But as it belonged to Grandmamma, this house and the five acres of land became mine.

◆ ◆ ◆

Joanne remembered her promise to McAllister. However, asking Elaine to check out some simple details for the manuscript—the locations of the illustrations, the sources of old books—that had nothing to do with her promise to stop probing into Alice's death.

"How are you?" Joanne asked when Elaine called.

"Truly, righteously fed up," Elaine answered. "You know, of course, that Calum is back home and in danger of losing a great job he's only been at for two weeks."

Joanne considered fibbing. Then didn't. "Yes, I know. If he returns soon, it should be fine." She didn't mention Lorna.

"Well, I'm coming down to start *my* new job no matter what. So if Calum chooses to stay at home . . ."

Usually, Joanne considered ultimatums dangerous. In the case of Calum Mackenzie, she conceded this might be the only strategy that would work; prizing him away from his mother would require all the wiles of a mother fox.

"I know the timing is bad. But the chance of a great job for her son, you'd think his mum would be thrilled."

Joanne could hear the despair in Elaine's voice.

"In his last job," the nurse continued, "she couldn't see how her turning up to a council meeting he was reporting on was embarrassing. 'The council chambers is a public place,' she'd say. She always had some excuse to 'pop in' when Calum was doing an interview in the tearoom or the golf club. 'Just happened to be passing by,' she'd say. Calum was right humiliated." Elaine sighed a long deep outbreath. "I've no right to criticize. It's just that she has her life, and we need ours, or we'll never— Sorry Joanne, I'm right frustrated."

This was the first time Joanne had heard Elaine voice doubts about her future with Calum. "I can't advise you. I'm hopeless at relationships." She was not able to talk about her parents to anyone other than her husband. As for her first marriage, apart from it being a disgrace to be a divorced woman, she believed discussing her former husband was disloyal to her children, and this stopped her from saying anything further.

"Anyhow, the old books you wanted to know about. I found out that Miss Ramsay bought the former library of a military family who'd lived in a grand house near Brora for centuries."

"Most were falling apart," the auctioneer had told Elaine. "Right dirty and dusty they were, and some in a foreign language."

"Thanks, that helps me," said Joanne, thinking, *though I've no idea how.*

"I don't suppose you'd come up here for my leaving party."

The way Elaine said this, so much quieter than her usual bubbling-burn-in-full-spate voice, made Joanne reply, "I'd love to come."

After a squeal of joy that made Joanne almost drop the receiver, Elaine told her the arrangements for the party. "It's in Mrs. Galloway's hotel, in the afternoon so the fittest of the old people can come. Only shame is Mrs. Galloway's mother won't make it. She's gone downhill since Miss Ramsay . . ."

Another unfinished sentence; Joanne wondered when they would be able to say "died" without shuddering at the manner of Alice's death. *Probably never,* she thought.

"As it's Saturday, why don't you bring the girls?" Elaine suggested. "The old dears love having children around."

Joanne didn't voice her reservations: a long journey for a short visit; the drive home would be in the dark; memories of Alice Ramsay; meeting Mrs. Mackenzie again. "Can't promise, but I'll ask them."

"Thank you thank you thank you," Elaine gushed, reminding Joanne how frustrating the young woman's situation was. It was best they leave for a while, best for their careers, best for them as a couple.

Joanne went back to pondering the final work needed on the manuscript. An index? The foreword? For the cover, she'd decided on a painting of the glen above Alice's home, where a splash of late heather glowed in an otherwise bronze-brown landscape.

When McAllister came home, she explained about Elaine's party.

"I'll come too," he said.

"But you'll hate it."

In his bachelor days, he would never have attended, but Joanne was teaching him that being part of a community meant more than just writing about it.

Instead of sharing his doubts that Calum would ever leave Sutherland, he told her Don was taking Lorna on as a trainee reporter. "On a trial basis for three months," he said. "She'll either be brilliant or terrify everyone into silence—her social skills can be abrasive."

"She'll be brilliant. As for being abrasive, some of those town and county councilors need a cheeky young woman to shock them."

"Her makeup's a bit confrontational."

Joanne burst out laughing. "I can't believe you said that. You sound like someone's granddad, not my sophisticated man-about-town."

"In that case, I'll need to live it up at this party in the wilds of Sutherland."

That the activities of the Man from the Ministry were obsessing him, he didn't share. Nor did he share his conviction that the man was telling as little of the truth as possible. He knew he'd have to tell Joanne the stranger wanted the manuscript.

But not yet, he told himself, *not before I've checked the legal situation*. That thought led to another. *Not that legalities stopped Stuart spying on my wife, perhaps on me, and on Miss Ramsay*. As for holding the Fatal Accident Inquiry in secret, the disposal of the body equally secretive, Stuart seemed able to make his own laws, even in Scotland.

✦ ✦ ✦

Elaine told no one, but her doubts about relocating had vanished; the more Mrs. Mackenzie clung to her son, the more determined she became to leave.

"The two of us, living away from home, with great jobs, it'll be wonderful." Finding time alone with Calum was a hundred times harder since the accident. "We can save money, then when we come back"—she was still certain they would return one day—"we will have enough money for our own place and not have to live with our families." *Your mother*, she meant.

Calum was wise enough to know his fiancée could never share a house with his mum. How to tell his mum was the problem.

Elaine thought of her own mother, a straightforward, caring woman with lovely eyes, who bore a strong resemblance to her daughter. She thought of the people she would miss—friends from school, colleagues from work, Nurse Ogilvie, Dr. Jamieson, and the more mobile of their charges.

Even knowing what a disaster Calum's parents' marriage was, she'd put aside her doubts about marrying into the Mackenzie family.

"Calum takes after his dad," she'd told her mother. "He's kind, really patient, and always sees the good in others. He's interesting to talk to as well." She meant interested in more than cars and Friday-night drinking until you fell over, which was all the other young men in town seemed to care about. Elaine loved her "Wee Man," as she called him in private.

Calum heard it as "Her Wee Man" and loved the possessiveness in the words. He never minded being small. "I can play golf with the best o' them. And I have you," he told her, "so why should I mind?"

✦   ✦   ✦

When McAllister and Joanne arrived at the hotel, they knew where to go from the balloons and the murmur of conversations competing with music from a gramophone.

Joanne was familiar with the dining room from her previous stay at the hotel. She led her family through the double swing doors and into Elaine's farewell party.

What struck her, after the pleasant surprise at seeing so many gathered to honor Elaine, was Alice Ramsay's painting. It now had pride of place on the center wall above the fireplace. And lit by a proper art gallery light, the heather, the willows, the birch, and the water in the lochan in the foreground glowed.

McAllister made straight for the ham sandwiches and a beer. Joanne went to join the circle of what she took to be fellow nurses around Elaine. Jean clung to her mother's side but was tempted towards the cake table by Elaine's mother.

Annie made a beeline for Calum. "Hiya!"

Calum now knew, and didn't mind, that Annie would ask the questions everyone wanted an answer to but daren't voice.

"Is your mother too sick to come to the party?"

"Her left leg is in plaster, and her broken ribs hurt. She's getting better but can't get around much."

"Good," Annie said. "I mean, it's good she's getting better." The girl crammed her mouth with the last of the sausage rolls before she made another blunder.

Joanne came over to say hello to Calum. "Elaine introduced me to your father. Such a nice man." She then worried that the remark might be interpreted as *in contrast to your mother* and escaped to talk to the doctor, who was on his own, balancing a cup of tea and a plate of sandwiches and looking miserable.

"Hello, Doctor. Joanne Ross. We met at the auction."

"Hello, Mrs. Ross . . ." He looked towards McAllister as though searching for an answer. Or a clue.

"Sorry, I'm also Mrs. McAllister. Ross is my professional name. Not that this is a professional occasion. I just wanted to say hello."

"A modern woman," he said. "I like that."

"Alice Ramsay was too."

"She was a wonderful woman. I miss her." His sorrow was clear and, Joanne decided, genuine.

"Elaine told me you are also leaving. Africa, isn't it?"

"Yes, Rhodesia. Doctors are needed there."

He saw Joanne look up through the strands escaping from a Kirby-grip that was failing to hold back her thick chestnut hair. In her eyes he read a question.

"Here they can always find another doctor. Other nurses, even, if it comes to that. But there will never be another Alice Ramsay. She brought joy and color into the lives of those she met."

"The old saying, we'll ne'er see her likes again, is how I feel about her."

"Absolutely." The doctor continued, "When I heard Alice referred to as 'thon witch,' I took it as a joke. Yes, she made up teas from herbs. Yes, she made up ointments. Aspirin comes from willow bark, after all, and for the older generations, their medications were homemade remedies."

Joanne said, "I'm beginning to think that if you are a strong, independent, and, worst of all, contented single woman, all it takes is a black cat, and you're a witch."

He nodded. "Right enough. Miss Ramsay knew why she was accused, who her accuser was, knew the charges should never have been brought. That poor woman, with her desperate need for a baby, she didn't want a trial either."

"Who did?" Joanne knew but wanted it confirmed.

"The husband. He gave evidence at the trial. Why anyone listened to him I don't know. Even the sheriff knew him as a right layabout; he's been up before the bench often enough." He added, unnecessarily, "Drink." The curse of the country, as Joanne well knew. "Alice wouldn't defend herself. Couldn't, she said. When she was charged, she had no choice but to hire a solicitor. You know the rest."

Around them, the noise of voices was rising, partly because of the shouts from the hard-of-hearing, partly because the high ceiling made sound echo.

Joanne liked the young doctor. She decided that the soft Highland cadence of his voice, his smile, and the way his steady grey eyes listened would reassure young and old that Doctor really did know best.

"This is your home?" she asked, wanting to change the subject, as every conversation seemed to be about Alice Ramsay.

"Farther north—Caithness." He went on, "Alice was certain that the woman—heavens, I've forgotten her name—was being beaten. She also knew there had been a previous miscarriage— two previous, as it turns out. The husband was, is, a brute, but only after a drink."

Joanne did not share her opinion that drink was never an excuse.

"He is also a gullible soul."

She knew this was shorthand for "not too bright."

"If it hadn't been for him sharing his troubles with Mrs. Mackenzie . . ."

Or Mrs. Mackenzie weaseling it out of him, Joanne decided.

". . . and Mrs. Mackenzie encouraging him, telling him it was all Alice's fault, he would never have gone to the police. To be fair, the police weren't initially interested. But then the husband found an ally in another local solicitor, a man renowned for encouraging litigation just so he can listen to his own voice in court."

He sighed. In small communities, where everyone knew everyone, the simplest of disputes between neighbors could fester, turning into long-drawn-out sagas of gossip, snubs, and vindictive quarrels with the original sins long twisted beyond recognition.

"The solicitor persuaded the fiscal to prosecute. I can't prove this, but I'm certain part of the reason to charge Alice was that both men are set against terminations of any kind, even when a mother's life is at risk. Alice was astonished at being charged. I remember her saying, 'This is nonsensical.'"

"I agree," Joanne said. "Reading about the trial, the charges seem so absurd. But tell me, why did Mrs. Mackenzie have it in for Miss Ramsay?"

Dr. Jamieson wasn't fazed by the abrupt change of thought. "Because Alice was friendly with Mrs. Galloway."

"That's all?"

He thought about his reply. "The enmity between Mrs. Galloway and Mrs. Mackenzie is understandable."

Not to me it's not, Joanne thought.

"Perhaps any friend of Muriel Galloway is automatically an enemy of Mrs. Mackenzie," Dr. Jamieson said. "Sorry, Elaine needs help."

From the way Elaine was gesturing towards the door, Joanne gathered the gentleman in the wheelchair needed the lavatory. Now.

McAllister knew he should chat with Calum. "So, Calum, when can we expect you in the office?" Calum looked so glum he hastily covered up his question. "I know how hard it must be for you leaving home, only a few days in a new job, then your mother having her accident, so take your time and don't worry about the *Gazette*." He could see from the young man's face he was not reassured. "Lorna has three months trial as a cadet reporter; she will cover local events until you come back." McAllister would have kicked himself, if that were possible whilst holding a cup of tea and a pie. Too late, he remembered Joanne saying, *When I'm told "don't worry," I worry all the more.*

Calum reached out to catch the pie that was in danger of sliding *splat* onto the carpet. "Thank you, Mr. McAllister. I will be in the office on Monday."

McAllister nodded. "Good, good."

But Calum wasn't listening. His mouth was imitating a goldfish, his eyes wide as though he'd seen a specter at the feast.

He had.

McAllister turned around.

The short, round figure leaning on two sticks but standing absolutely still stopped the conversation of those nearest the open double doors.

"Calum!" she called out.

Now everyone stopped talking. McAllister could see Mr. Mackenzie taking shelter behind the tea urn. Mrs. Galloway didn't move, standing guard over her dining room, arms folded.

One of the old men didn't have his hearing aid in and shouted, "Here comes trouble!" then sat back to enjoy the spectacle.

Elaine stepped forward. Her mother watched, confident her daughter could deal with Mrs. Mackenzie, a woman she had no time for. "Mum, it's lovely you could come. Let me get you a chair."

"Calum!" Mrs. Mackenzie shouted past Elaine. "Son, fetch your coat, we're going home."

Mr. Mackenzie stepped out. "We've no had Elaine's presentation yet. So my son, he'll be back later."

"He's no spending one minute more in the company o' thon Jezebel!"

Joanne was thinking, *That's a bit harsh when Elaine is so patient with her.*

The other guests turned to stare at Mrs. Galloway. They knew it wasn't Elaine who was the Jezebel. Mr. Mackenzie was at her side. He was as short as his son and just as upset.

In his grim *don't worry, I have this under control* tight-lipped smile—or was it a grimace?—Joanne saw pain. No, she corrected herself, humiliation.

Mr. Mackenzie must have felt her gaze on him, for he turned, caught Joanne's eye, and shrugged. Then smiled. Then, taking half a step sideways to close the gap between him and Mrs. Galloway, he linked arms with her.

Mrs. Galloway said nothing. But her silence spoke. She was standing proud, in her own hotel, amongst friends, out in the open, in full view, with her man. As bold as the figurehead on the

Cutty Sark, glorious in her best silk dress—albeit covered with an apron in a clashing pansy print—and even though this skirmish in a twenty-year battle had just commenced, it was clear Mrs. Galloway would always be the winner.

"You tried to kill me!" Mrs. Mackenzie shrieked at her. "I know it was your car that hit me. I know you want me dead. I know—"

"I drive a van," Mrs. Galloway pointed out.

"It *was* you! I know it was you. It had to be . . ." The sentence faded. In truth, Mrs. Mackenzie hadn't seen who knocked her over, had no explanation for the attempt to kill her, yet was certain that was what had been planned. For years.

Muriel had been her husband's childhood sweetheart. She'd lost him when she'd left the area. Returning as Mrs. Galloway but with no husband accompanying her, it was only a short time before the relationship with Mr. Mackenzie resumed. No one who knew all the protagonists involved was the least bit surprised.

"Mum. Mum. Please." Calum was shaking. "It's Elaine's special party."

Elaine thought her fiancé might cry. "We'll be back home in an hour or so," she said, "and I've saved you a piece of cake." She was not going to let her future mother-in-law win. Not again.

"How could you?" Mrs. Mackenzie turned on Elaine. "Having your party here instead of at my house? Inviting that whore?"

She had a big voice for such a wee woman. The shriek from Mrs. Galloway was even louder. "Whore? Whore? You get out of here this instant, you dried-up auld b—witch!"

"You let go of my husband, or I'll—"

"Or you'll what? He's been mine for near on twenty years, and he's never coming back! Look at your son. He can't wait to get away from you either."

"Mum, please." Calum took his mother's arm. "Sorry, Elaine," he said. "I'll take her home and be back soon."

As he propelled her out of the room, Joanne could see that the woman was far more mobile than she pretended.

"Sorry, Elaine," Mrs. Mackenzie called over her shoulder. Elaine was in no doubt that this was to placate her son; she had no intention, and never would have, of apologizing to Elaine. Mrs. Galloway had stolen her husband; no one was going to steal her son.

"Ladies, gentlemen, friends." There was a tapping of a teaspoon on a tumbler. Dr. Jamieson stood at the head of the table to make a speech. "Today is a day to say farewell to one of the best, one of the kindest people I know. Nurse Elaine."

The applause was loud and long, relieving the tension through hard claps, palm to palm, everyone wanting to show appreciation and support to Elaine.

"We will miss you," the doctor finished.

"Hear, hear" rang out around the room.

"Aye, lass, you'll be sorely missed," agreed an elderly gentleman with a thick thatch of white hair and a tweed jacket, its collar liberally sprinkled with a storm of dandruff.

"Don't leave us!" shouted an old lady with a walking frame decorated with little-girl-pink ribbon.

Dr. Jamieson could see Elaine was teary and tired yet happy. He picked up the large parcel, wrapped in Christmas paper left over from the previous year, and handed it to her. "This is from all of us. We'll miss you, but good luck in your new job."

Elaine oohed and ahed, didn't mention that she'd chosen the gift herself, and kept exclaiming, "This is just what I wanted!" She beamed at the residents of the nursing home. They, including the toothless Mr. Meikle, beamed back.

"I hear it's right cold in the south," she joked, "so I'll be needing this." She draped the tartan mohair stole across her shoulders—Mackenzie tartan, naturally—and thanked everyone for coming.

"If the lass still wants him, she needs to kidnap thon fiancé of hers and flit to the moon." This came from the old man, whose hearing may have deteriorated but not his intelligence.

Mr. Mackenzie heard. He turned to Mrs. Galloway. "I'm so sorry, ma dear."

She replied, "Wheesht!" and took his hand. "It's Elaine we should be sorry for. And your lad."

The scene between the women had shocked no one except the McAllisters.

Wouldn't have missed it for the world was the final judgment on the farewell do. The accusation of being deliberately run over by Mrs. Galloway was mostly dismissed. It would be gossiped about, and knowing Mrs. Mackenzie would never let go, they would hear the accusations repeated. Again and again.

But that's Mrs. Mackenzie for you was the general consensus. *Aye on about nothing.*

"Twenty years," McAllister said as he drove his family home. "No wonder Mrs. Mackenzie is bitter."

"I wish the girls hadn't been there." Joanne thought the children were asleep when she said this.

Jean was, her head on a pillow of piled-up overcoats. Annie wasn't; she loved listening in on adult conversations. "I'm glad we were there," she said. From the jerk of Joanne's head, she knew she'd said the wrong thing. "Us coming made Elaine happy." The girl knew how to soft-soap her mother.

"Yes. You're right. She's a lovely young woman," Joanne agreed.

Annie glanced up. They were passing through Invergordon.

In the streetlights she caught McAllister watching her in the driving mirror. He winked.

◆ ◆ ◆

When McAllister switched off the engine, they sat in silence for a moment. The only sounds the ticking of the engine as it cooled and a faint whisper of wind in the cypress tree.

"I'll lift Jean up to bed," he said.

"And I'll put the kettle on," Annie offered. She went ahead with McAllister, using her key to open the door and switch on the lights. He had her sister in his arms, nothing waking her.

"An atomic bomb wouldn't wake you," Annie had once said to her sister.

"What's an atomic bomb?" Jean had asked.

Annie followed the wireless news and felt an explanation was too scary for a nine-year-old. "It's a big, big bomb," she'd said, not admitting that the news had given her nightmares.

Joanne went straight to the sitting room. The fire was set but unlit and the room chilly. She sat on the sofa, easing off her shoes, and put her feet up.

She sighed.

Closed her eyes.

Then suddenly opened them, all senses on alert. A smell, a draft—a sense of something awry, amiss, disturbed, touched, altered—made her freeze. She heard her husband move above. From the kitchen, she heard her daughter run the tap. She gazed around her—the pictures, nothing different; the ornaments, all in place; the rugs, the chairs, the flowers, gladioli she should have thrown out this morning but hadn't time, nothing seemed out of place.

She smelled the room. Taking slow shallow breaths, breathing through her skin, her scalp, breathing between her eyes, she was certain: someone, something, had been here.

She went to the writing box. Still locked. She took the key and opened it. The perhaps Leonardo drawings were with Hector, as he wanted to photograph them and examine them with a strong magnifying glass. As for the manuscript, she couldn't be certain, but the folders seemed in order, and nothing seemed to have been removed.

She ached to call out to McAllister but didn't want to seem foolish.

"Night, Mum."

Joanne jumped.

"What's wrong?" Annie asked.

"Tired, that's all."

"It's been a long day." The girl turned away, not wanting her mother to sense her own fear. The long illness after Joanne's injury had terrified the child, terrified her into believing her mother would never again be the same. "She's not herself" was the phrase she'd used. It had taken her stepfather a while to see that Annie was right. It had taken time for Annie to understand that nothing was the same for any of them after the ordeal. Not her mother, not McAllister, not herself, although she would deny that if asked. Even her sister had become more clinging.

In a flash of insight beyond her years, Annie thought, Maybe that's what happened to Mrs. Mackenzie, something terrible, and she's never recovered.

She went to bed, where she would write up the day in her diary, resolving to remember her insight when she was an author, writing about people.

Joanne went up to their bedroom. About to put on her slippers, she stopped and began looking, sniffing, checking in drawers, smoothing out the bed linen. Here too, she thought. Someone has been in here.

She reached for the musical jewelry box on the dressing table, a present from the girls last Christmas. The box played "Greensleeves" when opened. It was switched off, and the box unlocked. Did I switch it off? Did I unlock it? She hated that she couldn't remember.

Her few items of jewelry were all there, including her previous wedding ring, which she couldn't bring herself to throw out or sell. The small gold thistle brooch with the purple amethyst—a present from Mrs. McAllister on their wedding day—a thin gold chain, her pearls inherited from her grandmother, they were all there.

Nothing was out of place. Nothing missing. Yet her certain dread crawled up her arms, pressing against her throat, pressing into the base of her skull, making her feel nauseated.

When she came downstairs, McAllister had a dram in his hand and was considering whether to light the fire. Even though only a few minutes past ten, early for him but an hour when most in the town were asleep, he was tired and wishing he'd set the bedroom fire as well as the one in the sitting room.

He was a bad actor. He listened to her suspicions, doing his best to disguise his skepticism. He didn't ask, How do you know? Why do you think that? He had the sense to not say, You're tired, perhaps you are imagining it.

Joanne accepted it was challenging for him, for anyone except their friend Jenny McPhee the traveler, to believe in intuition, believe the unbelievable. She held up her hands, palms outwards, to ward off his incredulity. "If you believe in me, trust me. I know someone was in our home when we were away. I know you doubt the sixth sense, but I am certain someone has been in the house."

To placate her, he began a conversation as to the who, the why, the when.

The when was easy. "Today," Joanne said. "This evening." The why she was equally certain of. "It's to do with Alice Ramsay." What part in the mystery of Alice she could not say.

And McAllister didn't want to speculate. Nor did he want to articulate his theories regarding the who, for that would require at least two more whiskies, and the room was cold, and he needed his bed.

Joanne's answer surprised him. "I think someone is after the drawings."

"Not the manuscript?"

"I immediately thought of Forsythe. He doesn't strike me as the burglar type, though. Maybe it's . . ." She shook her head. A strand of hair fell over her left eye. She blew it away. "I don't have a sense of danger. But I thought that the last time."

"He might have hired someone. Leonardo drawings are a major find to an art expert like him."

She stood. Yawned. Then hastily covered her mouth. "Excuse me."

He smiled. He loved everything about her, even her yawns. "Do you want cocoa?"

"No, thanks, I'm too tired." The explanation that it might be Forsythe had calmed her, and she knew she would now sleep. Such an idiot, that man, she told herself as she climbed the stairs to bed, but harmless.

McAllister bent over to switch off the table lamp. There was a spent match in the unlit fire. Why he picked it up he couldn't say. It was just a spent match, he was later to say to DI Dunne. He threw it back into the fire, then switched off the lights.

At the foot of the stairs, he froze. Went back to the sitting room. Switched on the overhead lights. Picked up the match. Looking at it, he understood that Joanne hadn't been imagining things.

"It's too short," he murmured. "It's from a pocket box of matches." He looked for their box of household-sized matches. It was underneath old copies of the *Gazette* in the wooden box along with a bundle of kindling.

He put the spent match on the mantelpiece. He took a deep breath. Now he sensed it, a disturbance of the air, in the fabric of the room.

He had a flash of him telling Dunne, No, nothing is missing, no signs of a break-in. But Joanne can sense these things. And I have a spent match that's the wrong size.

As evidence of a nonburglary, he knew it was flimsy. Yet he now believed someone had been in their home. Someone professional. But not quite professional enough.

"We will talk soon, Mr. Stuart, or whoever you are," he vowed.

And went to bed.

CHAPTER 17

Of course I said no. I told him I couldn't supply him with the documentation. He wanted the passports so desperately I knew it was wrong.

He reminded me of our family ties, talking about "people like us" and all that nonsense. I told him that meant nothing to me.

Then he'd explained just how deeply I was involved.

"Remember when I asked you about P's cover identity?" he'd asked. "Well, thanks to you, he was traced, and he's now dead. Remember that document I asked you to forge, the one in Arabic? A network was uncovered, and all the operatives disappeared. As for D, he wouldn't be sitting in his apartment in Moscow if it weren't for the documents you supplied."

He'd said all this in a matter-of-fact voice, as if he were discussing the prospect of rain for the Wimbledon Fortnight. But his eyes, they'd betrayed him. His eyes, brown, soft, pleading. I knew that look. Soft and endearing if you didn't know him. And the softer and more charming his behavior, the more dangerous he was.

That shattered me. In hindsight, I suspect he may have been bluffing. So many identity documents and passports were available, and by that time, I was involved in less mundane work.

I asked why he couldn't use the identities already provided—all three sets of documents. "We suspect a leak," he'd told me, "and being able to move without detection from our own people, this is my way of finding the traitor."

I did ask if he was one of the traitors. He'd laughed.
I still can't believe I believed him.

*   *   *

"No Calum, then," Don remarked before they began the Monday Morning Meeting.

"Seeing how half the calls are from his mother, he should look after the switchboard," Lorna said. "If he turns up, that is."

McAllister was inclined to agree but didn't say so. "Right, what have we got for this week?" he began.

"Lots of pre-Christmas and New Year advertising," Frankie told them.

"Just what I don't need." Don groaned.

"I've done a piece on the rape of our architectural heritage," Lorna began, "and I've some interesting stuff on who exactly will benefit from the building contracts—amongst the names is a well-known former councilor."

"Like it," Don told her, "but the 'rape' word is not in our vocabulary."

"It's almost 1960. Whyever not?" she protested.

"Because I say so," the deputy editor replied.

McAllister smiled. She'll do well, this young lass, he thought. And the battle of wills and wits between her and Don was sure to be entertaining.

He could see from their grins that Frankie and Rob agreed.

Hector was too busy with his negatives to notice anything.

Frankie had asked the woman who was a part-time book-keeper for the *Gazette* to work full-time. So Mrs. Brown had taken over the switchboard and the classified advertising. A quiet, nondescript middle-aged woman, she was a widow in need of the

236 • A. D. Scott

income. Frankie assured them she was efficient, but that was not what worried McAllister; he feared that when she was not in her place behind the reception desk, he might not recognize her.

Don agreed. "She'll no frighten the public," he told McAllister.

"What about Lorna?" the editor asked. "Are you not concerned she'll terrify the public?"

"She'll do that, all right," his deputy replied. "But bairns and grannies take to her."

Calum telephoned at noon.

"You should've called first thing," Don said.

"Sorry. I'm really sorry. Can I speak to Mr. McAllister?"

"McAllister?" Don looked across the table at the editor, who was thumping out an article on a proposal to phase out National Health orange juice.

"No, he's busy. You'll have to make do with me."

Calum was not offended; Mr. McAllister was a lofty being in his eyes. "Miss Ramsay's farmhouse was broken into. Even the floorboards were ripped up, and someone did something to the chimney; there's soot everywhere."

"You went to the place?"

"Aye, this morning. I heard about it from a pal in the police and went out with him."

"Local news from two counties away is not much use to us. Write it up anyhow, but I doubt we can use it."

"My old editor offered me my job back." That Mrs. Mackenzie had threatened the editor, over a matter some eight years ago involving a junior typist and a weekend in Ullapool, Calum would never know. The editor decided he was more afraid of Mrs. Mackenzie and what she could tell his wife than he was of some mysterious man who seemed to have vanished southwards down the A9.

"And?"

"Elaine, my fiancée, starts her training today at Raigmore. But my mother needs me."

"Well, it's straightforward: your mother or your fiancée. Your choice. But let me know your decision this week." Don hung up. "You got all that?"

McAllister answered, "I got the gist of it."

"I'm thinking that lad is more trouble than he's worth."

The editor did not disagree.

"He phoned to say there's been a break-in at the late Miss Ramsay's house."

McAllister told him of Joanne's certainty that they too had had an intruder. He explained why he agreed.

"A spent match, not very much," Don said. "But since your missus says someone's been there, well . . ."

McAllister could tell his deputy believed Joanne. And him— maybe. An old Highlander, Don McLeod knew there was more abroad than what could be seen or touched.

"Alive and dead, your Miss Alice Ramsay is at the heart of some great secret." Don knew that Joanne would not give up until she knew, or was thoroughly convinced she would never know, the mystery of the artist's death. Therefore, her husband wouldn't either. So he might as well become involved too. "Time to ask this man from London if he's responsible for these visitors."

"Visitors!" McAllister shot off his chair. "Joanne said there's a brush salesman pestering her."

"Aye, they're around this time o' year. They call on me an' all, but best to check." Don said this to footsteps already halfway down the stairs, hurrying for the door and home.

✦   ✦   ✦

"Brush salesman? You asked me to an urgent meeting to inquire about a door-to-door salesman?"

It was the next day. Stuart was implying he'd rushed to the Highlands on the overnight train, when McAllister knew he was a resident of a hotel on the north side of the river.

"My wife is certain someone is watching her. Certain someone has been in our house. So yes, I'm checking on a brush salesman."

"And now so am I," DI Dunne added.

"Mr. McAllister, I leave for London on the overnight train. I have finished my task. You will not be troubled again."

The editor knew he was being dismissed, and his frustration at the man's intransigence surfaced. "So was it you and your henchmen? First I find you attending a country auction. Then you threaten me. Spying on my home? A hit-and-run accident? Wrecking an empty house? Isn't it all a bit drastic? Seems to me, for someone so secretive, you are completely amateurish, flagging your presence wherever you go."

Stuart said nothing. But his silence said much.

It was then that McAllister understood that Stuart had told the truth about one thing—the man was indeed an "office wallah." His self-description said more than that; the very phrase indicated a man from a former colonial background, army perhaps, and private education and privilege certainly. He was everything McAllister despised—a man elevated to a job beyond his intelligence, hired, and promoted because of birth and education at the right schools. And, most of all, family connections.

McAllister continued, "Someone was, *is*, searching for something. It all connects with Alice Ramsay."

"That may be so. But you and the local police will never know." Stuart said this quietly, not boasting, not threatening, just stating a fact. His was a profession far removed from the life and experience of a small-town editor, of a small-town policeman.

"One final point. The Leonardo drawing, how does that come into all this?" McAllister almost missed the slight movement in the man's cheek. Was it a smile? A tic? An admission of heaven knew what?

"A fine example of a master at work," Stuart replied. "Gentlemen, please excuse me." He stood. "I am certain our paths will not cross again, so I will say good-bye." He was wise enough not to offer his hand to McAllister.

McAllister remained seated.

"The matter is over. You have my word." Stuart's face blank, voice firm, spoke as though in command of a regiment. "Good-bye, Inspector. Good-bye, Mr. McAllister."

When they were alone, McAllister quoted, "Ours not to reason why . . ."

The policeman couldn't resist finishing the quotation. "Ours but to do and die."

✦　✦　✦

Why the patrol officers stopped the car DI Dunne never discovered. How the small pouch of drawing implements was taken into custody was clearer; the chamois leather roll was in a compartment underneath the spare tire in the boot of the car.

"What made you search the car?" Dunne asked the constable.

The young police officer did not confess that it was his first time as a driver on road patrol and that he was overkeen to book someone, anyone. That the car was big and black and powerful, with English registration plates, and that he'd stopped the car out of curiosity he also kept to himself. "The car was speeding," PC Cameron said.

"By a lot?"

"No really. But I had to give it some wellie—sorry—I had to accelerate to overtake him."

He and his fellow policeman had used their flashing blue light and siren and were thrilled by the chase.

"When he got out the car, he was right unhappy." This was mostly untrue. The man had been quiet. Too quiet. Too cooperative. That seemed suspicious in a place where motorists would argue pink was purple to get out of a speeding charge. "Anyhow, me an' Allie thought we'd better check."

"You were being careful."

The constable worried that Dunne was reproaching him.

"Sergeant Patience says you can never be too careful."

"Quite right."

"We took him in. The sarge looked at what we found. We made a list, gave all his stuff back to him. Then the sergeant told the man to go to his nearest police station within seven days with his license and insurance."

"He didn't have those with him?"

"No. No license, no insurance, no ID."

"Why didn't you charge him with speeding?"

The young policeman blushed at the humiliation. "The motorist denied he was speeding. Sitting exactly on the speed limit, he said. An' he said that if we could overtake him in our patrol car, he couldney've been going that fast."

Dunne presumed the car had been speeding—slightly. He also knew that a foreigner from London, with the voice and demeanor of entitlement, would panic a young man on the first day in a job he had wanted and trained for ever since joining the police force.

"There was no one else in the car." This wasn't a question. Dunne already knew the answer.

"No, Inspector. He was alone."

The contents of the chamois roll had baffled the custody sergeant. He did not think to consult his inspector, so it was fortuitous that Dunne saw the contents listed on the charge sheet. By that time, the man had left.

"Aye, but we have his registration number and address," the sergeant said. "I'll check."

He left the sergeant peering at the booking sheet through half-moon spectacles, before reaching for the telephone. Good luck with that, the inspector thought.

Dunne called McAllister.

McAllister said, "I don't remember, exactly. Joanne will know. But I think a pen holder and nibs, Chinese calligraphy brushes, and an inkstone. No seals or stamps."

The sergeant had said he didn't examine the stamps but remembered some were in metal, a few were wood. There were seals and sealing wax. There was a box stuffed full of old paper. There was what looked like some receipt books, but they were in a foreign script. "Russian?" he'd guessed.

Dunne continued, "This fellow told Sergeant Patience he worked with museums rebinding old books and such like and these were the tools of his trade."

"Tools of the trade—maybe. *His* tools? Unlikely." McAllister sighed. An explanation was unlikely. "We know Miss Ramsay was a forger. And we know she worked in some branch of the security services in London. But did she continue to work for who knows who when she left? And does all this relate to her death?"

"Mr. McAllister . . ."

McAllister, alerted by the "Mr.," could guess what was coming.

"The verdict was suicide. The matter is over." Stated simply. Said as a matter of fact. The policeman was being neither judgmental nor encouraging. But the hidden rebuke was there. The question: Why are you letting your wife involve herself in an affair this dangerous?

"Joanne doesn't believe the woman committed suicide." Both men knew that the obsession of the living with the untimely dead could destroy even the sanest of survivors.

"Her opinion, your opinion, even mine, do not matter here. We are dealing with a government agency with powers way beyond our experience."

"Joanne is editing the manuscript Miss Ramsay was working on before her death." Here McAllister hesitated. The work on Alice's manuscript gave Joanne pleasure, purpose, perhaps an obsession. "Naturally, the life and death of Miss Ramsay are of interest."

"Is there a connection between the manuscript and her death?"

"Paintings of the local flora and fauna? I don't see how." McAllister lit another cigarette to help him think. "Miss Ramsay's house was vandalized. You said the man your constables stopped and searched was calm and professional. So would he wreck the house? Search thoroughly, yes. But Calum Mackenzie said windows were smashed, floorboards ripped up, pipes pulled out, water flooding the kitchen—the vandalism was done in anger."

McAllister heard the policeman groan before saying, "That's a matter for the Sutherland Constabulary."

"I told Calum Mackenzie the same." Both men felt it was yet another part of the puzzle.

"Stuart's departure is the end of it." Dunne's words were certain, his thoughts less so. "So I doubt we will ever know."

And therein lies the problem, McAllister didn't say.

CHAPTER 18

❦

I can't condemn Mrs. Mackenzie. Gossip is a form of currency, and without it, my job, and the lives of our operatives, would be impossible. To add veracity to a false identity, I relied on agents to provide me with current gossip, the slang, the jokes going around. That and the price of beer and bread and cigarettes.

What was the opinion of the man in the bar? The housewife in the market? I would pick a reference here, a piece of gossip there, and weave them into a new identity.

When I returned here, so many years later, I began to understand that Mrs. Mackenzie needed to be someone in the community. Being married and the owner of a prosperous local business brings her status. She trades information and feels needed. Unfortunately, she also embellishes the stories.

I tell her nothing. I smile. I'm polite. I pay my bills before they are due.

I should have known better. Nothing will satisfy her until she's discovered the minutiae of every moment of my life before coming up north to retire. (That's what I told her, and that is the truth. Mostly.)

No, I won't give her the satisfaction of my life's story. I've no wish to be a character in her dramas. In revenge, she encouraged, and exaggerated a ridiculous rumor. She calls me a witch instead of saying what she really wants to say: "a stuck-up bitch."

Foolish me for thinking I could be anonymous in a place where my family was once known. But the glen bewitched me.

✦ ✦ ✦

Although it was early evening, Calum was in bed in quiet despair. With Elaine gone, he could no longer look forward to their walks, their talks. If her shift was daytime, they would meet in the evenings and huddle up, cuddle up, on a sand dune or in the shelter of the rocks or in his father's car. If her shift was nighttime, in all weathers, they would spend afternoons at the beach or in the hills or drive up to Lairg, taking a picnic of digestive biscuits and cheese and pickle and lemonade. Or a flask of tea.

Once, Elaine brought a tea made from Miss Ramsay's herbs. He spat it out. "It's chamomile," she told him.

"Boiled garden weeds," he said.

Elaine laughed. Teased him for having no adventure in him. He gazed around at the loch, at the hills, at the high country up above Golspie, at the pass leading to the wildness of moorland around Garve, saying, "This is a grand adventure." And she'd agreed.

"Calum." The voice carried along the corridor, through two shut doors, past a small flight of stairs to a half landing, and through another sturdy door to his room, where Radio Luxembourg was transmitting faint sounds of music and voices through a thick haar of static. "Caa-lum."

When he could no longer ignore the macaw-like squawk, he climbed out of bed, put on his slippers, and pulled a jumper over his pajamas. In my pajamas at nine o'clock at night, he thought. Elaine would say I'm an old man before ma time. He yawned and went to his mother. "What's wrong?" he asked.

"Nothing's wrong. I just wanted company."

"I'm reading. And listening to the wireless."

"You can bring your book in here," she answered from her

throne in the high bed, with a mountain of pillows and cushions and rugs and a shawl. "Bring the wireless an' all. I feel like some music."

"Mum, I'm writing a—" Telling her he was writing to Elaine was not a good idea. "I'm trying to compose some articles for the *Highland Gazette.*"

"Surely you're not going back there? Not now you've been offered your old job back."

"I want to work on the *Gazette.* It's interesting, and I'll learn a lot." He knew he had to leave. The feeling of wanting to escape from her had come more and more frequently in recent weeks. And he hated himself for it. She was his mother. She was lonely. Not being in the shop, not serving the petrol, she had no one to talk to. Except him.

"That Elaine," Mrs. Mackenzie began, "she's determined to take you away from me."

"Mum." Calum stood.

She heard the warning and stretched out for his hand, his sleeve, anything to hold on to her boy.

He was out of reach. "Can I make you a drink?" he asked.

"No, thanks. I don't want to disturb you in the night." She would anyway, he knew.

"I'm leaving on Sunday so I can be back at the *Gazette* Monday morning. I've talked to the doctor, and the district nurse will come daily until you're up and about." He knew when she said nothing that she didn't believe he would leave her. "I want to be with Elaine, so even if I don't have a job on a newspaper, with my qualifications, I can always find work down there." He was proud of his daring.

"It's clear I'm not wanted." With a tremble in her voice, reaching into her sleeve for a hankie, she overplayed the pity-poor-me.

"It's only for a year. When me and Elaine are married, we'll settle back here." He knew not to mention they were saving for a house of their own or that his dad and Mrs. Galloway had promised to help them financially.

Elaine had agreed when they discussed it. "Of course we'll move back. But we're young, so let's have some fun first, then find a nice wee place and start a family." She had one in mind, a small terraced house across the cobbled lane from her mother. "We'll have our wedding in the cathedral, you can go back to your old job, and I'll go back to nursing—after our babies are at school, of course."

He'd blushed. She'd kissed him.

His anxiety lessened. He loved his mother. But knew they could not live with her.

+ + +

Next morning, after the drawn-out performance of taking his mother breakfast in bed, helping her downstairs, fetching the newspaper, tuning the wireless to the Home Service, lighting the fire, and promising to be back in time to make dinner—"twelve o'clock sharp, else ma stomach plays up"—Calum walked to the hotel where his dad had left the car for him, keys in the ignition.

About to set off for the glen, he changed his mind.

"Hello, Mrs. Galloway, how are you?"

"Grand, Calum. Yourself?" She didn't need to ask. She could see the shadows under his eyes. See the sag of his shoulders.

"Not too bad. I just dropped in to tell you I'm taking Dad's car. Miss Ramsay's house was broken into. Now the rain's stopped, I want to have a proper poke around. See if . . ." See if what, he didn't know.

"Can I come too?" she asked. "It's been a while since I was up there. The auction was the last time."

He didn't know why he'd hoped she would come with him but was grateful she'd offered. He liked Mrs. Galloway and was happy his dad was happy. Besides, he'd known little else. When he was growing up, his father would finish work, join them for supper, and be there for breakfast. It was only when he was nine, or was it ten, that he discovered from the school bully that his father spent his nights with Mrs. Galloway.

When they climbed out of the car, they buttoned their coats tight and pulled their hats down over their ears. The wind was brisk, the temperature in the low forties, but the sun was bright and the sky a deep blue that gladdened the heart.

"Listen." Mrs. Galloway stood still, her head to one side.

"What?" He could hear nothing except a rustle of bog cotton, a whisper of wind in distant pines, the faint sound of a Forestry vehicle climbing the track across the glen.

"A skylark. Alice's favorite. That's why she took the house, she said. The skylark enchanted her into falling in love with the glen all over again."

The five-bar gate had a new shiny lock. They climbed over and tramped up the track. From a distance, the house looked the same as Miss Ramsay had left it. Close up, it looked like it was suffering from a terminal injury: empty eye sockets for windows; the once bright blue door had fresh wounds slashed across the middle; the door handle had been gouged out; someone had nailed two planks of what looked like old floorboards across the doorframe to keep intruders out.

The back door was intact and locked. "I wonder if the key's in the same place." Mrs. Galloway checked under a stone near the outside stone sink cum drinking trough Alice had used to pound willow bark to make a sleep remedy. "Here it is."

"If someone knew Miss Ramsay, would they know where the key was kept?"

Mrs. Galloway thought about it. "A local would know that we seldom lock up hereabouts. An' if we do, we always leave a spare key handy."

Calum nodded in agreement. He pushed open the back door that led into the scullery. This area was intact. The coat stand, the floor-to-ceiling shelves full of tins and jam jars and shoe polish and balls of twine and a bag full of of bags, all the handy things you might need in the garden—it was typical of a farmhouse or cottage.

Mrs. Galloway opened the door to the kitchen. He joined her. It took a moment or so before either could speak, as sadness silenced them.

"We had some nice chats in this place," Mrs. Galloway began. "To see it like this . . ." Her eyes filled with tears, and Calum, seeing how shook up she was, patted her arm. The gesture was so like his father, a gesture of helplessness when confronted with a crying woman, the tears started to leak even more, but silently, running in rivulets down her cheeks, dripping down from the sides of her chin. She wiped her face with the sleeves of her coat. Taking a deep breath, she blew out noisily. "The court case, the gossip, Alice didn't deserve all thon nonsense."

That much of the nonsense had been broadcast to every passing motorist, every townsperson, every countryman and woman, had been discussed, dissected, and exaggerated by his mother, Calum knew. He was grateful he had never once heard Mrs. Galloway criticize his mother.

Dad's friend was what he called her. Elaine had giggled, saying, "Come on, Calum, she's more than just a friend."

Calum asked, "Do you think she did it?" He'd wanted to ask since they'd set out on the eight miles to Alice Ramsay's lair up the glen.

No explanation was needed. "I believed it at the time," Mrs. Galloway answered. "Alice was sensitive, artistic, she saw things differently from ordinary folk. Maybe the gossip and rumors was too much for her. Calum, I just plain don't know." She gestured around. "All this has got me to wondering."

"It's only eejits out for mischief."

"This far from the road? In this weather?" She was looking at the floorboards. They had been prized up at the nail joins, neatly, regularly. She thought this significant but couldn't grasp why. "It'll be a big job to put this lot back." She kicked a loose plank.

"Do you think someone will ever live here again?"

"You and Elaine could. It would be hard for your mum, though. She'd need a piggy-back up the track."

Calum grinned at the joke. Then, seeing his sort-of-step-mum's face, the twin lines between her eyebrows deepening at the thought of his mother, he said, "Likely to be snowed in in the winter, up here." He wanted to reassure her the suggestion was not taken badly. "But a lovely place in summer."

"Aye." She nodded, then smiled. "Up here, for three months it's spring, summer, an' autumn, and nine months it's winter."

They left none the wiser as to why someone would vandalize the house. Both had theories. Calum thought it was done for the hell of it. Mrs. Galloway thought someone was looking for something and, failing to find it, made their search look like the work of hooligans.

Calum dropped Mrs. Galloway off at the hotel, thanking her for coming with him.

"Calum, do something to please me. Call me Muriel."

He promised he would, although it would always be Mrs. Galloway when his mother was around.

"Your dad and me, we've been talking."

"Oh, aye?" He didn't want to hear.

Muriel Galloway sensed his reluctance to become involved. "When Elaine visits, let's the four of us have a meal out somewhere away from the town. Maybe Mr. Mackenzie and me could drive south to visit you."

"Thanks. Elaine and me, we'd like that."

"Us too." She smiled at him. "You're a good person, Calum. I'm only sorry you've had to put up with . . ." She gestured to everything and nothing. "With all this," she said quickly, before the words *your mother* escaped.

◆ ◆ ◆

The editor offered Calum the use of the office and a typewriter at the Sutherland newspaper. Calum thanked him, said he would write up an article on the vandalism of the house, then told him he would be returning to the *Gazette*.

"I like it, and I'm learning a lot from Mr. McAllister. He used to be a big-time journalist, you know."

When Elaine called that evening, he said the same.

"I know," she replied. "So make certain you're there on Monday morning; they won't wait forever. And I won't either."

That depressed Calum. And worried him. Never before had Elaine indicated she might not wait for him.

"Who was that?" his mother asked when he returned to the sitting room.

"Elaine."

"Oh. I thought it was something important the way you took so long."

Calum was oblivious to his mother's wee tricks of language and said nothing.

Next day, back in the comfortable and unchallenging atmosphere of his former office, he was typing his notes when the receptionist came in with a note.

"Don't tell me, it's my mother."

"No, your dad."

He phoned the garage. "Dad, how are you?"

"Calum, it's your mother. She apparently had a turn, but nothing serious. The doctor gave her an injection to calm her down, and Nurse Ogilvie says she's now sleeping."

"She was fine when I left an hour ago." He was unsure if it was serious or if she was pretending. "Thanks for telling me. I'll get home right away."

"No. Listen, son, come over here first."

Calum hurried the few hundred yards to the petrol station and garage.

"Hiya, Calum!" shouted Kirsty, a girl he'd been at school with and who was temporarily looking after the shop and the petrol pumps. He waved, having no breath to reply.

"What happened to Mum?" Calum was panting.

"Nothing," his father said. "Nothing at all."

"But the doctor? Nurse Ogilvie?"

"Someone telephoned her to tell her you were seen in my car with Muriel."

"No, that can't be right." Yet he knew it probably was. "With her leg in plaster, Mum can't make it into the hall to answer the phone."

"With your mother, you never know what she'll do." He spoke softly, more to the seagull that was sitting on a rusted wreck of a truck that had been there longer than he could remember and was now so spattered in seagull guano that it resembled some piece of art beloved by Dougald Forsythe. There was no bitterness in his voice, only resignation. He looked at his son, remembered what Muriel had said. He picked up a none-too-clean cloth to wipe the oil off his hands.

Calum noticed the oil and dirt ingrained beneath the fingernails. The palms of his hands and fingers would have made prints admissable in a court of law. This was one of the many faults Mrs. Mackenzie found in her husband. Mrs. Galloway reminded him that those same stained hands paid for her rival's home and her comfortable life.

Mr. Mackenzie had difficulty beginning what he wanted to say. He called out, "Kirsty, love, any chance of a cup of tea?"

"For two?" she asked as she stuck her head around the door to the workshop.

"Aye, that'd be grand."

"I need to check on Mum soon," Calum said.

"No yet."

The talk was the first heart-to-heart they'd ever had. They took the mugs of tea out the back door to a pile of used tires stacked up against the metal wall of the workshop. They sat on the tires conveniently piled for sitting and smoking and watching the waves only a long hop, skip, and jump from the workshed.

In a watery winter sun, they sat side by side. No wind, no rainclouds, temperature a balmy fifty degrees, they enjoyed this reprieve between weathers, and Calum wondered why they— he and his father, on their own together—didn't do this more often.

They stared towards the distant headland to the south. The suggestion of a finger pointing heavenwards was the lighthouse. Though often unseen in daylight, during the night the blinking light kept all who went to sea safe. For landlubbers, it was as natural as the landscape of sand dunes and coastal flats and the high hill with the statue of the Duke lording it over them. They watched the seagulls practicing their acrobatics; they watched the waves, soft calm grey-slate-blue, break in and out in the short North Sea swell.

They never once looked at each other.

"Muriel tells me we should have talked long before now," Mr. Mackenzie began.

"What for?" Calum asked. Remembering this was the kind of thing Elaine might say, he added, "Righty-oh."

"Your mother is a difficult woman. And it's partly my fault, partly to do with thon sad business wi' her father."

Calum knew his granddad had blown his brains out with a shotgun. Far gone with the drink was the explanation. He knew his mother had discovered the body. And didn't want to think about it. "Don't worry, Dad, I've known about you and Mrs. Gallo—Muriel—for years. Elaine's mum told me how you were childhood sweethearts, then her going off to the south and no one hearing from her for years."

"Four years and seven months."

"And she came back married."

"Aye, she did. So was I. Married. Only seven months married when she came back. Mr. Galloway was out of the picture by then. And I—we—knew we had ruined our lives. A year or so went by, but there was no use denying it—me and Muriel, we were meant to be together."

To Calum, this sounded like something a woman would say, and he understood his dad and Mrs. Galloway had discussed their fate, their story becoming a private legend. Or a justification.

"It was no your mum's fault. She was a lovely lass when she

was young, but she aye had a sharp tongue on her. As the years went by, it got worse, and well, I was lonely. So I took to going to the hotel for a wee drink or two most evenings."

Calum seemed to remember some fuss—*was I eight or maybe nine?*—when his father had been caught drunk driving and almost lost his license. The sheriff took into account his job—collecting and delivering vehicles for his customers was part of a garage operation—and let him off with a caution. As far as Calum knew, his father hadn't touched spirits since then.

"Then I took to staying out overnight." There was no need for him to say *staying overnight with Mrs. Galloway.* "Though I always had my tea and my breakfast with you and your mum."

Calum said nothing. This was the routine he'd grown up with. In the small community, where many households had been disrupted by war, by emigration, by the old way of life on the estates, in the woolen mill, on the fishing boats, fading, changing, ending, theirs was only one household amongst many where a maelstrom of anger and resentment was concealed behind Presbyterian ideals of respectability.

Calum was uncomfortable discussing his parents' personal life, even more uncomfortable at the thought of his father having a love life. *They're nearly fifty,* he thought, *far too old for all that stuff.*

"Why did Mum take against Miss Ramsay? She really had it in for her."

Mr. Mackenzie shook his head slowly, trying to make sense of the senseless. "It was not long after she came to live here. Miss Ramsay came into the garage in a right old state. Her brakes had gone spongy, and she'd nearly come a cropper on thon bends at the top o' the brae. Anyhow, apparently Miss Ramsay rushed past yer mum into the workshed, wi'out saying hello and all that. She wanted me to fix the Land Rover immediately, cos the tide was about to turn, and she needed to take pictures o' the mudflats for a painting she was working on."

As his wife would get worked up about nothing, he'd thought little of it at the time.

"When she told me, I asked, 'What of it?' Your mother was right angry. 'That woman, who does she think she is? Coming back here like she owns the place?'" He sighed. "Your mum never forgot being ignored. 'I was black affronted,' she said."

Calum smiled. "Artists get like that—really distracted sometimes." He was remembering Hector.

"Aye, so Miss Ramsay explained. 'Forget my own name when I'm working,' she told me. But there was no changing your mother's mind, and when she sets herself agin someone, she can be a right good hater."

"That's ridiculous," Calum said. But he knew his father was right. When Mrs. Mackenzie made up her mind, nothing would change it—not reason, not evidence, not even an abject apology.

"So, me and Muriel were thinking." Mr. Mackenzie had at last reached the point of the father-son chat. "What with you and Elaine leaving for new jobs, we can be together all the time."

"Divorce?"

"Oh, no! Nothing as drastic as that. Just carry on the same as now but me move in full-time to the hotel."

Calum could see no reason why not. Then again, he knew what his mother's reaction would be. "Does Mum know?"

"Not yet. We wanted to tell you first."

Calum could think of no objections. "Who do you think knocked Mum down?"

"Some eejit wi' too much drink in him. But your mother is

telling everyone it was Muriel." From his fist clenching and tapping his thigh, Calum could feel his father's anger.

"No one pays any notice to Mum's havering."

"Tell that to Miss Ramsay."

The bitterness in his dad's voice shocked Calum. "You can't think Mum had anything to do with—"

"Calum. Son. Elaine is the best thing ever to happen to you. You need to get away from . . ." He looked around at the home he loved dearly. "You need to make a life for you and Elaine away from a' this."

Calum looked at his dad, stared at the reflection he saw when he shaved, only with more lines and grey hairs. He saw a sadness he hoped would never happen to him. "Elaine agrees with you. But I can't just abandon Mum. I'm all she's got."

"She's not as helpless as you think." A seagull swooped close. Finding no food, it shrieked in disapproval. They both laughed. "Flying rats," Mr. Mackenzie said.

They went quiet again, contemplating their first-ever conversation.

Mr. Mackenzie sighed. "I made a marriage vow. I'll not put your mother through the shame of a divorce. But maybe we can—"

"Mr. Mackenzie, Mr. Beattie is on the phone asking when his van will be ready. What'll I say?" Kirsty shouted into the garage. Her voice was loud and carrying after years as a Girl Guide leader. She'd initially suggested she use her whistle whenever he was needed on the phone. Carried above the noise of the machines, she'd said. But Mr. Mackenzie told her a whistle would remind him of his old dad calling his gun dog, so no more was said.

"Calum, wait a wee minute, will you?" he asked. "I haven't finished yet."

"I have to get back to see how Mum is."

Mr. Mackenzie nodded. "An' I have to talk to auld Beattie. You know what he's like."

"Aye, I know."

Calum watched his father disappear towards the office, and for the first time, he acknowledged what Elaine meant when she said, "Like two peas in a pod, you and your dad."

Whatever else Mr. Mackenzie wanted to tell his son was left unsaid. And the chance to talk again never arrived.

◆ ◆ ◆

"The doctor says I've no to leave ma bed."

"What happened?"

"You broke ma heart, that's what happened."

Calum stared at her, stared at her wee brown eyes flashing malevolently, and he was reminded of a teddy bear his father had won at the Sutherland Highland Games, a bear bigger than his five-year-old self, a creature that had terrified him and had made his mum laugh and tease him and remind him of the incident in front of friends for years.

Elaine hadn't laughed. "I always hated those things," she'd told him when Mrs. Mackenzie brought up the incident." I had nightmares about one, a giant pink thing. I was terrified it would fall on me and stop me breathing."

"Calum?"

"Sorry Mum. I was remembering . . ."

"What were you doing wi' thon b—witch? She was the one caused ma accident, I know she was."

"Mum, you told the police you never saw the car."

That quieted her.

"How do you know someone was with me up the glen?"

"Ina phoned. She saw you. That woman, bold as brass, sitting alongside you for all to see. Inveigling you into leaving your job, your home."

There. He had her. "It's good you're able to make it to the phone."

"I had to practically crawl—"

"I'll be off now, Mum. Nurse Ogilvie is calling by later." He leaned over and patted her arm. "I'm sorry I wasn't back sooner, but I was at the office. I have a story to write." He hoped being back at the *Sutherland Courier*, if only temporarily, would placate her.

"Aye, see you later."

Her reaction astonished him. He was expecting tears, tantrums even. On the walk down the cobbled lane to the car and on the drive from the village the eight miles into the town, he was tormented by endless questions. *Why? What's she up to?*

"Stop it," he muttered. "She's your mother. She only wants what's best for you." But he had seen a side of his mother that everyone else saw, a side of her he had never acknowledged. *Dad's right. I have to get out of here.*

✦ ✦ ✦

Elaine had the weekend free, so Calum left on Friday, not Sunday as planned. "First time since I started nursing I've had two whole days off together. Let's do something."

"In November?" he'd asked.

"I want to go dancing at the Caley Ballroom on Friday night. And there's a film on at the La Scala I want to see, so we'll do that Saturday. On Sunday, we can drive out to Loch Ness and look for the monster. Or just walk round the Islands. There's heaps to do down here."

On the Monday, he was there for the morning news meeting and had little to contribute except the details on the break-in at Miss Ramsay's cottage.

"No use to us; it's a local matter," Don said. "Nothing else happening in the wilds of Sutherland?"

"No really," Calum replied.

Lorna was next. Using her notes, plus a folder thick with backing documents, she detailed her findings on the redevelopment of Bridge Street. Calum had no idea what she was talking about. He felt worse than useless when he saw Mr. McAllister, Mr. McLeod, Rob, Frankie Urquhart, and even Hector listening intently.

"This is the plan, and here's an artist's sketch of the building." Work had already started. "But see, if you look at it from another angle"—she turned the plan around—"if you're seeing it from downriver, it's a real eyesore set against the castle."

The discussions were lively and long, and Calum felt he had nothing to contribute, but just before midday, McAllister said, "Calum, can I have a word?"

As they went to the editor's office, Calum was more resigned than nervous. *Elaine will be disappointed, but I can see I'm not needed here. Not with Lorna being local and so good.*

"Calum, tell me what you found at Miss Ramsay's house."

He was bewildered, the question so unexpected that he hadn't an answer. "What we found?"

"We?"

"Me and Mrs. Galloway." Calum closed his eyes briefly. It was something he'd heard Hector say. *Close your eyes and see the picture. Then find the words.* "It was a mess, broken windows, smashed-up front door. Mrs. Galloway thought it couldn't be a local, because everyone knows you'd put a spare key somewhere handy."

"Good point."

Calum took courage from the way the editor was looking directly at him. *He's really listening.* "The floorboards were raised, and it seemed methodical."

"As though someone was searching for something?"

Calum sat back. He was bewildered by the implications. "Aye. They were looking for something and maybe got angry because they didn't find it."

"Or wanted the police to think it was local louts." McAllister took a long drag of his cigarette. He directed an equally long outbreath of smoke to the high ceiling, where it settled on the once white, now dirty rust-colored paint.

Calum waited for an observation, a comment, and some sort of enlightenment. None came. "What does it all mean?" he asked eventually.

"No idea," the editor replied.

The admission made Calum feel better than he had since he'd started the job on the *Gazette.* He was thinking, I'll find out.

"Thanks, Calum. I hope you can stay with us this time." He meant the remark as a last warning. "Now, find Rob. Tell him you'll cover this week's hearings at the sheriff's court.

Calum took the warning as such. At the end of a long Monday, when he called his mother at the promised one minute past six, trunk calls being cheaper then, he told her he would be in court most of the week but would call her at the same time every day. "I won't be back home for four weeks. Then we'll have a weekend all to ourselves," he promised.

"You know what's best, son."

The meekness of her reply would have made Elaine suspicious. All Calum could feel was relief. "If you hear anything interesting, you know, stories that might be of use to me, you can let me know."

"As I canny get out the house on my own, how would I hear anything?"

◆ ◆ ◆

When McAllister told her of the break-in at Alice's house and Joanne asked if he thought they were looking for the drawings, it was his turn to say, "I don't know."

"Well, whatever it is they're searching for, and whoever they are, I hope they find it and leave."

"So do I. Then we can get back to a quiet life."

"McAllister!" Joanne burst out laughing. "I never thought I'd hear you say that."

"A quiet life with you and the girls is growing on me."

CHAPTER 19

I can't believe they didn't foresee that I'd take insurance. I took nothing that wasn't mine, no papers, no documents—that isn't my way. They always underestimated me, never once looking at the women without whom the Service would not function.

When we were growing up, moving in the same social circles, meeting whenever our families decamped to Scotland for the opening of the grouse-shooting season on the twelfth of August, we were thrown together. They ignored me, me being a girl.

Later, at Cambridge, they ignored me except when they needed a female to accompany them to balls.

After I finished Art College, he heard of my talent for forgery when Daddy made a joke that I could probably forge a five-pound note if I set my mind to it. So he recruited me. "Good girl," he once said when I produced a pleasing piece of work, that copy of that Cyrillic stamp complete with double-headed eagle. Good girl—how patronizing!

What they also ignored was my almost photographic memory. Can't take that away from me. I only needed to memorize the details of four documents. That was more than enough to pin down the where, the when, and, of course, the who. The why was, is, a complete mystery to me. Despite the best education, their elite and ancient family, they betrayed our country, and dragged me into their duplicitous plot. Deluded fools.

Not that I care. They are gone now. Yet what kind of life do they now enjoy? One lived at the bottom of a vodka bottle, so I was told. And there is no shortage of vodka in Moscow.

❖ ❖ ❖

"I'm about to publish an article on the triumph of that great art arbiter Dougie Forsythe. Is there anything I should know?" Sandy Marshall hadn't said hello or how are you or any of the other opening conventions; he treated his best friend's wife exactly as he treated his oldest friend.

Joanne appreciated it. "I wish him all the success he deserves. His profit from the sale of the drawing will pay for the lairy cravats and velvet wes'coats," she joked.

"His dress sense will be forgiven when it comes out he purchased a genuine Leonardo da Vinci at a farm sale in Sutherland."

"It's only a wee drawing," Joanne said, "but very lovely." She was still disappointed that McAllister had been beaten at the auction.

"Museums in Italy and elsewhere have examples of the artist's notebooks and sketches, so the drawing is not that rare. But finding it where he did, that's a story in itself."

"It was a very profitable purchase."

"Aye, but it would fetch a lot more if it came in a complete notebook or with other drawings in the series."

"All I know is what I read in the encyclopedia in the library." Joanne had looked up as much as she could about Leonardo da Vinci, and there was a surprising amount.

"How about your writing? More stories coming out?"

"Sort of." She wondered if she should tell him. "Sandy, this manuscript Alice Ramsay left, it's lovely—watercolor illustrations of the flora of the glens, birds, their nests and eggs, and landscapes from the northeast. I've been working on it, and it's almost finished, but who would be interested in publishing work like that?"

"You know who would know?"

They said in unison: "Dougald Forsythe."

"He owes you. Have him look at it. But don't let it out of your sight."

"McAllister would rather drink arsenic than have to deal with that man again. I'll finish the manuscript first; then we'll see. Anyhow, I'm looking forward to reading how the great Dougald bested my husband at auction."

"Aye, the subs had to cut his article drastically in case McAllister decided to sue."

"I'm sure he will read it with great interest." They knew McAllister didn't care if he was shown as the loser in an auction; he was only annoyed at not winning the drawing for Joanne.

Returning to the manuscript, she decided it was time to ask for an outsider's opinion. But who?

She went back into the hall to telephone. Although not yet eleven in the morning, the light was November dark. Only five weeks to the solstice, the short northern days were cold, but as yet, no snow. Seen from the kitchen window, the snow cloaking Ben Wyvis made washing up enjoyable, but from the front of the house, the light gave no pleasure. Nor did the prospect of letting go of Alice Ramsay's manuscript.

She dialed the office. "Hector, who could we show the manuscript to? It's ready." Joanne found herself speaking to Hec in his own shorthand assuming he would know which manuscript.

"I'll contact that woman who's always asking me to publish a book o' ma photos."

"That's really exciting. When are you going to do it?"

"I haven't said yes. But she only wants the pretty ones—you know, castles and glens and such like, calendar stuff."

"Highland cows?"

"I do not take pictures of Highland cows!"

"Sorry." She remembered an almost stand-up fight when some advertiser wanted Hec to provide a picture of a Highland cow to advertise their milk.

"You don't get milk from Highland cows," he'd protested. But Don made him take the shot, telling Hec newspapers were a business, not an art form.

Next, she decided to finish emptying the last of Alice's books and papers. Though her husband had put away all those he wanted to keep, there was still a box filled with bundles of paper of varying age, thickness, and quality.

Pulling out one bundle, she began to sneeze.

I'll give it all to Hector, she decided. *He's the only person I know who might find a use for it.*

She untied the brown twine around a sheaf of documents. Some were very old. "Last century," she muttered, reading the dates on pages of accounts of parish finances in a village in northwest Sutherland. There was a bundle of lists—extracts from parish registers, she thought. Mostly births and deaths, mostly turn-of-the-century but some earlier, some later, Joanne felt a deep sadness as she read the details of the short lives of children in those times.

Before National Health Service was introduced, many families could not afford to pay a doctor, if they could ever get a doctor to come up to those remote glens and villages. One family up Strathfleet had lost three children in two years.

Knowing how fussy Hector was about dust around his cameras and equipment, she emptied the box, deciding to clean it before handing it over. A stout affair, it was a custom-made document box and still in good condition. And heavy. When she put it down on the kitchen table, she noticed the outside and inside base of the box were different heights, but so skillful was the construction she was reluctant to take it apart.

She jumped at the doorbell ringing loud and long, echoing through the hallway and up the stairs. An outline of a person could be seen through the stained-glass panels.

"Hector?" she shouted.

"Aye," came the answer.

"The door's open."

"No, it's no."

"Sorry." She unlocked the door, forgetting that, in a shiver of unease, she'd locked it.

Hec was at his most ridiculous. He was wearing a rust-colored tweed jacket that matched his hair, which in turn closely resembled the inside of a bird's nest minus the eggs. A black and white Clachnacudden supporter's scarf, lurid green bobble hat knitted by his granny and more appropriate on a teapot, a satchel he'd had since Miss Rose's class in primary school was slung across one shoulder, and one small camera around his neck, the strap being his old Academy tie, completed his outfit.

As she'd worked with him for two years, Joanne took no notice.

"Why's your door locked?" he asked.

"Oh, you know." She gestured vaguely to the street, the town, the world.

Looking around at the rhododendron bushes, the lilacs, and the many suitable places for lurking, he said, "Don't blame you. But if you took down yon gloomy old cypress, it'd make the place much lighter."

We might be moving to a place of light, she thought to herself.

"I brought you a photograph of one of the pages." Hec undid the folder, one of the stiff cardboard ones with string tied around a board circle he habitually used. "I've costed the color separations for printing." He reached into his bag and brought out a tiny notebook full of tiny writing. "It's not cheap to do it properly," he said as he pushed the notebook at her.

"I need my reading glasses for this, Hector."

"Times the page costs by—how many illustrations? Thirty?"

"So basic printing costs will be . . ." She named an outrageous sum.

He whistled. "Did you do that in your head?" Hec needed pencil and paper to work out basic arithmetic.

Staring at the amount, she calculated a similar sum should be factored in for manuscript setting, proofreading, binding, covers, all the processes leading to final publication. "We can't afford to do this ourselves. We need a publisher."

"Aye, but who'd be interested in a nice wee book o' nice wee paintings?"

"And who'd be interested in a nice wee drawing of a bird skeleton?"

They were quiet for a moment, thinking of the two small drawings locked up in Hector's studio-cum-washhouse.

"Joanne . . ."

From the way he drew out her name, quietly, hesitating, she knew this was not good news. Every time she'd been given unpleasant news, she'd heard this tone, a way of speaking, usually from a doctor or a priest or her mother-in-law, to impart tidings of doom. "The drawings are fake," she said.

"Are they?" His green eyes flashed greener in surprise.

"Sorry, I just assumed . . ."

"I've no idea if they are genuine or not. But I came across this when I was looking at pages from your manuscript." He opened another folder, this time with green ribbon holding it closed.

"Here's an original painting you gave me." It was a drawing of a red admiral butterfly on a marsh marigold. "The writing down the left side describes the habitat an' aa' that." He pointed without touching one of the butterfly's wings. "No detail. Seems it's no finished."

"I have another on the same subject, and it's much more detailed."

"When I examined it under a light, the heat exposed some more writing." He paused, before continuing in his lecturer's voice. "It's faint, and the writing is tiny, but you can make out a list of numbers and dates."

"Do you know what they are?"

"No idea."

"Do you think there is more?"

"Invisible writing? Hope so." He pulled a face, and, looking like a contestant in a gurning competition, he made her laugh, which pleased him, as he liked her laugh.

"What on earth is this all about?" She was speaking to herself, but Hector heard, and he too had no guesses.

When she later showed McAllister, he knew instantly. During their precious evening talking time, she handed him a copy of the list. He said, "Passport numbers."

As Joanne had never had a passport, Hector neither, they were unfamiliar with the numbering system. "Is it always similar sets of numbers?"

"Yes. Unless it's a diplomatic passport. Where did you find this?"

She handed him the pages with Alice's illustrations, with numbers and names inserted between the lines now visible. "Thanks to Hec," she explained.

"This is dynamite." He went to the bureau drawer where he

kept his important papers. Deeds of the house, birth certificate, passport, were in a locked metal cashbox in a locked drawer.

Using his battered but still current passport, he compared his numbers with the list. "Four of these look likely. The others might be foreign passports." He considered the implications. "Alice Ramsay's role was creating forged identities. Multiple identities are essential in that business."

Joanne did not need to ask what business; the stories of spies and of defections had been front-page news. Then came the Suez Canal crisis, the Hungarian crisis, the Cold War crisis, and the nightmare of nuclear oblivion, all of which she had tried to shut out. To Joanne Ross, the challenges of postwar life were hard enough without reading, and hearing, of the doom and gloom in the world outside of the Highlands. The *Gazette* and stories of two-headed sheep were what she preferred.

McAllister was a news addict, fascinated by both national and international concerns. As editor of a local newspaper, he tried to show interest, but his eyes would glaze over when others discussed town and county politics—unless they involved a scandal.

"Hector said there might be more invisible writing on other pages of the manuscript, but I couldn't let them out of my sight."

"Not afraid of burglars, then?"

"Don't say that, McAllister." She went over to the folder. She opened it to the illustrations. "There can't be anything hidden in these." She went to the kitchen and came back with another folder, this time in a brown paper bag.

He went to take it out and felt a faint tinge of flour on his hands. He smelled it. "Bread."

"The bread bin was all I could think of. Hector said he can expose hidden writing under studio lights, then photograph the results."

"Let's go." He stood, patting his pockets for the car keys.

"It's past nine o'clock, far too late for visiting." She could see how excited he was. "We don't have a babysitter, and I want to be there with you."

"Annie will still be reading. Tell her we will be gone for one hour. No more." He looked at her. "She's twelve."

"It's not that. If we go out now, she will insist on knowing why we're rushing out. I don't want to explain. Or lie."

He smiled. "But I'm desperate to know."

"Tomorrow."

"Yes, mum." He grinned. "Tomorrow."

✦　✦　✦

McAllister's patience was sorely tested but as it was deadline day, a visit to Hec's studio had to wait. As did sharing the information with the photographer. Joanne knew that if Hec was told the plan beforehand, he would pester the editor all day with *Can we go now?*

Now, Thursday morning, a slack day with only a postmortem on the previous edition, tidying up, and filling in the football pools scheduled, it was the ideal time to check the manuscript. Joanne walked to the *Gazette* office. She introduced herself to the new receptionist, whose name she promptly forgot, and congratulated Lorna, whom she brushed past on the stairs.

Lorna replied, "Thanks, Mrs. M, must be off, I've a meeting wi' . . ." The rest of the sentence was lost in the clatter of a delivery from the stationery agent.

"How's young Lorna coming along?" Joanne asked as she went into her husband's lair.

"A lot brighter than Calum," he replied.

"Wheesht," she said. But she was grinning. "Told you you should have hired a lassie."

"Did you?"

"Maybe. But nonetheless, I'm right."

"Always."

Already the shorthand of a married couple was developing. And she loved it. Loved how she could tease him. Make him laugh. Make him meals he appreciated. Talk about the children, the weather, discuss books, music, her work, the manuscript.

"The manuscript," she began.

"Hector!"

Joanne jumped. McAllister bellowing like a vexed Aberdeen Angus bull she had not previously experienced at such close range.

Don came in and winked at Joanne. "He's gone home to file negatives, so he said. You'll have to make do with me." He sat and lit up a Capstan Full Strength. "So how are you, ma bonnie lass? Time to go out for a drink with an auld man? Warm the cockles o' ma heart?"

"No, she hasn't," the editor replied. "We need to find Hector."

"Another time." Don was not offended, as McAllister had meant no offense.

She reached into her shopping bag, took out the folder, and handed Don a page. "Hector found invisible writing in Alice Ramsay's manuscript. We want to check if there's more."

"Like a spy story, this," Don said as he stared at the almost invisible list of numbers.

"What makes you think that?" McAllister asked. He was staring up at the portrait of a previous editor painted in Victorian times. The heavy dark oils were gloomy, thick, and of no artistic merit. But he liked it, liked the way it connected him to the high times of newspapers and the founding of the *Highland Gazette* in the 1860s.

Don was taking his time answering. Puffing away at his

cigarette, squinting through the smoke at the faded lists, he began, "I was joking. But now I come to think on it, there is this, then the visit from the man from London and all his threats of a D notice, then the encounters with a mysterious black car or cars, not forgetting thon matchstick."

"Ah. Right."

Don could see from McAllister's frown that he hadn't told Joanne about the matchstick. *None o' my business.* He continued, "There was also a mystery man, or is it men, hanging around. And for why? There's the fake artworks. Miss Ramsay's past profession and the—"

"Hang on," Joanne said. "What did you say? Matchstick?"

McAllister told her.

She was not happy.

"I forgot," he fibbed.

Don intervened. "The man from London, is he gone?"

"He said he was going last week." McAllister paused. "The only way of contacting him is through DI Dunne."

"Don't know if this is important enough to pass on," Don said, "but I wouldney mind a wee poke around to see what else we can discover."

"These are definitely passport numbers?" Joanne asked.

"Looks like," Don replied. "So you young things get Hector to do his magic, and if there is more invisible writing, let's us talk it out before we contact your mysterious contact."

"I was threatened with the Official Secrets Act if I discussed it," McAllister reminded them.

"Aye, but I wasn't." Don grinned, and they both knew threats from officialdom, particularly English officialdom, were like petrol on a bonfire to Don McLeod of the Skye McLeods.

* * *

In the car, driving along Tomnahurich Street, Joanne said little, until she couldn't hold it in any longer. "Matchsticks?"

"A burnt-out match. One. Single. Solitary. Small. Not from the big box in the log basket. I found it the night we came back from Elaine's farewell party."

"When I thought someone had been in the house, you let me believe I was going crazy imagining things." She said this calmly, as though pointing out the weather or a road sign or an announcement of the coming apocalypse in the classified advertisements.

"I didn't think."

"I don't want to fall out with you. So next time, share."

"I'm really sorry." He bit back a comment about her not sharing the drawings.

"Serves me right for marrying a confirmed bachelor." Joanne poked him in the arm and opened the car door before he could say more.

She walked quickly up the front path, past the rockery now denuded of all but heather. She walked around the side to the back garden. The house felt empty, but a notice on the door of the concrete washhouse said "RING BELL" with (if you must) written in red pen underneath. She rang the bell. McAllister came up behind, and she squeezed his hand.

He put an arm around her shoulders.

"What do you want?" Hec shouted.

"Your money or your life!" she shouted back.

"Have you brought more pages?" Hec opened the door a fraction.

"Hello, Hec. Yes, I'm very well, thank you for asking."

"Wipe your feet," Hec told McAllister.

McAllister looked down. Seeing Hec in slippers, he did as he was told.

Door shut and locked, his granny's blackout curtains left over from the war pulled to, Hector was working in the dim. Pools of brightness from overhead retractable lamps shone down over a table bench, and what looked like a microscope, cobbled together from a spare lens, was sitting in the middle. Under the lens was an enlarged print of a list of numbers.

Hec said, "Let's try another page."

Joanne handed him a page of practice handwriting.

"More numbers." With the small Leica, he took two shots. "That's enough. Next?"

Joanne and McAllister, mostly silent except for the odd "hmm" or "I see" or "interesting," watched as Hec did his magic with eight sheets, all of which had some form of numbers in lists, groups, or paragraphs.

When he'd finished, Hec asked, "That's the lot?"

McAllister answered, "Yes."

Joanne added, "Maybe." Answering the unsaid question, she continued, "If I wanted to really hide invisible writing, I'd put it in the middle of a picture—you know, in the gaps of color." She was imagining one of Alice's illustrations. "There's space between the lines of her writing and between paragraphs and drawings. I thought it was all artistic, done that way."

"For the composition." Hec felt his knees shoogle with excitement. "Brilliant, Joanne, brilliant. Maybe you could go home and fetch them?" He was less asking, more commanding his boss to run the errand. McAllister surprised himself by agreeing.

An hour and eleven minutes later, they found what Joanne

decided was "the treasure." "That the writing is in Russian is fascinating. But what's really interesting is how carefully it's hidden, the writing interwoven into drawing of the curlews and their nests. See how these tiny letters are placed between the twigs and feathers of the nest?"

"We could ask Peter Kowalski to translate," McAllister suggested.

"And put him and Chiara and the baby in danger?" Joanne was shaking her head. "No, please don't."

Peter, married to Joanne's best friend, was Polish, and he spoke and read Russian fluently. McAllister had once joked about him speaking five languages, and Peter had contradicted him, saying he spoke seven but only read and wrote five.

"Hector, when will the prints be ready?" McAllister asked.

"As soon as you get out ma road, I'll start. Say late this afternoon?"

"No. Tonight. Come to our place after supper," McAllister did not tell him that in sharing, he would be breaking the Official Secrets Act.

◆　◆　◆

The gathering was like old times, except Elaine joined them. She'd called to say she and Calum were going out but couldn't agree on a film. "What's that one you saw last week?" she'd asked Joanne.

"Don't. I thought I liked Doris Day, but she was so perfect it was nauseating."

"I wanted to see the Hitchcock, but Calum gets nightmares after scary films."

"Come round here," Joanne had said. "Is nine o'clock fine for you?"

"For me, yes. For Calum, no. His landlady locks up at nine

on the dot. And no passkey." She'd giggled. "Worse than being at home—almost."

The others had walked in without ringing the doorbell, so when it did ring, McAllister answered. It was Elaine. She'd put lipstick on and her hair up, needing to be herself after days and weeks and years of being Nurse Fraser—except with the old people where she was always Nurse Elaine—and McAllister almost didn't recognize her, as she'd gained a decade of sophistication.

Seeing the others, Elaine said, "Hope I'm not intruding." She grinned at Hec and Rob, who were sitting together on the sofa. "Budge up, lovebirds."

They moved without comment, Rob happy to have her so close, even if she was Calum's fiancée.

"So, what do we think?" Don asked again.

"We're trying to make sense o' these numbers," Hec explained, handing Elaine copies of the photographs.

"Right, Miss Ramsay's drawings. I'd recognize them anywhere." She was staring at the lines interspersed between Alice's handwritten notes on the curlew, its nesting habits and territory. "This is some kind of number system."

"One column is passport numbers," McAllister said.

"Right." Elaine was holding the print of the drawing at arm's length, as though she needed reading glasses. "In this list here"— she was looking at another photograph of a page with a long sequence of numbers—"the numbers of the passport identify the person, so the next set is the date of birth, and then date of death. The rest of the set is possibly a number-letter code." She looked up at Joanne. "I don't have a passport, but it's my dream one day to go abroad and— What? What have I said?"

"No, no, lass, you're doing grand." Don did his kind old granddad grin.

Elaine smiled back.

"What about these?" Joanne passed another photograph to the nurse.

"Same first code, then . . ." She stared.

"I get it." Rob was sharing the page with her and followed her finger as it rested on part of the set of numbers. "It's dates of birth of bairns. Babies." He added the obvious. "It's rare that a baby would have a passport."

"Explain again, lass," Don asked.

Only then did Elaine realize that almost everyone from the *Gazette* was there, barring Lorna, as neither Don nor McAllister was ready for an eighteen-year-old to join the crew, and they were all staring at her.

"Right, photo four," Elaine began. "See the dates of birth. Now, look at the list of passport numbers. They start with the three identifying numbers, then the date of birth, then a six-number code."

"No death dates," McAllister muttered, knowing that obviously that would not be checked when applying for a passport.

"How did you work it out?" Frankie Urquhart asked Elaine. He'd come to the meeting because he was curious, not because he had much to contribute to the proceedings.

She explained, "I'm trained in patient identification numbers, dates of birth, operation procedure numbers, medication codes, all the paperwork that goes with a hospital admission." She left out that the date of death was a number she'd had to enter more and more regularly in the Old People's Home, especially as winter set in. "What's this all about?" Elaine addressed her question to Joanne.

"Not sure" was the answer.

"Long story," McAllister added.

"Well, you can't show me these," Elaine lifted the two photos up, "then leave me hanging."

"It can't leave this room. And above all, don't tell Calum," the editor warned.

"Because Mrs. Mackenzie can read her son's mind." Elaine smiled. They all smiled back.

It took half an hour to tell her and another half to discuss the possibilities thrown up by Elaine's insight. When the clock struck ten thirty, she said, "I have to go, I've a curfew."

"I'll drive you back," McAllister offered.

"Sorry I can't give you a lift," Rob added. "The bane o' my life is with me."

Hector chortled at the old joke.

Frankie said, "I'll take you. I need to get back anyhow, make sure my wee sister is no reading in bed till midnight."

They said good night, and Joanne saw them to the door.

"Night, Frankie. Night, Elaine. Come and visit on your next day off."

"I'd like that." Elaine was hovering on the doorstep.

Joanne fancied she could see Elaine's brain working, trying to decide whether to ask.

"Do you think there's any connection between Miss Ramsay's death and Mrs. Mackenzie's accident?"

"I don't know." Joanne had thought about it often and could see how there might be a link. A car, in the dark and the rain, had hit her. Had Mrs. Mackenzie seen something? Was the intention to kill her? Was it a sheer accident? Or had she invented a story that ended up putting her in danger? Joanne had no answers. Nor did the local police. "We may never know."

"She has enough enemies," Elaine said, "but enemies who would want to kill her? I can't see it."

When it was only the three of them, and after Joanne had yawned once too many times and gone to bed, McAllister poured a nightcap for himself and his deputy.

"A grand bunch," Don said, toasting their young friends and colleagues.

"They are that." McAllister raised his glass. An Islay malt this time, the clear oily burnt peat and seaweed flavored liquid rolled over his tongue. He remembered his one trip to the island, when the mist was so dense, the rain so heavy, there was nothing to do but hole up in the hotel and sample the bottles of malt, starting at the top left, working down to the bottom right of three shelves, ending up with a horrific bar bill.

"So," Don asked, after he'd had his private moment of reminiscence, involving his late wife, a wondrous few days in Skye, and an Islay malt, "what do we think?"

"I think this is what whoever they are has been looking for."

"Aye, but who are they? And what would Miss Alice Ramsay be wanting with those numbers?"

McAllister appreciated Don's Highland way of putting words together and smiled. "Insurance?"

"Blackmail?"

"Maybe she was continuing her trade up the glen and—"

He said, " 'Maybe,' and, 'If,' and, 'But,' and 'Perhaps'—I'm hearing too many doubts to be comfortable."

"We do know Miss Ramsay was known to some or all of the traitors who escaped to Moscow."

"Guy Burgess, Kim Philby, Donald Maclean." Don and every other journalist in the Kingdom knew the names by heart.

"There were, are, rumors that not all the traitors were revealed."

"And Alice Ramsay's information might lead to them?"

"Or her."

"Her? She might be the traitor? That's too deep for us." Don was deeply suspicious of government agencies, official or otherwise. As a newspaperman, he always assumed there were stories beneath the stories. He believed he was honor bound to expose those who tried to keep everything and anything from the public. He loathed how those self-same self-serving officials believed they knew best.

"Aye, and they still believe in the divine right of the aristocracy to rule over us peasants," he'd told McAllister—more than once.

"Those birth certificates used to create a new identity, the chances of them being discovered are as remote as the parishes they come from." Don was metaphorically tipping his hat to Miss Ramsay.

"The method used to hide the information, hiding it in plain sight, that's clever."

"Aye, yet so simple thon clever chappies from Intelligence couldney see it."

"Because we have the manuscript."

"You will have to inform them."

McAllister agreed with Don. He went to bed unhappy that they would have to share the manuscript. Although fearful of Joanne's reaction to the news, he was pleased at the thought of showing Stuart what the professionals had missed and what a group of Highland amateurs had found.

Until twenty past three in the morning.

What woke him he didn't know—wind in the trees, an owl shriek, too many cigarettes. He went quietly downstairs, checked that the manuscript was locked tight in the box, then went to make tea.

Handing the manuscript over to a man who had yet to return one of Joanne's favorite paintings would be more than hard for her. It was her link to a woman she'd admired from afar. It was a project in which she was learning how an author organized a manuscript. It gave her an understanding of how competent she was. And it gave her pleasure.

So how do I tell them what we've discovered and make sure Joanne keeps the manuscript?

He still had no answers.

CHAPTER 20

❧

D once proposed to me. Ridiculous. Who would marry such a womanizer? The American woman, that's who. Daddy thought the marriage absurd. "Not one of us," he'd said. But she stayed with him, even joining him in Russia.

It was good Daddy didn't live to learn of the betrayal—he would have been deeply embarrassed. Now what does our family have? Our name. That is enough, Grandmamma would have said. "Our name is ancient and noble, our titles go back centuries, our reputation is for selfless service for king and country."

Those old values and that way of life are gone. Yet many of the aristocracy can't face the truth. "We can't even afford a full complement of staff," Mummy had said.

"You have a housekeeper, a maid, and a cook," Alice reminded her. That didn't appease her. With no lady's maid, she'd had to learn how to fasten her own buttons. Without a butler, she could no longer entertain, or so she believed.

I doubt there are butlers in Moscow.

"What do you mean, you can't contact him?" McAllister could barely hold the telephone steady. His face a shade of puce beyond angry, he yelled, "I'm coming over!"

He marched up the staircase, ignoring the call of "You can't go there," from the constable at the front desk, and into the detectives' room. No one stopped him. Not because they knew him, more that they recognized there was more chance of turning around the *Queen Mary* in the Forth & Clyde Canal.

DI Dunne beckoned him into the interview room. He too was looking like he wanted to throttle someone. Only the hair on his regimental short-back-and-sides was unmoved, every other part of him hurting from the humiliation. Speaking in his quiet minister-of-the-church-comforting-the-bereaved voice, this time the bereaved being himself, he said, "The person calling himself Stuart cannot be traced."

A local policeman in a small Highland town would have no influence in Westminster, McAllister knew. "Well, we guessed that was not his real name." McAllister felt cold and clammy in the small of his back. *This is not good.* "There must be another way of finding him. Wasn't he introduced to you by your chief constable?"

"Yes, and he was asked to give Stuart assistance by the chief constable of Sutherland-shire."

"I bet your boss was also told to put the fear of the Almighty into that meddlesome editor."

The editor was right, but Dunne only nodded. As he didn't smoke, he concentrated on the grimy wall with water stains blooming under a window that leaked imperceptibly into the tiny room. "We move to new headquarters soon," he said, "then all this history will be demolished."

"The *Gazette* building too," McAllister said.

"I'm sure the security forces in London will never be moved out miles from the town center to an industrial estate where the wind can cut a man in half."

"They deserve to be sent to Siberia. There they would find out what the Cold War is really about."

"Agreed. But what do we do now?"

McAllister acknowledged the "we." "Correct me if I'm wrong. First, the *Gazette* publishes that photograph. Next, the chief constable of Sutherland contacts your boss. Your boss orders you to cooperate with the man. I think you need to remind him of that so—"

"So he can shift the blame to Sutherland." The inspector felt lighter. "I like that suggestion." He looked at McAllister and, seeing the smug grin, was about to say, *Don't quote me*.

The editor preempted him with hands held up in submission, saying, "Not that I'd ever publish that. But too good not to pass on to Don McLeod." His deputy and keeper of the town's secrets would add it to his treasure chest of information, to be used cautiously, with immaculate timing, and to the advantage of the *Gazette*.

"Do you have contacts in London in, you know, secret circles?" Dunne sounded as though he still read the *Eagle*.

"No, but I have a friend who might. Can I use this phone?" McAllister didn't say, but he felt safer using a police phone than the one at the newspaper. Or home. He dialed Sandy. "I need your help."

"It better be good. I've a front page just fallen foul of the legal department and nothing newsworthy to replace the story," Sandy growled.

"That man I told you about, from the mysterious branch of government, we're trying to reach him, and it seems he doesn't exist."

"Hold on." McAllister could hear Sandy, although with a hand over the receiver, shouting down some junior reporter, saying, "I want it verified, and I don't care how. You have precisely thirty minutes." There were background mumbles. Sandy shouting "Out!" before turning back to his caller and in a totally normal voice saying, "Right, where were we?"

McAllister didn't bother with the long version—he'd talk to his colleague later—only a request that they track down Stuart.

"You say you have a photo of him?"

"Yes, but hard to identify anyone from the shot."

"Get it down to me," Sandy said. "I'll make some calls and get back to you."

"I owe you."

"Make sure there's a front page in it for me, then we're square," he said, and hung up.

Like Don's treasure chest, on a much larger scale, or Mrs. Mackenzie on a village level, Sandy Marshall's vault of information was vast, making him one of the most powerful men in Scotland.

Dunne stood. "I need to make calls."

McAllister understood how tricky the next few hours would be for the policeman. "Aye. And if it looks like the blame will be dumped on you, remind your chief constable, and the sheriff in Sutherland and his chief constable, that you were ordered to help this Stuart character. Also ask why they were so keen to jump to his commands. Remind them that I met him, as did you, and both my deputy and I know everything."

He knew Dunne would never threaten his superiors. Not even nicely. That was why he would never rise to a higher rank. Good man, no ambition was the verdict on Detective Inspector Dunne.

McAllister went back to the office and sent Hector home to print copies of the photo to mail to the *Herald*. He then thought over who he knew in London who might help. Unsuccessfully.

Hector returned close to tears. "No, I've no idea what

happened to it." Sniff. Sniff. "No, I haven't lost it. Or misplaced it. I'm meticulous about my work."

For once, Rob made no joke about Hec using a big word, agreeing with the photographer's insistence he would never mislay a negative. "What was it filed under?" he asked instead.

"Negatives. *Gazette.* Date of publication."

"So if you knew what you were looking for, you could find it?"

"Easy-peasy."

"Don't you lock up?" Lorna asked.

"Ma cameras and lenses, they go in a safe. But no the filing cabinets. I lock the outside door wi' a padlock, but . . ."

"Simple to open if you know what you're doing," Rob finished.

"Was that all that was missing?" McAllister asked.

"I think so."

The reporters' room was crowded with Calum, Lorna, Rob, Frankie, Don, and McAllister squeezed together, watching Hector behaving as though he were about to pull a rabbit from the hand-crocheted string bag.

"This is all the photos and negatives and film relating to Miss Alice Ramsay." He dumped the files onto the table. "You have them." He thrust them towards McAllister. "I'm no having anyone break into my place and mess wi' ma files."

Lorna looked bewildered. Calum also.

"Thanks, Hec," the editor said. "Sorry you were . . . alarmed."

"Alarmed? I'm no alarmed, I'm fair scunnered."

"Rightly so." Rob mock-thumped him on the back. "And no one has the right to upset my friend."

McAllister took the files into his office.

Don joined him. "A fine mess an' aa' that." He lit up.

For once, McAllister didn't join him; Joanne had asked him to cut down, meaning stop. He didn't think it possible but would try. For her. "So what do you think?"

"Until we track down your missing man, there's not a lot to say."

"And if we don't—can't?"

"It's because he's not there to be found. Then it gets very interesting indeed."

"I hoped we'd had enough of interesting," McAllister said. But he said it with a Grim Reaper grin.

Which his deputy returned. "Interesting is what makes great front pages."

◆　◆　◆

Sandy called back late that afternoon. "I've spoken to the most senior person I know. He passed me on to some anonymous person in London, who passed me on to a police officer from Special Branch. Apparently someone you know, Superintendent Westland."

"We've met." McAllister said nothing more. Seconding a senior police officer was a major development, but he would not speculate on the why of it until he and the superintendent had spoken.

"I was warned not to interfere. Ordered not to publish. Or to investigate," Sandy added.

"You make your own decisions."

"That's right—except when the lawyers poke their noses in."

McAllister could hear the interest in his friend's voice.

"I love a good spy story," Sandy said. "A female traitor would be an even better headline."

"Hold on. Who said anything about Alice Ramsay being a traitor? This is all sheer speculation; we know nothing about her except—"

"Just kidding. But she was a key employee in a covert branch of the secret service establishment. She is from one of the premier aristocratic families in Britain. So if it turns out she is also a traitor, who wouldn't want the story?"

"You'll be slapped with a D notice."

Sandy knew as well as McAllister that it was impossible to publish when the crown solicitors issued the order on grounds of national security. "Keep in touch," Sandy said.

They left it at that.

McAllister was about to leave for home when DI Dunne called.

"Glad I caught you," the inspector said. "Tomorrow morning, two gentlemen will be here to interview you and Mrs. McAllister."

As he still thought of Joanne as Joanne Ross, McAllister had a moment of panic. *Now my mother is involved?*

"Will nine o'clock suit you? They will come straight to my office from the train."

"Nine is fine. But here in our office."

"The *Gazette* is not suitable."

Instantly, McAllister was mindful that his phone, here and at home, might be tapped. "I am not having Joanne questioned in your wee interview room. If they want to meet us, they can pay for a room in the Station Hotel." McAllister was adamant. He would not have his wife interviewed in the police station. She'd had enough of police and interviews and being a witness after she was attacked and imprisoned not even six months since.

"I'll arrange it." Dunne was also aware that Joanne Ross was fragile. *But not as fragile as her husband thinks.*

✦ ✦ ✦

"Good to meet you again, Mr. McAllister." Superintendent West-land turned to Joanne. "And you, Mrs. McAllister. Congratula-tions on the marriage." Westland, in a uniform with many insignias of rank, smiled.

Joanne and McAllister had been involved in helping to re-solve a case of child abuse some years back, and the superinten-dent had been sent to the Highlands to solve the case.

Westland continued, "Good to meet you, DI Dunne," and shook his colleague's hand. "I was asked to accompany this gentle-man and to vouch for his identity. I will also be reviewing the circumstances surrounding the death of Miss Ramsay."

"I'm glad," Joanne said. She did not notice the formal word-ing; McAllister did.

Circumstances surrounding? Does he mean to look at the FAI? The hasty cremation? Or the death itself?

The large man, muscle not fat, was dressed in the Civil Ser-vice uniform of navy-blue suit, with highly polished black shoes on feet that seemed incongruously large and more accustomed to boots. With a briefcase and a bowler hat, he was as clichéd and as out of place as a kilted Highlander in London.

He first introduced himself to Joanne. "Roland Hennessey. My credentials." He held out an ID card and a letter with an im-pressive crest and an equally impressive address: the Ministry of Defense.

McAllister gestured to Westland. "I hope someone checked his ID." Hennessey ignored him, but both policemen smiled.

Mr. Hennessey asked, "Do you prefer I address you as Joanne Ross or Mrs. McAllister?"

"Mrs. McAllister." She wanted the protection of her status.

Turning to McAllister, he said, "Honored to meet you. I've been reading some of your Spanish Civil War reporting. Most enlightening."

McAllister knew he was saying *I've read your file*, but he was flattered nonetheless. He also knew, from the suit, that Mr. Hennessey might now be an office man, but from his hands and handshake and eyes that flicked to take in everything and everyone, even the hotel's tartan carpet, he was much more than that.

"First, we need to get the police work out of the way," Westland said.

The police work was almost an hour of intense questioning from both visitors, the witnesses being all three locals.

"Establishing the identity of Stuart . . ." Hennessey was saying.

"And his driver . . ." Superintendent Westland added.

". . . is of paramount importance."

"So are you saying Stuart isn't with your lot?" McAllister needed to ask directly, needed to know if he—they—had been fooled.

"I can't answer that."

"Can't, Mr. Hennessey? Or won't?"

Westland was sitting opposite McAllister. He leaned back slightly in his chair, observing the exchange and enjoying it.

"Mr. Stuart was employed by a department of a service that does not exist in any public record." Hennessey spoke quietly, his words well chosen. He knew McAllister knew how to interpret "was" and "in any public record." It still didn't clear up what Alice Ramsay's role was. But McAllister knew how to wait.

They took a break. The superintendent and DI Dunne disappeared. McAllister guessed they were conferring from a Scottish-policeman point of view. He hoped so, as the secretive Secret Service perspective was stifling. And annoying.

They returned five minutes later with a waitress pushing a trolley with tea, coffee, and scones. Hennessey was delighted. "I'm addicted to good scones," he said as he helped himself to one.

"Spent time in Scotland, then?" McAllister asked. Hennessey gave the look of a small boy caught out in the pantry. "Your pronunciation of 'scones,'" the newspaperman explained.

"Got me. Yes, I trained with one of your rugged regiments in equally rugged country."

"You'll know the Highlands, then," McAllister said, guessing it was with the Lovat Scouts but receiving no confirmation.

Another intense hour of questioning relating to the break-ins, including the disappearance of Hec's negatives, followed. Then a sandwich lunch. In early afternoon, the questioning turned to Miss Alice Ramsay and her artworks.

Joanne was exhausted. She was almost teary when the subject of the paintings came up. "They still haven't returned one of my paintings. One I really liked."

There it is again, McAllister thought, *the mysterious* "they." He was becoming annoyed with Hennessey and the never-ending questions.

"Do you have any other artworks by Miss Ramsay?" Hennessey asked.

"Yes," Joanne answered. "The pages we told you about come from the manuscript and the loose papers we found in Alice's writing box. There are also two small drawings that might be by Leonardo da Vinci."

McAllister said nothing. This was his wife's decision. And he respected that.

"Hector Bain sent the drawings to an art expert in Edinburgh. We are waiting to hear if they are genuine."

"Do you believe they are?"

"I don't know." To her, the drawings, genuine or otherwise, meant a great deal. The image of a bird wing, pulled open to illustrate how every bone, every feather of such an insubstantial yet sublime creature—a skylark, she fancied—was miraculous. She felt humbled by the craftsmanship of a true artist and inspired by the illustration of the miracle of flight.

"We will need to check the manuscript and drawings but only to see if there is anything hidden. After that . . ." Mr. Hennessey shrugged.

"I need to leave," Joanne said quietly. "The children will be home soon."

"When would it be convenient to study the manuscript?" Hennessey asked.

"Will you take it away?"

"I can examine it in your presence."

"Come to our house tomorrow morning. We can go through it together. That is, if you're staying?"

"Thank you, Mrs. McAllister."

McAllister drove her home. Both knew that Hennessey needed no permission to take the manuscript. Both appreciated his asking.

After the McAllisters had left, DI Dunne with them, Superintendent Westland remarked to the man he'd only met last night on the train. "Good people. Intelligent too."

"More than can be said for our lot," Hennessey replied.

Westland thought well of his companion for admitting it.

✦   ✦   ✦

The following days were intense, with bad weather, hours of questions, and Joanne having to recount, again and again, the same events. At first, it was interesting, then boring, then confusing. She wanted to say, loudly and frequently, *We've already been over that, twice at least*, but instead, decided to enjoy the sessions.

Using her author's eye, she would try to recall the small details of everything and everyone connected to Alice.

Hennessey was accompanied this time by Detective Constable Ann McPherson, whom Joanne knew.

"I'm here because my shorthand is the best in the station," McPherson explained.

"It's the small unremembered details that might be important," Hennessey explained before the questions started.

Over many cups of tea and a batch of scones Joanne had taken out of the oven just as the doorbell announced her visitors, she was impressed by his patience, his ability to keep to the point, and his ability to eat a plate of scones and still have room for seconds of the shepherd's pie she'd made for the family dinner but served to the unexpected lunch guests.

"Are these numbers connected to the spy scandal?" Joanne eventually asked.

"I can't say," Hennessey replied.

She tried again. "And are the drawings in the style of Leonardo da Vinci genuine?"

"That I don't know, but I promise to find out."

Joanne stated her version: "A talented artist, retires from her job as . . ." She paused, not wanting to know exactly what Alice did, as it all sounded too fantastical. "A government employee. She has a family connection to this part of Scotland. So she settles in Sutherland, using her birth name, renovates the home she inherited, and works on her paintings in peace and quiet. She ends up in court, accused of deliberately causing a miscarriage, which leads to accusations of witchcraft."

The snort from Hennessey was loud.

And appropriate, Joanne thought. "The trial is reported in the local press," she continued. "I read it. Then I drive up to meet her and . . ." Here she stopped. Remembering. *I wanted to meet her because I wanted to meet a real live witch living near the town where the last witch in Scotland was put in a barrel of boiling tar and burnt alive.*

"And?" Hennessey asked.

I'm no better than Mrs. Mackenzie, she didn't say. "And this leads to me talking to Dougald Forsythe, who then uses what I emphasized was background information in an article in a national newspaper. He also reveals the whereabouts of Alice Ramsay, the artist."

"Not your fault," Hennessey interjects. But Joanne does not accept his opinion.

"Forsythe's article leads to someone"—"persons unknown" was a police phrase that always made Joanne smile—"discovering her. Perhaps killing her."

"And now we are here to investigate." Hennessey did not respond to the last sentence.

Ann McPherson intervened. "Sir, the appointment with the chief constable is at three o'clock, and it's now half past two."

"Thank you, Sergeant." He stood. As did Joanne and Ann.

The three of them were of an almost equal height, and Joanne was reminded that Alice too had inherited those tall northern genes.

"Is treason still a hanging offense?" She shuddered as the word escaped into the air, polluting the already abysmal day. The thought was haunting her. Although abolished for all other crimes, capital punishment was still the sentence for betraying your country.

He looked at her in surprise. She saw his eyes were like her eyes, that muddy green common in the north.

"Technically, yes. But it is unlikely to come to that."

Because it is unlikely it will ever come out, she thought, or it will be dealt with in other equally secretive ways.

"Thank you, Mrs. McAllister, for being so helpful. And for the magnificent scones."

"Sorry for the gruesome question."

"I'll need to take seven pages from the manuscript and these loose sheets with the numbers." He ended by writing out an official receipt, with Ann McPherson cosigning as witness. "Good luck with Miss Ramsay's manuscript. To have it published would be a wonderful homage to a fascinating woman."

Joanne made a fresh pot of tea, then sat and thought. It had been intense, and too much thinking gave her a headache. So she went to the piano, and almost an hour later, in the middle of a tricky passage in the Shubert, the girls came home.

From the kitchen came Annie's voice. "Who ate all the scones? There's only one left."

Joanne smiled. *Caught out by a twelve-year-old, Mr. Hennessey.* "I'll make pancakes instead."

◆   ◆   ◆

That night, even McAllister was too tired to talk. "So, to summarize, a talented forger and artist, but was Alice a traitor?"

Joanne was shocked at that suggestion.

"We're meeting tomorrow, probably for the last time. We'll know more then."

"Oh, really?" Joanne asked. "This is the secret intelligence service. Why would they tell us anything?"

"Because, dear wife, no professional spy would be unwise enough to leave a nosy journalist and a budding author with unanswered questions."

"I'm sure we'll be fed a plausible story. True or otherwise." Joanne sighed. "I know Mr. Hennessey and Superintendent Westland are the best we could hope for. But all I want is to find out what happened to Alice."

CHAPTER 21

◦◦◦

He meant those threats. Didn't work. Then he tried charm, tempting me with the Hermitage. I laughed. Exposure means little to me, but it would devastate my maiden aunts. What fun!

Then I considered the loss of freedom to walk the glens, to paint under a great open sky, to hear the skylark. Those I will not risk losing.

"Please," he'd asked, "give it to me as a keepsake."

"I don't have it," I said. "I burned it."

But he knew I was lying. That was my best work. I did it in a frenzy of lust, wine, and inspiration, and it is good. "My version of The Last Supper," I told him. Which it turned out to be; not a last supper, exactly, but the last of those summer evenings amongst friends. He, they, knew what I had seen—even if I didn't. Not then. Drinking, laughing, talking until dawn, reading poetry with the moon reflecting on the river, we were friends, family—with a side serving of betrayal.

That drawing might be dangerous, but it is my only keepsake of those intoxicating times.

◆ ◆ ◆

Calum Mackenzie was lost in his new home. The streets in the center of town he'd conquered. He recognized the names of the outlying suburbs, thanks to the book of maps Elaine bought him. He and Elaine had gone out to the Holm Mills to buy him a jumper, a red one, so he knew the road to the south side of Loch Ness.

"A change from all that blue your mother buys you," she'd said. He'd told her his mother insisted red did not suit him. Elaine laughed.

Now, in his red jumper, underneath a tweed jacket more suitable for an octogenarian than a twenty-two-year-old, he watched as McAllister went into his office, Don and Rob and Hector following.

"What's going on?" he whispered to Lorna when they were alone.

"Search me." She shrugged her shoulders and grinned. Her black-lined eyes sparkled and her pale lipstick shone as she teased, "Feeling left out, are ye?"

"No, but there's been lots o' comings and goings. We're reporters on the *Gazette*, so . . ."

"So?" she asked. "If you want to impress the bosses, get out, talk to people, don't wait for information to come to you."

"Oh. Right. Thanks." He'd never met anyone like Lorna. He wanted to say, *But I don't know anyone down here*. Without his mother to keep him abreast of the gossip, the developments, the traffic, and the farm and glen and sea news, he had no contacts and no ideas. In this town of strangers and strangeness, he was lost. But he didn't share that; Lorna was only seventeen, and a girl.

"Talking of which, I'm off to the hospital. There's an introduction to the new head surgeon come up from England, plus a graduation ceremony for the nurses in the specialist unit."

"My Elaine's one o' the nurses; maybe I should cover that."

"Too bad. I asked for an invitation, so it's my story."

He knew he should have followed up. Elaine had told him of the event a week ago. Even Hector would be there. He was staring at the phone, in a dwam of self-pity, when it rang. "*Highland Gazette*."

"Calum, I've—"

"Mum, we agreed. I phone you after six o'clock. No phone calls to the office."

"Well, if you don't want to know about the police going back to search Miss Ramsay's house and the byre, I'll just keep ma mouth shut."

He sighed, reached for his notebook, and began. "Tell me. But it's unlikely to be used, as the story is local to Sutherland."

"You've been offered your old job back."

"Mum, we've been over that."

"Fine." She sniffed. "I know when I'm not wanted." He was about to hang up when she said, "I was thinking about the car that hit me. I'm certain it was black, but I couldn't see the person behind the wheel. It was in here one time for a flat tire, and right muddy it was, so your dad washed it. The driver, this English fellow, he paid cash, said he didn't need a receipt, but you know me, always efficient, so I wrote down the numberplate."

Much like trainspotters, his mother often whiled away a slow afternoon writing down the registration number of passing cars. Calum saw it as a harmless hobby, until Elaine had joked that Mrs. Mackenzie could use the information to point out that someone was not where they should be and could lose their job, marriage, and reputation if discovered. "Mum would never do anything like that," he'd said.

"Calum? Calum? You there?"

"Give me the number. Then I have to go. I've an appointment in ten minutes."

He scribbled it down, made a promise to come back on Saturday. "Just this once," he said, and escaped.

There was no appointment, no story, no work—or at least none he thought Don McLeod would be interested in. So he left for the Italian café that was all the rage amongst the young professionals of the town.

He was walking through the Victorian market when he admitted to himself that he didn't like coffee. As there was no one he wanted to impress, he made for the tea shop Rob had introduced him to. Best bacon rolls, Rob told him, and as Calum chewed on one, he agreed.

It also had the best view of the station car park, and this Calum enjoyed. His father had hoped his son would follow him as a mechanic, taking over the business one day. But Calum preferred trains—big, puffing, spitting, gleaming steam engines. And Calum liked people watching—running for trains, coming out with luggage; happy alone, happy with family, unhappy with family; on a visit to the capital of the Highlands for the doctor, a solicitor, or the courthouse. People watching was something he and Joanne had in common.

He was counting out the coins to pay for his lunch when he saw the car arrive. Just another big black car, he thought, but I may as well check.

With little enthusiasm, he walked towards the car, where someone, hat on, overcoat also, was sitting with a newspaper open over the steering wheel, smoking, waiting.

The numberplate was the one his mother had given him, the same number he'd asked his policeman pal back home to investigate. Inquiring about it had raised questions. Brought forth officials. And intrigue. And maybe, possibly, perhaps, that same car and driver had knocked over his mother.

Calum's breath wouldn't come. The bacon roll and two industrial-strength cups of tea weighed down his stomach, slowing his legs. He turned away. Lost.

He returned to the *Gazette*. There was nowhere else to go.

"Mr. McAllister, I—"

"Not now, Calum."

"Don't look at me either, laddie, I'm away out," Don said before he even asked.

"Sorry, Calum. Catch you later, yeah?" Rob was off and running down the stairs in a clatter of boots and a jangle of keys.

Lorna was still out. Hector also. Frankie Urquhart was no help, as this was editorial, not advertising, and conversations with Frankie needed to be in ten-second bursts between phone calls. Friends and colleagues in Sutherland wouldn't take him seriously, not when he mentioned the inquiry involved his mother.

Still, Calum couldn't shake the fear that the car was important. So he did what he knew he shouldn't do. He called his mother.

✦ ✦ ✦

Joanne put the pie in the oven, then decided to invite Don for supper, promising him an apple pie for pudding. It took him five minutes for the ten-minute drive from his home on Church Street to their home off Crown Drive.

Two extra helpings of pie later, he and McAllister were sitting either side of the fire, saying little and, so full, moving less. "No update on the Stuart fellow, him who was impersonating a spy?" Don asked.

"Who calls himself Stuart," McAllister reminded him. "None. Only speculation on our part. After all, Hennessey has never stated that Stuart is an imposter."

"A right tricky lot, them spies." Don had never believed that the earlier revelations of a spy ring in the British secret services told the full story. And accepted he would never find out. "So we won't be having him as a front-page scoop. Pity."

"There is a story we might be able to use. Dougald Forsythe, the art expert, is in a spot of bother."

"Him who beat you to the drawing?"

"Don't remind me!" McAllister paused. "A second opinion is saying that his very expensive drawing is a master forgery." How they could run the story in the *Gazette* was problematical. So he explained to Don what had happened and the dilemma of how to make it relevant to their readers. "We need to word it so it not only connects to the *Gazette* but is syndicated to the *Herald* and other newspapers with our byline," McAllister began.

"Our intrepid reporter Joanne Ross discovered the drawing, and—"

"I'm not having my wife splashed about on the front page of—"

"Since when did you make decisions for me?" Joanne came in carrying a tea tray. She bumped the door shut with her hip and said, "Put another log on the fire, McAllister, it's winter. Or hadn't you noticed?" She put down the tray, turned her back on her husband, and asked Don, "So what's this about?"

He told her.

"I like it. Forsythe is not connected with spies, so the gentlemen from the government can have no objections."

"As far as we know," Don agreed.

"But the publicity?" McAllister asked.

"Joanne Ross believes in the public's right to know. It's Mrs. McAllister who wants a quiet life," she said. "Use the auction as background, then reveal the drawing is fake."

"Yes, but how did we discover it is fake?"

"Blame Hector," she said.

"Now, that is a brilliant idea," Don said, mentally composing a headline for an article yet to be written.

◆ ◆ ◆

Superintendent Westland knew the geography of the town and knew the senior staff on the *Gazette*. He well remembered Don McLeod. "A useful man to have on our side," he remarked to DI Dunne.

"And the reverse," the policeman replied.

The superintendent met Don in the pub on Baron Taylor's Lane. After a sip of the excellent draft beer, he asked Don, "Would it be possible to leave for the Baltic countries from here without anyone knowing?"

"Aye. Danzig always did good trade with Scotland. As for all thon Soviet countries, you could ship out from here no bother. What your reception on arrival will be depends."

For both of them the idea of a spy escaping from this small town to fame and fortune, or infamy and a Soviet pension, was intriguing. Thrilling, even.

"Didn't thon traitors escape via France? Maybe on documents forged by Alice Ramsay?" Don was enjoying the thought. Not that he approved of traitors and spies, but the machinations of governments he had no time for.

"On a cross-channel ferry via France." The superintendent sighed. "Pretty embarrassing for the spy agencies. Thank goodness I'm just a mere police officer sent to escort the expert from Westminster."

Don thought "mere police officer" was twaddle, and he doubted that escorting a senior spy was all the superintendent was here for. Here sits a very senior policeman, who is accompanying a very senior spy, Don thought, and I will never be allowed to publish the story.

"Can you ask if anyone knows anything at the harbor?"

"I have already, and no, no one saw nothing out of the ordinary."

The police officer laughed. Whether at Don's convoluted grammar or that the journalist was one step ahead of him was not the point; if there had been an escape by boat, Don McLeod would have heard.

* * *

"Mrs. McAllister, thank you so much for allowing me into your home again."

The sentiment was meant to reassure. But Hennessey's voice, dark with hidden power, made her wary. Plus, she was annoyed; she had had to bake again and vacuum the house, interfering with her newfound lust for writing.

"I have some good news. There is no objection to you keeping Miss Ramsay's versions of the Leonardo drawings."

"So Hector was right—they are fakes."

"Not exactly fakes," Hennessey said. "I believe 'executed in the style of' is the term."

"Good enough to fool some of the experts." Joanne smiled.

"Oh, yes," he said. "Our Alice was the best."

He took a seat at the table, where Joanne had laid out the manuscript, divided into chapters, making eight piles of paintings and commentary. In a separate pile, she'd put out the miscellaneous notes, partial paintings, and fragments of paper with Alice's various handwriting styles. Then came a bundle of documents, official-looking—they seemed to be for reference. Finally, still in a cardboard box, were stacks of paper, cut-up notebooks, cannibalized old books, pages from parish registers.

Hennessey was an organized searcher and a fast reader, but it took close to two hours before he finished.

Joanne left him at his task and went on with her own work—making a pot of soup, preparing pastry, all the boring household chores that she chose to enjoy, using the monotony to think about her own writing. *What if the postman is a bearer of information but not in a gossipy way? A man or woman who binds a community together, not divides? What if he too is subjected to an injustice, just as Alice was? Just as I was—and maybe still am. Perhaps the postie is a foreigner? Perhaps he writes poetry?* She wrestled with plots, with character, with how to link the ideas, and two hours vanished.

She knocked on her own sitting-room door. "Mr. Hennessey, a cup of tea?"

"Love one." He stood, stretched, saying, "I'll join you in the kitchen, if I may?"

The scones were cooling on a wire rack. "Cheese scones, raisin scones, and over there are plain old-fashioned tattie scones."

"My granny made tattie scones and served them with Ayrshire bacon."

"So you are Scottish." She laughed.

"Wheesht," he said in a Highland accent. "That is a state secret."

She half-believed him.

"I've finished with the manuscript. As I said, I'll need to take a few pages for examination by the experts, but only two of the pages are important to the work."

"The bird's nest is the one I particularly want back. But what will happen with the finished manuscript, I've no idea."

"I could contact some publishers who might be interested in the project."

"Mr. Hennessey," she began, and seeing those eyes, the watchful missing-nothing looking-right-at-you eyes, she hesitated.

He waited.

"If you tell me what you're looking for, I might be able to help." In her nervousness, it came out in a rush, and she laughed a little gurgle of a laugh. "Sorry, maybe it's too important for me to know."

"No." He was still. Very still. It was as though the cogs were turning. Or the scales balancing. As though he was giving every consideration to why she should, or should not, know. "I can't tell you everything. Actually, I can't tell you much at all. And I promised your husband you would not be exposed to danger."

She rolled her eyes, and he liked her the more for it.

"You have been excellent in your suggestions, so yes, you might be able to help, but purely with ideas."

This time, he didn't see her eyes, although Joanne was equally annoyed at Hennessey treating her as though she were a clever dog.

He was leaning back in the kitchen chair in a movement similar to her husband. "I am looking for a drawing. There have been references to it in a letter. And in a conversation recalled by friends. The subject is a group of young men, four friends, at a dinner table. This drawing could supposedly reveal—"

"I don't want to know," Joanne declared.

He sensed her fear and ignored it. "It is a small drawing, done in pencil, sketched at a dinner party. Do you have any ideas where she would hide it?"

"Perhaps it was hidden in the back of a picture and Mr. Stuart found it?"

"No. No, it wasn't."

How can he know that? She was longing to ask.

Hennessey continued, "If you think of something, please let me know." He saw her nod agreement, and he was certain that finding the whereabouts of Alice's drawing by herself would be a very tempting quest for Joanne Ross.

"Thank you again," he said. "Especially for the scones. I will be off down south tonight, so in case we don't meet again, write to me here when the manuscript is ready to show a publisher." He handed her a simple card with a post office box number in Westminster.

When he was safely gone, and when her heartbeat had returned to near normal, Joanne leaned against the kitchen dresser and sighed. "Phew." She had lied. She knew exactly where to look but couldn't think how to search for the drawing without alerting anyone. Then Calum saved her.

◆　◆　◆

In town for grocery shopping, she first stopped by the *Gazette* office; not because she needed anything, more for the company.

McAllister told her that Dougald Forsythe now knew he'd bought an expensive fake and that the *Gazette* and the *Herald* were about to print the story. She almost felt sorry for Forsythe. "He's too ridiculous to be a real villain," she said.

"He tried to cheat us," McAllister reminded her.

"Aye, and he exposed Alice. But you can't blame a fox for getting in amongst the chickens."

In the reporters' room, she listened in on a discussion between Lorna, whom she liked more and more, and Calum, whom she had less and less patience with. But still liked.

"Lorries are the best. Or commercial travelers—if you're a lad. Not always so nice if you're a girl, as they're always making passes," Lorna was telling Calum.

"Don't blame them, you're really pretty," he replied.

When Lorna said, "That doesn't make it acceptable," Joanne was impressed, but could see Calum hadn't a clue what she meant.

"I'm teaching Calum to hitchhike," Lorna explained. "Telling him the best spots to wait for a lift."

"Clachnaharry for northbound," Joanne said. "Out past Raig-more on the A9, before it gets too steep. If it's the Aberdeen road, I've no idea."

Lorna laughed. "You pick up hitchhikers?"

"Always," Joanne replied.

"I can't afford more than one trip a month home," Calum told them, "and my mother is up to high doh, so I promised I'd come home on Saturday."

"I get the feeling she's always up there," Lorna said. "I used to take the calls, remember?"

"If you really need to see your mum, I'll take you up. Then you can take your chances on a lift back on Sunday."

He jerked up; the stool he was perched on wobbled. His smile and the Labrador-puppy-grateful-for-a-bone eyes made Joanne see him as a seven year old, not twenty-two. "Really? You mean it about giving me a lift?"

"Saturday morning, eight o'clock at your digs will get us to Sutherland when?"

"Around eleven thirty, twelve, depending on the rain. And if we take the high road, it's shorter. But the A9 is easier."

"Calum, Mrs. McAllister knows where she's going." Lorna was not being rude; five years younger, she had more common sense than him, and he knew it.

Joanne popped in to give her husband a hug, saying, "Must run, shopping and all that."

He hugged her back. "Me too, editorial an' aa' that."

She felt guilty for deceiving him. But excited by her idea. Once home, she dialed.

"Sutherland Arms."

"Mrs. Galloway, Joanne Ross here." She explained her mission, accepted the invitation to lunch, put down the phone. Then worried how, and what, and how much she should tell her husband.

It was he who said, "I hear you're giving Calum a lift home. Want me to come too?"

"No, I'll be fine."

He knew she was determined to go and guessed that it had something to do with Alice Ramsay. From guilt, from curiosity, she would go north, with or without him. The consequences could be nothing. Or could awaken yet another visit from the shadows.

She didn't see the concern on his face as he turned away. But she sensed it and knew she was being stubborn. "You're right. I could do with a second driver."

"How can I resist such a charming invitation?"

◆　◆　◆

They dropped the girls off at their grandparents', picked up Calum, and once more set off up the A9 northwards. Joanne never tired of the Highland roads, never tired of the spectacle of the firths and rivers and mountains and sea lochs and forests and moors of her native land.

At the turnoff at Alness, she stared at a deep winter-blue sky and hoped the cold, clear day was set to last. They were on the high ridge road—shorter in miles but longer in time—to Bonar Bridge, the crossing point over the Dornoch Firth to the county of Sutherland, when she became aware of an uneasiness in her stomach. She drew into a lay-by at the top of the pass, with the view to the mountains of Sutherland ahead and below the long, wide mudflats of the firth that divided the counties.

"I need to stretch my legs," she explained. As they stood staring at the view, she felt hot in the cold air. *What are we doing? Why can't I leave well alone? Why am I so obsessed with Alice Ramsay?*

"Bonnie, isn't it?"

She jumped. She'd forgotten Calum was with them, as no one had spoken much on the journey.

"It is," she agreed.

McAllister reached for a cigarette. Then put the packet of Passing Clouds back. Joanne wanted him to cut down on his smoking, and the air felt like pure oxygen. I'm behaving like a married man, he thought, and didn't mind.

At the hotel, Calum thanked them for the lift.

"Time for a beer?" McAllister asked him.

"Best not," the young man replied.

"Don't tease him," Joanne said as she watched Calum, shoulders slumped, walk across the square towards home.

"I think I'll take a walk to the golf links. See you back here in an hour."

"Aye," she said. "The bar there will be open by now." And, grinning, she waved him off to the clubhouse, where he could view the links and think his ungentlemanly thoughts about golf, "the ruination of a good walk" one of his more polite descriptions of the ancient game.

She'd told him she needed to ask Mrs. Galloway about the manuscript. Why she hadn't told him her real plan was hard to admit. Her desire to find the treasure—to beat the professional searchers, to show him, and them, that she had a full working brain again—she knew was childish. He might even say dangerous.

Mrs. Galloway was at reception. "You made good time," she commented. "I'll fetch us a cup of tea."

"That would be lovely." Joanne took off her coat, settled into a chair in the lounge, where a good fire was warming the high room with large bow windows that looked across the town square. For once the passersby were not hurrying, the trickster of a sun fooling the locals into lingering in the bright, hard, yet cold sunlight.

After chatting, the conversation mainly centered around Calum and how he was faring, and with no mention of his mother, Joanne told Mrs. Galloway why she was here.

"I just need a quick look." True, she told herself, no deceit there.

"I'll call Nurse Ogilvie and tell her to expect us." She'd sensed a tension in Joanne—the hand to her hair, the way she sat forward in the chair—and wanted to help, if only by keeping her company.

They went in Mrs. Galloway's van. "Easier, as I know the way."

Joanne asked, "Have they caught whoever knocked over Mrs. Mackenzie?"

"She's on about it being someone in a big black car that did it."

"A big black car." Joanne stared at the gates of a sizable grey stone house, set back from the road at the end of a driveway that transformed into a tunnel when the oak and beech and elm and sycamore trees were in leaf. *I shouldn't be here.* "She says it was a big black car?" *I should have told McAllister why we're really here.*

"Aye, but you never know with her."

Joanne wanted to turn back. She wanted to drive, fast, to the golf clubhouse, tell McAllister it was all a mistake, and drive home to her children, to her home, to a life without spies and mysteries and death.

"Mrs. McAllister. Or is it Joanne Ross?" Nurse Ogilvie had on a professional smile. She did not want the residents distressed, and everything to do with the death of Alice Ramsay upset them. "How can we help you?"

Muriel Galloway felt the chill in the nurse's voice and said, "I'll off and say hello to Mum." In the car, she'd told Joanne how her mother had always recognized Alice Ramsay, how she was hoping that today her mother would recognize her, her own daughter.

"I'd like to examine Miss Ramsay's picture and perhaps use it in a book of her work."

"I see." As she nodded, the nurse was examining Joanne, making her doubts about the excuse clear. "It'll need taking down, then."

The handyman was called. "This is the second time in two weeks someone has asked to see this picture," he told her.

Joanne felt sick. "Oh, aye, and who was that?"

"A detective, so he said. Had a policeman's badge, but he was English."

Too late. I'm too late. "Did he say anything about the picture?"

"No. Poked around the back o' it. But nothing else."

The handyman was up the stepladder, unhooking the painting, when a shriek—a banshee wail was how Joanne later described it—cut through the muggy, overheated room.

"Alice, Alice, they're stealing your picture!"

The man handed the painting to Joanne.

The sobbing woman was pulling at her hair, spittle flying out as she continued to shout, not words but shrieks. Nurse Ogilvie was trying to calm the woman, when other residents started to cry, to moan, to rock in their chairs. Two nurses bustled in, summoned by the brass hand bell used for emergencies. It seemed a perfect illustration from a Victorian novel on Bedlam and its inhabitants, and although not usually callous, Joanne was glad of the distraction, giving her time to examine the frame and the backing.

After levering out three tacks from a corner, she slipped the scalpel she'd borrowed from Hector into the back, between frame and tape. Slicing through, she peeled away the heavy card backing. Nothing. She lifted more tacks, pulled away another few inches of backing. Still nothing.

"Let me," the handyman offered. With the back completely off, it was obvious there were no other pictures concealed behind the original. A fire blanket of disappointment made her miss what the man said.

"Finished?" he was asking.

"Sorry about the mess."

"I can fix it up later." In his outdoor overalls, he was hot and red in the stuffy airless room, and the sound of patients' cries reminded him that he too might end up an elderly baby dependent on strangers.

"Thank you." She too needed to leave the room. "God's waiting room" was a common description of old people's homes. A God lacking in charity, McAllister would have said.

Mrs. Galloway came back. She too looked like she'd been crying. "The nurse thought I should leave. Mother is not her best today," she said. That her mother stared at the wall, saying nothing, recognizing no one, was a body without a mind or a soul, she didn't share.

Joanne could see her blotchy face, her red eyes, and her hair no longer in its perfect hairspray-set waves, and all she could do was reach for her hand and hold it.

Muriel Galloway squeezed back. "It's strange she took to Alice. Maybe it was that Alice said nothing. Didn't fuss and never chatted—she just sat with the old dears and sketched." On the short drive to town, she continued, "I'm sorry you didn't meet my mother when she was all here. Lovely woman. Kindness itself. What with Mr. Mackenzie and all that, I caused her a lot of grief. It's no wonder she doesn't want to know me."

"No, it's not that. It's a condition." Joanne became passionate when mental health was discussed, confessing that formerly, she too would joke about the inmates of asylums, those with illnesses not understood and always feared. "I went through it myself briefly. Your mind goes, and it's terrifying."

Joanne could see it was no comfort. Thinking to distract her, she asked, "Has anyone been to ask you about your painting?"

"No really. Wait. After the auction, thon art expert came in for a drink and asked to look at it. We were right busy in the public bar, so I told him where it was and left him to it."

Forsythe? What did he want?

"I love the paintings; they remind me of her. We were good pals when we were young, and it was a pleasure to get to know her again when she moved back here. Alice was never a snob. It made no difference to her that I was a hotel landlady and she was an aristocrat."

"Did Alice know Mrs. Mackenzie back then?"

"We only saw her on summer holidays, when her family and friends were up here for the grouse shooting. All us children would play together, out all hours in those long nights."

"And nothing . . ." Joanne paused to think how to phrase the question. "Nothing *important* happened when you were children?"

"Important enough for someone to want to kill her, you mean?"

Joanne had forgotten how sharp Mrs. Galloway was. And forgotten that she too had doubts. "No," she began slowly, thinking out loud. "But I've found often that it's the small things, what seems a silly childhood game or a trick or . . ." *Humiliation*, she was about to say. "They can poison people's lives."

"Big things too, like stealing their husband." Mrs. Galloway began to laugh. "Sorry, shouldn't laugh, but I'm right happy. We've decided, what with Calum living away from home, we—Mr. Mackenzie and me—are finally going to live together."

No mention of divorce. Or remarriage. Only "live together." And from Mrs. Galloway's voice and her smile and the way she held her head up, looking straight at Joanne with no sense of shame, she wished them happiness.

"Congratulations. Take it from me, a divorced woman . . ."

Mrs. Galloway's mouth dropped at that.

"You will not regret it. And to heck with what anyone says."

"Thank you, Joanne."

Mrs. Galloway fetched the ladder and took down the picture. Joanne laid it on a dining-room table, facedown, to examine it.

"Looks like someone has had a go at removing the back," Mrs. Galloway said. "Why on earth?" She saw Joanne flush. "Maybe best not to know."

They removed the back. Joanne checked the layers of backing board. Nothing. "That's my theory shot to pieces," she said.

"What are you looking for?"

"Mrs. Galloway—Muriel—I don't want to involve you in something that could bring trouble to your door." It was a trivial phrase to describe the horror of being watched, having the telephone line tapped, the house broken into and searched, her and McAllister's private lives examined, to sense that someone was there in the shadows over her shoulder.

Muriel looked at Joanne. Her eyes said it all, but she added, simply and clearly, with no doubts, no hesitation, "I want to know why Alice died."

"Me too."

Joanne did not want to breathe, to break the spell, the magic of mutual understanding, the awfulness of saying out loud what they had both been avoiding. *Someone killed Alice.*

"There's a drawing Alice did of me in my bedroom. Only Mr. Mackenzie knows about it."

Standing in the large bow window of the bright, airy bedroom with a view over the graveyard, the intimacy of the room disturbed Joanne. The his and her sides of the bed. The scent of sleep. Above all, the tender eroticism of the drawing hanging above the high wood headboard made her feel an intruder into their lives. Their love.

"It's beautiful," she whispered.

"Aye. I told Alice it was far too flattering."

Once Joanne might have agreed. Yet in the lines around the half-closed eyes, in the hair tumbling over freckled shoulders, in the tilt of her neck, in the soft folds of skin between the barely covered breasts, a different Muriel, perhaps the real Muriel, glowed.

Mrs. Galloway went over to the drawing and took it off the wall. "Right, let's get it down and check." She was embarrassed. And delighted. She'd wanted to show off the portrait to someone. Yet she knew no one she could share such an intimate portrait with. Until now.

Joanne removed small brass tacks with small electrical pliers. Next, she prized off an outer board of thin plywood.

"She framed it herself," Mrs. Galloway said. "Very handy with carpentry tools was Alice."

Joanne felt the extra layers and wished she were alone. But nothing would make Mrs. Galloway leave, not now it was clear there was something behind the picture.

"It's a drawing," Muriel whispered.

They took the portrait down to the empty dining room. Joanne turned back the protective cover and stared. The scene was a dinner party. The setting she guessed was Mediterranean, until she saw the outline of a minaret through an open arched doorway.

Three of the men were leaning inwards, heads almost touching. "Conspirators" was the word Joanne immediately thought of. To one side of the frame, as separate as Judas and drawn in profile, was an older man. "Observer," she would say of him, but he, the fourth man, would be hard to identify.

"May I take this?" Joanne asked.

"Will it help find her killer?" It was clear Mrs. Galloway was reluctant to let the drawing go.

"You really don't believe she killed herself?" Joanne needed to know it wasn't only her who doubted the official verdict.

"I always found it hard to credit. And—"

"Ah, there you are." McAllister walked in, smelling of beer and wind. "What's that? Another of Alice's paintings?"

Joanne jumped. Caught out, she blushed, saying, "I had this idea that maybe I should check—you know."

"Good thinking. We've come all this way to give Calum a lift to see his mother, so why not?"

When he smiled, Joanne guessed that he'd foreseen there was more to their journey.

"May I see?"

Mrs. Galloway said, "It's a fine drawing."

"It is," Joanne agreed.

"You look really beautiful," McAllister said.

Muriel Galloway blushed and said thank you and desperate to have his attention elsewhere she pushed the other drawing towards him.

"Ah. This really *is* special." From McAllister's voice and the way he sat down, staring at the subjects, Joanne could sense his fascination. "I think perhaps I recognize—"

Joanne nudged him. He looked at her. And at Muriel Galloway. "On second thoughts, I'm not so sure."

"Is this what everyone is looking for?" Joanne asked.

"Perhaps." He was staring at the back of the drawing. In pencil was a list of numbers. They began with a letter, followed by a single digit, a slash, then a string of numbers. There were twelve in all. The column of numbers was scrawled, the spacing close, and not every symbol completely formed. This was written in a hurry, he decided.

"What's it about?" Muriel Galloway asked.

"Best you don't know," he replied. "But we need to take it, and I can't guarantee you'll get it back."

"I don't want it." Mrs. Galloway had seen in McAllister's face a hint of fear. And excitement. His long, hard stare, as though trying to guess not who the men were but *what* they were, scared her. "As long as I get to keep my portrait, no, I don't mind."

"Thank you." He added, "I will try to keep where it was discovered secret." Top secret, he was thinking. He glanced up at Joanne. Saw her sitting slumped in the dining chair, elbows on the table, head resting on her hands. "It's time we left. Long drive ahead. Thank you again."

"I've made soup—won't you have some before you set off?" Mrs. Galloway asked.

"Sorry." He took Joanne's arm with one hand, steering her out to the car. In the other, still between the protective sheets of paper, was the drawing. "Sorry," he said again as he went to open the driver's door. "We'll stop in Tain or Dingwall for something to eat. But I need to get out of here."

"I want to drive. You need to think. And smoke. But with the windows down."

Joanne kept to the main coastal road; the climb over the shorter but tortuous route over the pass she knew would not be safe. Not in her condition of excitement with a strong dash of fear. The first hour of the drive, they said little. It was when she felt the ache in her shoulders, noticed her knuckles tight around the steering wheel and drained of blood that she knew she needed to stop. Invergordon, there was sure to be a café there. There wasn't. It being Saturday afternoon, nothing was open; it was half closing day for shops and too early for the pubs.

Just past the town, she drew into a lay-by on the shoreline of the firth. "Need to stretch my legs," she said.

"Me too," he answered.

Although chilly, it was clear. Fluffy clouds were reflected in the still, flat water of the firth. Spreading clouds of rotting bladder seaweed made picking their way over shingle difficult. McAllister paused, searched the sea stones, and picked out four flat skimming stones. He handed two to Joanne.

He threw first. "Six."

She threw next. "Eight!"

His turn. "Seven."

Her turn. "Six." She laughed. "Thirteen skips to fourteen. I win!"

"One more throw settles it."

"No, let's get home."

Just before the main bridge into town, they stopped for a fish supper. They decided to eat the fish and chips—which came wrapped in an old issue of the *Gazette*—on a bench facing the river and the castle.

"I needed that," she said, licking the grease from her fingers. "I was starving."

When they arrived home, after she'd switched off the engine, she didn't move, just sat, staring into shadows. She whispered, "Is it safe?"

With the girls at their grandparents' for the night, with no lights on, no music coming from the sitting room, and no smoke from the chimney, all life had departed from their home.

"I'm pretty sure it is, but . . ." He told her, "I have a plan. Move over, I'll drive."

She laughed when he registered them as Mr. and Mrs. Smith and told the receptionist, "No, no luggage."

She loved the clean sheets, the endless hot water, and the suggestion that this was a belated honeymoon.

She understood when he said, "Tomorrow. Time enough to talk about it tomorrow."

But she insisted the drawing, in the envelope, in her handbag, be placed between their pillows.

◆ ◆ ◆

That McAllister was asking to meet in his solicitor's office made DI Dunne curious. But not worried.

When he heard what McAllister had to say, he was shocked. "You did what?" It came out louder than the policeman intended.

"We found a drawing by Miss Alice Ramsay. I believe it is what Hennessey and his colleagues were searching for. I had it photographed and copies printed. Four are in sealed envelopes and placed with reliable people. They will only be opened on my personal say-so."

"You were told to drop the matter. You were reminded of the Official Secrets Act. Do you know what you've done?"

"Not really," McAllister said. "But I've given up trusting anyone—even you, Inspector."

Angus MacLean had agreed to be a silent witness yet found it hard not to smile when John McAllister, respectable editor of a local newspaper, implied that a senior policeman who he now knew to be with Special Branch, a senior representative of the Foreign Office, and a local detective renowned for his integrity were untrustworthy.

"So where is the original drawing?"

"In a bank vault. Not that I expect that to be a problem for those shady branches of the security services. But it will be difficult and time-consuming, and what can they do to me without raising a hell of a fuss?"

"Clap you in irons in the castle dungeons?" the solicitor joked.

DI Dunne frowned. "What are you hoping to achieve, Mr. McAllister?"

McAllister heard the "Mr." and knew the policeman was distancing himself. "I don't want to know about spies or betrayals or state secrets. I want my family left in peace. I will not have my wife scared to be alone in her own house. And I want the death of Miss Ramsay explained."

So that Joanne can stop obsessing over it, he would never say. But DI Dunne guessed.

McAllister added, "Inspector, you have been witness to most of the interviews. You must have the measure of these people." He needed a cigarette but had left the packet in the office as part of his cutting-down regime. "It didn't occur to me until after we found the drawing that this is what Hennessey hoped for. He couldn't risk any more searches, so he described the portrait in detail to my wife. He guessed, rightly, that she couldn't resist looking for it."

DI Dunne didn't contradict him.

Here McAllister took a deep breath and spoke as though

being interviewed. "I wish you to pass on this information, Inspector. I will be keeping the original drawing until I have an explanation, an apology, and a guarantee that this is the end of the matter." He stood. "No doubt, I will be hearing from them soon."

"No doubt," echoed Angus MacLean.

DI Dunne left. From his deep sigh, they could hear, and see, he was not happy.

As they shook hands, the solicitor said, "I have news on your bid for the house."

✦　✦　✦

When McAllister returned home, Joanne asked, "Did you do what we agreed?"

"I did. Now we wait." He put his hands on her shoulders, facing her. "I have other news."

She was too scared to look up at him.

And feeling her tremble, understanding her fears, he quickly said, "I'm afraid we didn't get the house."

She said, "Is that all? I thought you were about to tell me something serious."

He hugged her. Held her close. Felt her shake. He stepped back, looked at her. She began to smile. Then laugh. "You're hopeless, McAllister. That's twice you've lost a bid. Next time, I'm taking charge of business."

He agreed.

"It's only a house, McAllister. No one's life is at stake."

CHAPTER 22

❧

My oh my, they are all so fixed in their public-schoolboy code of conduct they can never envisage that a woman could be intelligent enough to outwit them.

Though now that they suspect I know, I could lose everything; traitors cannot afford to leave loose ends.

It was such fun in the beginning. I've known D since we were children, when we would join the adults for the shooting season.

We children were sent by train, with our governesses, with the baggage, with all the accoutrements for the deer stalking, and salmon fishing, and hiking, plus our frocks for tea-parties and, of course, the Hunt Ball.

The Hunt Balls were a de facto marriage market. Us sweet young things—awkward, blushing, barely educated, potential breeding stock— were on display much like slave women in a marketplace.

Even sheltered in our Swiss finishing schools, we girls knew who was available, who their family was, their lineage, their income, and which marriage would consolidate the family fortune—or lack thereof. Some of our chums were marrying Americans for their fortunes.

Meeting up again as adults in those prewar years, working in affiliated services, attending the same parties in Cairo, and Istanbul, and Paris, to say nothing of our social life at home, what fun we had. The champagne bills must have been astronomical.

Sisters, wives, husbands, cousins, friends; we all knew one another well.

Or so we thought.

⋆ ⋆ ⋆

Don McLeod had heard many bizarre tales in his life but none quite as bizarre as this.

"If it hadn't been for Westland vouching for him, I was beginning to think Mr. Stuart—if that was his name—and our newest spy, Mr. Hennessey, are from one and the same department."

"Perhaps they are."

"We have no way of knowing." McAllister was speaking through the smoke steaming out of him like a kettle on the boil. His voice indicated the same held-in pressure.

Don knew to sit back, let his editor release the pressure, and only then would they begin at the beginning, analyzing every moment, every incident, every nuance of the scandal, knowing they could never print.

"I'd like you to keep this safe." McAllister handed Don an envelope with the original drawing. "Put it in a bank, maybe, but not in my name."

"Nor mine." Don thought for a second. "I'll put it in the Darts Club deposit box. I'm on the committee, but my name's on nothing official."

When Don left, McAllister began a systematic series of phone calls to everyone he could think of. As casually as he could, and knowing a great many explanations, or lies, would be needed, he'd say, "I'm researching a piece about the lack of investment in the Highlands. Along the lines of 'we pay the same taxes as everyone, but what do we get?'"

The editor of the *Sutherland Courier* suggested that upgrading the A9 from the lowlands to John o' Groats was a priority. "And a new bridge across the firth," he added.

The answers were different, but all were of the same ilk.

After he'd heard McAllister out, and realizing he had no idea why the editor had called, Angus MacLean said, "You are investigating the allocation of government money and thinking you might ruffle a few feathers. Got it." He recognized a cover story when he heard one.

"I hope not," McAllister replied.

Peter Kowalski, friend and prominent businessman-about-town, was next to receive a baffling phone call from McAllister. "You are trying to find out how exactly the government in London spends our taxes?"

"Exactly. Although it might stir up some unwanted attention from some governmental—"

"I never discuss politics," Peter said. *On the telephone*, he meant. A Polish refugee who had escaped the Nazis, Kowalski was now settled, and safe, in the Highlands and more aware than most of the powers of secret services of all varieties.

McAllister left a message for Sandy Marshall. Then, last, he wrote a letter to the chairman of the board of the *Gazette*, again stating his articles might stir up controversy but that he was doing his job as an investigative journalist believing it would increase the standing, and the circulation, of the *Highland Gazette*.

He had alerted all the people he could think of and felt better. *So if I should disappear or be knocked over by a car, someone will check.*

◆　◆　◆

The police constable tried Calum Mackenzie's lodgings.

"He came back yesterday, and he's at work, as far as I know," the landlady said.

Next, he tried the *Gazette*.

"Aye, Calum was in first thing this morning. Haven't seen him since." Don didn't add that he'd told Calum to leave and only come back when he had an article worth publishing. "Chase a cat up a tree, then call the fire brigade if you have to!" he'd shouted at Calum.

"I believe his fiancée works at the hospital," the policeman said.

"Aye, so I heard. Anything I can help you with?"

"No thanks Mr. McLeod, it's personal."

When the constable left, Don lit up. He knew that look of panic-stricken dread; cadet reporters experienced it when doorstepping the newly bereaved. People of the first half of the war-torn twentieth century knew it from a knock on the door, a uniform, a telegram. Don knew that the young constable's face would burn, words scorching his throat, how he would wake up in the night, reliving that part of his job he would never become cynical about, breaking the news to the oblivious wife, husband, children, family. He knew it only became easier to bear if, or most likely when, the policeman or the reporter lost his humanity. Or took to drink.

Whatever it is Calum lad, I'm sorry I was so hard on you. He groaned. He picked up the phone and called Joanne on the off chance Calum was there. Engaged. Ten minutes later, the telephone still engaged, he decided to walk over for a cup of tea. Maybe check up on Joanne whilst there; not that he'd tell her that—Joanne became pretty feisty if she thought she was being protected.

Joanne recognized the shape through the glass. "Hold on, Sandy, Don's at the door."

She put a hand over the mouthpiece and called out, "Come on in. Won't be a sec."

Don went to the kitchen and put on the kettle.

She returned to her phone call. "Really, Sandy, that man's got the hide of a rhinoceros."

"I know. But at least one mystery is solved. He and Miss Ramsay knew each other at the College of Art."

"Was that the name she went by? Alice Ramsay?"

"I don't know. Why?"

"You need McAllister to explain."

"Aye, well. I also checked up on Hennessey. He is with the Foreign Office, though which department is impossible to know." Sandy was aware his line might be tapped in spite of the laws and safeguards that prohibited tapping a newspaper telephone.

"I don't want to think about those men," she said. "But thanks for letting me know about Forsythe."

"Buy tomorrow's newspaper. Dougald Forsythe blows his own trumpet so well he should take up politics."

"Heaven forfend."

Don was reading yesterday's *Scotsman* when Joanne joined him, saying, "That was Sandy Marshall. He was telling me about Mr. Forsythe. He's donated the Leonardo drawing to the School of Art as an example of a master forgery. He says he knew all along and only wanted to show up the art establishment. According to Sandy, he's making out that he's an all-round great guy and only— What's wrong? Is it McAllister?" She dropped to the chair.

"I left McAllister punching the life out of his typewriter. No, nothing's wrong, I'm only here for a cup of tea."

The doorbell rang. The front door opened. Whoever was there was not a stranger. "Joanne? Hello?"

"In the kitchen."

Elaine was in her uniform. She was a mess of hair escaping her nurse's cap, pink-rimmed eyes, and a smear of snot on the collar of the blue dress. She would not look out of place in a portrait of Highlanders fleeing Culloden. "I can't find Calum. I've no idea where he went. How am I going to tell him? He'll never cope."

"What is it?" Don asked. Remembering the policeman who'd been to the office looking for Calum, he knew he'd been right to be uneasy.

"Excuse me a moment." Elaine went to the sink, wetted a hankie, wiped her eyes, then began. "Sister called me into her office. Told me to call my mum." She'd been terrified that the bad news concerned her family.

The telling was secondhand, but in her mind's eye Elaine was there, in the hotel she'd worked in as part-time receptionist, housemaid, and waitress on Saturdays from when she was fourteen until she'd left school. She'd known everyone at the gathering since she was a baby. As she repeated the story to Joanne and Don, she did the voices, the gestures. Perhaps not word-for-word accurate but certainly sentiment-perfect, Elaine spoke the picture, word-painted the scene.

"Last night at the hotel, it was a going-away do for Mrs. Byrne, the chiropodist. She's flitting to Aberdeen as her husband has a new job. Mum was there with my auntie and a bunch of friends. No one asked *her* to the do, because no one wanted her there. The excuse was that she needs a wheelchair."

Joanne and Don didn't need to be told who *her* was.

"They never saw her come in. She tells Calum she can't walk much, but last night she was mobile enough to get herself to the hotel and scream and shout and carry on."

"Poor Calum."

"Aye, poor Mrs. Galloway an' all." Elaine began to cry again. "I still don't understand how it could have happened."

The doorbell rang. Don said, "I'll get it." He came back with Calum.

"What are you doing here?" Calum was staring at his fiancée, could see something was badly wrong, but daren't ask.

"Sit down, lad." Don gestured to the chair next to Elaine.

Calum looked at her.

Reaching into her sleeve for the already sodden hankie, she was unable to look back at him.

"Mum! Is she aa' right?" Calum felt Elaine's hand cover his. He saw Mrs. McAllister looking down at the tablecloth. He felt every second of the *tick-tock* from the clock in the hallway. "Tell me."

Elaine accepted that part of a nurse's duties was breaking bad news. Doctors were hopeless at it, Matron told them. Men were hopeless at it, was Elaine's opinion.

Speaking quietly, with a calm and wisdom of the wise woman she would surely become, she said, "My mum was at a party in the hotel with Mrs. Galloway and about eight or nine others. Your mum wasn't invited, but she came anyway. She was furious she was left out." *Even though she would have refused the invitation*, Elaine and Calum knew. "There was a scene, and your mother accused Mrs. Galloway of running her over."

"She doesn't mean it. Sorry, Elaine, but Mum sometimes makes things up." He told her this as though it were news.

"I know, Calum. I've always known." She continued, hand over his. "Your mum was hysterical, saying over and over that Muriel was driving the big black car that ran her over and tried to kill her."

That it was checking up on the same car that Calum had lost his job over Elaine did not know.

"There's more." Heads almost touching, they formed a universe of Calum and Elaine; no one else existed. "Your dad heard the commotion. He came in, and when he understood he said to your mother, 'It was me. I was driving the car. I was the one who tried to kill you. I'm only sorry I didn't do a proper job.'"

Elaine paused to let the information sink in. She was wondering if her own relationship would withstand the disaster, and decided it would.

Elaine—via her mother—now knew how they had talked, planned, decided; at last, they were to be together. Now this—Mrs. Galloway's dear wee man would be put on trial and jailed for attempted murder. She was certain Mrs. Mackenzie would report her husband to the police, if only to devastate Muriel. And everyone in the hotel in Sutherland and in the McAllisters' kitchen knew it too.

Calum was bouncing. His knees were uncontrollable; his eyes moved here and there, fixing nowhere. "Dad's just saying that to shut Mum up. He'd never ever harm anyone."

"Your dad said he borrowed the big black car. It was in for a service. He waited for your mum to lock up. Then he drove at her from behind, with the lights out. He knocked her over, didn't check if she was alive but hoped she was dead."

Elaine's mother told her that when he said that, Mrs. Mackenzie fainted. *Or pretended to faint—you never know what's real with that woman.*

"He put the car back in the garage, then went back to the golf clubhouse. It all took only twenty minutes, so your dad said, and no one noticed him gone, as it was a right busy night there."

"Where is Dad now? Have the police charged him or what?"

"No. No one's said anything to the police about your dad's confession."

Don knew that in small communities, an unspoken code of silence could descend. The police would know but be unable to prove anything.

"Early this morning, still dark, apparently, your dad took his car and left the hotel. Mrs. Galloway said he was driving down here to speak to you."

Elaine left out her conversation with Mrs. Galloway. *He wanted to tell Calum himself. Wanted to speak to him before thon witch poisoned her son against his dad.* The rest of the conversation had consisted of wailing and crying and sobbing. Elaine was hearing the pain even now.

"Calum, there was an accident. Black ice, the police said. The car went off the road at thon steep stretch before Bonar Bridge."

"He's dead." Calum's voice was flat.

"He is."

Joanne rose. Feeling like an intruder, she went to the sitting room, leaving the couple to themselves.

Don joined her. "Bad do," he said.

Joanne was sitting in her husband's chair. She needed the scent of him. No comment was necessary.

Five minutes later, Elaine came in. "There's a train at ten past the hour. We need to go home."

"I'll give you a lift to the station," Don said.

Elaine telephoned her ward sister to explain. With Calum holding her hand, unable to speak, they left for the station.

In the kitchen with the undrunk cups of tea and the residue of heartbreak, Joanne understood she needed release. She went into the sitting room, opened the piano, and began to play. At first, she played a Liszt sonata. Then she began to hum. Without any intention, the music changed. It flowed through her fingers, and she began to half-sing, half-hum. It was half a minute or so before she recognized the song.

"Westlin Winds" was perhaps her favorite Burns song, an autumn song, although now it was winter. She knew most of the words, but the fourth and fifth verses she struggled to remember correctly, and in struggling she was distracted. But some lines of the last verse she knew. Spoken, she'd call them soppy or maudlin. Sung, they were tender and true.

> *We'll gently walk and sweetly talk*
> *Till the silent moon shines clearly,*
> *I'll grasp thy waist and, fondly pressed,*
> *Swear how I love thee dearly*

McAllister could hear the piano from the garden gate. Closing the front door quietly, he stood in the hallway and felt the notes and the lyrics penetrate his skin. And his heart. He knew then that all would be well with his Joanne.

CHAPTER 23

I didn't want the responsibility of a dog. But he found his own way up here, so he can find his own way back. The hens I can always set loose. They'll survive for a time—as long as a fox doesn't find them.

I'll need to climb into the barn rafters for the emergency rucksack. One spare set of clothes and extra passports, that's all I need. I'll take the small folding painting box I had custom-made in London. It fits the cover of eccentric lady artist. I'll be sorry to leave the camera, though. It has an excellent lens. I remember clearly the day I bought it in that small shop near Potszdamer Platz in Berlin.

No maps, no camera, and no mementos, travel as lightly as possible. No identifying objects, unless they are part of one's cover. Remember your tradecraft—Moscow Rules, we called them.

If I ever have to leave in a hurry, I will not be parted from my walking boots. Someone who knows their job would be able to identify me from them. It's a risk I will have to take. If I have to leave, I will abandon the manuscript. That would hurt.

The walk out of the glen, over the hills, and crossing the hours and hours of peat bogs and heather and bracken in the high country, is one I've walked twice—but only in early and late summer. Then it's down to the opposite coast and the railway line—or a boat. For part of the way, I can use the old drover's road. Overnight campsites where the men would rest the sheep or the cattle are still there—if you know how to look. A cluster of trees—birch, willow, hawthorn, running water, shelter amongst rocks or a fold in the earth, that's where the drovers and traveling people would rest on the long trek to the livestock auctions in Tain or Dingwall.

But in winter, it's a much harder and riskier hike. I'm not as fit as I once was. Hence the boots.

She opens the tin of dubbin, wipes off the dust, and begins applying a fresh coat of the waterproof emulsion. Finished, she stands the boots on a sheet of newspaper to dry thoroughly.

"Be prepared," she says to the dog.

Boy Scouts motto. She remembers telling them, more than once, that the service reminded her of the Boy Scouts. Spies, secret agents, plotting, and planning, they are boys masquerading as men, reliving their childhood fantasies of daring or dastardly deeds, believing themselves invincible. And untouchable. Until someone is killed. Or turns traitor.

◆ ◆ ◆

With the house to herself, Joanne stood at the kitchen window, seeing nothing, no hills, no mountains, no distant smudge of forest, no sky, no discernible clouds, only a dome of thick, smooth grey, much the color of an army blanket unwashed for years. She went into the hallway to telephone; she still saw nothing, only the hook where the still life with red onions had hung. The mirror she ignored. She went to pick up the receiver. Stopped.

"I'm with Superintendent Westland. I'll be back in about an hour," he'd said—an hour ago.

She knew then that their plan had worked. If the superintendent was back again, someone somewhere wanted that drawing. It had begun. And she desperately wanted it ended.

The doorbell rang at half past eight. Late enough for Jean to be in bed, early enough for Annie to be up.

Joanne wanted to ignore it, but when it rang a second time, she knew she must answer, or her daughter would worry.

"Mum," Annie called out, "I'll go."

"Stay in the dining room," Joanne snapped. "Shut the door, and don't come out until I tell you."

The girl was terrified. This was the voice and these were the words her mother used when her father was drunk, with his fists ready to lash out at his wife. Annie said nothing but pressed herself against the dining-room door, listening for whoever had frightened her mum.

"Oh, it's you. McAllister will be here any minute."

"Can I come in?"

Annie sensed her mother's hesitation.

"Your husband said to meet here."

The girl knew it must be safe when her mother said, "Sorry. Yes. Of course. Come into the sitting room."

Joanne came into the dining room, where Annie was pretending to do her French homework, and said, "It's best you go to your room now."

Annie looked up, was about to protest, saw her mother's forced smile and decided not to argue. "All right."

"Thanks. We will explain in the morning."

A scant five minutes later, Annie was in her room when McAllister's car arrived. She watched him and the big man in a police uniform walk down the path.

When I'm a writer, I'm going to have adventures like McAllister, she decided.

Annie waited, watching. An hour and ten minutes later, she awoke, in a folded-up position against her bedroom windowsill, her neck stiff and feet frozen. A car door slammed. The car drove off. She heard the front door being locked. She heard her mother come upstairs. Then McAllister's heavier tread. Now she could sleep in her bed.

* * *

Next morning, still dark and only half past six, Annie heard the toilet flush, then footsteps going downstairs. She put on her dressing gown and slippers. As she yawned, she saw a cloud form and noticed ice on the inside of the window. Soon be Christmas, she thought.

McAllister was alone in the kitchen. "Want some coffee?" he asked when she came in.

"Mum says I'm too young."

He poured her a cup anyhow but added milk.

She sipped it and pretended she liked it. "What's going on?"

"An expert wants to discuss the manuscript your mum has been working on."

"This is about Miss Ramsay, the artist."

Annie Ross was observant and relentless and needed to know what was happening to feel safe. Through eavesdropping in doorways, listening for pauses, for the breaking off of a conversation, staying quiet, watching whilst buried in a book, she would review conversations and situations and judge if her mother was in harm's way.

"Yes, Miss Alice Ramsay, the artist." *And who knows what else besides?* McAllister did not lie, nor did he dismiss her concerns. Occasionally, like now, he would silently curse her father for having caused his children and his wife perpetual anxiety.

"Will mum be back tonight?"

"They've said she will *probably* be back tonight. But no promises."

Annie hated open-ended sentences ending in "soon" or "it's nothing" or "we'll see" and words like "probably" and "promise." Her first nine years of life in a household scarred by alcohol and violence, both physical and mental, had programmed her to disbelieve adults. When told everything would be "fine," she was ready for the worst.

"I'm going back to bed to read," Annie said when Joanne came in. "See you tonight, Mum." She left quickly, but not before Joanne could see her eyes.

"Annie looks as scared as me." Joanne tried to smile. But failed. She was furious with herself for starting the whole debacle. And more furious still with these mysterious men and their secret scandals concerning distant strangers, how they came to the Highlands, tainting the glen with death.

"I'll look after her. You ready?" He nodded at her carpetbag, where he knew that, along with a change of clothes and a book or three, his wife would have packed her knitting.

Reading his mind, she joked, "I've put in my Shetland steel knitting needles. A brilliant weapon against spies and traitors, don't you think?"

She passed the hall mirror to fetch her coat. There stood a stranger, a faded, anxious, middle-aged woman in a none-too-smart blouse, with hair looking like she'd stepped in from a force ten hurricane. She went upstairs to change, to brush her hair, before giving up and putting on a Fair Isle beret—anything to waste time until Hennessey and Superintendent Westland came to fetch her. And to avoid talking to her husband lest he change his mind. She had agreed to go with them, no questions asked.

So had McAllister. "But only because of Superintendent Westland's assurances," he'd told Hennessey the previous night. "And only if the superintendent accompanies you."

"Joanne?" Hennessey had looked at her for confirmation, and she liked him better for it. He understood she was a woman who made her own decisions.

"I'm coming with you because you have given your word this will be the end of it." *Make sure it is* went unsaid. "And yes, I insist that Superintendent Westland comes too." She could see it wasn't in Hennessey's original plan and was pleased they had won one small victory.

She put on red lipstick for courage. She dabbed on McAllister's cologne for consolation, but her best blouse was in the ironing pile. "Drat and blast and . . ." She set up the ironing board and ironed the bits that would show. "Hennessey—if that's your name—I hope you appreciate the effort," she murmured, knowing the effort was for her alone.

◆ ◆ ◆

Joanne came home near midnight. She hugged her husband, then went upstairs to kiss the girls. McAllister opened some wine. When she returned, they settled by a fire of spitting spruce logs to talk.

She sipped the wine and didn't shudder. "I'm beginning to like this." She smiled, holding up the glass and staring at the fire through the ruby liquid.

"Salut." He raised a glass to her. "Since we aren't buying a new house just yet, let's go to Paris and drink wine in Montmartre."

"We flew to Ireland today."

"Did you now?" He was not expecting that.

"Not that anyone said we were in Ireland, but the weather was so clear I recognized the geography and the sea crossing over the Mull of Kintyre. I've never flown before. Scotland is really beautiful." She nodded at the memory.

He watched her, saw her trying to unravel a story so big she was unsure how to begin.

"I'm surprised they didn't make me wear a blindfold."

With that joke, he knew she was fine.

"I was given a present." She passed him an envelope. "Open it."

Between the hard outer cover and the frontispiece, on paper torn from a sketchbook with the perforations uneven, was a pencil portrait of Joanne. In her wool jacket with her Celtic cross brooch, her hair escaping from the Fair Isle beret, in the half-smile, the searching eyes, it was more than a good likeness; it captured the passion and compassion of his wife.

"It's wonderful."

"Turn it over."

The line of overly familiar writing said, "We should have been friends, but alas." The signature said, "Alice Ramsay."

"Did you know?"

"It was why I agreed to your going."

"You should have told me."

"I know. But that was also part of the agreement. Alice Ramsay wasn't sure if, given a choice, you'd want to meet her again."

Their voices had been low. Their thoughts racing. "Perhaps," she acknowledged. She sipped the wine. That and the fire began to thaw her insides. She settled back in the chair, ready to tell a tale that she was yet to fully understand.

"We landed on a small airstrip outside a town in what I imagine was Northern Ireland. The men, in RAF uniforms, were expecting us. Hennessey showed some papers. Superintendent Westland and I were ignored. Then a big black car arrived, and we were driven through lovely countryside—a bit like here but less wild—for just under an hour." She didn't tell him that on the journey, there and back, barely five words were spoken between the three of them.

"We drove through high gates set in a high stone wall. There was a lodge house and a security barrier, and the papers were checked again." She said nothing about how trapped she'd felt. In the small aeroplane, in the car, she'd scared herself thinking, *I know no one here. I don't have change for the phone. If there are phones. I am completely alone.* Even Westland was no longer a supportive Scottish policeman. *He is one of them.*

"A mile or so on, we reached a biggish loch and a smallish baronial castle with long lawns going down to the water's edge. It looked rather grand until we went closer. Then you could see how badly maintained it was. There were dogs running around. Not nice family dogs, big Alsatian guard dogs. The man who called them away was in uniform. I don't know which branch of the army . . ." Joanne's speech was fading, but he knew she needed to finish, else she would not sleep properly.

"Then you met Alice?"

"Sorry." A roll of the shoulders, a sip of wine, her neck relaxed, and he was glad. "We were shown into a sitting room. I stood in the middle, probably with my mouth open, and stared. Hennessey said, 'I believe you have met. Mrs. McAllister, Miss Ramsay, we'll leave you to it.'"

"Westland knew. I could see he knew. I was furious with Hennessey, with all of them. I told him so, and all he said was to ring if I needed him, pointing to a bell next to the mantelpiece marked 'Butler.'"

"What was Miss Ramsay doing?"

"Nothing. Sitting by the fire, legs crossed, watching, waiting. When the men had left, she said, 'Hello, Joanne, I never thought we'd meet again.' I said, 'Me neither.'"

As she said it, McAllister could hear her *Me neither.* That slightly perplexed, slightly cross expression that usually preceded an offhand remark like *me neither* or *you're kidding* or *oh, really* he knew to be her well-brought-up-daughter-of-the-manse way of hiding anger.

"You were so persistent in your belief that I would not take my own life you had my colleagues worried. Good for you." Alice smiled.

Not *former* colleagues, Joanne noted as she waited and watched. This is not the person I remember, she thought, but I can't fathom how just yet.

"I can only offer a partial explanation. I hope it is enough."

Joanne said nothing, just waited.

"I joined the service in the mid-nineteen-thirties, not long after I'd left art school. We 'gals' were recruited in an informal way, through family connections and acquaintances. They were particularly interested in women like me who spoke languages, had traveled abroad, so we already knew our way around the continent.

"Initially, I was a clerk listening in to German radio chatter, translating documents, and all that. From meetings, discussions, and the circulation of top-secret documents, we were excluded, even though we knew the content. They believed only men could decipher the intelligence. Ha! What arrogance!

"Then my talent for drawing came up. I used to do party sketches to amuse my friends. The head of my section also discovered my photographic memory." She was shaking her head. "Serves me right for being such a show-off. It would have been much, much safer if I'd stuck to being a lady artist."

"Is that how you met Dougald Forsythe?"

"He was plain Douglas then. Dougie to his friends. Yes. After school in Switzerland, I didn't know what to do, so I enrolled in the Glasgow School of Art—it has an excellent reputation for drawing. We were lovers until I overheard him showing off in a bar that I was his 'posh totty.'"

Again, Joanne noticed that smile, a knowing smile, a smile that said, *What a fool I was.* "It went both ways. He was definitely not one of us."

"He can be charming." Joanne was remembering his heavy hair, his wide smile, the way he spoke on the phone, implying the possibility of an affair.

"Oh, yes. Charm aplenty. But unscrupulous in the way a man from an impoverished family, with huge ambition and not enough talent, can be." She reached for the bell rope and pulled.

Superintendent Westland quickly appeared.

"Would you order fresh tea?" Alice asked. "And sandwiches?" She didn't ask what Joanne would prefer. And she did not seem aware she was treating a very senior policeman as a butler.

"Is there anything I can get you, Mrs. McAllister?" he asked.

"I'm fine," she replied. And they smiled at each other with their eyes only.

The pause in the telling felt like the interval in a play. Their theater was this large high-ceilinged room, with long casement windows looking out over a stone terrace and the loch beyond. The theatrical backdrop was a layer of mountains aching to be painted. The silence was not uncomfortable; neither had much to say to the other outside of the story.

When the tea came, after they ate and drank and chatted about the weather being delightfully clear for December, Alice continued. She spoke rapidly. She wanted the meeting over with.

"My wartime activities I can't discuss. Nor the present debacle. Official Secrets Act, you know."

This remark had a tinge of superiority to it that Joanne didn't appreciate. But she let it all pass. And Joanne could well believe

Alice's account of working for the government. In her own brief stint as an army messenger, some officers treated her as an object to be patted, physically and metaphorically. "Good girl," they'd say, in the same tone as they'd say "Good dog."

"Of course, it was disastrous when Guy Burgess and Donald Maclean went missing."

Joanne sensed a hesitation over the name Donald, but couldn't be certain.

"I felt there was something not quite right in the department for years but assumed the big boys knew what they were doing. When it was revealed those two were traitors and in Moscow, so much codswallop of denials and damage limitation was published. The prime minister made a statement assuring the public that that was an end to it. But I and a few others were never convinced."

Alice leaned forward. In her sturdy corduroy trousers, stout brown boots, Aran jumper, closely clipped hair, and a body that was feminine, yet not, her face resembled a classical statue. Not marble. Perhaps basalt. Joanne also saw that Alice might pass as a man.

"I am—was—only an intelligence operative whose department reinvented people, creating an imagined past with all the documents and folderol to complete the new identity."

"Much like an author," Joanne commented.

"Absolutely."

"So why did—"

"There was suspicion that there was a third man who'd warned Maclean and Burgess that they were about to be uncovered. It couldn't be proved. In fact, in a formal inquiry, it was dismissed as paranoia. Before I left, I told Ruraidh my plans."

She saw Joanne's question.

"Oops. Security breach. Forget the name, or we may have to lock you in the Tower."

"Mary Queen of Scots was locked in the Tower."

"I also mentioned that I agreed with the third-man theory. He expressed no opinion, only asked if I'd shared this with anyone else. My head of division, I said. As my superior is so senior, and such a brilliant operative, and a charming, well-connected man, I knew I was safe. But still I felt uneasy and wanted out of the service."

She said she remembered Burgess as a fop but a funny and entertaining man. Maclean she'd known as a child, and she had been besotted with him as a young woman. "I told them Burgess and Maclean had broken my faith. They accepted that, as everyone connected with the service was feeling the same. Then I retired to the glen to paint."

"So what were you doing with those lists of numbers? And why fake your death? And who helped you escape? And Stuart, is he a . . ." *Goodie or baddie*, she was about to say, then realized she was being silly. What with traitors, break-ins, invisible ink, forgeries, and fake artworks, she felt she was in a spy novel, not in the reality of a cold winter in late 1959.

Alice began to laugh. "My dear Joanne. Stop right there. You know I can't tell you. And I should warn you, it is unwise ever to ask these questions even of your friends."

Joanne smiled in acceptance. "I had to ask."

"I know. As for Stuart, my dear friend and colleague Mr. Stuart, again I can't answer, because I really don't know." Alice turned her head away.

Joanne fancied she saw her eyes brighten. No, she dismissed the thought. Perhaps, she reconsidered. No, she thought again, he couldn't be! Yet it made sense. Ruraidh and his lot, they were the rescue team. Stuart had to be a traitor. Or at least in cahoots with the traitor.

"Joanne, there is no point in continuing to speculate. If you did perhaps stumble on some incident, some scrap of information, please, don't explore further. Enjoy your life. Do not live always looking over your shoulder. I have only myself to look after. You have children."

Joanne felt the threat in the mention of her children. That shook her, making her want to run home as fast as possible. "I brought the manuscript," she said. "As you requested."

Alice nodded, understanding Joanne's stiff posture, her clipped voice. "Thank you. I've been told you put a lot of work into it. We're sorry it will never see the light of day." The cliché rolled out, the meaning that it would never be published clear, yet there was no indication that Alice cared.

"I've also handed over the drawing of the men. Why is it important?"

"You could ask Hennessey—but don't expect an answer," Alice said. "You are owed an explanation. They could possibly shoot me for telling you—sorry, joke." She stood. "I need a whisky. You?"

Joanne shook her head and watched as Alice went to the decanter and poured a Don McLeod–sized dram of amber liquid.

Alice continued, "I know you will have seen the numbers on the back of the drawing. That is what they wanted. Just before the outbreak of war, I was on assignment in Cairo and came across the list in Donald's bedroom."

Joanne longed to know what Alice was doing in the spy's bedroom but didn't ask.

"One small drawing, one short list of agent identification numbers, but enough to trap a spy, and look at all the trouble that simple sketch has caused. Goodness knows how they weren't caught sooner. So careless. So unprofessional. Later that night, I met them dining together. They were absolutely sloshed and didn't even notice me spying from another table. Later in my room, I did a quick sketch of the four men. I remembered most of the numbers perfectly and wrote them on the back of the paper."

Joanne had the feeling that Alice was pleased to talk but needed to remain aloof; the professional self was paramount.

"It is a conceivable coincidence that three of those men could be together. Two of them were close friends, and the three worked in different but connected sections of the service. The fourth man's identity I didn't and still don't know. I now know he was their contact, the man who recruited those wretchedly naive idiots to commit treason." Abruptly she stood, and the bitter word hung between them, making the bright, high-ceilinged drawing room feel claustrophobic.

Joanne stared out at the midafternoon sun, about to drop behind the hills, departing with a burst of red-gold reflections in the loch. *Or is it "lough"?*

Alice valued light. Walking in it, memorizing it, painting it—subtle changes in light enchanted her. She stood. "Let's walk. Never know when we will have another afternoon like this."

Taking a well-worn track that circled the loch, Alice began, "I miss the house. I miss the glen. Unfortunately, returning is not an option. I was persecuted by that Mackenzie woman—though God knows why—I became a victim of Dougie's self-aggrandizement, and my cover was blown and my whereabouts revealed in that newspaper article. That is how they found me. So no. No going back." Alice kicked a broken branch of oak lying across their path.

Nice boots, Joanne thought.

They'd walked the circumference of the water. It was colder than it looked from indoors. Joanne, aware the audience was about to end, attempted more questions.

"Who faked your death?"

Alice said, "Sorry, I can't tell you."

"The paintings I bought at the auction, what do you want me to do with them?"

"Keep them." Alice relented. She stopped, shaded her eyes with one hand, and stared towards a blood-red sun fast disappearing into a mountain with a curiously fractured peak. "The paintings were part of my cover. The drawing Dougie bought is a very good fake, if I do say so myself." She smiled. "And a Civil Service pension is paltry. The paintings, when I occasionally sell one I make clear they are studies, and they are very popular. The still life with onions, that one I'm holding on to—my pension fund."

"So it's an original?"

"Couldn't you tell?" The slight hint of condescension hurt, and Joanne was glad they had arrived back at the castle.

Hennessey came out to meet them. Superintendent Westland followed.

"Ladies, sorry, but we need to leave."

Alice turned to Joanne and held out her hand. "Thank you for all you have done for me. And you are correct. I would never take my own life." Their hands met. Alice stepped closer. "Please don't tell anyone I am alive. It would put me in enormous danger."

"I won't." Looking at Alice, seeing into her eyes, sensing her loneliness and her courage, Joanne took back all thoughts of Alice Ramsay being difficult, being unfriendly. *She can't afford friends,* Joanne now knew. "I saw your drawing of Muriel Galloway. It's beautiful."

Alice stared into the far distance—perhaps to her kitchen in the house in the glen in the northern wilds. "Yes, it is good, isn't it?" She smiled. "That house, the glen, they made me a better person. I miss them." She gave Joanne a quick hug. "Good-bye, Joanne Ross. Have a wonderful life."

She walked quickly up the steps to the doors large enough to allow through a knight in shining armor, on horseback.

She did not look back.

The car ride to the airstrip, the flight home in the dark, went by fast. Hennessey did not come with them. Superintendent Westland opened the box of sandwiches, along with two slices of a rich fruitcake, on the flight.

"Miss Ramsay made the cake," he said. "And Hennessey sent a gift for McAllister." The bag clinked. Joanne knew that whatever it was, it was alcoholic. "There is also this for you." He handed over an envelope of stiff card, just the size of the drawing she had delivered to Alice.

"I'm not sure I want it, whatever it is," she said.

He shrugged and tackled another sandwich.

The flight was short. The drive from the aerodrome to town was not much shorter. Westland walked Joanne to her front door.

"I leave tomorrow," he said, "but I'll call by McAllister's office before I go."

"You'd better," she said. "Else McAllister will come looking."

"Good night, Joanne." He was about to say, *Well done*, but didn't. She has been underestimated and patronized enough, he thought.

◆　◆　◆

Next morning, Joanne met McAllister at the *Gazette* office. She'd slept through the girls leaving for school, even though both of them had tiptoed to her bed to make certain she was there.

"Told ya," McAllister had joked, throwing back at them another of Annie's catchphrases.

Inside his private lair, Joanne sat with a cup of tea, while McAllister leafed through the messages the receptionist had delivered on his arrival, tossing most into the wastepaper bin.

Don was looking at the bottle McAllister had given him, saying, "It's only as different from whisky as the spelling."

"W-H-I-S-K-E-Y," she read out. "I never knew that spelling."

"May I come in?" Superintendent Westland was in civvies—checked Vyella shirt, knitted tie, thick brown corduroy trousers, and the ubiquitous tweed jacket. His hat, however, was not a deerstalker, just a plain flecked-brown-trout-colored workaday tweed flat cap. "Thanks for waiting," he said as he took a chair.

"Hennessey threatened to haul me in under the Official Secrets Act if I tell anyone," McAllister growled. "Don said he'd resign if I don't."

"So I told him," Joanne said.

"Right," Westland said. "Well, I'm off duty. And I didn't hear any of that."

"So who was Mr. Stuart?" Don asked.

"That would definitely be breaking the Official Secrets Act," Westland warned.

"That means he doesn't know." Joanne laughed.

Don shook his head. "Heavens above—spies and traitors and treachery in a wee Highland community."

"Aye," Joanne said, "and that's only Mrs. Mackenzie."

It came out lighter than intended. *That woman caused her husband's death.* She was grateful for the laughter nonetheless.

Westland began. "Joanne is right. I don't know who he is or which department he works in. I do know he is a bona fide government employee. Hennessey too, but in some branch of the

Foreign Office. When the spies were discovered, there were huge repercussions, and I did hear that a veritable war broke out among the various intelligence services. Lots of finger pointing over who knew what and who should have been able to intercept them."

McAllister had spoken with Sandy. "A wee bird in Glasgow via other wee birds on Fleet Street says the relationship with the American agencies is still precarious."

"No doubt," Don said.

"I was in London at that time, working on the Fleet Street desk of the *Herald*," McAllister added. "The scandal was catastrophic. Two of their best men disappeared. No one knew where. Prime ministers, politicians denying everything. The Americans going ballistic. D notices as thick as a manuscript delivered to us at the *Herald* and to every newspaper, wireless station, and television. Nothing could be reported. But we knew. Or guessed. 'Diplomats Missing' was all the information we were allowed to print."

"Then they turned up in Moscow," Don remembered. "Three years later that the truth came out."

"Some of the truth came out," McAllister corrected him.

"I couldn't say," Westland said. "As you know, the death and the disposal of Miss Ramsay were ..."

"Unusual." Don supplied the word.

"So my investigation is concluded," the policeman said. "Naturally, my findings will not be made public. And the matter is over."

"For us, but not for Calum," McAllister said.

"And poor Mrs. Galloway," said Joanne.

Don couldn't let it go. "Who was spying on McAllister and Joanne?"

"I didn't ask," Westland said. As they wouldn't tell me, he didn't say.

"I've had enough of it all," Joanne declared. "The subject is now closed."

"Aye, lass, but what about—"

"Don McLeod, when I say the subject is closed . . ."

"It's closed." He sighed and looked towards the bottle of Jameson. "Is it too early for a wee drop of the Irish?"

"Never," McAllister said, and fetched the glasses.

"This stuff any good?" She took a mouthful from McAllister's glass, swallowed, coughed, coughed some more, and said, "Jings, this'll put hair on yer chest."

EPILOGUE

~

It should have been her. Still, if I can't have him, neither can she.

Who does she think she is? All that carry-on at the funeral. Me, I'm his wife, it says so on the gravestone I had done for him.

I told her she was no welcome in the church or the graveside, but Calum insisted she come. Got quite shirty when I said she was nothing but a whore.

At the graveside she wasn't crying, but she was shaking worse than a sparrow in a storm. Calum was holding her arm. I soon put a stop to that.

Mind you, I narrowly missed falling into the grave wi' ma pretend fainting fit. I was moaning an' crying an' that, and Elaine comes over an' slaps me. Much harder than necessary, I might add. Then she's telling Calum that's what you do for hysteria, and he does nothing. Just like his dad, that son o' mine. I'll deal wi' Nurse Elaine soon enough. Can't have history repeating itself.

Then, after the graveside bit, Calum tells me the funeral tea is to be at the hotel. I refused to go, saying everyone was coming to ours, as I was his wife and I had everything prepared.

But they all went back to her place like it was her that was the widow, no me.

Even Calum went. But he did say he was coming back to his old job. And he's promised he'll always look after me. He's a good boy, is my son.

◆   ◆   ◆

Four weeks later and three weeks short of Christmas, Joanne was staring into Simpson's shoe-shop when the woman next to her said, "I'd love those fur-lined boots, but they're much too dear on a nurse's salary."

"Elaine!"

"Hiya, Joanne." They grinned at each other.

"Do you have time for coffee?"

Elaine turned to look at the clock on the Church Street spire. "I'm meeting a friend at the Ness Café in half an hour, so let's go there."

Elaine told Joanne about the funeral. "It seemed like the whole county was there." Then she told Joanne about the will. "He left *her* the house. But Muriel, Mrs. Galloway, gets the business— the garage, the shop, the lot."

"Good."

"Aye. Everyone's relieved they'll no have *her* poking into their affairs when all they want is a gallon of petrol."

Joanne could sense there was more. "How's Calum?"

"He's back at the local paper. I broke off our engagement."

Joanne wasn't surprised.

"I feel really bad about it, but . . ." Elaine looked out the window. Remembering the last talk with Calum still upset her. It had been worse than painful for him; he'd been completely shocked. All she had felt was relief that a decision was finally made. He was convinced she would come back to him. *Give it time*, he'd told her. *When you come back, when everything's settled down . . .*

"Calum said he has to live with his mum because she's got no one and no money coming in. He said when we're married, we could share her house, because there was plenty of room for us and her. I said, 'No, I'm never going to live with your mother.'"

She'd said worse than that. She could still feel the words that had escaped, the sentences there was no turning back from.

"It was awful, Joanne. I told Calum his mother's gossiping and lies as good as killed Miss Ramsay." She would never confess that she'd added, *And killed your dad.* "He said she's had to put up with years and years of people laughing at her, gossiping how her husband was living with another woman."

"I know how that feels." Joanne didn't mean to say it, but it popped out.

"Aye, a divorce is still a huge disgrace," Elaine agreed. "What Calum finally said, and what makes me feel guilty every time I think about it, was 'Elaine, I know what she's like, but she's my mother.'" She sighed. "Calum's a saint. He is a good, kind man, and his mum's hysterics pass him by, like words lost in a wind. I feel dreadful about breaking off the engagement. But I can't. I just can't." She felt the heat in her cheeks and changed the subject. "I've signed up to be here for a year, so I moved into Calum's lodgings. It'll do fine until me and some nurse friends find a house to share."

"I'm glad for you, Elaine." Joanne was about to say, *Don't carry the corrosive burden of guilt, it is too destructive.* But a belief in Elaine's good sense stopped her. She wanted to tell Elaine that Alice was well, except she knew that after the last time, she would never betray Alice Ramsay.

A car drew up and beeped the horn.

Elaine jumped up. "Sorry, my friend is here. I have to run." She opened a purse to leave money for the coffee.

Joanne refused. "My treat."

Elaine hugged her and ran to the car. Frankie Urquhart got out and opened the passenger door for her.

Joanne smiled. "Good luck, Elaine, you deserve it."

◆   ◆   ◆

Sutherland Courier, 15 December: "Rowan House, part of the estate of the late Miss Alice Ramsay, has been gifted to the Scottish Society of Watercolorists for use as a residential retreat. Those wishing to apply for a residency can do so at the following address. . . ."

◆   ◆   ◆

31 December 1959. I can't quite believe it—Hogmanay and the end of a decade, the beginning of . . . of what?

McAllister is in the sitting room with Don McLeod waiting for the bells to ring in 1960. The girls are in bed, but we promised we'd wake them to see in the New Year with us. McAllister has made his special mulled wine. Annie will want some, but it is really alcoholic—as I found out last Hogmanay.

Here I am, in the kitchen as usual, trying to compose a list of my New Year's resolutions, only I don't know what to write. All I can think of is the last months, the last year. Best summed up by: "I married him."

Alice Ramsay is no longer haunting me, especially not here in my spicy warm kitchen. My obsession has evaporated. Yet I will always remember her. Always remember how I learned what I already knew.

It will be my New Year's resolution: Do as you would be done by.

ACKNOWLEDGMENTS

A huge thank you to Anna Moi and Laurent Schwab for lending me their delightful home in Correze in South West France as a writing place. Anna, I miss our conversations.

To Susan and Paul, strangers who became friends and who made me so welcome in their adopted home village in South West France.

To Randy of Randy's Books, Hoi An, Vietnam—thank you for the excellent feedback on this manuscript and unending willingness to talk books.

Elka Ray—once again an astute reader, and wonderful friend.

MangoMango Duc and Ly—the food, the coffee, the love—couldn't do this without you guys.

Sarah Durand McGuigan—I miss you.

Sarah Cantin—my oh my, what a fresh outlook on life you have—and a deeply caring and intelligent editor you are.

Judith Curr—thank you for the faith, the support, and the wonderful Atria team you have gathered around you. Truly appreciated.

And lastly to the people of Dornoch and Golspie: I have played fast and loose with geography and was, and am, overwhelmed by the kindness and warmth of the people in Sutherland. If there is any resemblance to anyone (alive or dead), in this novel, or if I have offended anyone, please remember this is fiction. I made it all up. Except for the witch.

IF YOU ENJOYED *A KIND OF GRIEF*, GO BACK AND FIND OUT HOW IT ALL BEGAN...

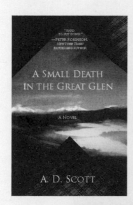

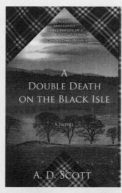

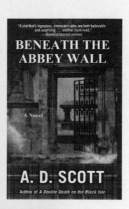

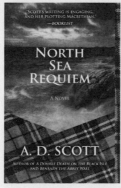

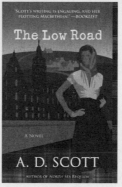

PROUDLY PUBLISHED BY ATRIA BOOKS

Pick up or download your copies today!